PENGUIN BOOKS

DRAGONLANCE® PRELUDES
VOLUME ONE:
DARKNESS & LIGHT

Paul B. Thompson remembers clearly the first real book he ever read, a prose translation of the *Iliad*. This was followed by *The Arabian Nights' Entertainment*, and his tastes were set for life. His first novel, *Sundipper*, was published in 1984. The next year Thompson began collaborating with Tonya Carter. Thompson and Carter have also written *Red Sands*, a novel in the TSR style, and have contributed to the DRAGON-LANCE® anthology *Love and War*. *Darkness and Light* is their second novel together.

Tonya R. Carter attended the University of North Carolina at Chapel Hill, where she met her husband, Greg, and her collaborator, Paul Thompson. After college she visited England and Ireland. There, in spite of her red hair and Irish ancestry, she was mistaken for an Australian several times. This prompted her to take up Gaelic studies on her return to the States. In addition to her collaborative work, she has written a number of fantasy, horror and science-fiction stories, including 'To Hear the Sea-Maid's Music'. When not writing, she enjoys shopping for books, travelling and skiing.

D1385836

DragonLance® saga

PRELUDES

VOLUME ONE

Darkness & Light

**Paul B. Thompson and
Tonya R. Carter**

Cover Art
JEFF EASLEY

PENGUIN BOOKS
in association with TSR, Inc.

PENGUIN BOOKS

Published by the Penguin Group
Penguin Books Ltd, 27 Wrights Lane, London W8 5TZ, England
Penguin Books USA Inc., 375 Hudson Street, New York, New York 10014, USA
Penguin Books Australia Ltd, Ringwood, Victoria, Australia
Penguin Books Canada Ltd, 2801 John Street, Markham, Ontario, Canada L3R 1B4
Penguin Books (NZ) Ltd, 182–190 Wairau Road, Auckland 10, New Zealand

Penguin Books Ltd, Registered Offices: Harmondsworth, Middlesex, England

First published in the USA by TSR, Inc., 1989
Distributed to the book trade in the USA by Random House, Inc.,
and in Canada by Random House of Canada Ltd
Distributed to the toy and hobby trade by regional distributors
Published in Penguin Books 1989
5 7 9 10 8 6 4

TSR, Inc.
PRODUCTS OF YOUR IMAGINATION™

Printed in England by Clays Ltd, St Ives plc

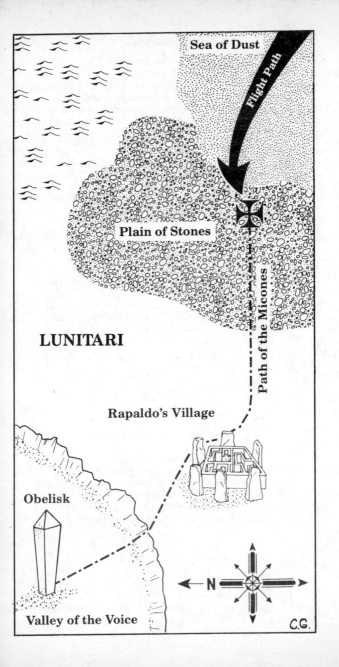

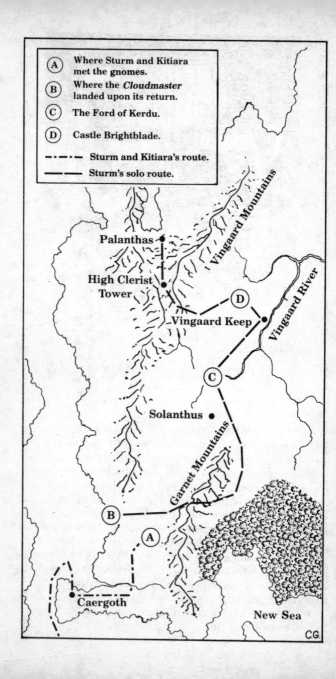

A Where Sturm and Kitiara met the gnomes.

B Where the *Cloudmaster* landed upon its return.

C The Ford of Kerdu.

D Castle Brightblade.

—··— Sturm and Kitiara's route.

—·— Sturm's solo route.

Palanthas

Vingaard Mountains

High Clerist Tower

D

Vingaard River

Vingaard Keep

C

Solanthus

Garnet Mountains

B

A

Caergoth

New Sea

C.G.

Chapter 1

Separate Ways

AutumN painted Solace iN gay colors. EacH porch, each window, was filled with red, orange, and yellow foliage, for the shops and houses of Solace were nestled among the stout branches of a vale of vallenwood trees, well above the mossy ground. Here and there were clearings in the treetown. These were the town's commons, where there might be a market one week and a traveling carnival the next.

On this bright afternoon three figures stood in a sunlit clearing—two men and a woman. Two swords played back and forth, flashing with fire when the sun's rays caught them. Two figures circled warily, feinting with sudden flicks of their naked blades. The third one stood back, watching. The swords scraped together with a kiss of tempered steel.

"Well met!" said Caramon Majere, the onlooker. "A very

neat parry, Sturm!"

The tall young man with the drooping brown mustache grunted a brief acknowledgment. He was rather busy. His opponent sprang forward, lunging at his chest. Sturm Brightblade cut hard at the onrushing point, backpedaling as he swung. It missed him by a scant inch.

Sturm's foe wobbled as she came down off balance, her feet too far apart.

"Steady, Kit!" Caramon called. His half-sister recovered with the practiced grace of a dancer. She brought her heels together with a smack of boot leather and presented Sturm with only her slim profile as a target.

"Now, my friend," she said. "I'll show you the skill that comes from fighting for pay."

Kitiara cut tiny circles in the air with her sword tip. Once, twice, three times—Sturm watched the deadly motion. Caramon watched, too, open-mouthed. At eighteen, he was the size of a full-grown man, but he was still a boy inside. The wild and worldly Kitiara was his idol. She had more drive and dash than any ten men.

From his place, Caramon could see every nick in the edge of Kitiara's blade, mementoes of hard-fought battle. The flat of the blade was shiny from frequent and expert polishing. By contrast, Sturm's sword was so new that the hilt still showed the blue tinge from the smith's annealing fire.

"Watch your right," said Caramon. Sturm closed his free hand over the long pommel and awaited Kitiara's attack square on, as a Solamnic Knight would.

"Hai!" Kitiara whirled on one leg, cleaving the air with an upward sweep of her sword. Caramon's breath caught as she carried her swing forward. Sturm did not move. Her sword would complete its arc at his neck. Caramon shut his eyes—and heard a solid ring of steel. Feeling foolish, he opened them again.

Sturm had parried straight across, hilt to hilt, with no finesse at all. He and Kitiara stayed locked together with their sword points high. Kitiara's wrists shook. She stepped in and braced her sword arm with her empty hand. Sturm forced her guard down. Her face paled, then flushed red. Caramon knew that look. This friendly bout was not going to her liking, and Kitiara was getting angry.

Vexed, she shifted her stance and strained against Sturm's greater size and strength. Still her hilt fell. The knobbed quillon of Sturm's new sword brushed her chin.

With an explosive gasp, Kitiara ceased the struggle. Both sword points stabbed into the green sod.

"Enough," she said. "I'll buy the ale. I should've known better than to let you bind up my guard like that! Come on, Sturm. Let's have a tankard of Otik's best."

"Sounds good to me," he replied. He freed his blade and stepped back, breathing heavily. As he moved, Kitiara thrust the flat of her weapon between his ankles. Sturm's feet tangled, and he sprawled backward on the grass. His sword flew away, and in the next instant Kitiara stood over him holding thirty-two inches of steel poised at his throat.

"Combat is not always a sport," she said. "Keep your eyes open and your sword firmly in hand, my friend, and you'll live longer."

Sturm looked up the blade at Kitiara's face. Sweat had stuck dark curls of hair to her forehead, and her naturally dark lips were pressed firmly together. Slowly they spread in a lopsided smile. She sheathed her weapon.

"Don't look so downcast! Better a friend knock you down as a lesson than an enemy cut you down for good." She extended a hand. "We'd better go before Flint and Tanis drink all of Otik's brew."

Sturm grasped her hand. It was warm and calloused from gauntlets and sword grips. Kitiara pulled him up until they were nose to nose. Although a head taller and fifty pounds heavier, Sturm still felt like a callow youth beside her. But her bright eyes and engaging smile dispelled his anxiety.

"I see now how you've managed to prosper as a fighter," he said, stooping to retrieve his sword. He buried the blade in its sheath. "Thank you for the lesson. Next time I will keep my feet out of reach!"

"Later, will you teach me some of your moves, Kit?" asked Caramon eagerly. He carried a short sword himself, a gift from his adventurous sister. She'd picked it up on one of her many battlefields. Flint Fireforge, who knew metalwork as few did, said that Caramon's sword had been made in southern Qualinesti. Only by clues such as this did her friends know where Kit's wanderings had taken her.

"Why not? I'll tie one hand behind my back to make it fair." Caramon opened his mouth to retort, but Kitiara clapped a hand over his lips. "Now, to the inn. If I don't get a draft of ale soon, I'll perish!"

When they reached the base of the great vallenwood tree that supported the Inn of the Last Home, they found their friend Flint sitting at the bottom of the ramp. The dwarf had a split of kindling in his massive, knobby hands and was shaving off hair-thin slices with a single-edged knife.

"Well, you came back with your skin whole," said Flint, eyeing Sturm. "I half-expected to see you carrying your head under your arm."

"Your confidence in me is enormous," the young man replied sourly. Kitiara halted and draped an arm across Caramon's broad shoulders.

"Better watch yourself, old dwarf. Our Master Sturm has an uncommonly strong arm. Once he learns not to hold to outdated knightly codes—"

"Honor is never outdated," said Sturm.

"Which is how you landed flat on your back with my sword at your neck. If you would—"

"Don't start!" groaned Caramon. "If I have to hear another debate on honor, I'll die of boredom!"

"I won't argue," Kitiara said, slapping her brother on the rump. "I made my point."

"Come with us, Flint. Kit's buying," said Caramon. The elderly dwarf rose on his stumpy legs, sweeping a cascade of white wood slivers off his lap. He straightened his clothing and tucked his knife back in his leggings.

"No ale for you," Kitiara said to Caramon with mock-maternal sternness. "You're not old enough to drink."

Caramon ducked under her arm, sprinted up to Sturm, and said, "I'm eighteen, Kit."

Kitiara's face showed surprise. "Eighteen? Are you sure?" Her 'little' brother was an inch or so taller than Sturm.

Caramon gave her a disgusted look. "Of course I'm sure. You just haven't noticed that I'm a grown man."

"You're a baby!" Kitiara cried, whipping out her sword.

"Any more out of you and I'll spank you!"

"Ha!" Caramon laughed. "You can't catch me!" So saying, he dashed up the stairs. Kitiara returned her sword and bounded after him. Caramon's long legs covered the steep boards quickly. Laughing, he and his sister disappeared around the tree trunk.

Flint and Sturm ascended more slowly. A light breeze rustled through the tree, sending a shower of colored leaves across the steps. Sturm gazed out through the branches at the other tree homes. "In a few weeks, you'll be able to see clear to the other side of the commons," he mused.

"Aye," said Flint. "It's strange not to be on the road right now. For more years than you've been alive, boy, I've tramped the roads of Abanasinia from spring to autumn, plying the trade."

Sturm nodded. Flint's announced retirement from his itinerant metalworking had surprised them all.

"It's all behind me now," Flint said. "Time to put my feet up, maybe grow some roses." Sturm found the image of the bluff old dwarf tending a rose garden so unnatural that he shook his head to dispel the thought.

At the level platform midway up to the inn proper, Sturm paused by the railing. Flint went a few steps beyond before halting. He squinted back at Sturm and said, "What is it, boy? You're about to burst to tell me something."

Flint didn't miss a thing. "I'm going away," said Sturm. "To Solamnia. I'm going to look for my heritage."

"And your father?"

"If there is any trace of him to be found, I shall find it."

"It could be a long journey and a dangerous search," Flint said. "But I wish I could go with you."

"Never mind." Sturm moved away from the rail. "It's my search."

Sturm and Flint entered the door of the inn just in time to receive a barrage of apple cores. As they wiped the sticky pulp from their eyes, the room rocked with laughter.

"Who's the rascal responsible?" roared Flint. A gawky young girl, no more than fourteen, with a head of robust red curls, handed the outraged dwarf a towel.

"Otik pressed some new cider, and they had to have the

leavings," she said apologetically.

Sturm wiped his face. Kitiara and Caramon had collapsed against the bar, giggling like idiots. Behind the bar, Otik, the portly proprietor of the inn, shook his head.

"This is a first-class inn," he said. "Take your pranks outside, if you gotta pull 'em!"

"Nonsense!" said Kitiara. She slapped a coin on the bar. Caramon wiped the tears of laughter from his eyes and stared. It was a gold coin, one of the few he'd ever seen. "That will ease your temper, eh, Otik?" Kitiara said.

A tall, well-favored man stood up from his table and approached the bar. His motion was oddly graceful, and his high cheekbones and golden eyes eloquently proclaimed his elven heritage. He picked up the coin.

"What's the matter, Tanis?" Kitiara asked. "Haven't you ever seen gold before?"

"Not as large a coin as this," Tanis Half-Elven replied. He flipped it over. "Where was it struck?"

Kitiara lifted her mug from the bar and drank. "I don't know," she said. "It's part of my wages. Why do you ask?"

"The inscription is Elvish. I would say it was minted in Silvanesti."

Sturm and Flint came over to examine the coin. The delicate script was definitely Elvish, Flint said. Far-off Silvanesti had practically no contact with the rest of Ansalon, and there was much curiosity as to how an elvish coin managed to drift so far west.

"Plunder," said a voice from the corner of the room.

"What did you say, Raist?" asked Caramon. In a corner of the inn's common room a pallid figure could be seen. Raistlin, Caramon's twin brother. As usual, he was immersed in the study of a dusty scroll. He rose and moved toward the group; the colored light filtering through the inn's stained-glass windows gave his pale skin odd tints.

"Plunder," he repeated. "Robbery, rapine, booty."

"We know what the word means," said Flint sharply.

"He means the coin was probably stolen in Silvanesti and later turned up in the coffers of Kit's mercenary captain," said Tanis.

They passed the coin from hand to hand, turning it

around and feeling the heft of it. More than its crude monetary value, the elven coin spoke of far-off places and distant, magical people.

"Let me see," said an insistent voice from below the bar. A small, lean arm thrust between Caramon and Sturm.

"No!" said Otik, taking the coin from Tanis's hand. "When a kender gets hold of money, you can kiss it a quick good-bye!"

"Tas!" cried Caramon. "I didn't see you come in."

"He was in the room the whole time," Tanis said.

Tasslehoff Burrfoot, like most of his race, was both clever and diminutive. He could hide in the smallest places, and was known to be light-fingered—"curious," as he said.

"Ale all around," said Kitiara, "now that my credit is good." Otik filled a line of tankards from a massive pitcher, and the friends retired to the great round table in the center of the room. Raistlin took a chair with the others, instead of returning to his scroll.

"Since we are all here," Tanis said, "someone ought to make a toast."

"Here's to Kit, the founder of the feast!" said Caramon, raising his clay mug of cider.

"Here's to the gold that pays for it," his sister responded.

"Here's to the elves who coined it," offered Flint.

"I'll drink to elves in any form," Kitiara said. She smiled over her mug at Tanis. A question formed on his lips, but before he could speak it, Tasslehoff stood on his stool and waved for attention.

"I say we drink to Flint," said Tas. "This is the first year since the Cataclysm that he won't be on the road."

A chuckle circled the table, and the old dwarf reddened. "You whelp," he growled. "How old do you think I am?"

"He can't count that high," said Raistlin.

"Well, I'm a hundred and forty-three, and I can lick any man, woman, or kender in the place," Flint declared. He thumped a heavy fist on the table. "Care to test me?"

He had no takers. Despite his age and short stature, Flint was powerfully muscled and a good wrestler.

They toasted and drank from then on with good cheer, as afternoon became evening and evening became night. To stave off tipsiness, one of Otik's large suppers was ordered. Soon the table was groaning under platters of squab and venison, bread, cheese, and Otik's famous fried potatoes.

The red-haired girl brought each platter to the diners. At one point, Caramon put his gnawed chicken bones in her apron pocket. The girl responded gamely, dropping a hot potato slice down Caramon's collar. He squirmed out of his chair as the girl skipped back to Otik's kitchen.

"Who the blazes is she?" asked Caramon, wiggling the crispy potato slice out his shirttail.

"She is in Otik's care," said Raistlin. "Her name is Tika."

The night passed on. Other patrons came and went. It grew late, and Otik had Tika light a fork of candles for the friends' table. The merry banter of the early evening gave way to calmer, more reflective conversation.

"I'm going tomorrow," Kitiara announced. By candlelight her tanned face seemed golden. Tanis studied her and felt all the old pangs return. She was a most alluring woman.

"Going where?" asked Caramon.

"North, I think," she answered.

"Why north?" Tanis asked.

"Reasons of my own," she said, but her smile softened the flat answer.

"Can I go with you?" Caramon said.

"No, you can't, brother."

"Why not?"

Kitiara, seated between her half-brothers, glanced at Raistlin. Caramon's gaze went from her to his twin. Of course. Raistlin needed him. Though twins, they were not much alike. Caramon was a genial young bear, while Raistlin was a studious wraith. He was frequently ill and had an uncanny habit of antagonizing large, belligerent types. After the birth of the twins, their mother had never recovered her strength, so Kitiara had fought for young Raistlin's health. Now it was Caramon who watched out for his twin.

"I'm leaving, too," put in Sturm. "North." He glanced at Kitiara.

"Foo," said Tasslehoff. "North is dull. I've been there. Now east, there's the way to go. There's lots to see in the East—cities, forests, mountains—"

"Pockets to pick, horses to 'borrow'," said Flint.

The kender stuck out his lower lip. "I can't help it if I'm good at finding things."

"Someday you'll find from the wrong person, and they'll hang you for it."

"I have to go north," Sturm said. He leaned forward, resting his chin on his hands. "I'm going back to Solamnia."

They all stared at him. They knew the story of Sturm's exile from his homeland. Twelve years had passed since the peasants of Solamnia had risen against the knightly lords. Sturm and his mother had escaped with only their lives. The knights were still despised in their own country.

"Could you use a good right arm?" offered Kitiara. Her offer caught everyone by surprise.

"I wouldn't want you to go out of your way," said Sturm, noncommittally.

"North is north. I've been east and south and west."

"Very well then. I'd be honored to have you with me." Sturm turned from Kitiara to Tanis. "What about you, Tan?"

Tanis pushed a hunk of bread through the remains of his dinner. "I've been thinking of doing some travel myself. Nothing specific, just a trek to see some places I haven't seen. I don't think my journey will take me north." He looked at Kitiara, but her gaze was directed at Sturm.

"That's the idea," Tasslehoff said briskly. His right hand dipped into his fur vest and came out with a flat copper disk. He rolled the disk over the back of his knuckles. It was an exercise he sometimes did to keep his fingers nimble. Not that he needed practice. "Let's go east, Tanis, you and me."

"No." The flat turn-down froze the copper disk midway across the back of the kender's small hand. "No," said Tanis again, more gently. "This is a trip I must make alone."

The table was silent again. Then Caramon let out a single great hiccup, and the laughter returned.

"Pardon me!" said Caramon, reaching for Kitiara's tankard. She was not fooled. As his hand closed around the pewter stem, she rapped his wrist with her spoon. Caramon snatched his hand back. "Ouch!" he protested.

"You'll get worse if you try it again," said Kitiara. Caramon grinned and made a fist.

"Save your energy, brother," Raistlin said. "You'll need it."

"How so, Raist?"

"Since everyone has decided to undertake journeys, this seems like a good time to announce one of my own."

Flint snorted. "You wouldn't last two days on the road."

"Perhaps not." Raistlin folded his long, tapering fingers. "Unless my brother goes with me."

"Where and when?" asked Caramon, pleased to be going anywhere.

"I cannot say where just now," Raistlin said. His pale blue eyes stared fixedly at his nearly untouched plate of food. "It may be a long and perilous voyage."

Caramon jumped up. "I'm ready."

"Siddown," Kitiara said, dragging on her brother's vest tail. Caramon plumped down on his stool.

Flint sighed a great, gusty sigh. "You're all leaving me," he said. "I'll not go a-tinkering this season, and all my friends are going their own way." He sighed again, so heavily that the rack of candles flickered.

"You old bear," Kitiara said. "You're feeling sorry for yourself. There's no law that says you have to stay in Solace by yourself. Don't you have any relatives that you can impose on?"

"Yes," Tasslehoff added, "you can visit your gray-bearded, I mean gray-haired, old mother.

The dwarf bellowed his outrage. Those sitting closest to Flint—Caramon and Sturm—slid quickly away from the furious dwarf. Flint banged his tankard on the tabletop, sending a splash of ale at Tasslehoff. Rivulets of sticky golden ale ran off the kender's nose and soaked into his topknot of wild brown hair. He rubbed the brew from his eyes.

"Nobody makes sport of my mother!" Flint declared.

"Not more than once, anyway," Tanis observed sagely.

Tas wiped his face on his sleeve. He picked up his own scaled-down tankard (it was empty) and tucked it under his arm like an absurd helm. Assuming an air of injured dignity, he declaimed, "Now we must fight a duel!"

Kitiara said gleefully. "I'll be your second, Tas."

"I'll stand for Flint!" Caramon cried.

"Who has choice of weapons?" asked Tanis.

"Flint's challenged; it is his choice," Sturm said, smiling.

"What'll it be, old bear? Apple cores at ten paces? Ladles and pot lids?" asked Kitiara.

"Anything but ale mugs," Tas quipped, his pose of haughty dignity replaced by his usual grin. The laughter didn't stop until Tika returned.

"Shh! Shh, it's late! Will you people be quiet!" she hissed.

"Go on, before someone spanks you," Caramon said, without turning to look at her. Tika slipped in behind his stool and made horrid faces at him. The others laughed at her. Caramon was puzzled.

"What's so funny?" he demanded.

Tika deftly lifted the dagger from Caramon's belt sheath. She raised it over her head with a terrifying grimace, as though to stab Caramon in the back. Tears ran down Kitiara's face, and Tas fell off his chair.

"What?" shouted Caramon. Then he snapped his head around and spied Tika in midgrimace. "Aha!" He started after her. The girl darted around the nearby empty tables. Caramon blundered after her, upsetting chairs and stumbling against stools.

Otik appeared from the kitchen with a lamp in his hand. His nightshirt was askew and his sparse white hair was standing up in comic tufts. "What's this row? Can't a man get some sleep around here? Tika, where are you, girl?" The red-haired girl peeked over the rim of a table. "You were supposed to hush them, not join in the party."

"That man was chasing me." She pointed at Caramon, who was busy studying the candle-lit rafters.

"Go to your room." Tika went regretfully. She cast a last grin back at Caramon and stuck out her tongue. When he started toward her, she flipped his dagger at him. It struck the floor quivering, inches from his feet. Tika vanished through the kitchen's swinging doors.

Otik planted his fists on his hips. "Flint Fireforge! I expected better of you. You're old enough to know better. And you, Master Sturm; a well-bred fellow like you ought to know better than to be roistering this late at night." Flint looked properly abashed. Sturm smoothed his long mustache with his right forefinger and said nothing.

"Don't be an old sop," said Kitiara. "Tika was very amusing. Besides, this is a going-away party."

"Everything is amusing to people who've got four kegs of ale in their bellies," growled Otik. "Who's going away?"

"Well, everybody."

Otik turned back to the kitchen. He said, "Well, for pity's sake, go quietly!" and left.

Caramon returned to the table. Through a gaping yawn he said, "That Tika's the ugliest girl in Solace. Old Otik'll have to put up a big dowry to get her married off!"

"You never know," said Raistlin with a glance at the kitchen. "People change."

It was time to part. There was no reason to delay any longer. Sensing this, Tanis stood with folded hands and said, "Though we friends will separate, our good wishes cannot be diminished by time or distance. But to keep the circle in our hearts, we must come together again, each year on this day, here in the inn."

"And if we cannot?" asked Sturm.

"Then five years from today, everyone here tonight shall return to the Inn of the Last Home. No matter what. Let's make this a sacred vow. Who will take it with me?"

Kitiara pushed back her stool and put her right hand in the center of the table. "I'll take that vow," she said. Her eyes fixed Tanis in a powerful hold. "Five years."

Tanis lowered his hand on hers. "Five years."

"Upon my honor, and in the name of the house of Brightblade," Sturm said solemnly, "I vow to return in five years." He placed his sword hand on Tanis's.

"Me, too," said Caramon. His broad palm hid even Sturm's hand from sight.

"If I am living, I will be here," said Raistlin, with a strange lilt in his voice. He added his gracile touch to his brother's.

"And me! I'll be here waiting for all of you!" So saying, Tasslehoff stepped up on the tabletop. His tiny hand rested next to Raistlin's, both lost on Caramon's wide hand.

"Lot of confounded nonsense," Flint grumbled. "How do I know what I'll be doing five years from now? Could be a lot more important than sitting in an inn, waiting for a pack of errant rascals."

"C'mon, Flint. We're all taking the oath," said the kender.

"Hmph." The old dwarf leaned over and set his age- and work-worn hands around the others. "Reorx be with you until we meet again," he said. His voice caught, and his friends knew him for the sentimental old fraud he was.

* * * * *

They left Flint at the table. The twins departed. Tanis, Kitiara, and Sturm strolled to the foot of the stairway. Tasslehoff trailed after them.

"I will say good night," said Sturm, with a glance at Tanis. "But not good-bye." They clasped hands. "Kit, my horse is stabled at the farrier's. Will you meet me there?"

"That's good. My beast is there, too. Sunrise tomorrow?" Sturm nodded and looked around for Tas.

"Tas?" he called. "Where did he get to? I wanted to say good-bye."

Tanis gestured toward the inn above. "He went back up, I think." Sturm nodded and strode away into the cool night. Tanis and Kitiara were left with the crickets, which sang from the massive trees, a symphony of hundreds.

"Walk with me?" asked Tanis.

"Wherever you like," Kitiara replied.

They strolled a dozen paces from the inn before Kitiara took the opportunity to slip her arm through Tanis's. "I have a thought," she said slyly.

"What's that?"

"That you should stay with me tonight. It may be five years before we see each other again."

He halted and drew his arm free. "I cannot," said Tanis.

"Oh? And why not? There was a time not so long ago when you couldn't keep away from me."

"Yes, in between the times you spent far away, campaigning for whoever would pay you."

Kitiara lifted her chin. "I'm not ashamed of what I do."

"I don't expect you to be. The point is, I've come to realize more and more clearly that you and I are of two worlds, Kit. Worlds that can never hope to be reconciled."

"So what are you saying?"

"I had a birthday while you were gone. Do you know how old I am? Ninety-seven. Ninety-seven years old, Kit! If I were a human, I'd be a withered ancient. Or dead."

She eyed his willowy form appreciatively. "You're not withered or ancient."

"That's the point! My elvish blood will extend my life far beyond the normal span of humans." Tanis stepped closer and took her hands. "While you, Kit, will age and die."

Kitiara laughed. "Let me worry about that!"

"You won't. I know you, Kit. You're burning your youth out like a two-ended candle in a gale. How do you think I feel, knowing that you might be killed in battle for some petty warlord, while I would live on and on without you? It has to end, Kit. Tonight. Here and now."

Though it was dark, and the white moon, Solinari, was hidden by boughs of vallenwood, Tanis saw the hurt in Kitiara's expression. It was there but an instant. She mastered it and forced a superior smile.

"Maybe it's just as well," she said. "I never did like being tied down. My poor fool of a mother was like that—she never could get along without a husband to tell her what's what. That's not my style. I take after my father. Burning in the wind, am I? So be it! I ought to thank you, Tanthalus Half-Elven, for holding a mirror up to the truth—"

He interrupted her tirade with a kiss. It was a gentle, brotherly kiss on the cheek. Kitiara glared.

"It's not what I want, Kit," Tanis said with great sorrow. "It's how it must be."

She slapped him. Being the warrior she was, Kitiara's slap was no light tap. Tanis staggered and put a hand to his face. A thin smear of blood showed in the corner of his mouth.

"Keep your pretty gestures," she spat. "Save them for your next lover, if you find one! Who will it be, Tanis? A full-blooded elf maiden? But no, the elves would despise you as a half-breed. You need a female version of yourself to love." She marched away, leaving Tanis staring. "You'll never find her!" Kitiara called from the darkness. "Never!"

The crickets had quieted under Kitiara's shouts. In their own time they began to sing again. Tanis stood alone in the night, finding no comfort in their song.

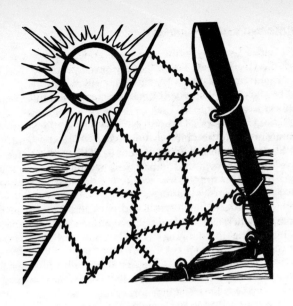

Chapter 2

High Crest

The sky had not yet lost its violet hue when Sturm reached the farrier's shop. Tirien, the farrier, had his establishment in a vallenwood tree. The winding ramp to Tirien's shop was doubly wide and strongly braced for horses. Tirien, ruddy-faced from leaning over forge fires, and with heavily muscled arms and shoulders from wielding his farrier's hammer, was already up and about when the knight arrived.

"Sturm!" he boomed. "Come in, lad. I'm just straightening some nails." Tirien's helper, a boy named Mercot, plucked a red-hot spike from the furnace with a pair of tongs. He set the bent nail in the groove atop Tirien's anvil, and the brawny farrier smote it twice. Mercot flicked the straight nail into a bucket of water. A serpent's hiss and a wisp of steam arose.

"I need my horse, Tirien," said Sturm.

"Right. Mercot, fetch Master Brightblade's animal."

The boy's eyes widened. Rings of soot around them made him look like a startled owl. "The chestnut gelding?"

"Aye, and be quick about it!" said Tirien. To Sturm he continued, "Reshod him, as you asked. A good mount."

Sturm paid his bill while Mercot led Tallfox, his horse, to the lower platform. Sturm had bought Tallfox from a Quekiri tribesman only a few weeks before, and he was still learning the horse's manners.

He shouldered his bedroll and pack and descended the ramp to where Mercot had tied his mount. Tirien's hammer rang out again, banging twisted scrap iron into arrow-straight horseshoe spikes.

Sturm distributed his baggage over Tallfox's sides and rump. He filled his water bottle and heard, "You're late."

Kitiara was slouched in a corner under the livery's eaves. She was wrapped to her ears in a red horse blanket.

"Am I?" asked Sturm. "The sun is just rising. When did you get here?"

"Hours ago. I slept here," she said, casting off the blanket. Underneath, Kitiara still wore the clothes she'd had on the previous night. She stretched her arms and braced the knots out of her stiff back.

"Why in the gods' names did you sleep here?" asked Sturm. "Did you think I'd forget and leave without you?"

"Oh, not you, noble friend. It seemed like a good place to sleep, that's all. Besides, Pira needed a shoe repaired."

Sturm led Tallfox down to the ground. He swung into Tallfox's saddle and waited for his companion. Kitiara came loping down the ramp, leading a rather nondescript brown and white spotted mare.

"Something wrong?" she asked, mounting beside Sturm.

"I just imagined that you would prefer a fiery stallion for your mount," he replied. "This, ah, quaint animal doesn't suit you at all."

"This 'quaint animal' will still be walking a steady pace long after that beast of yours is no more than bones and hide," Kitiara said. Her fitful sleep had not improved her temperament since her parting with Tanis. "I've been on six campaigns with Pira, and she's always carried me home."

"My apologies."

They rode out of Solace, north by east. The new sun pierced the hills around Solace and warmed the air. Sturm and Kitiara breakfasted simply, on jerky and water. The fine dawn became an even finer morning, and Kitiara's spirits rose.

"I can't be unhappy on the road," she said. "There's too much to see and do."

"We should be on guard as well," Sturm said. "I heard travelers in the inn say there were brigands about."

"Tshaw. Peasants on foot may have reason to fear brigands, but two warriors, armed and mounted—it's the robbers who'd best be afraid!" Sturm made polite assent, but still kept his eyes on the horizon and his sword hilt handy.

Their route was simple enough. Once clear of Solace's hills, the two would turn northwest and make for the coast. On the shore of the Straits of Schallsea was a small fishing port called Zaradene. From there Kitiara and Sturm could easily take passage to Caergoth in southern Thelgaard. North of Caergoth lay Solamnia proper, their ultimate destination.

Such was their plan. But plans, as said the sage wizard Arcanist, are like figures drawn in sand: easily made and just as easily disturbed.

The forests and hills of Abanasinia thinned with the miles. Kitiara filled the hours with tales of her past adventures.

"My first hire was with Mikkian's Marauders. They were a bad lot. Mikkian was a low-born lout from Lemish. He had the bad fortune of always losing parts of himself in battle—an eye, an arm, half an ear. Pretty ugly he was, and mean! I walked into his camp, sure of my skill with a blade. In those days, I had to pretend to be a boy, else the churls would have ganged up on me," she said.

"How does one go about getting hired as a mercenary?"

"In Mikkian's band, there was only one way: kill one of his men. Mikkian had only so many openings on his payroll, and he wouldn't expand it for anybody." Kitiara wrinkled her nose at the memories conjured up by Mikkian. "Worthless rogue! The foot soldiers made a big ring and put me in it with a snaggletoothed axeman called—now what was his name? First man I ever killed. Trigneth? Drigneth? Some name like that. So we went at it, axe against sword. It was not a pretty fight, I tell you. We had to stay in the dead center of the ring, or Mikkian's boys would poke us with daggers and spear points. Trigneth—Drigneth?—fought like a woodcutter, chop, chop, chop. He never laid an edge on me. I got him with a straight thrust, right through the neck." She regarded Sturm. He looked shocked.

"How long were you with Mikkian's company?" he asked, finally.

"Twelve weeks. We sacked a walled town near Takar, and Mikkian finally lost a part he couldn't do without." Sturm raised an eyebrow. "His head," said Kitiara. "That was the end of the Marauders. It was every man for himself, and the whole company broke up, looting and killing. The towns-folk rose up and fought back, wiping out the whole damn gang. Save for yours truly." She smiled crookedly.

Kitiara had a deep fund of such stories, all exciting and nearly all bloody. Sturm found himself confused. He'd known her for about two years now and was no closer to understanding her. This handsome, bright woman pos-sessed no small measure of wit and charm, and yet was enamored with war on its basest level. He had to admit he marveled at her strength and cunning—but he feared Kiti-ara a little, too.

The road petered into a path, and after a score of miles it merged into a stretch of sandy pine barrens. The air grew still and heavy with moisture. They camped in the barrens that night, and the wind gave them their first smell of the sea.

Pine knots made an acrid, smoky campfire. As Kitiara fed the flames, Sturm watered the horses. He returned to the dim circle of firelight and squatted on the sand. Kitiara handed him a cold mutton joint. Sturm gnawed the pep-pered meat, and Kitiara leaned back, her feet to the fire and her head pillowed by her bedroll.

"There's Paladine," she said. "See?" She pointed to the

heavens. "Paladine, Mishakal, Branchala," she said, naming each constellation in turn. "Do you know the sky?"

"My boyhood tutor, Vedro, was an astrologer," Sturm said, not really answering. He lifted his eyes. "It is said that the will of the gods can be divined by the movement of the stars and planets."

"What gods?" Kitiara replied lazily.

"You don't believe in the gods?"

"Why should I? What have they done for the world lately? Or for me ever?"

Sturm could tell she was baiting him, so he decided to drop the subject. "What is that group there?" he asked. "Opposite Paladine?"

"Takhisis. The Queen of Darkness."

"Oh, yes. The Dragonqueen." He tried to see the authoress of evil, but to him it was only a spatter of stars.

The white orb of Solinari climbed above the horizon. In its glow, the sandy hillocks and solitary pines were pale ghosts of their daytime selves. Not long after, in the middle quadrant of the sky, a red glow of equal size appeared.

"Now that I know," said Sturm. "Lunitari, the red moon."

"Luin to the Ergothites, Red-Eye in Goodlund. A strange color for a moon, don't you think?" said Kitiara.

He tossed the naked mutton bone aside. "I didn't know there were proper colors for moons."

"White or black are proper. Red means nothing." She propped her head up so that Lunitari was directly in her line of sight. "I wonder why it's red?"

Sturm reclined on his bedroll. "The gods ordained it so. Lunitari is the abode of neutrality, of neutral magic and illusion. Vedro theorized that the color came from the blood sacrificed to the gods." He offered this cautiously. "Other philosophers claim the red color represents the heart of Huma, the first knight of the Dragonlance." There was only silence from his companion. "Kit?" he said quietly. A rasp from the shadows revealed the result of his lecture. Kitiara was asleep.

* * * * *

The village of Zaradene was a low, brown smudge on the gray-white shore. There were perhaps fifty weatherworn houses of varying size, none with more than two stories. Sturm and Kitiara rode down the face of a steeply sloping dune toward the village. On the way, they had to thread through lines of sharpened stakes, buried in the sand with the points slanting out. Here and there the stakes were scorched by fire.

"A hedgehog," Kitiara remarked. "A defense against cavalry. The villagers must have been raided not long ago." Behind the stakes was a shallow trench, which was spotted with black clots of blood, soaked into the sand.

The faces of the people of Zaradene were not friendly as Sturm and Kitiara rode up the single sandy track that was the main street. Sullen eyes and work-gnarled hands clenched into fists seemed to be everywhere.

Kitiara reined up and dismounted in front of a sagging gray tavern that bore the name Three Fishes. Odd white posts and rafter ends showed between the weatherworn clapboards. Sturm tied Tallfox to one of the posts. It was bone, from some enormous, long-dead sea creature.

"What do you suppose it was?" he asked Kit curiously.

Kitiara glanced at the bone and said, "Sea serpent, maybe. Come. There'll be shipmasters in here."

The Three Fishes tavern was well filled with patrons for so early an hour. The first master that Kitiara approached growled "Mercenaries!" and spat at her feet. She almost drew her blade on him, but Sturm caught her wrist. "Cut one, and we'll have to fight them all," he muttered. "Be patient. We must have a boat to cross the straits."

They tried half a dozen sea captains and were rebuffed each time. Kitiara was fuming. Sturm was puzzled. He'd voyaged before, and knew that mariners usually liked to take on a few passengers. They paid better than fishing or cargo did, took care of themselves, and didn't take up much deck space. So why are the masters of Zaradene so hostile? he wondered.

They drifted to the bar. Kitiara called for ale, but all the barkeep had was black wine of Nostar. After a sip of the bitter vintage, Sturm shoved his cup aside. Better to be thirsty, he thought.

Kitiara plunked one of her Silvanesti coins on the dirty bar. Even in the dim tavern, the glow of gold caught the barkeep's eye. He came to the end of the bar, where Sturm and Kitiara leaned.

"You want something?" said the man. A sheen of sweat coated his shaved head.

"Words," said Kitiara. "Merely a few words."

"For that amount of gold, you can have all the words you want." The barkeeper tucked his greasy rag under his arm. Sturm wondered idly which was dirtier, the rag or the barkeep's canvas shirt.

"What happened here?" asked Kitiara.

"They don't like mercenaries here. Ten nights ago, horsemen attacked the village. Carried off everything they could grab, including some women and children."

"Who were they?" Sturm asked. "Did they wear insignia?"

"Some say they wasn't true men at all," said the barkeeper. "Some say they had hard, dark skin and—" He looked from side to side to see if anyone else was listening. "—and some say they had tails!"

Sturm started to ask another question, but Kitiara stopped him with a glance. "We need to buy passage to Caergoth," she said. "Will anybody in Zaradene take us?"

"Dunno. Some of them lost heavy in the raid. They'd as like to slit your throats as take you to sea."

The barkeep went back to dispensing his awful wares. Sturm surveyed the room. "I don't like this," he said. "Raiders with tails? What sort of monsters could they have been?"

"Don't take that one's mutterings too seriously," Kitiara said. "The farther you get from safe havens like Solace, the wilder and weirder the tales you'll hear." She tossed back the Nostarian wine without a shudder. "Skinhead is right about one thing; we have no friends in this room."

From behind their backs, a voice said, "Be not certain of that, me hearties."

Sturm and Kitiara faced the speaker. He was a full head shorter than Kitiara, with sharply pointed features and a clean, boyish face—signs of elven blood. Kitiara saw a flash of Tanis as she had last seen him, blood on his lips, his cheek red from her slap, staring at her in shock.

"Tirolan Ambrodel, at your service." He bowed from the waist. "Mariner, map maker, gem cutter, and piper." Tirolan reached for Kitiara's hand and raised it to his lips. He didn't kiss it, but touched it to his forehead. She smiled.

Sturm introduced them both and asked, "Can you provide us with transport to Caergoth, Master Ambrodel?"

"Easily, sir. Me craft, *High Crest*, is laden with dunnage for that very port. Will it be just the two of you?"

"And two horses. We're traveling light," Kitiara said.

"For two passengers and two horses, I shall require five gold pieces—each."

Sturm gaped at the high price, but Kitiara laughed scornfully. "We'll give you four gold pieces for the both of us," she said.

"Eight for both," countered Tirolan.

"Five," she said. "And we'll pay in Silvanesti gold."

Tirolan Ambrodel's arched brows bunched over his thin nose. "True gold of Eli?"

Kitiara picked up the coin from the bar and flashed it in the mariner's face. Carefully, almost tenderly, Tirolan reached for the elven gold. He held the coin, caressed it, and ran his fingertips over the worn inscription. "Very fine," he said. "Do you know that this coin is more than five hundred years old? Minted just before the Lords of the East withdrew into the forest, severing all ties with the human world. How many of these relics have you tossed away for meat and wine?"

"I had a dozen," said Kitiara. "Now I have five. They are yours if you ferry us to Caergoth."

"Done!"

"When do we sail?" asked Sturm.

"The tide ebbs with the first moon's rise. When the silver moon clears the grip of the sea, we up anchor! And away." Tirolan slipped the coin into a suede pouch on his belt. "Now, follow me, and I'll take you to the *High Crest*."

Sturm dropped some coins on the bar, and they exited the tavern. They led Tallfox and Pira through the streets of Zaradene, following as Tirolan Ambrodel led. People turned from them everywhere they went. One old crone uttered a charm against bad luck as Tirolan passed.

"The natives are very superstitious," he said. "Anything or anyone foreign is believed dangerous these days."

Sturm looked back at the circle of stakes in the dunes above the town. "They have reason to be afraid," he said.

Zaradene had a single decrepit wharf. Sturm was uncertain the warped planks would hold Tallfox's weight, but Tirolan assured him that it was safe. Cargo far heavier than horses passed over the wharf every day, he said.

"Where's your boat?" asked Kitiara.

"Me ship is beyond the headland, yonder."

"Why anchor so far out?" Sturm asked.

"Me vessel and crew are not well liked in Zaradene. When we must call here, we moor in deep water so as to avoid trouble with the natives."

A wide, shell-like lighter was tied to the pier. A man lay asleep in the stern, a ragged cap over his face. Tirolan jumped into the lighter, startling the man into wakefulness.

"This your boat?" said Tirolan in a loud, cheerful voice.

"Uh, yeah."

"Well then, hop to it, man. You can earn your grog money for the week."

The horses were led to a gangplank. Kitiara spoke soothingly to Pira, and the mare entered the rocking lighter without too much trouble. Tallfox, on the other hand, balked completely. Sturm wrapped the reins around his fists and tried to drag the terrified animal into the boat.

"No, no, that's not the way," said Tirolan. He hopped to the narrow gunwale and walked agilely to the foot of the gangplank. "May I, Master Brightblade?" Sturm reluctantly gave over the reins. Tallfox began to calm the moment Tirolan's slim hands stroked his neck.

Tirolan spoke soothingly to the horse. "Strong as you are, and you're afraid of a little boat ride? I'm not afraid. Am I better than you? Am I braver?" To Sturm and Kitiara's astonishment, Tallfox shook his head energetically and snorted. "Then," continued Tirolan in quiet, golden tones, "step down and take your place with your friends." The chestnut gelding stepped daintily into the lighter and stood quietly next to Pira. Their tails switched gently in time with the rocking of the boat.

"How did you do that?" asked Kitiara.

Tirolan shrugged. "I have a way with animals."

After sculling away from the pier, the boatman raised a tattered lateen sail. The lighter skimmed between bobbing fishing craft and past the few major merchant ships in the harbor. The laden boat ran uneventfully all the way to the southern headland. Then the wind died, and the boatman went back to his sweep.

Dark slate-and-indigo clouds piled up on the southern horizon. Against the blue and green of the sea stood the white hull of the *High Crest*. Its shape was quite unlike the other boats in Zaradene harbor. The sheer line rose from the low, sharp bow to a high poop. The single lofty mast was painted white, too, and in the freshening air, a green pennant rippled from the masthead.

"Me vessel," said Tirolan proudly. "Isn't she beautiful?"

"I've never seen a white ship before," said Sturm.

"It's very handsome," Kitiara said. She frowned privately at Sturm and gestured to him.

Amidships, they huddled between their mounts. "This is getting stranger by the minute," whispered Kitiara. "An elven captain, shunned by the local folk, a strange white ship anchored far from other vessels. There's more to this than meets the eye. I'm glad I lied about how many gold coins I have."

Sturm said, "I agree. The way he charmed Tallfox wasn't natural. I think he used a spell." To Sturm, steeped in the Solamnic tradition, there was no worse sign than the use of magic.

Kitiara put a hand to his shoulder and said, "Keep your sword handy."

"All is well?" called Tirolan, over his shoulder.

"Very well," said Kitiara. "Oh, your ship is big!"

They were now only a hundred yards from it, and the *High Crest* filled their view. The white ship rode steadily in the waves, anchored at both bow and stern. The deck and rigging were empty, but a boarding ladder hung over the bulwark, waiting. Tirolan snared a dangling rope and tied the lighter fast to the *High Crest*.

"Ho, there, me hearties! Show yourselves," he sang out in a clear tenor. The ship's ghostly inactivity vanished in a flurry of bare feet and whoops. A score of agile sailors, all sharp-featured and beardless, poured onto the deck. Sturm found himself seized by eager hands and hauled to the deck. Kitiara followed, carried by four smiling sailors. She laughed, and they set her on her feet beside Sturm.

A sailor with white hair (yet quite young looking) approached Tirolan and bowed to him. "Hail, Kade Berun!" said Tirolan.

"Hail hail, Tirolan Ambrodel!"

"We've two fine horses to bring aboard, Kade. See to it, will you?"

"Horses! I haven't seen horses since—" Kade Berun glanced at Sturm and Kitiara. "—since we left home." He shouted some orders in a strange tongue, and the lively sailors rushed to the rail overlooking the lighter. They looked at Tallfox and Pira with unconcealed admiration. The chatter ceased.

"Sling a boom!" called the boatman in the lighter. "I'll fasten the harness and you can hoist them up!"

The *High Crest* crew did so and they all were quickly aboard the ship. Beneath the rapidly setting sun, the sailors fell to quickly and soon had the *High Crest* ready for sea.

The sail was raised, a fat triangle of brilliant green fabric. The *High Crest* stirred and stood out from the Abanasinian headland. Tirolan took the wheel and buried the ship's bow in the tossing waves of the Straits of Schallsea.

Kitiara discarded her black leather jerkin. The breeze stirred her light linen blouse. She closed her eyes and ran her fingers through her short black curls. When she opened her eyes, she spied Sturm brooding by the bowsprit.

"Cheer up!" she said, whacking him on the back. "The wind is fair and Tirolan seems to know his trade. We'll be in Caergoth in no time."

"I suppose," Sturm answered. "But I can't help being worried. The last time I made a sea voyage in these waters was as a boy. There was magic on that ship, and things went badly for my mother and me for a time."

"But you came through, didn't you?"

"We did."

"Then be calm! You're a knight in all but the ceremonial sense, going to reclaim your rightful heritage. Maybe you don't realize it, but I've got family in Solamnia, too."

"The Uth Matars?"

She nodded. "I've not had contact with them since my father left us. In all my travels, I've never penetrated the Solamnic Plain. When you declared your intention to go north, it seemed as good a time as any to do some exploring up there." She raised an eyebrow. "The Uth Matars are a knightly line, too, you know."

"No, I didn't." He realized he knew so little about her, really.

She left him by the bowsprit and went below. Sturm slipped the strap off his chin and removed his helmet. The twin brass horns were smudged; he'd have to polish them tonight. For now, he cradled the helmet against his chest, and let the sea wind wash through his long, tangled hair.

Chapter 3

The Severed Head

"Hail, Captain Tirolan," said Sturm, blinking in the
bright morning light.

"Hail, hail, Sturm Brightblade! We've reached the cape of
Caer in splendid time. Did you rest well?"

"Well enough. Why have we anchored so far from the
harbor?" Sturm asked.

Kade handed his captain a loose, hooded coat, which
Tirolan slipped on. "The city folk here are even less fond of
elves than those at Zaradene. Here comes one of me boys
now with a lighter for you," he said.

"I'll tell Kit we're going."

He lifted the latch on the cabin door and bulled right in—
to find that Kitiara was up and dressing. A linen blouse,
beautifully embroidered with red and blue, slid up over her

bare shoulders. She'd already exchanged her heavy corduroy riding pants for baggy Ergothic-style trousers. He could not help but stare.

"I'm just about ready," she said. "How does the city look?"

He swallowed and said, "We're a mile or two out. Tirolan fears the anti-elf sentiment in Caergoth. He's rowing ashore to scout things, and I'm going with him."

"Good." She picked up her sword belt and buckled it around her hips. "I'm ready, too."

The four of them lowered the horses with a block and tackle. Kade held the painter line, while Tirolan, Sturm, and Kitiara climbed down into the boat. The first mate cast them off, and Tirolan dug in with the oars.

It was a sultry morning, hotter than any they'd had yet, and a steamy calm hung over the water. No one spoke as Tirolan rowed toward the hazy line of the coast.

Caergoth was a major port, and the watercraft thickened as they drew nearer. Skiffs and dories, ketches and pinnaces plied to and fro, laden with fish, crab, and clams; larger boats shuttled goods from the big merchant ships at rest in the main harbor.

Tirolan swung his arms untiringly back and forth, maneuvering the yawl between the bigger vessels skillfully. Kitiara craned her neck to see up the steep side of an Ergothic argosy. A quartet of sailors in woolly caps leaned over the rail and hooted at her. She waved gaily and said to Sturm, "I'd like to see how bold they'd be if we faced each other with swords in our hands."

Once clear of the heavier ships, the trio noticed a very strange vessel drawn up to the deep-water docks. It was high and square, with a pair of what looked like wagon wheels attached to each side. The short mast was very thick, and a signal fire seemed to be burning from its top. A patch of grimy smoke drifted away from the ugly ship.

"What in the world is that?" asked Tirolan.

Creeping nearer, they saw that a heavy boom had been rigged to the craft's starboard side. A barge lay alongside it, and two enormous wooden crates were already on it. A third crate, fully as large as Tirolan's yawl, was slowly being hoisted off the deck of the queer, smoking ship.

"It's going to fall," said Tirolan. "Watch."

The boom swung out, revealing that the crate was wrapped up in a cargo net. Clusters of small figures heaved against the weight of the crate—in vain. The net sagged, a corner poked through, and the crate ripped free and crashed into the water, just missing the loaded barge. A string of little people, shrieking in high-pitched voices, tumbled over the side. Tirolan chuckled loudly.

"I should've known," he said. "Gnomes."

Sturm knew the little people only by reputation. They were incessant tinkerers, makers of weird machinery, and purveyors of endless theories. Disdaining magic, gnomes were the most fervent technologists on Krynn. For centuries, the gnomes and the Knights of Solamnia had maintained a pact of mutual aid, since both groups distrusted the workings of magic.

Tirolan rowed around the stern of the gnome ship. Kitiara pointed to an endless string of letters painted across the stern, along the side, under the bow—it was the name of the ship. The portion on the stern read, *Principle of Hydrodynamic Compression and Etheric Volatility, Controlled by the Most Ingenious System of Gears Invented by the Illustrious Inventor, He-Who-Utters-Polynomial-Fractions-While-Sleeping* and on and on.

"Should we lend a hand?" Sturm asked.

"Not unless you want to get wet," said Kitiara. Sure enough, the gnomes on the barge who tried to rig up a life line succeeded only in falling overboard themselves. Tirolan rowed on.

"I wonder what the crates contain," Sturm said as the gnomish pandemonium passed astern.

"Who knows? A new machine to peel and core apples, perhaps," said Tirolan. "Here's the dock."

The elf captain shipped his oars, and the yawl coasted in to the dock. Sturm slipped the bowline over a cleat, and the three of them climbed the short ladder to the platform.

With a large block and tackle, anchored to the dock for loading and unloading cargo, they easily transported their horses to the dock and shore.

"Where to now?" asked Sturm.

A row of grog shops and taverns lined the wharf, and beyond them were great warehouses.

"I don't know about you fellows," Kitiara said, gazing at the line of public houses, "but I'm starved."

"Can't you wait?" objected Sturm.

"Why should I?" She hitched her sword belt into its proper angle and set off, trailing her horse behind her. Tirolan and Sturm reluctantly followed.

She chose, for no obvious reason, a tavern called The Severed Head. Kitiara tied her horse outside, kicked the door open, and stood there, surveying the room. Figures stirred in the dim recesses. An odd, fetid odor wafted out the door.

"Faw!" said Tirolan. "That smell is not human."

"Come, Kit, this is no place for us." Sturm tried to take her by the elbow and steer her away. But Kitiara would have none of it. She jerked her arm free and stepped in.

"I'm tired of barren roads and snug ships," she said. "This looks like an interesting place."

"Be on your guard," Sturm muttered in Tirolan's pointed ear. "Kit's a good friend, but long months of the quiet life in Solace have made her reckless." Tirolan winked and followed Kitiara inside.

There wasn't an actual bar in The Severed Head, just a scattering of tables and benches. Kitiara swaggered to a table near the center of the room and threw one leg over the back of a chair. "Barkeep!" she shouted. In the darkness, heads swiveled toward her. Sturm saw more than one pair of eyes glowing in the shadows. They were red, like the coals in a farrier's furnace.

Sturm and Tirolan sat down warily. A squat, lumpish creature appeared by Kitiara's elbow. It puffed like a leaky bellows, and each breath brought a fresh wave of foulness.

"Uhh?" said the lumpish creature.

"Ale," she snapped.

"Uh-uh."

"Ale!" she said a little louder. The creature shook its upper body in negative fashion. Kitiara slapped the tabletop. "Bring the specialty of the house," she said. This elicited an affirmative grunt. The servant trundled around.

"Double-quick!" Kit screeched, and the creature ambled off.

Something rose out of the tavern's shadows. It stood a good half-head taller than Sturm and was at least twice as wide. The shambling hulk approached their table.

"This is not a place for you," said the hulk. Its voice was deep and hollow.

"I don't know," Kitiara said airily, "I've been in worse."

"This is not a place for you," it repeated.

"Maybe we should go," said Tirolan quickly. "There are many taverns." He eyed the door, gauging the distance to it.

"I already ordered. Sit down."

The hulk leaned over and rested a hand, as big as a dinner plate and with four fingers, on the table. The hand was dry and scaly. "You go, or I send you out!" said the hulk.

Tirolan sprang up. "There's no need for trouble—" The creature's other arm shot out, catching the elf in the chest. Tirolan staggered back. His hood fell off his head, revealing his elven features. There was a general intake of breath in the room. The hiss was enough to make the hair on Sturm's neck bristle.

"*Kurtrah!*" said the menacing creature.

Sturm and Kitiara stood smoothly but quickly. Swords flicked out of sheaths. Tirolan produced an elvish short sword, and the three closed together, back to back.

"What have you gotten us into?" Sturm asked, keeping his blade on guard.

"I just wanted a little fun," Kitiara replied. "What's the matter, Sturm? Do you want to live forever?"

A three-legged stool hurtled out of the dark. Sturm knocked it aside with his blade. "Not forever, but a few more years would be nice!"

Somewhere in the gloom, steel glinted. "Move for the door," Tirolan said. "There are too many of these things in here to fight." A clay mug shattered on an overhead beam, showering them with shards. "And I can barely see them!"

"It would be nice to have a candle or two," admitted Kitiara. One huge figure moved out of the shadows toward her. It wielded a blade as wide as her palm, but she parried, disengaged, and thrust into the darkness. Kitiara felt her sword point strike flesh, and her attacker howled.

"Candle? I can do better than that!" Tirolan said. He whirled and jammed his sword into the center of their table. He began to sing in Elvish, hastily and shakily. The blade of his weapon glowed red.

Two creatures closed on Sturm. He beat against their heavier weapons, making a lot of noise but accomplishing nothing. "Tirolan, we need you!" he barked. The elf sang on. The short sword was nearly white now. Smoke curled up from the tabletop. An instant later, the table burst into flame.

The enemy stood out in the first flash of fire. There were eight of them, great, brawny lizardlike creatures in thickly quilted cloaks. The light dazzled them, and they retreated a few steps. Kitiara gave a battle cry and attacked.

She avoided a cut by her towering opponent and brought the keen edge of her sword down on the creature's arm. The big sword clattered to the floor. Kitiara took her weapon in both hands and thrust it deep into her foe's chest. The creature bellowed in rage and pain, and tried to get her with its clawed hand. She recovered and thrust again. The creature groaned once and fell on its face.

Sturm traded cuts with two creatures. The burning table filled the room with smoke, and the creatures backed away, gasping. Tirolan, on Sturm's right, was not doing well. He'd recovered his now-cool sword, but the short weapon was doubly outclassed. Only his superior nimbleness was saving him from being cut down.

With a bang, the creatures stormed the tavern door and smashed it aside. Flames had spread down the table's legs to the tinder-dry floor. "Out, out!" Sturm cried. Kitiara was still dueling, so Sturm grabbed her by the back of the collar and pulled her away.

"Let go! Leave me alone!" She threw an elbow at Sturm. He blocked the blow and shook Kitiara.

"Listen to me! The place is burning down around your ears! Get out!" he cried. Reluctantly, she complied.

The smoke billowing from the upper-story windows had drawn a crowd of curious Caergothians. Tirolan, Sturm, and Kitiara erupted into the street ahead of the flames. Sturm scanned the watching crowd, but the strange lizard creatures were gone.

The three of them leaned on each other and coughed the rancid smoke from their lungs. Gradually, Sturm became aware of the silence of the crowd around them. He lifted his head and saw that they all were staring at Tirolan.

"Elf," someone said, making the word sound like a curse.

"Trying to burn down our town," said another.

"Always causing trouble," added a third.

"Back to the boat," Sturm murmured to Tirolan. "And watch your back."

Kitiara offered Tirolan's fee, but he took only half. The elvish sailor started off as Sturm and Kitiara mounted their horses. He stopped, though, turned, and tossed a shiny purple carved gem to Kit. A wink of his eye made her smile. "A gift," was all he said. The three of them then parted.

Chapter 4

A Hint of Purple

Kitiara and Sturm rode up a winding trail to the sand cliffs overlooking the bay. The *High Crest* had shrunk to toy size in the distance. After a last look at the elf ship, they turned their horses inland.

They soon reached the road outside the walls of Caergoth. From the sutlers and traders who lined the road they bought bread and meat, dried fruit and cheese.

The road ran as straight as an arrow east. Domed and cobbled, it was one of the few public works remaining from pre-Cataclysmic times. Kitiara and Sturm rode side by side down the center of the road. Its shoulders were fairly thick with travelers on foot, at least for the first ten miles or so from the city. By mid-afternoon, they were alone.

They said little. Kitiara finally broke the silence saying, "I wonder why there are no travelers on the way to Caergoth."

"I was puzzled by that myself," said Sturm. "A bare road is a bad sign."

"War or robbers beset empty roads."

"I've heard no rumors of wars, so it must be the latter." They paused by the side of the road long enough to don their mail shirts and helmets. No sense catching an arrow when they were so close to reaching Solamnia.

The eerie desolation persisted to the end of the day. Now and again they passed the burned-out remains of a wagon or the blanched bones of slaughtered horses and cattle. Kitiara rode with her sword across her saddle.

They were tired from the day's morning mayhem and decided to camp early. They found a pleasant clearing in a ring of oaks, a hundred yards from the road. Tallfox and Pira were tied to a picket line to graze on grass and broom straw. Sturm found a spring and fetched water, while Kitiara built a fire. Dinner was bacon and hard biscuit toasted over the fire. Night closed in, and they moved closer to the flames.

Smoke wound in a loose spiral toward the stars. The moons were up. Solinari and Lunitari. Souls rise up like smoke to heaven, Sturm thought.

"Sturm."

Kitiara's voice brought him out of his reverie. "Yes?"

"We'll have to sleep in turns."

"Quite so. Ah, I'll stand watch first, all right?"

"Suits me." Kitiara circled around the campfire with her bedroll. She unrolled it beside Sturm and lay down. "Wake me when the silver moon sets," she said.

He looked down at the mass of dark curls by his knee. Veteran that she was, Kitiara soon dropped off. Sturm fed the fire from a handy pile of kindling and sat cross-legged, with his sword across his lap. Once Kitiara stirred, uttering faint moans. Hesitantly, Sturm touched her hair. She responded by snuggling closer to him, until her head was resting on his crossed ankles.

He never felt the lethargy creep over him. One minute Sturm was awake, facing the fire with Kitiara asleep in front of him, and the next thing he knew he was lying facedown on the ground. There was dirt in his mouth, but for some reason he couldn't spit it out. Worse, he couldn't seem to move at all. One eye was mashed shut against the ground. With tremendous effort, he was able to open the other.

He saw the fire still burning. There were several pairs of legs around it, clad in ragged deerskin leggings. There was an odd, unpleasant smell, like singed hide or burning hair. Kitiara was beside him, lying on her back, her eyes closed.

"Nuttin' but food," said a scratchy, bass voice. "Dere's nuttin' in dis bag but some lousy food!"

"Me! Me!" said another, shriller voice. "Me find coin!"

One pair of legs ambled out of Sturm's sight. "Where da coins?" He heard a tinkle of metal. One of Kitiara's last Silvanesti gold coins dropped on the ground. The shrill speaker said "Ai!" and dropped on his hands and knees. Then Sturm saw who—what—they were.

There was no mistake. The pointed heads, angular features, gray skin, red eyes—they were goblins. The smell was theirs, too. Sturm tried to muster all his strength to stand, but it felt as though bars of lead were piled on his back. He could see and feel enough to know he wasn't tied. That, and the suddenness with which he was taken, meant that someone had cast a spell on him and Kitiara. But who? Goblins were notoriously dimwitted. They lacked the concentration necessary for spellcasting.

"Stop your bickering and keep searching," said a clear, human voice.

So! The goblins were not alone!

Hard, bony hands grabbed his left arm and rolled him over. Sturm's one open eye stared into the face of two of the robbers. One was warty and had lost his front teeth. The other bore scars on his neck from a failed hanging.

"Ai! Him eye open!" squawked the warty one. "He see!"

Scarface produced an ugly, fork-bladed dagger. "I fix dat," he said. Before he could strike the helpless Sturm, another brigand yelped. The others quickly converged on him.

"I found! I found!" babbled the goblin. What he had found was the arrowhead amethyst Tirolan had given Kitiara. She had tied a string around the carved shoulders of the stone and had been wearing it around her neck. The finder held it up and capered away from his fellows. They slapped and clawed at him for the pale purple stone.

"Let me see that," said the man. The dancing goblin halted and contritely carried the amethyst into the shadows beyond the fire. "Rubbish," said the man. "A flawed bit of crystal." The arrowhead arced through the air. It hit the dirt between Sturm and Kitiara and bounced into Kitiara's slack and open palm. The goblins scampered over to retrieve it.

"Leave it!" the man commanded. "It's worthless."

"Pretty, pretty!" protested Warty. "Me keep."

"I said leave it! Or shall I get the wand?"

The goblins—Sturm estimated there were four—shrank back and gibbered.

"We'll take the coins and the horses. Leave the rest," said the robbers' human master.

"What about da swords?" said Scarface. "Dese is good irun." He held out Sturm's sword for his leader to see.

"Yes, too good for you. Bring it. It will fetch good money at Trader Lovo's. Get the woman's, too."

Warty hopped over to Kitiara. He kicked her arm aside and bent over to draw the sword, which lay under her. As he did, her hand clamped around the goblin's ankle.

"Wha?" said the wart-faced goblin.

Kitiara yanked his leg out from under him, and the goblin went down with a thud. In the next instant, she was up, sword in hand. Warty groped for his dagger, but never drew it. With one cut, Kitiara sent his ugly head bouncing away.

"Get her! Get her, you miserable wretches! It's three against one!" yelled the man from the shadows.

Scarface pulled a hook-bladed bill off his shoulder and attacked. Kitiara knocked the clumsy weapon away repeatedly. The other two goblins tried to circle behind her. She turned so that the fire was at her back.

Sturm raged against the spell that kept him helpless. A goblin's foot passed within easy reach of his right hand, but he couldn't even flex a finger to help Kitiara.

Not that she needed any help. When Scarface lunged with his bill, she lopped the hook off. The goblin stared stupidly at his shortened shaft. Kitiara thrust through him. "Now it's two to one!" she said. She leaped over the campfire, landing between the last two robbers. They screeched in terror and dropped their daggers. She cut one down as he stood there. The last goblin ran to the edge of the clearing. Sturm heard him die among the oaks. There were a few other sounds— feet running, loud breathing, and a howl of pain.

"Thought you could get away, eh?" Kitiara said. She had caught the hidden magic-user and brought him back into the firelight. He was a gaunt fellow twice Sturm's age, dressed in a shabby gray robe. Tools of his art dangled from a rope tied around his waist: a wand, a bag of herbs, amulets wrought in lead and copper. Kitiara kicked the magician's legs out from under him, and he sprawled in the dirt beside Sturm.

"Take the spell off my friend," Kitiara demanded.

"I-I can't."

"You mean you won't!" She poked him with her sword.

"No, no! I don't know how! I don't know how to take it off." He seemed ashamed. "I never had to take a paralysis spell off before. The goblins always cut their throats."

"Because you ordered them to!"

"No! No!"

Kitiara spat. "The only thing worse than a thief is a fool weakling of a thief."

She raised her blade to her shoulder. "There's only one way to break the spell that I know of." She was right, and when the magic-user was dead, the leaden feeling vanished from Sturm's limbs. He sat up, rubbing his stiff neck.

"By all the gods, Kitiara, you're ruthless!" he said. He looked around the campsite, now a bloody battlefield. "Did you have to kill them all?"

"There's gratitude for you," she said. She wiped her blade on the tail of the dead magician's robe. "They would have cheerfully cut our throats. Sometimes I don't understand you, Sturm."

He remembered the goblin's fork-bladed dagger and said, "You have a point. Still, killing that scruffy magician was no honorable deed."

She slid her blade into its sheath. "I didn't do it for honor," she said. "I was just being practical."

They gathered their belongings from where the robbers had scattered them. Sturm saw Kitiara pick up the amethyst necklace. "Look," she said. "It's clear."

In the light from the fire, Sturm saw that the once-purple stone was now ordinary, transparent quartz. "That explains it," he said. "You were able to move when the amethyst fell into your hand, yes?"

The light dawned on her. "That's right. I was wearing it over my blouse and under my mail—"

"When it touched your skin, the paralysis spell was broken. The dissipation of the spell bled all the color from the stone. It's just an arrowhead-shaped piece of quartz now."

Kitiara slipped the loop over her head. "I'll keep it, just the same. Tirolan probably never realized he was saving our lives when he gave me the stone."

Their baggage recovered, Sturm began to gather dead wood from the circle of oaks and heaped it on the fire. The flames leaped up. "Why are you doing that?" asked Kitiara.

"I'm making a pyre," said Sturm. "We can't leave these corpses lying about."

"Let the vultures have them."

"It's not out of respect that I do this. Evil magicians, even one as lowly as this one, have the unhappy habit of returning undead to prey on the living. Help me put them on the pyre, and their menace will truly be over."

She agreed, and the goblins and their master were consigned to the flames. Sturm flung dirt on the embers, then he and Kit mounted their horses.

"How do you know so much about magic?" asked Kitiara. "I thought you despised it in all forms."

"I do," Sturm replied. "Magic is the greatest underminer of order in the world. It's difficult enough to live with virtue and honor without the temptation of magical power. But magic exists, and we all must learn to deal with it. For myself, I have had many talks with your brother, and I've learned some things I've needed to defend myself."

"You mean Raistlin?" she asked, and Sturm nodded. "His lectures on magic always put me to sleep," she said.

"I know," said Sturm. "You go to sleep awfully easily."

They turned the horses toward the new morning's sun and rode away.

Chapter 5

Cloudmaster

The day after the robbers' attack was oppressively humid. Tallfox and Pira needed frequent watering, for their heads would sag and their gait falter. They entered a district of orchards and farms, with a good view from the road on all sides. Kitiara and Sturm discarded their mail for shirt-sleeves, and by noon Kitiara had pulled her blouse loose and tied the tails together around her waist. Thus cooled, they paused in a fig grove for lunch.

"Too bad they're green," said Kitiara, pinching an imma-ture fig between her thumb and forefinger. "I like figs."

"I doubt that the orchard's keeper would share your enthusiasm unless you paid for what you ate," said Sturm. He hollowed a large biscuit and filled the hole with chopped, dried fruit and cheese.

"Oh, come on. Haven't you ever snitched apples or pears? Stolen a chicken and roasted it over a bark fire, while the farmer hunted for you with a pitchfork?"

"No, never."

"I have. And few things in life taste as sweet as the food you season with wit." She dropped the fig branch and joined Sturm under the tree.

"You never considered what your witty little thefts might do to the farmer, did you, Kit? That he or his family might go hungry for a night because of your filched meal?"

She bristled. "A fine one you are to talk, Master Brightblade. Since when did you ever work for the food that went into your belly? It's very easy for a lord's son to speak of justice for the poor, never having been poor himself."

Sturm counted silently until his anger subsided. "I worked," he said simply. "When my mother, her handmaid Carin, and I first arrived in Solace twelve years ago, we had some money that we'd brought with us. But soon it ran out, and we were in dire straits. My mother was an intensely proud woman and would not take charity. Mistress Carin and I did odd jobs around Solace to put food on the table. We never told my mother."

Kitiara's prickly demeanor softened. "What did you do?"

He shrugged. "Because I was able to read and write, I got a job with Derimius the Scribe, copying scrolls and manuscripts. Not only was I able to earn five silver pieces a week, but I got to read all sorts of things."

"I never knew that."

"In fact, I met Tanis at Derimius's shop. He brought in a ledger that he kept for Flint. Tanis had spilled some ink on the last pages and wanted Derimius to replace them with new parchment. Tanis saw a sixteen-year-old boy scribbling away with a gray goose quill and inquired about me. We talked and became friends."

This statement was punctuated by a roll of far-off thunder. The sultry air had collected in a mass of blue-black thunderheads piling up in the western sky. They were moving quickly eastward, so Sturm crammed the last of his lunch in his mouth and jumped to his feet. He mumbled something through bread and cheese.

"What?" said Kitiara.

"—horses. Must secure the horses!"

Lightning lanced down from the clouds to the hills where the robbers had been vanquished. Wind blew out of the upper air, swirling dust into Sturm and Kitiara's eyes. They tied Tallfox and Pira to a fig tree, and hastily rigged their blankets as a shelter to keep the rain off. Down the road Kitiara could see a wall of rain advancing toward them. "Here it comes!" she said.

The storm broke over the fig grove with all its fury. Rain hammered the skimpy screen of blankets down on their heads. In seconds, Sturm and Kitiara were completely soaked. Rain collected between the rows of trees and filled the low places. Water climbed over Kitiara's toes.

Tallfox couldn't bear it. A nervous beast by nature, he reared and neighed as the storm played around him. His terror infected the usually stolid Pira, and both horses started straining against their tethers. A bolt of lightning hit the tallest tree in the orchard and blasted it into a million burning fragments. The horses, driven beyond terror, tore free and galloped away, Tallfox fleeing east and Pira veering north.

"After them!" Sturm cried above the din.

He and Kitiara splashed off after their respective mounts. Tallfox was a long-legged sprinter, and he galloped in a straight line. Pira was a hard-cornering dodger. She wove among the leafy fig trees, changing direction a dozen times in twenty places. Kitiara stumbled after her, cursing her favorite's agility.

The orchard ended in a gully. Kitiara slid down the muddy bank and into calf-deep water. "Pira!" she called. "Pira, you pea-brained nag, where are you?" All she got for her shouting was a mouth full of water. She scanned both sides of the gully for tracks. In the lightning's glare Kitiara saw a strange thing. An angular black shape, like a warrior's shield, was silhouetted against the clouds, some forty feet overhead. The dazzling glow faded, but not before she saw a long line trailing below the shield to the ground. Kitiara slogged forward, not knowing what she would find.

Tallfox easily outran his master, but Sturm was able to follow the chestnut's prints in the mud. A wall of closely growing cedar saplings blocked the end of the orchard. There was only one gap wide enough for a horse to pass through, and sure enough, Sturm found Tallfox's trail there. He plunged into the dense tangle of evergreen. Broken saplings told well which way his horse had gone.

The lightning was unusually active overhead. It crackled and pulsed from cloud to cloud. One prolonged stroke illuminated a wonder to Sturm's eyes: an enormous bird fluttered in the storm wind. The bird wobbled from side to side, but never flew off. Another bolt of lightning crackled, and he saw why. Someone had tied cords to the bird's feet.

Kitiara climbed a hill of solid mud. Her hair was plastered to her head, and her clothing felt as if it had absorbed a ton of water. At the top of the hill, she could see down into a wide clearing. There was no sign of Pira. There was, however, plenty to see.

In the center of the clearing was a thing such as Kitiara had never seen. It was like a huge boat with large leather sails furled along each side. There were no masts, but the prow was long and pointed, like a bird's beak, and there were wheels on the underside of the hull. Above the boat, tied to it by a rope netting, was a big canvas bag. A huge egg-shaped bag squirmed and writhed in the wind like a living thing. A swarm of little men surrounded the boat-thing. Beyond them, a couple of tall poles rose straight up from the ground. From the tops of these four poles, long ropes whipped about, and at the end of the ropes were more of the 'warrior's shields' that Kitiara had seen.

At the same time, Sturm emerged from the cedars on the opposite side of the same clearing. He gaped at the thing. Wordlessly, he headed toward it.

A little man in a shiny hat and long coat greeted Sturm. "G-greetings and felicit-tations!" he said cheerily.

"Hello," said a bewildered Sturm. "What is going on here?" Even as he spoke, a bolt of lightning struck one of the 'birds' tethered on a pole (the same thing Kitiara had mistaken for a shield). Blue-white fire coursed down the line to the pole. From the pole, it flashed along another line a foot off the ground, until it reached the boat-thing, where it vanished. The boat swayed on its wheels, then settled back.

"D-Doing? Well, charging up, as you c-can see," said the little man. When he flipped the wide brim of his hat back, Sturm saw his pale eyes and bushy white brows and realized that he was a gnome. "It really is a w-wonderful storm. We're so l-lucky!"

Kitiara wandered around the odd-looking craft, warily keeping her distance. By one especially vivid bolt of lightning, she saw Sturm talking to the little fellow. She cupped her hands around her lips and yelled, "Sturm!"

"Kit!"

She joined him. "Did you find the horses?"

"No, I was hoping they ran to you."

She waved her arms in great circles. "I fell in a ditch!"

"So I see. What are we going to do?"

"Ahem," said the gnome. "D-do I understand that you t-two have lost your m-means of transportation?"

"That's right," said Sturm and Kitiara in unison.

"Fortuitous f-fate! Perhaps we can help one another." He flipped the brim of his hat down again. A tiny torrent of water spilled down his coat. "Will you c-come with me?"

"Where are we going?" asked Sturm.

"For n-now, out of the w-weather," said the gnome.

"I'm for that!" said Kitiara.

The gnome led them up a ramp into the left side of the boat. The interior was brightly lit, warm, and dry. Their guide removed his hat and coat. He was a mature male of his race, with a fine white beard and bald pink head. He gave Sturm and Kitiara each a towel—which, being sized for gnomes, was no bigger than a hand-towel. Sturm dried his hands and face. Kitiara loosened some of the mud from hers, wrung out the towel, and tied it scarf-fashion around her head.

"F-follow me," said the gnome. "My c-colleagues will join us l-later. They're busy now g-gathering the lightning."

With this amazing statement, he led them down a long, narrow passage between two banks of machinery of unfathomable purpose. All the rods, cranks, and gears were skillfully wrought in iron or brass and carefully hollowed out. Their guide came to a small ladder, which he ascended. The upper deck they entered was subdivided into small cabins.

Hammocks were slung from hooks, and all sorts of boxes, crates, and great glass demijohns were packed on every inch of floor space. Only a narrow track down the center of the passage was clear for walking.

They climbed a second ladder and were in a house built in the center of the deck. There were portholes in the walls, and Sturm could see that rain still lashed at them. The deck-house was split into two large rooms. The forward room, where they entered, was fitted like a ship's wheelhouse. A steering wheel was set at the bow end, which was extensively glazed with many glass panels. All sorts of levers sprouted from the floor and ceiling, and there were mysterious gauges labeled *Altitude*, *Indicated Air Speed*, and *Density of Raisins in Breakfast Muffins*.

Kitiara introduced them. The gnome's eyes widened, and he smiled benignly when he learned that Sturm was the son of an ancient Solamnic family. Ever curious, he inquired after Kitiara's antecedents. She turned his query aside and described their journey so far, their goal, and their general frustration at having lost their horses.

"P-perhaps I can be of s-service," said the gnome. "My name is He-Who-Stutters-Ap-propriately-in-the-M-midst-of-the-Most-Abstruse-Technical-Explanations—"

Sturm interrupted, knowing the length of gnomish names. "Please! What do those not of the gnomish race call you?"

The gnome sighed, and said very slowly, "I am often c-called 'Stutts', a wholly inadequate approximation of my true n-name."

"It has the virtue of brevity," said Sturm.

"B-brevity, my dear knight, is no virtue to those who love knowledge for its own s-sake." Stutts folded his stubby fingers across his round belly. "I should like to offer you a p-position, if, under the circumstances, you are i-interested."

"What sort of position?" asked Kitiara.

"My c-colleagues and I arrived here today from Caergoth." The awkward spectacle of the gnome ship in Caergoth harbor came to the humans' minds. "We c-came to this region of Solamnia because the weather patterns are well known for v-violent thunderstorms."

Sturm brushed his drying mustache with his fingers. "You were seeking a storm?"

"P-precisely. The lightning is vital for the operation of our m-machine." Stutts smiled and patted the arm of his chair. "Isn't it a b-beauty? It is called the *C-Cloudmaster*."

"What does it do?"

"It f-flies."

"Oh, of course it does," Kitiara said with a chuckle. "Very ingenious of you gnomes. What does that have to do with Sturm and me?"

Stutts's small face flushed a deeper shade of pink. "Ahem. W-we've had a bit of b-bad luck. You see, in calculating the op-optimal lift-to-weight ratio, someone failed to consider the effect of the *Cloudmaster* coming to r-rest on soil in an advanced state of hydration."

"What did you say?"

"We're st-stuck in the mud," said Stutts, turning pink again.

"And you want us to dig you out?" asked Kitiara.

"For which we will g-gratefully fly you to any point on Krynn that you wish to go. Enstar, B-Balifor, or far Karthay—"

"The Plains of Solamnia were where we were headed," said Sturm. "That's as far as we need to go."

Kitiara swung an elbow into Sturm's ribs. "You're not taking this little lunatic seriously, are you?" she hissed from the corner of her mouth.

"I know gnomes," he replied. "Their inventions work with surprising regularity."

"But I don't—"

Stutts hopped up. "You'll want to d-discuss it. May I suggest you clean up, have a good m-meal, and then d-decide? We have a cleansing station on board like nothing you've s-seen before."

"I'm sure of that," Kitiara muttered.

They agreed to bathe and dine with the gnomes. Stutts pulled a light chain that hung from the ceiling by the steering wheel. A deep-throated AH—OO—GAH! echoed through the flying ship. A young gnome in greasy coveralls and with very bushy red eyebrows appeared.

"Show our g-guests to the cleansing station," said Stutts. The bushy-browed gnome whistled a string of notes in reply. "No, one at a t-time," Stutts said. Bushy-brows whistled again.

"Does he always talk like that?" queried Kitiara.

"Yes. My c-colleague—" Here he recited about five minutes of gnome-name. "—has evolved the theory that spoken l-language was derived from the songs of birds. You may call him—" Stutts paused and looked at the bushy-browed fellow, who tweeted and chirped. Stutts continued, "—Birdcall."

Birdcall took Sturm and Kitiara below deck to the stern. There, with whistles and gestures, he indicated two cubicles on either side of the corridor. The doors bore identical signs that read:

Rapid and Hygienic Cleansing Station
Perfected and Provided to the Flying Ship *Cloudmaster*
By the Guild of Hydrodynamic Masters and Journeymen
And the Apprentices of
Mt. Nevermind
Level Twelve
Sancrist
Ansalon
Krynn

Sturm looked from the door to Kitiara. "Do you think it works?" he asked.

"Only one way to find out," she replied, pulling the filthy towel from her head and dropping it on the floor. She stepped through the door and it swung shut behind her with a soft click.

The tile walls inside the cleansing station were covered with writing. Kitiara squinted at the hand-painted script. Some of it ran sideways, and some of it was upside down. Most of the writing concerned proper and scientific bathing procedure. Some of it was nonsense—she saw a line that declared, "The absolute value of the density of raisins in the perfect muffin is sixteen." And some of the writing was rude:

"The inventor of this station has dung for brains."

She peeled off her outer clothing and put it in a convenient wicker basket. Kitiara stepped to a raised wooden platform. There was a ghastly, rubbery hissing sound, and water began to spray from a pipe above her head. It caught her by surprise, so she clamped a hand over the spouting end. No sooner had she stopped one spray than another started from the wall on her left. That one she plugged with a finger. Then the real melee began.

With mud and water trickling down her face, Kitiara heard a rattling and squeaking behind her. She twisted around without unstopping the spouts. A square tile on the wall had popped open, revealing a jointed metal rod that was unfolding and reaching out for her. On the end of the rod was a round pad of fleece, rapidly spinning. Wheels and pulleys set along the jointed rod made the sheepskin turn.

"What a time to be without a sword!" Kitiara said aloud. The rod wavered and came toward her. It was a moment of decision. She accepted the challenge and released the pipes. Water gushed out, sluicing the mud from her body. Kitiara grappled with the whirling fleece, grabbing it with both hands. The pulleys whined and the cords twanged.

Finally she succeeded in snapping the rod off at the first joint. The water stopped. Kitiara stood, panting, as the water drained through slots in the floor. There was a knock on the door.

"Kit?" Sturm called. "Are you finished?"

Before she could reply, a heavy piece of cloth dropped from the ceiling over her head. She yelled and threw fists at her unseen attacker, but all she hit was air. Kitiara pulled the cloth off her head. It was a towel. She dried off and wrapped herself in it. Sturm was in the corridor, likewise swathed in a dry blanket.

"What a place," he said, grinning more widely than Kitiara had ever seen him do.

"I'm going to have a few words with Stutts!" she declared.

"What's wrong?"

"I was attacked in there!"

Stutts appeared. "Is there a p-problem?"

Kitiara was about to voice her outrage, but Stutts wasn't

actually speaking to her. He bustled on by and opened a panel in the wall. Inside, a rather harried-looking gnome lay in a tangle with a three-legged stool. At the gnome's waist level was a hand-crank, labeled Cleansing Station Number 2—Rotary Washing Device.

"Is that what I was fighting?" Kitiara said.

"Looks that way," said an amused Sturm. "The poor fellow was just doing his job. The fleece is like a washcloth, only he does the scrubbing for you."

"I can do my own scrubbing, thank you," she said sourly.

Stutts mopped his face with his sleeve. "This is all v-very distressing. I must ask you, Mistress Kitiara, to not d-damage the machinery. Now I shall have to write a report in qui-quintuplicate to the Aerostatics Guild."

"I'll keep an eye on her," Sturm said. "Kit has a tendency to bash things she doesn't understand."

Birdcall came down the corridor whistling furiously. Stutts brightened. "Oh, g-good. Time for d-dinner."

* * * * *

The gnomes dined in the rear half of the deckhouse. A long, plank table was suspended from the ceiling, as on an ocean-going ship, but the gnomes had 'improved' on the sailors' arrangement by hanging their seats from the ceiling, too. They swung happily from side to side. Thus, Sturm and Kitiara had to squeeze into narrow chain swings just to sit at the table. Dinner proved ordinary enough: beans, ham, cabbage, muffins, and sweet cider. Stutts apologized; they had no scientifically trained cook on board. The warriors were grateful for that.

The gnomes ate rapidly and without conversation (because it was more efficient). The sight of ten bowed, balding heads, accompanied only by the sound of spoons scraping on plates, was a little unnerving. Sturm cleared his throat and said, "Perhaps we ought to introduce ourselves—"

"Everyone knows who you are," said Stutts without looking up. "I s-sent out a memorandum while you were b-being cleansed."

"Then you can introduce your crew to us," said Kitiara.

Stutts's head snapped up. "They're n-not crew. We are c-colleagues."

"Pardon me!" Kitiara rolled her eyes.

"You are p-pardoned." He spooned the last of his beans swiftly into his mouth. "But if you insist." Stutts slipped from his swinging seat and walked down the row of eating gnomes. He gave a yawningly elaborate profile of each of his colleagues, including the name by which "those not of the gnomish race" could call each one. Sturm distilled all of this into a short mental list:

Birdcall, chief mechanic in charge of the engine,
Wingover, Stutts's right-hand gnome; in charge of actu-
     ally flying the machine,
Sighter, astronomer and celestial navigator,
Roperig, expert with rope, cord, wire, cloth, and so forth,
Fitter, Roperig's apprentice,
Flash, collector and storer of lightning,
Bellcrank, chief metal worker and chemist,
Cutwood, in charge of carpentry, woodwork, and all
     non-metal parts,
Rainspot, weather seer and physician by designation.

"How did you come to build this, uh, machine?" asked Sturm.

"It is part of my Life Quest," said Wingover, a taller-than-average gnome with a hawklike nose. "Complete and successful aerial navigation, that's my goal. After years of experimenting with kites, I met our friend Bellcrank, who has discovered a very rarefied air, which, when enclosed in a suitable bag, will float and support other objects of weight."

"Preposterous," said Sighter. "This so-called ethereal air is humbug!"

"Listen to the stargazer," the tubby Bellcrank said with a sneer. "How do you think we were able to fly to this point from Caergoth, eh? Magic?"

"The wings supported us," Sighter replied with heat. "The lift ratios clearly show—"

"It was the ethereal air!" retorted Rainspot, who sat by Bellcrank.

"Wings!" shouted Sighter's side of the table.

"Air!" cried Bellcrank's allies.

"Colleagues! C-colleagues!" Stutts said, holding up his hands for quiet. "The p-purpose of our expedition is to establish with scientific accuracy the c-capabilities of the *Cloudmaster*. Let us not argue needlessly about theories until the d-data is available."

The gnomes lapsed into sullen silence. Rain drummed on the skylight over the table. The hostile silence lingered for an embarrassing length of time. Then Rainspot lifted his eyes to the dark panes and said, "The rain is stopping." A few seconds later, the steady thrumming ceased completely.

"How did he know that?" asked Kitiara.

"Theories differ," said Wingover. "A committee is meeting even now on Sancrist Isle to study our colleague's talent."

"How can they study him when he's up here?" Sturm wondered. He was ignored.

"It's his nose," Cutwood said.

"His nose?" Kitiara asked.

"Because of the size and relative angle of Rainspot's nostrils, he can detect changes in relative air pressure and humidity just by breathing."

"Hogwash!" Roperig said.

"Hogwash," echoed Fitter, the smallest and youngest of the gnomes, from his place by Roperig.

"It's his ears," continued Roperig. "He can hear the rain stop falling from the clouds before it reaches the ground."

"Unmitigated tommyrot!" That was Sighter again. "Any fool can see it's his hair that does it. He can feel the roots uncurl when the moisture in the air falls—" Bellcrank, sitting opposite Sighter, snatched up a muffin from the table and bounced it off his rival's chin. Flash and Fitter pounced on the fallen muffin and broke it open.

"Twelve, thirteen, fourteen," Flash counted.

"What's he doing?" Sturm asked.

"C-counting raisins," answered Stutts. "That's his current project: to determine the world average density of raisins in muffins." Kitiara dropped her face into her hands and moaned.

* * * * *

The dinner debacle over, the gnomes left the flying ship to dismantle their equipment in the meadow. Kitiara and Sturm, now dry, dressed in enough clothing to hike back to their campsite in the fig orchard and pick up their gear. The storm had blown itself out, and stars showed in the ragged holes between the clouds.

"Are we doing the right thing?" asked Kitiara. "These gnomes haven't got all their bootlaces tied."

Sturm glanced back at the queer machine lying cockeyed in the muddy field. "They are lacking in common sense, but they're tireless and creative. If they can get us to the high Plains of Solamnia in a day, then I, for one, don't mind helping to dig them out of the mud."

"I don't believe that thing can fly," she said. "We never saw it fly. For all we know, the storm blew it here."

They reached the sodden remains of their camp and packed up their scattered belongings. Kitiara hoisted Pira's saddle on her shoulder. "Blast that horse," she said. "Raised her from a filly, I did, and she never looked back once she got loose. I'll bet she's halfway to Garnet by now."

"Tallfox was a bad influence, I fear. Tirien warned me that he was skittish."

"It may be that Tallfox had the right idea," Kitiara said.

"How so?" said Sturm.

She slung the damp bedroll over the saddle. "If the gnomes can do half the things they claim, we may end up wishing we'd run away in the storm, too."

Chapter 6

1,081 Hours, 29 Minutes

"Higher! Higher! Get that balk in place!" Sturm grunted against the massive weight of the gnomes' flying ship. He and Kitiara strained against a rough-hewn lever they'd made over the gnomes' protests. Crude levers! the gnomes protested. Bellcrank claimed that any gnome could invent a device ten times better for lifting heavy objects. Of course, it would take a committee to study the stress analysis of the local wood, as well as to calculate the proper pivot point for raising the ship.

"No," Kitiara had insisted. "If you want us to help get your ship out of the mud, then we'll do it our own way." The gnomes had shrugged and rubbed their bare pates. Trust humans to do things the crudest way.

The gnomes rolled several large rocks up to the hull. These would be the fulcrums. After Sturm and Kitiara had made the ship level, the gnomes shoved short, thick timber balks into place to brace it upright. It was slow, sweaty labor, but by noon of the day after the storm, the flying ship was finally on an even keel.

"A problem," Wingover announced.

"Now what?" Kitiara asked.

"The landing gear must have a firm surface on which to roll. Therefore, it will be necessary to construct a roadbed. Here; I've made calculations as to how much crushed stone and mortar we'll need—" Kitiara plucked the paper from his hand and tore it in two.

"I've gotten wagons out of mud before," she said, "by putting straw or twigs in the ruts."

"Might work," Sturm said. "But this thing is very heavy."

He spoke to Stutts, who promptly removed the protesting gnomes from their important (though completely useless) 'improvement' work and set them to gathering windfall branches and brushwood. They all turned out except Bellcrank, who was busy with his pots of powders and vials of noxious liquids.

"I must attend to my first task, generating the ethereal air," he said, pouring iron filings from a keg. "When the air bag is filled, it will help lighten the ship."

"You do that," said Kitiara. She leaned against the hull to watch. She didn't like strenuous work. Work was for dullards and peasants, not warriors.

The gnomes returned with a scant armful of brush. "Nine of you, and that's all you have?" Sturm said incredulously.

"Roperig and Sighter disagreed on which kind of sticks to bring, so in the spirit of cooperation, we didn't pick up either of their choices," Wingover said.

"Wingover," Sturm said pleadingly, "please tell Roperig and Sighter that the kind of wood doesn't matter in the least. We just want something dry for the wheels to run over." The tallish gnome dropped his bundle of sticks and led his fellows back to the woods.

Meanwhile, Bellcrank had managed to enlist Kitiara's aid in inflating the *Cloudmaster*'s air bag. On the ground beside the ship he'd set up a big clay tub, five feet wide. He poured powdered iron and other bits of scrap metal in the tub and smoothed the pile out around the edges. "Lower away!" he told Kitiara, and she set a domed wooden lid, like the top half of a beer barrel, on top of the ceramic tub. Bellcrank worked around the outside, poking a long strip of greased leather into the joint. "It must be tight," he explained, "or the ethereal air will seep out and not fill the bag."

She hoisted the gnome up and set him on top of the barrel. With a corkscrew, Bellcrank popped a large cork in the top of the barrel. "Hand me the hose," he said.

"This?" asked Kitiara, holding up a limp tube of canvas.

"The very thing." She gave it to him, and he tied it over the neck of a wooden turncock. "Now," said Bellcrank, "for the vitriol!"

There were three very large demijohns sitting in the tall grass. Kitiara stooped to pick one up. "Oof!" she gasped. "Feels like a keg of ale!"

"It's concentrated vitriol. Be careful not to spill it; it can burn you very badly." She set the heavy jug down by the tub.

"You don't expect me to pour that stuff in there, do you?"

Bellcrank said, "No indeed! I have a most efficacious invention that will circumvent such tiresome duty. Hand me the Excellent Mouthless Siphon, would you?"

Kitiara cast about but saw nothing that resembled an Excellent Mouthless Siphon. Bellcrank pointed with his stubby finger. "That, there; the bellows-looking item. Yes." She gave him the mouthless siphon. Bellcrank put the beak of the bellows into the demijohn and pulled the handles apart. The sinister brown liquid in the jug sank by an inch.

"There!" the gnome said triumphantly. "No sucking on tubes. No spillage." He pushed the beak into the hole in the barrel where the cork had been, and emptied the vitriol. "Ha, ha! Gnomish science overcomes ignorance again!"

Bellcrank repeated the siphoning four more times before Kitiara noticed vapor escaping from the leather hinges of the Excellent Mouthless Siphon. "Bellcrank," she said hesitantly.

"Not now! The process has begun, and it must be kept

going at a steady pace!"

"But the siphon—"

A drop of vitriol seeped through a hole that it had eaten in the hinge of the siphon, and splashed on Bellcrank's shoe. He carelessly flung the siphon away and began hopping around on one foot, trying desperately to pry the shoe off his foot. The vitriol ate the buckle strap in two, and with a mighty kick, Bellcrank flung the shoe away. It missed the returning Fitter's nose by a whisker.

"Oh, Reorx!" said Bellcrank sadly. The Excellent Mouthless Siphon was a pile of steaming fragments.

"Never mind," Kitiara said. She wrapped her arms around the vitriol jug and planted her feet firmly. "Hai-yup!" she grunted, and raised the demijohn to Bellcrank's level. He guided the jug's mouth, and soon a steady stream of the acrid fluid was spilling into the ethereal air generator.

The hose from the keg to the air bag swelled. The sagging bag itself began to fill out and grow firmer inside its web of netting. Soon all the rope rigging and tackle was taut. The bag strained against the confining ropes. At Bellcrank's signal, Kitiara lowered the heavy demijohn.

Sturm came around the bow with the other gnomes. "The ruts are full of brush," he said.

"The bag is full of ethereal air," said Bellcrank.

"My back is killing me," said Kitiara. "What next?"

"We f-fly," said Stutts. "All colleagues to their flying st-stations!"

Stutts, Wingover, and the two humans went into the forward end of the deck house. The other gnomes lined the rail.

"Release ballast!" cried Wingover.

"Release b-ballast!" Stutts called out an open porthole. The gnomes took up long, sausage-shaped bags that lined the rail. The ends opened, and sand poured out. The gnomes flung sand over the side, getting as much in their own eyes as they did out of the ship. This went on until Sturm felt the deck shift under his feet. Kitiara, wide-eyed, grabbed the brass rail that ran around the wheelhouse at the gnomes' shoulder height.

"Open front wings!" cried Wingover.

"Opening f-front wings!" Stutts replied. He leaned against

a lever as tall as he was and shoved it forward. A rattle, a screech, and the leather 'sails' that Kitiara and Sturm had noticed on the hull unfolded into long, graceful batlike wings. The goatskin covering the bony ribs was pale brown and translucent.

"F-front wings open," Stutts reported. Wind caught in them, and the ship lifted an inch or two at the bow.

"Open rear wings!"

"Opening rear w-wings!" A slightly wider and longer pair of leather-clad wings blossomed aft of the deckhouse.

"Set tail!"

The gnomes on deck ran out a long spar and clamped it to the stern. Roperig and Fitter clambered over the spar, attaching lines to pulleys to hooks. They unfolded a fan-shaped set of ribs, also covered in goatskin. By the time they finished, the *Cloudmaster* was swaying and bucking off the ground.

Wingover flipped the cover off a speaking tube. "Hello, Birdcall, are you there?" A shrill whistled answered. "Tell Flash to start the engine."

There was a sizzle and a loud crack, and the deck quivered beneath their feet. Wingover twirled a brass ring handle and threw another tall lever. The great wings rose slowly in unison. The *Cloudmaster* lost contact with the ground. Down came the wings, folding inward as they came. The flying ship lurched forward, its wheels sucking free of the mud and bouncing over the scattered brush. The wings beat again, faster. Wingover grasped the steering wheel in both his small hands and pulled. The wheel swung toward him, the bow pitched up, the wings flapped crazily, and the *Cloudmaster* was borne aloft into the blue afternoon sky.

"Hurray! H-Hurray!" Stutts said, jumping up and down. The *Cloudmaster* climbed steadily. Wingover eased the wheel forward, and the bow dropped. Kitiara yelled and lost her footing. Sturm let go of the handrail to try to catch her, and he fell, too. He rolled against one of the levers, knocking it out of place, and the wings instantly stopped moving. The *Cloudmaster* wobbled and plunged toward the ground.

There were several seconds of stark terror. Sturm disentangled himself from the lever and hauled back on it. The wings sang as the taut skin bit the air. Stutts and Kitiara, in a knot, rolled to the rear of the room. Shakily, Wingover steadied the ship.

"I think passengers ought to leave the wheelhouse," Wingover said. His voice shook with fear. "At least until you get your air legs."

"I agree," said Sturm. From his hands and knees he grabbed the handle of the door and crept out on deck. Kitiara and Stutts crawled out behind him.

The rushing wind was strong on deck, but by taking firm hold of the rail and leaning into it, Kitiara found it tolerable. The wings flexed up and down in close harmony. Kitiara slowly straightened her legs. She looked over the side.

"Great Lord of Battle!" she exclaimed. "We must be miles and miles straight up!"

Stutts boosted himself to the rail and hung his head over the side. "N-not as high as all that," he remarked. "You can st-still see our shadow on the ground." It was true. A dark oval sped across the treetops. Sighter appeared with his spyglass, and he promptly announced their altitude as 6,437.5 feet.

"Are you certain?" Kitiara asked.

"Please," said Sturm, "take his word for it."

"Where are we headed, Sighter?" asked Kitiara.

"Due east. That's the Lemish forest below. In a few minutes, we should be over the Newsea."

"But that's seventy miles from where we were," Sturm said. He was sitting on the deck. "Are we truly flying that fast?"

"Indeed we are, and we shall go faster still," Sighter said. He strolled forward, his spyglass stuck to one eye as he surveyed the world below.

"It's wonderful!" Kitiara said. She laughed into the wind. "I never believed you could do it; but you did. I love it! Tell the whistler to go as fast as he can!" Stutts was almost as excited, and he agreed. He turned to re-enter the wheelhouse. Sturm called to him, and he paused.

"Why are we heading east?" Sturm asked. "Why not north and east—toward the Plains of Solamnia?"

Stutts replied, "Rainspot s-says he feels turbulence in that direction. He f-felt it wouldn't be prudent to fly through it." He disappeared into the wheelhouse.

"Sturm, look at that!" Kitiara said. "It's a village! You can see the housetops and chimney smoke—and cattle! I wonder, can the people down there see us? Wouldn't that be funny, to swoop down on their heads and blow a trumpet—ta-ta! Scare them out of ten years' growth!"

Sturm was still sitting on the deck. "I'm not ready to stand up yet," he said sheepishly. "I was never afraid of heights, you know. Trees, towers, mountaintops never disturbed me. But this . . ."

"It's wonderful, Sturm. Hold the rail and look down."

I must stand up, thought Sturm. The Measure demanded that a knight face danger with honor and courage. The Knights of Solamnia had never considered aerial travel in their code of conduct. I must show Kit that I am not afraid. Sturm grasped the rail.

My father, Lord Angriff Brightblade, would not be afraid, he told himself as he faced the low wall and rose to his haunches. Blood pounded in Sturm's ears. The power of the sword, the discipline of battle, were of little help here. This was a stronger test. This was the unknown.

Sturm stood. The world spun beneath him like a ribbon unspooling. Already the blue waters of the Newsea glittered on the horizon. Kitiara was raving about the boats she could see. Sturm took a deep breath and let the fear fall from him like a soiled garment.

"Wonderful!" she exclaimed again. "I tell you, Sturm, I take back all the things I said about the gnomes. This flying ship is tremendous! We can go anywhere in the world with this. Anywhere! And think of what a general could do with his army in a fleet of these devices. No wall would be high enough. No arrows could reach you up here. There's no spot in the whole of Krynn that could be defended against a fleet of flying ships."

"It would be the end of the world," Sturm said. "Cities looted and burned, farms ravaged, people slaughtered—it would be as bad as the Cataclysm."

"Trust you to see the dark side of everything," she said.

"It happened before, you know. Twice the dragons of Krynn tried to subjugate the world from the sky, until the great Huma used the Dragonlance and defeated them."

Kitiara said, "That was long ago. And men are different from dragons." Sturm was not so sure.

Cutwood and Rainspot climbed a ladder to the roof of the wheelhouse. From there they launched a large kite. It fluttered back in the wind from the wings, whipping about on its string like a new-caught trout.

"What are you two doing now?" Kitiara called out.

"Testing for lightning," Cutwood responded. "He smells it in the clouds."

"Isn't that dangerous?" Sturm said.

"Eh?" Cutwood put a hand to his ear.

"I said, isn't that—"

The brilliant white-forked bolt hit the kite before Sturm could finish. Though the sun was shining and the air clear, lightning leaped from a nearby cloud and blasted the kite to ashes. The bolt continued down the string and leaped to the brass ladder. The *Cloudmaster* staggered; the wings skipped a beat, then settled back into their regular rhythm once more.

They carried the scorched Rainspot into the dining room. His face and hands were black with soot. His shoes had been knocked right off his feet, and his stockings had gone with his shoes. All the buttons on his vest were melted as well.

Cutwood lowered his ear to Rainspot's chest. "Still beating," he reported.

The ship's alarm went AH—OO—GAH! and the speaking tube blared, "All colleagues and passengers come to the engine room at once." Stutts and the other gnomes filed toward the door, with the humans trailing behind.

Stutts paused. "What ab-bout him?" He indicated the unconscious Rainspot.

"We could carry him," Sighter said.

"We can make a stretcher," said Cutwood, checking his pockets for paper and pencil to draw a stretcher design.

"I'll do it," Sturm said, just to end the discussion. He scooped the little man up in his arms.

Down in the engine room, the ship's entire company collected. Sturm was alarmed to see Wingover there. "Who's steering the ship?" he asked.

"I tied the wheel."

"Colleagues and passengers," Flash said, "I beg to report a fault in the engine."

"You needn't beg," said Roperig. "We'll let you report."

"Shut up," said Kitiara. "How bad is it?"

"I can't shut it off. The lightning strike has fused the switches in the 'on' position."

"That's not so bad," Sighter said. Birdcall warbled in agreement.

"But we can't fly around forever!" Kitiara said.

"No indeed," said Flash. "I estimate we have power to fly for, oh, six and a half weeks."

"Six weeks!" cried Sturm and Kitiara in unison.

"One thousand, eighty-one hours, twenty-nine minutes. I can work out the exact seconds in a moment."

"Hold my arms, Sturm; I'm going to throttle him!"

"Hush, Kit."

"Could we unfasten the wings? That would bring us down," said Roperig.

"Yes, and make a nice big hole when we hit," Bellcrank observed tartly.

"Hmm, I wonder how big a hole it would be." Cutwood flipped open a random slip of parchment and started figuring on it. The other gnomes crowded around, offering corrections to his arithmetic.

"Stop this at once!" Sturm said. Kitiara's face was scarlet from ill-concealed rage. When the gnomes paid him not the least heed, he snatched the calculations from Cutwood. The gnomes broke off in midbabble.

"How can such clever fellows be so impractical? Not one of you has asked the right question. Flash, can you fix the engine?"

A gleam of challenge grew in Flash's eyes. "I can! I will!" He pulled a hammer from one pocket and a spanner from another. "C'mon, Birdcall, let's get at it!" The chief mechanic chirped happily and followed on Flash's heels.

"Wingover, where will we go if we keep flying as we are now?" Sturm asked.

"The wings are set on 'climb', which means we'll keep going higher and higher," Wingover replied. The gnome wrinkled his beaky nose. "It will get cold. The air will thin out; that's why vultures and eagles can only fly so high. Their wings are too small. The *Cloudmaster* shouldn't have problems with that."

"Everyone will have to dress warmly," said Sturm.

"We have our furs," Kitiara said, having mastered her anger at the situation. "I don't know what the gnomes can wear."

"Oh! Oh!" Roperig waved a hand to be recognized. "I can make Personal Heating Apparatuses out of materials I have in the rope locker."

"Fine, you do that." Roperig and his apprentice hurried away with their heads together. Fitter listened so intently that he walked under an engine part and into the door frame.

Rainspot moaned. Forgetting his burden in the excitement, Sturm had tucked him under one arm like a loaf of bread. The gnome coughed and groaned. Sturm set him on the deck. The first thing Rainspot did was to ask for his kite. Cutwood explained how it was lost, and tears welled up in Rainspot's eyes. As they trickled down his cheeks, they scored clean tracks in the soot.

"One thing more, Wingover," Kitiara said. "You said the air would get thin. Do you mean as it does on very high mountaintops?"

"Exactly like that."

She planted her hands on her hips and said, "I once led a troop of cavalry over the high Khalkist Mountains. It was cold, all right, and worse, our ears bled. We fainted at the slightest exertion and had the worst headaches. A shaman named Ning made a potion for us to drink; it eased our way."

"What a primitive shaman can do with m-magic, a gnome can do with t-technology," said Stutts.

Sturm looked out the engine room porthole at the darkening sky. A rime of frost was already forming on the outside of the glass. "I certainly hope so, my friend. Our lives may depend on it."

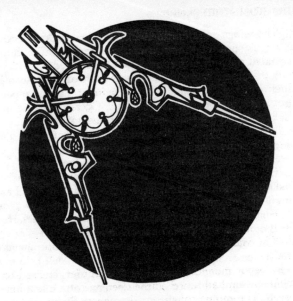

Chapter 7

Hydrodynamics!

It was quiet on deck. Sturm worked his way around the starboard side to the bow. Sighter had mounted a telescope on a spindle there, and Sturm wanted a look around. It wasn't easy moving in his thick fur coat, hood, and mittens, but he decided that it was no worse than being in full body armor.

The flapping of the wings scarcely could be heard as the *Cloudmaster* climbed steadily upward. The flying ship had pierced a layer of soft white clouds, which left a coat of snow on the deck and roof. Once it cleared the cloud layer, however, the rush of air over the wings swept the snow away.

Great pillars of vapor stood around them, fat columns of blue and white that looked as solid as marble in the moons' light. Sturm studied these massive towers of cloud through Sighter's spyglass, but all he could see was their sculpted surfaces, as smooth and still as a frozen pond.

He hadn't seen a gnome in over an hour. Wingover had tied the steering wheel again, and they'd all disappeared below to work on their inventions. Occasionally he heard or felt bangs and crashes under his feet. Kitiara, fully and fetchingly buried in her fox fur coat, had gone to the dining room and stretched out on the table for a nap.

Sturm swung the telescope left, over the pointed prow. Solinari shone between two deep ravines in the clouds, silvering the airship with its rays. He scanned the strange architecture of the clouds, seeing in them a face, a wagon, a rearing horse. It was beautiful, but incredibly lonely. He felt at that moment like the only man in the world.

The cold crept through his heavy clothes. Sturm clapped his hands on his arms to stir his blood. It didn't help much. Finally he abandoned his frosty post, and returned to the dining room. He watched the sleeping Kitiara sway gently with the motion of the ship. Then he smelled something.

Smoke. Something was burning.

Sturm coughed and wrinkled his nose. Kitiara stirred. She sat up in time to see the entry of a bizarre apparition. It looked like a scarecrow made of tin and rope, but this scarecrow had a glass jar on its head and smoke coming out of its back.

"Hello," said the apparition.

"Wingover?" asked Kitiara.

The little scarecrow reached up and twisted the jar off its head, and the hawkish features of Wingover emerged. "What do you think of Roperig's invention?" he asked. "He calls it the Refined Personal Heating Apparatus, Mark III."

"Mark III?" said Sturm.

"Yes, the first two prototypes were not successful. Poor Fitter has a burn on his . . . well, he'll be standing at dinner for a while. That was Mark I. The Mark II took off most of Roperig's whiskers. I warned him not to use glue on the Perfect Observation Helmet."

Wingover held out his arms and spun in a circle. "Do you see? Roperig sewed a continuous coil of rope to a set of long underwear, then varnished the whole suit to make it water-tight and airtight. The heat comes from a tin stove, here." He strained to point at a miniature potbelly stove mounted on his back. "A fat tallow candle provides up to four hours of heat, and these tin strips carry the warmth all over the suit." Wingover finally dropped his arms.

"Very ingenious," said Kitiara flatly. "Has anything been done about the engine?"

"Birdcall and Flash can't agree on the cause of the damage. Birdcall insists the fault lies in Flash's lightning bottles, while Flash says the engine is fused in the 'on' position."

Kitiara sighed. "By the time those two agree on what to fix, we'll have run out of sky."

"Could anything fly as high as we are now?"

"There's no reason why another flying ship couldn't get this high. It's largely a matter of aerodynamic efficiency." He thumped a dial or two and added, "I suppose a dragon might get this high. Assuming they still existed, that is."

"Dragons?" Sturm repeated.

"Dragons are a special case, of course. The really big ones, Reds or Golds, could achieve very high altitudes."

"How high?"

"They had wingspans of 150 feet or more, you know," said Wingover, enjoying his lecture. "I'm sure I could do a calculation, based on a fifty-foot animal weighing forty-five tons—of course, they couldn't glide worth shucks—"

"It's freezing on the inside now," interrupted Kitiara, scratching the frost off a small pane of glass. She breathed on the cleared spot, and it instantly turned milky white.

Stutts started up the ladder from below, but his Personal Heating Apparatus caught on the ladder and there were some moments of struggle to free him.

"Everything sh-shipshape?" he inquired.

"The controls are fine," Wingover responded, "but we're still going up. The height gauge has gone off the dial, so Sighter will have to calculate how high we are."

Stutts clapped his rope-wound hands together. "P-perfect! That will make him very happy." The gnomes' leader whistled into the voice tube. "N-now hear this! Sighter r-report to the wheelhouse!"

In seconds, the little astronomer came banging up the ladder, tripped on the top rung, and fell on his face. Kitiara helped him stand and saw why he was so clumsy. He had pulled his jar-helmet on in such a way as to cover his face with his long beard. Stutts and Kitiara worked and twisted to get the jar off. It came away with a loud pop!

"By Reorx," Sighter gasped. "I was beginning to think my own whiskers were trying to choke me!"

"Did you b-bring your astrolabe?" asked Stutts.

"When am I without it?"

"Then g-go up on the roof and shoot the stars. We need to know our exact p-position."

Sighter snapped his fingers. "Not a problem!"

He went out of the deckhouse through the dining room. They heard his feet stomping across the roof.

"Uh-oh," said Wingover, staring dead ahead.

Sturm said, "What is it?"

"The clouds are closing in. Look!"

They had flown into a box canyon of clouds. Even if Wingover put the wheel hard about, they would still plow into a cloud bank. "I'd better tell Sighter," Sturm said. He went to the door, meaning to shout up at the gnome on the roof. About the time he cracked the door open, the *Cloudmaster* bored into a wall of luminous white.

Frost formed quickly on Sturm's mustache. Snow swirled around him as he cried, "Sighter! Sighter, come down!" The frozen mist was so thick that he couldn't see a foot beyond his nose. He would have to go get Sighter.

He slipped twice on his way up the ladder. The brass rungs were encased in ice, but Sturm knocked it off with the butt of his dagger. As he cleared the roof line, a blast of frigid air stung his face. "Sighter!" he called. "Sighter!"

The rooftop was too treacherous to stand on, so Sturm crept forward on his hands and knees. Flakes of snow collected in the gap between his hood and coat collar, melted, and ran down his neck. Sturm's hand slipped, and he almost rolled right off the roof. Though there was four feet of deck on either side, he had the horrible idea that he would tumble right off the ship and fall, fall, fall. Cutwood would calculate how big a hole he'd make.

His hand bumped a frost-rimed boot, and Sturm looked up. Sighter was at his post, astrolabe stuck to one eye and completely covered with half an inch of ice! Snow was already drifting around his feet.

Sturm used his dagger to chip away the ice around Sighter's shoes. His Personal Heating Apparatus, Mark III must have blown out, for the gnome was now stiff with cold. Sturm grabbed the little man's feet and pulled—

"Sturm! Sturm, where are you?" Kitiara was calling.

"Up here!"

"What are you doing? You and Sighter get inside before your faces freeze off!"

"It's too late for Sighter. I've almost got him loose—wait, here he is!" He passed the stiff gnome over the edge of the roof to Kitiara's open arms. With commendable agility, he then scooted down the ladder and hurried back inside.

"Brr! And I thought winters at Castle Brightblade were cold!" He saw that Rainspot was on hand to doctor the frozen Sighter. "How is he?" asked Sturm.

"Cold," said Rainspot. He pinched the tip of Sighter's beard with a pair of wooden tweezers. A quick snap of the wrist, and the lower half of Sighter's beard broke off.

"Dear, dear," Rainspot said, clucking his tongue. "Dear, dear." He reached for the astrolabe, still in place at Sighter's eye, with Sighter's hands clamped to it.

"No!" Kitiara and Sturm yelled. Trying to break the instrument loose would probably take Sighter's eye with it.

"T-take him below and thaw him out," said Stutts. "S-slowly."

"Someone will have to carry his feet," said Rainspot. Stutts sighed and went over to help.

"He's g-going to be very angry that y-you broke his b-beard," he said.

"Dear, dear. Perhaps if we dampened the edge we could stick it back on."

"Don't be st-stupid. You'd never get it aligned p-properly."

"I can get some glue from Roperig—"

They disappeared down the hatch to the berth deck. Sturm and Kitiara heard a loud crash, and both rushed to the opening, expecting to see poor Sighter broken to bits like a cheap clay vase. But, no, Stutts was on the deck, Sighter cushioned on top of him, and Rainspot was hanging upside down with his feet tangled in the rungs. "Dear, dear," he was saying. "Dear, dear."

They couldn't help but laugh. It felt good after spending so much time worrying whether they would ever walk the solid soil of Krynn again.

Kitiara stopped laughing first. "That was a crazy stunt, Sturm," she said.

"What?"

"Rescuing that gnome. You might have been frozen yourself, and I'll wager you wouldn't thaw out as easily as Sighter will."

"Not with Rainspot as my doctor."

To his surprise, she embraced him. It was a comradely hug, with a clap on the back that staggered him.

"We're coming out of it! We're coming out!" Wingover yelled. Kitiara broke away and rushed to the gnome. He was hopping up and down in delight as the white shroud peeled away from the flying ship. The *Cloudmaster* emerged from the top of the snow squall into clear air.

Ahead of them was a vast red globe, far larger than the sun ever appeared from the ground. Below was nothing but an unbroken sheet of cloud, tinged scarlet from the moon's glow. All around, stars twinkled. The *Cloudmaster* was flying headlong toward the red orb.

"Hydrodynamics," Wingover breathed. This was the gnomes' strongest oath. Neither Sturm nor Kitiara could improve on it just then.

"What is it?" Kitiara finally said.

"If my calculations are accurate, and I'm sure that they are, it is Lunitari, the red moon of Krynn," said Wingover.

Sighter appeared in the hatch. His hair was dripping, and his broken-off beard fluttered when he spoke. "Correct! That's what I discovered before the snowstorm hit. We're a hundred thousand miles from home, and heading straight for Lunitari."

Chapter 8

To the Red Moon

The ship's complement assembled in the dining room. Reactions to Sighter's announcement were mixed. Basically, the gnomes were delighted, while their human passengers were appalled.

"How can we be going to Lunitari?" Kitiara demanded. "It's just a red dot in the sky!"

"Oh, no," said Sighter. "Lunitari is a large globular celestial body, just like Krynn and the other moons and planets. I estimate that it is thirty-five hundred miles in diameter and at least 150 thousand miles from Krynn."

"This is beyond me," Sturm said wearily. "How could we possibly have flown so high? We haven't been gone more than two days."

"Actually, time references are difficult to make at this altitude. We haven't seen the sun in a long time, but judging from the positions of the moons and stars, I would say we have been aloft for fifty-four hours," Sighter said, making a few jottings on the tabletop. "And forty-two minutes."

"Any other r-reports?" asked Stutts.

"We're out of raisins," said Fitter.

"And flour and bacon and onions," added Cutwood.

"What does that leave for food?" Kitiara asked. Birdcall made a very unbirdlike squawk. "What did he say?"

"Beans. Six sacks of dried white beans," said Roperig.

"What about the engine?" asked Sturm. "Have you figured out how to fix it?"

Tweet-tweedle-tweet. "He says no," Bellcrank translated.

"The lightning bottles are holding up quite well," Flash reported. "My theory is, the cold, thin air offers less resistance to the wings, therefore, the engine doesn't have to work as hard."

"Rot!" said Bellcrank. "It's my ethereal air. All that flapping impedes our flight. If we lopped off those silly wings, we could have flown to Lunitari in half the time."

"Aerodynamic idiocy! That big bag is just a big drag!"

"Stop it!" Sturm snapped. "There's no time for these ridiculous disputes. I want to know what happens when we reach Lunitari." Ten pairs of gnome eyes looked at him and blinked. They do it in unison, he thought, just to unnerve me. "Well?"

"We land?" said Wingover.

"How? The engines won't shut off."

The room fairly buzzed with the brains of gnomes furiously thinking. Roperig began to shake. "What does a ship in distress do when it's driven toward the shoals?" asked Roperig feverishly.

"Crash and sink," said Bellcrank.

"No, no! It throws out an anchor!"

Sturm and Kitiara smiled. Here was something they could understand. Never mind lightning bottles and ethereal air—throw out an anchor!

"Do we have an anchor?" asked Fitter.

"We have a few grappling hooks about this big," Wingover replied, holding his hands out, about a foot apart. "They won't stop *Cloudmaster*."

"I'll make a big one," Bellcrank vowed. "If we scrap a few ladders and iron fittings . . ."

"But what if we don't get the engine shut down?" Sturm said. "No anchor in the world will stop us."

Kitiara cocked her head and regarded Stutts severely. "What about it?" she asked.

"How l-long will it take you to m-make an anchor?" asked Stutts.

"With help, maybe three hours," said Bellcrank.

"When will we h-hit Lunitari?" Stutts asked Sighter.

Sighter scribbled across the table, around one corner, and up the other side. "As it stands now, we will hit Lunitari in five hours and sixteen minutes."

"Flash and B-Birdcall will keep working on the engine. If n-no other course is open, we m-may have to smash the engine b-before we can set down."

The gnomes erupted with cries of consternation. The humans objected, too.

"How will we ever get home if you wreck the engine?" demanded Kitiara. "We'll be marooned on Lunitari forever."

"If we c-crash, we'll be on L-Lunitari a lot longer than that, and enjoy it a lot less," Stutts said. "W-we'll be dead."

"Fitter and I will make a cable for the anchor," said Roperig, heading below.

"I'll fill the deckhouse with our blankets and pillows," Cutwood offered. "That way, we'll have something to cushion us when we crash, er, land."

The gnomes dispersed to their tasks, while Sturm and Kitiara remained in the dining room. The scarlet expanse of the moon was visible through the skylight. Together they looked up at Lunitari.

Sturm said, "Another world. I wonder what it's like."

"Who can say? The gnomes could give you theories; I'm just a warrior," said Kitiara. She sighed. "If we end up marooned there, I hope there will be battles to be fought."

"There are always battles. Every place has its own version of good and evil."

"Oh, it doesn't matter to me who I fight for. Battle is my virtue. You can't go wrong with a sword in your hand and a good comrade at your side." She slipped a thickly gloved hand into Sturm's. He returned her grip, but could not dispel the anxiety that her words caused.

*   *   *   *   *

The gnomes, when aroused, had formidable amounts of energy. In less time than it takes to tell, Bellcrank had forged a monstrous anchor with four flukes and a huge weight made of miscellaneous metal parts from all over the ship. In his zeal to add weight to his creation, Bellcrank took ladder rungs, doorknobs, spoons from the dining room, door hinges, and only by threat of force could he be discouraged from removing half of Wingover's control knobs.

Roperig and Fitter wove an appropriately stout cable; indeed, their first offering was too thick to thread through the eyelet that Bellcrank had fashioned in the anchor. Cut-wood filled the dining room so full of pillows and blankets that it was hard to walk across to the wheelhouse.

Lunitari grew visibly larger with each passing hour. From a featureless red globe, it had developed dark red mountain peaks, purple valleys, and wide scarlet plains. Stutts and Wingover debated endlessly as to why the moon was so dominated by red hues. As usual, they resolved nothing.

Kitiara made the mistake of asking how it was that they seemed to be flying straight down at Lunitari when they had been going up since leaving Krynn.

"It's all a matter of relative reference," Wingover said. "Our 'up' is down on Lunitari, and the 'down' on Lunitari will be up."

She set aside her sword, which she'd taken out to polish and sharpen. "You mean, if I drop a stone from my hand on Lunitari, it will fly up in the air and eventually fall on Krynn?"

Wingover opened and closed his mouth silently three times. His expression grew more and more puzzled. Finally, Kitiara asked, "What will keep our feet on the moon? Won't we fall back home?"

Wingover looked stricken. Stutts chuckled. "The same p-pressure that held you to the fertile soil of K-Krynn will allow us to walk normally on L-Lunitari," he said.

"Pressure?" asked Sturm.

"Yes, the p-pressure of the air. Air has weight, you know."

"I see," said Kitiara. "But what keeps the air in place?" Now it was Stutts's turn to look stricken.

Sturm rescued them from their scientific quandary. "I want to know if there will be people there," he said.

"Why not?" Wingover said. "If the air thickens and gets warmer, we might find quite ordinary folk living on Lunitari."

Kitiara drew the whetstone down the length of her blade. "Strange," she mused, "to think that people like us live on the moon. I wonder what they see when they look up— down?—at our world."

Birdcall whistled for attention from the deck below. Bellcrank had removed the ladder halfway down, so the chirping gnome couldn't reach a rung to pull himself up. Stutts and Sturm reached through the open hatch and hauled him out. Birdcall twittered a lengthy exposition, and Stutts translated.

"He says he and F-Flash have figured out a way to disengage the engine before we land. They will c-cut the main power cable a hundred feet up, and t-time the wing beats so that the wings will l-lock in their extended position. That way, we can glide in to a landing."

"And if they don't?"

Birdcall held up one hand with the fingers flat together. His hand dived into the open palm of his other, making a crunching noise when they smacked together.

"We have l-little ch-choice but to try." The others agreed. Birdcall dropped to the deck below and hurried down to his engine. Roperig and Fitter pooled the anchor and cable on the deck by the ship's tail. Cutwood, Sighter, and Rainspot boxed up their most valuable possessions—tools, instruments, and the big ledger with all the entries on raisin density in muffins—and buried them amidst the pillows in the dining room.

"What can I do?" Sturm said to Wingover.

"You could throw out the anchor when we say."

"I can do something, too," Kitiara said.

"Why don't you go to the engine room and help Flash and Birdcall? They can't tend the engine and cut the power cable at the same time," said the gnome.

She raised her sword until the hilt was level with her chin. "Cut it with this?" she said.

"Certainly."

"Right." Kitiara slipped the sheath over the blade and started down the abbreviated ladder. "When you want the cable cut, hit that crazy horn," she said. "That will be my signal."

"Kit," Sturm said quietly, making her pause. "May Paladine guide your hand."

"I doubt that I'll need divine aid. I've chopped through thicker things than cable!" She smiled crookedly.

There was nothing in view now but Lunitari. Though Wingover didn't change course, the moon seemed to sink from overhead to bows-on. As the minutes sped by, the red landscape spread to every horizon. Soon the airship was flying with the purple sky above and the red soil below.

The altitude gauge was working again. "Seventy-two hundred feet. Four minutes to contact," said Wingover.

A line of jagged peaks flashed by. Wingover spun the wheel hard to port. The wings on the starboard side flicked past the sharp spires with scant feet to spare. The *Cloudmaster* careened farther, almost onto its side. Soft thumps and muffled yells came from the dining room.

"Whoa-oh-oh-oh!" Wingover cried. "More bumps coming up!"

The prow smashed into a lofty pinnacle and carried it away. A cloud of red grit and dust hit the wheelhouse windows. Wingover frantically pushed levers and turned the wheel. The flying ship went nose up, then tail up. Sturm staggered back and forth. He felt like a pea being rattled in a cup.

The cliffs fell away to reveal a landscape of flat mesas divided by deep ravines. The ship was down to a thousand feet. Sturm opened the door. Melted ice ran along the deck outside. "I'm going aft!" he said. Wingover bobbed his head rapidly in reply.

He stepped out the door just as Wingover banked the

Cloudmaster in that direction. Sturm almost pitched head-first over the rail. The scarlet world roared past at terrifying speed, much faster, it seemed, than when they were cruising through the high clouds. He felt a rush of vertigo, but it quickly succumbed to his will. Sturm staggered aft, bouncing from the rail to the wall of the deckhouse. He glimpsed a queerly distorted face at one of the dining room portholes. It was Fitter, his bulbous nose and ruddy lips smashed flat against the pane.

The wind whipped at Sturm as he neared the anchor. The hinged tail bowed and flexed under Wingover's control. Sturm wrapped an arm around the tail's hinge post and held on.

The tableland was replaced by a featureless plain. The dark red soil was smooth and unrippled. At least Paladine had favored them with an uncluttered place to land the fly-ing ship! Sturm let go of the rudder post and cradled the anchor in his arms. Bellcrank had done a good job; the big hook weighed nearly as much as Sturm. He wrestled it to the rail. They were very low now. The ground resembled a sheet of marble, painted the color of blood.

Do it, Wingover. Blow the horn now, thought Sturm. They seemed too low. He's forgotten, he thought. We're too low. He forgot to sound the horn! Or had he himself failed to hear it in the rush of wind and the pounding of his heart?

After a second of indecision, Sturm heaved the anchor over. The multicolored rope, woven from everything Roperig could find—cord, curtains, shirts, and gnomish underwear—spilled after the hook, loop after loop. Roperig said he'd made 110 feet of cable. More than enough. The skein rapidly shrank. With a snap, it ran out, and the heavy scrap metal anchor streamed out behind the flying ship. Sturm had dropped it too soon.

He moved forward, watching the hook drop closer and closer to the red soil. By the door to the wheelhouse, Sturm paused, expecting the anchor to bounce and shatter as it hit, but it did neither. The anchor sank into the surface of the moon, plowing a wide, deep furrow.

He threw open the door. Wingover had his hand on the horn cord. "Don't do it!" Sturm yelled. "The ground below—it's not solid!"

Wingover snatched his hand away from the cord as if it had burned him. "Not solid?"

"I dropped the anchor, and it's flowing through the plain as though it were in water. If we land, we'll sink!"

"We don't have any time left. We're less than a hundred feet up now!"

Sturm went to the rail, staring desperately at the soft ground. What to do? What to do!

He saw rocks. "Hard to starboard!" he sang out. "Solid ground to starboard!"

Wingover spun the wheel. The right rear wing touched Lunitari. It dipped into the dust and came out unharmed. Sturm could smell the dirt in the air. The rocks thickened, and the smooth, scarlet dust gave way to a stony plain.

AA-OO-GAH!

The *Cloudmaster* quivered like a living thing. The leather bat-wings lifted in a graceful arc and froze there. Sturm threw himself through the door and landed on his belly. He covered his head tightly with his hands.

The wheels touched, spun, and snapped off with brittle, wrenching sounds. When the hull of the flying ship plowed into Lunitari, the bow bucked, rose, and jerked to port. Sturm careened across the deck. The *Cloudmaster* tore along, trailing a wake of dirt and stones. Finally, as if too tired to continue, the flying ship settled to a creaking, grinding stop.

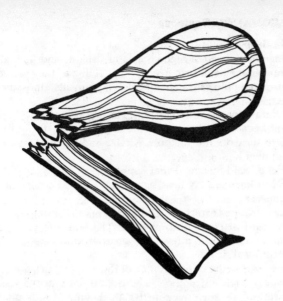

Chapter 9

Forty Pounds of Iron

"Are we dead?"

Sturm uncovered his head and lifted it. Wingover was jammed through the spokes of the steering wheel, his short arms squeezed tightly against his chest. His eyes were just as tightly closed.

"Open your eyes, Wingover; we're all right," said Sturm.

"Oh, Reorx, I'm stuck!"

"Hold on." Sturm grabbed the gnome's feet and pulled. Wingover protested all the way, but when he was finally free, he forgot his discomfort and said, "Ah! Lunitari!"

The gnome and the man went out on deck. The rear door of the dining room banged open, and the other gnomes piled out. Wordlessly, they surveyed the barren landscape. Aside from a distant hump of hills, Lunitari was flat all the way to the horizon.

One gnome gave a high chortle of delight, and they all scampered inside. Sturm heard things flying as they sorted through the pillows for their tools, instruments, and notebooks.

Kitiara appeared on deck with Flash and Birdcall. They hadn't been able to see from the engine room, being too busy to stare out the porthole. Kitiara had a fine goose-egg bruise over her right eye.

"Hello," said Sturm. "What happened to you?"

"Oh, I knocked my head against an engine fitting when we crashed."

"Landed," he corrected. "Did you break the fitting?"

His rare attempt at humor left Kitiara silent for a moment. Then they threw their arms around each other, grateful for their lives.

The ramp in the starboard side of the hull dropped down, and the whole gang of gnomes boiled out onto the red turf. Kitiara said, "I guess we'd better go down and look after them, before they hurt themselves."

The gnomes were lost in their specialties by the time Kitiara and Sturm joined them. Sighter scanned the horizon with his spyglass. Bellcrank and Cutwood were filling jars with scoopfuls of red dirt. Rainspot stood apart from the rest, his nose and ears tuned to the weather. He reminded Kitiara of a hunting dog. Stutts was rapidly filling pages in his pocket notebook. Wingover walked around the hull of the *Cloudmaster*, kicking the tight wooden planks now and then. Roperig and Fitter examined their anchor line and measured the amount that it had stretched when pulled taut. Birdcall and Flash were in a heated discussion. Sturm overheard something about 'wing camber variance' and listened no further.

He scooped up a handful of Lunitarian dirt. It was flaky, not granular like sand. As it fell from his fingers, it made a tinkling sound.

"Do you smell what I smell?" asked Kitiara.

He sniffed. "Dust. It'll settle," he said.

"No, not that. It's a feeling more than a smell, really. The air has a tingle to it, like a draft of Otik's best ale."

Sturm concentrated for a moment. "I don't feel anything."

Stutts bustled over. "Here are m-my preliminary findings," he said. "Air: normal. Temperature: c-cool but not cold. No sign of w-water, vegetation, or animal life."

"Kit says she feels a tingle in the air."

"Really? I h-hadn't noticed anything."

"I'm not imagining it," she said tersely. "Ask Rainspot, maybe he's noticed."

The weather-wise gnome came running when called, and Stutts asked for his impressions.

"The high clouds will dissipate soon," said Rainspot. "Humidity is very low. I don't think it has rained here in a very long time, if ever."

"Bad news," Kitiara said. "We haven't much water left on the ship."

"Do you sense anything else?" Sturm queried.

"Yes, actually, but it's not a weather phenomenon. The air is somehow charged with energy."

"Like l-lightning?"

"No." Rainspot pivoted slowly. "It's constant, but very low in intensity. It doesn't feel harmful, just . . . there." He shrugged.

"Why don't we feel it?" Sturm asked.

"You're not the sensitive type," Kitiara said. "Like old Rainspot and me." She clapped her hands. "So, Stutts, now that we're here, what do we do?"

"Explore. Make m-maps and study local conditions."

"There's nothing here," said Sturm.

"This is only one small l-location. S-suppose we had landed on the Plains of Dust on Krynn. W-would you then say that there is nothing on Krynn but s-sand?" Stutts asked. Sturm admitted that he would not.

Stutts called his engineers, and Flash and Birdcall trotted up. "St-status report."

"The lightning bottles are two-thirds empty. If we don't find some way to refill them, we won't have enough power to fly home," Flash said. Birdcall sang his report, and Flash translated for the humans. "He says the engine was shaken loose from its mountings by the hard landing. But the cut power cable can be patched."

"I have an idea about that," said Wingover, who'd joined them. "If we install a switch at that juncture, we can bypass the fused setting damaged by Rainspot's lightning."

"My lightning!" the weather gnome protested. "Since when do I make lightning?"

"Switch? What kind of switch?" Cutwood asked. The sound of disputation had drawn him and Bellcrank.

"A single throw-knife switch," said Wingover.

"Ha! Listen to the amateur! Single-throw! What's needed is a rotary pole switch with isolated leads—"

Kitiara let out a blood-curdling battle cry and swung her sword around her head. The silence that followed was instant and total.

"You gnomes are driving me mad! Why don't you just appoint someone to each task and be done with it?"

"Only one mind on each task?" Sighter was scandalized. "It would never get done right."

"Perhaps Bellcrank could make the switch," Fitter suggested timidly. "It will be made of metal, won't it?"

Everyone stared at him, mouths open. He edged nervously behind Roperig.

"Wonderful idea!" Kitiara said. "Brilliant idea!"

"There isn't much spare metal left," Wingover said.

"We could salvage some from the anchor," Rainspot said. The other gnomes looked at him and smiled.

"That's a good idea," said Cutwood.

"Fitter and me'll pull in the anchor," Roperig said.

They picked up the thick cable hanging down from the tail and hauled away. Fifty feet away, where the field of stones gave way to the deep dust, the buried anchor leaped ahead in dusty spurts. Then the hook caught on something. The gnomes strained and pulled.

"Want some help?" called Sturm.

"No—uh—we can do it," Roperig replied.

Roperig slapped Fitter on the back and they turned around, laying the rope over their shoulders. The gnomes dug in their toes and pulled.

"Pull, Roperig! Heave ho, Fitter! Pull, pull, pull!" shouted the other gnomes.

"Wait," said Kitiara suddenly. "The rope is fraying—"

The hastily woven cable was coming undone just behind Fitter. Twine and strands of twisted cloth spun away, and the two gnomes, oblivious, braced their backs against it.

"Stop!" This was all Sturm had time to shout before the rope parted. Roperig and Fitter fell on their faces with a plunk. The other end of the cable, weighted down by the anchor, snaked away. Bellcrank and Cutwood took off after it. The roly-poly chemist tripped over his own feet and stumbled. The ragged end of the cable whisked out of his reach. Cutwood, with surprising verve, leaped over his fallen colleague and dived for the fleeing rope. To Sturm's amazement, he caught it. Cutwood weighed no more than fifty or sixty pounds, and the anchor weighed two hundred. As it continued to sink into the red dust, it dragged Cutwood along with it.

"Let go!" Sturm shouted. Kitiara and the gnomes echoed him, but Cutwood was already in the dust. Then, as the others looked on in horror, Cutwood upended and disappeared. They waited and watched for the carpenter gnome to surface. But he did not.

Bellcrank got up and took a few steps toward the rim of the rock field. He was shouted to a halt. "You'll go in, too!" Kitiara said.

"Cutwood," said Bellcrank helplessly. "Cutwood!" A ripple appeared in the motionless dust. It roiled and grew into a hump of crimson grit. Slowly the hump became a head, then developed shoulders, arms, and a squat torso.

"Cutwood!" was the universal cry.

The gnome slogged forward heavily, and when he was waist-high out of the dust, everyone could see that his pants had ballooned to twice their usual size. The waist and legs were packed with Lunitarian dust. Cutwood stepped to firmer ground. He lifted one leg and shook it, and a torrent of grit poured out.

Bellcrank rushed forward to embrace his dusty friend. "Cutwood, Cutwood! We thought you were lost!"

Cutwood responded with a mighty sneeze, which got dust on Bellcrank, who sneezed right back, prompting Cutwood to sneeze again. This went on for some time. Finally, Sighter and Birdcall came forward with improvised Dust-

Free Face Filters (handkerchiefs). The siege of sneezing overcome, Cutwood lamented, "My suspenders broke."

"Your what?" asked Bellcrank, sniffling.

Cutwood pulled up his deflated pants. "The anchor dragged me under. I knew it was taking me down, but I couldn't let all our scrap metal get away. Then my suspenders broke. I tried to grab them and the rope jerked out of my hands." He sighed. "My best suspenders."

Roperig walked around Cutwood, plucking at his baggy trousers. "Give me your pants," he said.

"What for?"

"I want to do some structural tests. There may be an invention in them."

Cutwood's eyes widened. He quickly removed his rusty twill trousers and stood by in blue flannel long johns.

"Brrr! This is a cold moon," he said. "I'm going for another pair of trousers, but don't you invent anything until I get back!" Cutwood hurried to the *Cloudmaster* with showers of dust still cascading from his shoulders.

Sturm took Kitiara aside. "Here's a pretty problem," he said in a low voice. "We need metal to repair the engine, and all our scrap was lost in a lake of dust."

"Maybe Bellcrank could salvage a bit more from the flying ship," Kitiara said.

"Maybe, but I don't trust him not to ruin the whole ship in the process. What we need is more metal." He faced the crowd of gnomes who were busy examining Cutwood's pants as if they were the find of a lifetime. Now and then a gnome would turn his head and sneeze.

"Oh, Bellcrank? Would you come over here, please?" Sturm said.

The gnome scurried over. He stopped, pulled out a handkerchief stained with grease and chemicals, and blew his nose loudly. "Yes, Sturm?"

"Just how much metal do you need to fix the engine?"

"That depends on what type of switch I make. For a double throw, rotary pole—"

"The very least you'll need, in any case!"

Bellcrank chewed his lip a moment and said, "Thirty pounds of copper, or forty pounds of iron. Copper would be easier to work than iron, you see, and—"

"Yes, yes," Kitiara said hastily. "We don't have forty pounds of anything except beans."

"Beans wouldn't work," Bellcrank offered.

"All right. We'll just have to find some metal." Sturm looked around. The high clouds were beginning to thin, and the twilight that had persisted since their landing was beginning to brighten. The sun that warmed Krynn was rising higher in their sky. Taking that direction as east (for convenience), they could see a distant range of hills far off to the north.

"Bellcrank, would you know iron ore when you saw it?" said Sturm.

"Would I know it? I know every ore there is!"

"Can you smelt it?"

The germ of Sturm's idea spread to the gnome, and he smiled widely. "A fine notion, my friend. Worthy of a gnome!"

Kitiara slapped him on the back. "There you are," she said. "A few days in the air and you start thinking like a gnome."

"Never mind the wit. We've got to organize an expedition to those hills to see if there is any metal there."

Bellcrank ran back to his fellows to share the news. Exclamations of joy rang across the empty plain. Cutwood, coming down the ramp from the *Cloudmaster*, was nearly bowled over as his fellows charged up. He was carried back inside with them. The thumps and crashes that always signified gnomish enthusiasm were not long in coming.

Kitiara shook her head. "Now see what you've done."

*   *   *   *   *

The first argument began over who would go on the trek and who would stay with the flying ship.

"Everyone can't go," Sturm said. "What food and water we have won't sustain us all on a long march."

"I'll st-stay," Stutts said. "*Cloudmaster* is m-my responsibility."

"Good fellow. Who will stay with Stutts?" The gnomes

looked at the purple sky, the stars, their shoes, anywhere but at Sturm. "Whoever stays will get to work on the ship."

Birdcall whistled his acceptance. Hearing him agree, Flash said, "Oh, well, burn it! No one understands the lightning bottles but me. I'll stay."

"I'll stay behind," Rainspot offered. "I don't know much about prospecting."

"Me, too," Cutwood said.

"Hold your horses," Kitiara objected. "You can't all stay. Rainspot, we need you. We'll be out in the open, and if storms threaten, we'll want to know beforehand."

The gnome grinned and placed himself by Kitiara. He gazed happily up at her, pleased that someone needed him.

"Three should be enough to watch over the ship," Sturm said. "The rest of you get your belongings together. No one is to take anything more than he can carry on his back." The gnomes all nodded vigorous affirmatives. "After we eat, we'll all get some sleep and start fresh in the morning."

"When is morning?" asked Bellcrank.

Sighter unfolded his tripod and clamped his telescope in place. He studied the sky, searching for familiar stars. After a lengthy perusal, he announced, "Sixteen hours. Maybe more. Hard to tell." He snapped the telescope tube shut.

"Sixteen hours!" said Kitiara. "Why so long?"

"Lunitari doesn't sit in the same part of the heavens as Krynn. Right now, the shadow of our home world is over us. Until we move clear of it, this is all the light we'll get."

"It will have to do," Sturm said. To Fitter, who as the youngest gnome had permanent kitchen duty, he said, "What is there to eat?"

"Beans," said Fitter. Boiled beans, seasoned with their last tiny bit of bacon, was dinner, and it promised to be their breakfast, too.

Sturm squatted under the overhang of the flying ship's hull and ate his bowl of beans. As he ate, he tried to imagine what lay beyond the dust and stones. The sky was not black, but purple, lightening at the horizon to a warm claret. Everything was wrought in tones of red—the dirt, the rocks; even the white beans seemed vaguely pink. Was all of Lunitari like this, lifeless? he wondered.

Kitiara sauntered up. She'd shed her heavy furs for a less confining outfit. The hip-length jacket and leggings she'd retained, and had slung her sword over her left shoulder, as the Ergothites often did. In that position, it freed the legs for walking.

"Good, huh?" she said, dropping down beside Sturm.

"Beans are beans," he replied, letting them fall from his spoon back into the bowl. "I've eaten worse."

"So have I. During the siege of Silvamori, my troops' menu was reduced to boiled-boot soup and tree leaves. And we were the besiegers."

"How did the people in the town fare?" Sturm asked.

"Thousands died of starvation," she said. The memory did not seem to trouble her. Sturm felt the beans turn to paste in his mouth.

"Don't you regret that so many died?" he asked.

"Not really. If a thousand more had perished, the siege might have ended sooner, and fewer of my comrades would have died."

Sturm all but dropped his bowl. He stood up and started to walk away. Kitiara, puzzled by his reaction, said, "Are you through? Can I finish your beans?"

He stopped, his back to her. "Yes, eat them all. Slaughter spoils my appetite." He mounted the ramp and disappeared into the *Cloudmaster*.

A quick flush of anger welled within Kitiara. Who did he think he was? Young Master Brightblade presumed to look down on her for her warrior's code.

The spoon Kitiara had clenched in her fist suddenly snapped. The pieces fell from her fingers. She stared at them, her anger dissolving as quickly as it had come. The spoon was made of sturdy ash wood. But it broke cleanly where her thumb had pressed on it. Kitiara's eyebrows rose in amazement. Must be a defect in the wood, she thought.

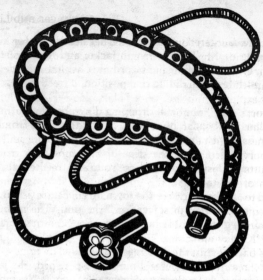

Chapter 10

The First Lunitari Exploration March

The gnomes emerged from the ship after a few hours' nap, staggering under a burden of tools, clothing, instruments, and other less identifiable rubbish. Kitiara spied Roperig and Fitter pushing a four-wheeled cart between them.

"What have you two got there?" she asked.

Roperig dug in his heels to stop the cart. "A few essential things," he said. He had a coil of rope over his left shoulder that was so thick he couldn't turn his head in that direction.

"This is ridiculous. Where did you get this contraption?"

"Fitter and me made it. It's all wood, you see? No metal." Roperig thumped the rear wall of the cart with his foot.

"Where did the wood come from?" said Kitiara.

"Oh, we knocked out a few of the inside walls in the ship."

"Great suffering gods! It's a good thing we're going on this march. Otherwise, you gnomes would have the whole ship dismantled before long!"

The explorers mustered on the plain below the *Cloudmaster*'s port side. The gnomes, in their usual endearing earnestness, lined up like an honor guard on parade. Despite the bleakness of their situation, Sturm couldn't help but smile at the goofy, ingenious little men.

"Stutts has asked me to lead this march to the hills, in search of ore to repair the flying ship, and you all have agreed to follow my directions. My, ah, colleague, Kitiara is to be equally responsible. She's had considerable experience in forays like this, and we should all be guided by her wisdom." Kitiara did not acknowledge his compliment, but leaned back against the ship's hull and looked on impassively, one hand resting on the pommel of her sword.

"Sighter estimates the distance to the hills as fifteen miles. We should reach them at about the time daylight breaks, isn't that right?"

Sighter checked a column of numbers scrawled on his shirt cuff. "Fifteen miles in six hours; yes, that's right."

Sturm looked down the line of his 'troops.' He couldn't think of anything else to say. "Well, let's get going," he said, embarrassed. So much for his first speech as a leader.

Fitter and Roperig ran around their makeshift cart, fitting long poles into prepared brackets on the front and back. Bellcrank and Cutwood placed themselves on the pole in front, while Roperig and Fitter took up positions at the rear.

"A four-gnome-power exploratory wagon," said Wingover admiringly.

"Mark I," added Rainspot.

"Move out," said Kitiara impatiently. With no more fanfare than that, the First Lunitari Exploration March began. Stutts, Birdcall, and Flash waved from the roof of the deckhouse as their colleagues marched away. From their high perch, they watched the expedition's progress long after the *Cloudmaster* was lost to the marchers' view in the fluid mauve shadows.

* * * * *

Kitiara lifted the water bottle to her parched lips. The cool, sweet water of Krynn trickled between them. Just a sip, she thought. These two pints are all you've got.

Sturm set a good pace with his strong, long stride. He'd traded his fur hood for his war helmet, a fine Solamnic piece of iron and leather, with two brass horns sprouting from the temples. He strode along on the right of the marching gnomes. Kitiara, on the left and a pace farther back, adopted an easy, economical lope that would not tire her quickly.

They marched steadily for almost two hours. Sturm called for a rest, and the gnomes on the cart loudly protested. They wanted to make the journey in one go, but Sturm insisted. They would reach the hills soon enough.

They sat in a circle with the cart at their backs. Kitiara rather pointedly sat away from Sturm. He sighed inwardly. What should he make of the woman?

The Measure of the Solamnic Knights held that women were always to be treated with courtesy and respect, even if their behavior had not earned it. That was clear enough. Sturm had great respect for Kitiara as a warrior. It was her moral laxity that troubled him. She lived with such two-fisted gusto, fighting and loving with an abandon he could not understand. But what allegiances did she make? It is the ties we make that anchor us against adversity, he thought. She mocked piety and the gods. She'd participated in raids and killing that lacked justice and honor. Where did Kitiara's heart lie?

Sturm leaned back against the cart. How had his mother and father gotten along when they first met? They loved each other very much, though they were both proud and independent. He saw again the scene in the courtyard of Castle Brightblade, when his parents had seen each other for the last time. They embraced, but did not kiss, as the snow fell about them.

Snow.

A chill flashed over Sturm so hard and so fast that his teeth chattered. The crimson landscape of Lunitari swam before his eyes and faded. He was in the midst of a howling snowstorm! The countryside was unfamiliar, but he knew that it was Krynn.

He saw a line of men, four in all, wading through the thigh-deep snow. They were wrapped in old blankets and strips of fur, and in the gaps in their cloaks, he could see the rusty glint of armor. Scabbards banged into their legs as they labored through a desolate, icy forest.

"Sturm? Sturm!"

He blinked and saw Kitiara bending over him. "What?" he said weakly.

"What's the matter with you? You've been staring into space and groaning. Are you sick?" she asked.

He put a hand to his face. His skin was ice cold! "I don't know," he said. "All of a sudden I felt as if I were somewhere else."

The irritation left Kitiara's expression. She said, "Where?"

"I-I don't know. It was Krynn—there was a snowstorm, and there were men. They were lost in the woods." He shook his head to clear his mind. "I don't understand."

"Neither do I. Shall I ask Rainspot?" The weather seer had some knowledge of medicine.

"No, I'm all right now." He stood. The thin, cool air of Lunitari felt balmy to him. Sturm inhaled deeply and exhaled. "Let's get moving," he said.

The gnomes hopped up and assumed their places around the cart. Roperig and Fitter pushed and Bellcrank and Cutwood pulled to get the cart started. But while they had rested, the weight of the cart had sunk the wheels into the spongy turf. The cart rocked a little, but refused to roll out of its ruts.

"Suffering gods," Kitiara complained. She stepped between Bellcrank and the cart's side and gripped the push-pole with her left hand. "Heave away!" she said. She leaned away, tendons standing out in her neck, and . . . Crack! The pole snapped right where Kitiara held it. She and Bellcrank tumbled backward.

"She broke the wagon!" Fitter said.

"Nonsense. That pole is solid garnerwood, two inches thick," said Sighter, picking at the shattered stump.

"Must be defective," Wingover said.

"Nope," Sighter said. "Sound as the slopes of Mt. Never-mind." He squinted up at Kitiara, who still held the broken-off pole in her hand. "You broke it with one hand."

Wordlessly she held the pole in both hands, straight out in front of her. Bending her elbows in, Kitiara bent the pole. The wood splintered with a loud crack.

"I had no idea you were so strong," said Sturm.

"Neither did I!" she replied, equally astonished.

"Here," said Bellcrank, picking up one of the pieces of the pole from where Kitiara had dropped it. "Break it again." The piece was less than a foot long. Kitiara had to use her knee for a brace, but she snapped even that short length.

"Something is happening here," said Sighter, narrowing his eyes. "You've gotten undeniably stronger in the twenty hours we've been on Lunitari."

"Maybe we're all getting stronger!" Cutwood said. He grasped another bit of the pole and tried to bend it. His flor-id face turned quite purple, but the wood did not so much as crack. Similar efforts by the others, including Sturm, showed no increase in strength. Kitiara beamed.

"Looks like you're the sole beneficiary of this gift, what-ever it is," said Sturm evenly. "At least it will be useful. Can you free the cart?"

She snapped her fingers and swaggered around the rear of the cart. Kitiara flattened one hand against the cargo box and shoved. The cart leaped out of its ruts, almost running Fitter and Wingover down.

"Careful!" said Sturm. "You've got to learn to handle this newfound strength, or you may hurt someone."

Kitiara wasn't listening. She ran her hands up and down her arms again and again, as if to feel the power radiating from her strangely augmented muscles.

"I don't know why it happened or how, but I like it," she said. Sturm noticed a new swagger in her walk. First his weird dream (it had been so real), and now Kit's new strength. All was not natural on the red moon.

Four hours later the hills were well within range. Close up, they had an oddly soft appearance, rounded, as though a giant hand had smoothed them.

Kitiara took over the lead when Sturm's step faltered. He

was tired, and his meager breakfast of beans and water wasn't enough to keep him at his best. In fact, as the marchers approached six and a half hours out from the *Cloudmaster*, Kitiara ran ahead to be the first to reach the hills.

"Kit, wait! Come back!" Sturm called. She waved and sprinted on.

The gnomes let the cart coast to a stop at the foot of a hill. Kitiara shouted and waved from the top. She skidded down the slope, coming to a halt by bumping into Sturm. He caught her arms. Panting, she smiled at him.

"You can see a long way from up there," she gasped. "The hills go on for miles, but there are wide trails running between them."

"You shouldn't go off on your own like that," Sturm said. Kitiara lost her smile and shook herself free of his grasp.

"I can take care of myself," she said coolly.

The gnomes flopped down where they stood. Uphill tramping had considerably dampened their ardor for the march. Against all advice, they rapidly drank up their meager water supply and were soon wishing for more.

"If only we could find a spring," said Wingover.

"Or if it rains, we could spread our blankets and catch the water," said Sighter. "Well, Rainspot? Might it rain?"

The weather seer, lying flat on his back, waved one hand feebly. "I don't think it has ever rained here," he said flatly. "Though I wish to Reorx it would."

At his words, a wisp of vapor, no denser than steam, abruptly formed over the exhausted gnome. The vapor expanded, thickened, and turned into a small white cloud, three feet wide. The gnomes and humans watched, speechless, as the white cloud went murky gray. A single droplet fell on the motionless Rainspot.

"That's not funny," he complained. Rainspot's eyes opened in time to catch the tiny shower that fell from his personal rain cloud.

"Hydrodynamics!" he exclaimed.

The other gnomes crowded in under the little cloud, their round, upturned faces ecstatic as the raindrops pelted them. Sturm came over. He swept a hand through it and it came out sopping wet. Then, as quickly and mysteriously as it had come, the cloud faded away.

"This smacks of magic," Sturm said.

"I didn't do anything," Rainspot insisted. "I just wished it would rain."

"Maybe you have the power to grant wishes now," said Wingover. "Like Kitiara has gained strength."

The gnomes took up this theory and besieged their poor colleague with a barrage of requests. Wingover wanted a rib roast. Cutwood asked for a bushel of crisp apples. Bellcrank wanted a roast pig and apples. Roperig and Fitter wanted muffins—with raisins, of course.

"Stop, stop!" Rainspot pleaded tearfully. He couldn't bear so many demands at once. Sturm shooed the shouting gnomes away. Only Sighter remained, staring at the weeping Rainspot.

"If you can wish for anything, wish for a switch to repair the ship with," he said sagely. The others—Sturm and Kitiara included—were surprised by his wise suggestion.

"I-I wish for a new switch to repair our engine," Rainspot said loudly.

"Made of copper," said Cutwood.

"Iron," muttered Bellcrank.

"Shhh!" said Kitiara.

Nothing happened.

"Maybe you have to use the same formula each time," said Wingover. "How exactly did you wish for rain?"

"I said something about Reorx." Reorx, creator of the gnomish race, was the only deity the gnomes worshiped.

"So try again and mention Reorx," said Sighter.

Rainspot drew himself up—all thirty inches of him—and declared, "I wish to Reorx that we had a copper—"

"Iron."

"—switch to repair our engine with!"

Nothing happened.

"You're useless," said Bellcrank.

"Worse than useless," added Cutwood.

"Shut up!" Kitiara snapped. "He tried, didn't he?"

"I'm sorry," the weather seer said between sniffles. "I wish it would rain again. Then everyone would be happy." Hardly had he said this than a new cloud formed over his head.

The rain poured down on Rainspot, making a puddle in the red dirt of Lunitari. It seemed insulting somehow, as if Reorx were teasing the gnome. Rainspot then did a rare thing: He got mad.

"Thunder and lightning!" he cried. The cloud flashed once, and a puny clump of thunder sounded.

"Ha, some storm!" said Roperig.

"It proves one thing," said Sighter. "The limits of Rainspot's power. He can make it rain. That's all."

"Useless, useless," said Bellcrank.

"Shut up," said Kitiara. "Rainspot's ability is very useful." The gnomes regarded her blankly. "We need water, don't we?"

As usual, once the gnomes were sparked off, they embraced a new concept with exasperating enthusiasm. Planks were torn off the sides of the cart and pounded into the ground with Cutwood's mallet. Roperig ripped their blankets into long triangles and sewed these together, leaving a hole in the center of the resulting circle of cloth. The edges of the blanket were nailed to the upright planks. One of Fitter's canvas buckets was put under the hole in the center of the blanket.

"Rainspot, sit in the middle and wish for rain," said Wingover. Rainspot complied, and the water was captured by the improvised funnel and led to the waiting bucket. Rainspot sat on the soggy blanket, soaked and bedraggled, wishing over and over for rain.

"I wish for rain." The cloud formed and sprinkled him. "Wish for rain." Water ran in the bucket. The gnomes changed buckets and filled it, too. "Rain," said the sodden, tired gnome. Poor Rainspot didn't enjoy it at all, but he wished for plenty of water to save them from the agonies of thirst.

"Happy to do my part," he said flatly when they finally let him off the blanket, squishing in his shoes all the way.

"I wonder who will get it next," Wingover said as they plodded into the first gully.

"Get what?" said Bellcrank.

"We seem to be acquiring new powers," Sighter said. "Kitiara's strength, Rainspot's rainmaking. The rest of us may get new abilities, too."

Sturm pondered Sighter's claim. His dream (if it was a

dream) had been so vivid. Was it part of this mysterious process, too? He asked Sighter if he could think of a reason why they should be affected like this.

"Hard to say," said the gnome. "Likely, there is something on Lunitari that has done this to them."

"It's the air," said Bellcrank. "Some effluvium in the air."

"Piffle! It's all due to the red rays reflecting off the ground. Red light always has strange effects on living creatures. Remember the experiments done by The-Clumsy-But-Curious-Doctor-Who-Wears-The-Tinted-Lenses-In-Frames-On-His-Face—"

"Hush!" said Kitiara. She held up a hand. The others watched expectantly. "Do you feel it, Rainspot?" she asked.

"Yes, ma'am. The sun's coming up."

A brace of shooting stars raced across the heavens from west to east. The crests of the red hills glowed, and a subtle ringing sensation filled the air. They all felt it. The line of sunlight crept down the hillsides toward the shadowed ravines. As the explorers watched, the soft, spongy covering of the hills writhed. Bumps appeared in the turf. The bumps moved in an unpleasantly animal fashion, twisting and swelling under the crimson carpet. The explorers had to hop about to avoid the moving bumps. Then a single spear of pale pink poked through the turf. It grew longer and thicker, rotating in slow circles as it pushed itself toward the sunlight.

"What is it?" breathed Fitter.

"I think it's a plant," Cutwood replied.

More pink spears bored through the ground and climbed on wine-colored stalks. Other bumps erupted into different types of flora. Fat, knobby puffballs sprang up and inflated themselves. Carmine sticks popped after growing straight out of the turf, and dozens of spiderlike flowers floated to the ground from their ruptured stems. Toadstools with purple spots on top and lovely rose gills underneath emerged and grew visibly as the explorers looked on. By the time the sun shone fully into the ravine, every inch of the hillsides was covered with weird, pulsating life. Only a narrow track at the bottom of the ravine, still shadowed by the surrounding hills, was clear of the speedily growing plants.

"An instant forest," said Sighter.

"More like an instant jungle," said Sturm, observing the clogged path ahead of them. He drew his sword. "We'll have to cut our way through."

Kitiara drew her sword. "It's an insult to honest steel," she said, eyeing the garish plants with distaste, "but it has to be done." She raised her arm and slashed into the growth crowding the path on the right. With her greater strength, she had no difficulty hewing the pink spears and spider-sticks cleanly off.

Kitiara stepped back. The chopped-off parts lay on the ground, wriggling.

The stumps oozed red sap that looked amazingly like blood. She noticed her sword was smeared with the same fluid. Holding the blade near her nose, she sniffed.

"I've been in many battles," she said. "I know the smell of blood, whether it be human, dwarven, or goblin." She dropped the blade from her face. "This is blood!"

The gnomes thought this was terribly interesting. They bunched together over the bleeding stumps, taking samples of the bloodsap. Bellcrank picked up the shorn length of a spiderstick. It popped, and eight white flowers burst out. Bellcrank yowled in pain. Each tiny flower had ejected a thorn into his face.

"Hold still," Rainspot said. With a pair of bone tweezers, he plucked the thorns from his colleague's face.

The gnomes filled fifteen jars and boxes with specimens of the Lunitarian plants. Sturm and Kitiara had a head-to-head talk and opted to travel a little farther. If they didn't find any ore by nightfall, they would return to the ship.

Steeling themselves, they started hacking. The plants groaned and screamed; when severed, they bled and twitched horribly. After a mile of this, Kitiara said, "This is worse than the massacre of Valkinord Marsh!"

"At least they don't appear to suffer long," Sturm said, but the screams and blood were wearing on him.

The gnomes wandered through the path the humans had cut, poking and sniffing and measuring the dying plants. For them it was, as Cutwood said, "better than a train of gears." The trail led down a broad draw. Being well shaded from the low sun, there were fewer plants growing there, and Sturm called for a break. Kitiara borrowed a bucket from the gnomes' cart and filled it with rainwater. She dipped a soft rag in the water and wiped the sticky bloodsap from her blade. The sap dissolved easily. She lent Sturm the rag and he cleaned his weapon.

"You know," she said, as he rubbed the sap off his sword hilt, "I'm no coward, and I'm certainly no delicate lady who faints at the sight of blood, but this place is disgusting! What kind of world is it where plants grow before your eyes and bleed when they're cut?"

"How's your sword arm?" Sturm asked. "How does it feel? I noticed that you're not even breathing hard. Look at me; I'm tired, as you should be, having swung a heavy sword for more than a mile through that weird jungle!"

"I feel fine. I feel—strong. Want to wrestle?"

"No, thank you," he said. "I wouldn't like to trust a broken arm to gnomish medicine."

"I won't hurt you," she said mockingly. Kitiara's smile faded. She scraped a shallow line in the turf with her heel. "What are you so worried about? We're alive, aren't we?"

"There are strange forces at work here. This new strength of yours is not normal."

Kitiara shrugged. "Lunitari isn't my idea of paradise, but we haven't done badly so far."

Sturm knew this was true. So why did he feel such foreboding? He said, "Just be wary, will you, Kit? Question what comes to you—especially what seems like a great gift."

She laughed shortly. "You make it sound like I'm in personal danger. Are you afraid I'll fall into evil ways?"

Sturm stood and emptied the sap-stained water from the bucket. "That's exactly what I'm afraid of." He wrung out the rag and left it to dry on a stone, then walked away to speak with Wingover.

The empty canvas bucket sat by her boot. Where Sturm had poured out the water, the turf was dark and slick. It looked like so much blood. Kitiara wrinkled her nose and kicked the bucket away. The toe of her boot split the fabric and sent the bucket soaring over the tops of the pink and crimson foliage.

Chapter 11

The Crusty Pudding Plant

The trail wound between the hills in no particular direction. Among the fast-growing plants, there was no way for the adventurers to identify landmarks or remember where they'd been. Sturm discovered that the path they had made grew tall again after they had passed. The explorers were virtually cut off in the living jungle.

Sturm halted the party finally and announced that they were lost. Sighter promptly tried to find the latitude by shooting the sun with his astrolabe. Even though he stood on Sturm's shoulders, the sun was too low for him to sight correctly, and he fell over backward trying. Fitter and Rainspot picked Sighter up and dusted him off, for he'd fallen on a puffball and was coated with pink spores.

"Useless!" Sighter said. Spores got up his nose and mouth and he coughed in fits and starts. "All I can tell you is that the sun is setting."

"We've not had but four or five hours of daylight," Wingover protested.

"The position of Lunitari in the heavens is eccentric," the astronomer gnome explained. Rainspot tried to dab the dust from his face with a damp rag, but Sighter swatted his hands away. "The nights are very long and the days very short."

"We haven't found any ore yet," Bellcrank said.

"True," said Wingover, "but we haven't tried digging, either."

"Digging?" said Roperig.

"Digging," said Sturm firmly. "Wingover's right. Pick a spot, Bellcrank, and we'll dig to see what we can find."

"Could we make supper first?" the tubby gnome asked. "My stomach's so empty!"

"I don't suppose an hour will matter too much," said Sturm. "All right, we'll camp here, eat, then dig."

The gnomes fell to in their cheerfully scatterbrained way. Roperig and Fitter unpacked the cart in a very simple way: they upended it. Fitter was buried in the mound of junk and came out with his favorite clay kettle.

"Supper will be ready in a jiffy!" he said brightly. The other gnomes hooted derisively.

"Beans! Beans! Beans! I'm sick of beans," Cutwood said. "I'm sick, sick, sick of beans, beans, beans."

"Shut up, you dumb carpenter," said Sighter.

"Ah-ah-ah," Kitiara warned, as Cutwood picked up a mallet and tiptoed up behind Sighter. "None of that."

Fitter took a hatchet and chopped a plank off the side of the cart bed. Sturm saw this and said, "Have you been burning pieces of the wagon all along?"

"Of course," said the gnome. "What else is there?"

"Why don't you try some of the plants?" said Bellcrank.

"They're too green," Wingover said. "They'd never burn."

"Start a fire with the kindling you've got and lay the green plants on top. When the fire dries them out, they'll burn," Kitiara said.

Fitter and Cutwood scavenged along the trail and

returned with double armfuls of chopped Lunitarian flora. These they dumped on the ground by the wagon. Fitter built an arch of pink spear plants over the smoky fire. Within a few minutes, a tantalizing aroma filled the air. The hungry band surrounded Fitter.

"Fitter, my lad, I never would've believed it, but that bean pot smells just like roast pheasant!" said Wingover.

"Your gears are slipping," said Roperig. "It smells like fresh-baked bread."

"Roast venison," said Sturm, wrinkling his nose.

"Sausages and gravy!" Bellcrank said, licking his lips.

"I haven't even put the beans in yet," Fitter declared, "and it smells like raisin muffins to me."

"It's those things," Rainspot said, pointing to the pink spears. The parts nearest the flames had darkened to a rich brown. The sap had oozed out and hardened in streaks along the stalk.

Sighter picked up one spear by the raw end. He sniffed the cooked tip, and very gingerly bit it. Chewing, his suspicious frown inverted. "Pudding," he said with a catch in his voice. "Crusty pudding, like my mother used to make."

The gnomes tripped over each other in a rush to try the other spears. Sturm managed to save one from the first batch. With his dagger, he sliced the roasted portion in two, stabbed a piece, and offered it to Kitiara.

"It looks like meat," she said, then nibbled off a bit.

"What does it taste like to you?" asked Sturm.

"Otik's fried potatoes," she said, amazed. "With lots of salt."

"A most unique experiment," Sighter commented. "To each of us, this plant tastes like our favorite food."

"How can that be, if it's all the same plant?" Kitiara asked, munching vigorously.

"My theory is it has to do with the same force that has given you your strength and Rainspot his rainmaking ability."

"Magic?" asked Sturm.

"Possibly. Possibly." The word seemed to make Sighter uncomfortable. "We gnomes believe that what is commonly called 'magic' is just another natural force yet to be tamed."

The rest of the pink spears were rapidly consumed. For their size, the gnomes were hearty eaters, and finished the meal lying about the camp, holding their bellies. "What a feast!" exclaimed Bellcrank.

"One of the finest," Roperig agreed.

Sturm stood over them, fists on his hips. "A fine lot you are! Who's going to help dig now?"

"Nap first," Cutwood mumbled, wiggling around to get comfortable.

"Yes, must rest," said Rainspot. "To ensure proper digestion. And adequate relaxation of the muscles." Soon the little clearing rattled with the high-pitched snores of seven sets of lungs.

The sun sank rapidly below the hill. When the light diminished to a deep amber glow, the tangle of plants began to wither. Almost as quickly as they had sprouted with the morning sun, they now shriveled. Spear tips dried and fell off. The spider flowers curled up and bored into the soil. The puffballs deflated. The toadstools crumbled into powder. By the time the stars came out, nothing remained above the ground but a fresh layer of red flakes.

Kitiara said, "I think I'll stand watch for a while. Get some sleep, why don't you, then you can relieve me later."

"Good idea," he said. Sturm was suddenly aware of how very tired he was. Constant wonders had dulled his senses, and hacking through the daylight jungle had worn him out. He spread his bedroll beside the upturned cart and lay down.

A full Krynnish day they'd marched, and still no sign of any ore deposits. He wondered what would happen if they dug into one of the hills and still found none. There was one desperate measure that they could resort to: He and Kitiara still carried their swords and armor. The gnomes could very likely forge new parts from the steel and iron of these. But he wanted that to be their last possible choice.

The air of Lunitari, never warm, grew chillier. Sturm shivered and pulled his furry cloak up to his chin. The lining was wolf fur. He and Tanis had hunted in the mountains of Qualinost last winter and had done very well. Tanis was a dead shot with a bow.

He heard the arrow's hum.

Sturm was on Krynn suddenly, and it was daytime, though cold and overcast. He was in a forest, and there were four men moving through the trees ahead of him. Two men carried a third between them, his arms across their shoulders. When Sturm got closer he saw why: the carried man had an arrow in his thigh.

"Come on, Hurrik! You can make it!" the leader was saying. Sturm couldn't see the fourth man's face, but he heard him urging the others on. There was a crackle in the dead brush behind him. Sturm looked back and saw dim figures in white flitting among the trees. They wore wolfskin cowls and carried bows. He knew who they were: the dreaded Trackers of Leereach. Hired huntsmen who would track down anyone or anything for a price.

"Stay with us, Hurrik! Don't give up!" the leader whispered urgently.

"Leave me, my lord!" the wounded man replied.

The leader stood with his men. "I'll not leave you to those butchers," he said.

"Please go, my lord. They will want to give me to their master, and that will give you time to get away," Hurrik said. There was blood on his armor. Sturm could see it smeared across the man's coif.

The two men carrying Hurrik propped him against a tree. They drew his sword for him and wrapped his fingers around the grip. Sturm could see his face, waxen from loss of blood.

The trackers stopped. A snickering whistle rattled through the forest. The prey was turning, at bay. The signal meant close in for the kill.

The leader, his face still hidden from Sturm, drew a long dagger from his belt and put it in the wounded man's left hand. "Paladine protect you, Master Hurrik," he said.

"And you, my lord. Now hurry!" The three unhurt men ran away as fast as their armor would allow. Hurrik raised his sword with pain-filled effort. A wolf's head parted a stand of ripe holly. "Come out," said Hurrik. "Come out and fight me!"

The tracker was having none of it. Coolly, he nocked an

arrow and let fly. The broadhead found its mark. "My lord!" Hurrik cried.

The leader paused to look back to where his comrade had died. Sturm saw his face.

"Father!"

He returned to Lunitari with that scream. Sturm was lying on his stomach, his bedroll in knots. Wearily, he sat up to find Kitiara watching him.

"I had a nightmare," he said, ashamed.

"No," she said. "You were awake. I saw you. You've been thrashing about and moaning for a long time. Your eyes were wide open. What did you see?"

"I was—I was on Krynn again. I don't know where, but there were trackers. They were after some men, one of whom was my father."

"Leereach Trackers?" Sturm nodded. Sweat stood out on his lip, though the air was cold enough for his breath to show.

"It was real, wasn't it?" he said.

"I think it was. This may be your gift, Sturm. Visions. Like my strength, this is what Lunitari has given you."

He shuddered. "Visions of what? The past? The future? Or am I seeing the present in far-away places? How can I tell, Kit? How can I know?"

"I don't know." She combed through her black curls with her fingers. "It hurts, doesn't it? Not knowing."

"I think I shall go mad!"

"No, you won't. You're too strong for that." She rose and came around the dying fire to sit by him. Sturm refolded his blanket and lay down. These visions which had been thrust upon him were maddening. They smacked of magic and tormented him without warning. However, Sturm found himself trying to fix every detail in his mind, going over and over the terrible scene; there could be a clue to his father's fate hidden in these specters. Kitiara laid a hand on his chest and felt the rapid beating of his heart.

Chapter 12

SOME OF OUR GNOMES ARE MISSING

THE GNOMES RECOVERED FROM THEIR POST-PRANDIAL lethargy and bounced around the camp, shouting and tossing tools to each other. Bellcrank found a long dowel and scratched a mark on the side of a hill. "There's where we dig," he announced.

"Why there?" asked Cutwood.

"Why not?"

"Wouldn't it be better to go to the top and drive a shaft straight down?" suggested Wingover.

"If we wanted to dig a well, maybe, but not when we're prospecting for iron," Bellcrank said. After lengthy discussion about such esoteric matters as geological strata, sedimentation, and the proper diet of miners, the gnomes discovered that all they had to dig with was two short-handled wooden scoops.

"Whose are these?" asked Sighter.

"Mine," Fitter spoke up. "One for beans, one for raisins."

"Isn't there a proper shovel or spade in the cart?"

"No," said Roperig. "Of course, if we had some iron, we could make our own shovels—" Cutwood and Wingover pelted him with dirty socks for his suggestion.

"If scoops are what we have, scoops it'll have to be," said Bellcrank. He offered them to Cutwood and Wingover.

"Why us?" said Cutwood.

"Why not?"

"I wish he'd stop saying that," Wingover said. He shoved his sleeves above his elbows and knelt by the circle that Bellcrank had scratched in the turf. "Oh, rocks," he sighed.

"You'd better hope to Reorx we strike rocks," said Cutwood, "else we'll be digging all day."

The gnomes gathered around as their two colleagues fell to. The upper layers of flaky red fluff were easily scraped away. The diggers flung scoopfuls over their shoulders, hitting Sighter and Rainspot in the face. The gnomes withdrew to a cleaner observation point.

Bellcrank bent down and grabbed a handful of the soil that Wingover had tossed back. No longer dry and spongy, this dirt was hard, grainy, and damp. "Hello," he said. "Look at this. Sand."

Sturm and Kitiara examined the ball of damp sand that Bellcrank had squeezed in his small fist. It was quite ordinary sand, tinged pale red.

"Ugh! Ow, here's something," Cutwood grunted. He kicked a large chunk of something out of the tunnel. The thing wobbled down the slope a little way and stopped. Fitter picked it up.

"Feels like glass," he said. Sighter took it from him.

"It is glass. Crude glass," Sighter said.

More bits of glass came out of the hole, along with sand, sand, and more sand. Wingover and Cutwood had tunneled headfirst into the hillside and now only their feet showed in the opening. Sturm told them to stop digging.

"It's no use," he said. "There's no ore here."

"I must agree with Master Brightblade," said Bellcrank. "The whole hill is likely one big pile of sand."

"Where does the glass come from?" Kitiara asked.

"Any source of heat can melt sand into glass. Lightning, forest fire, volcano."

"That's not important," Sturm said. "We dug for iron and found glass. The question is, what do we do now?"

"Go on looking?" said Fitter timidly.

"What about Stutts and the others?" Kitiara asked.

"Strip my gears, I forgot about our colleagues," said Roperig. "What shall we do?"

Sturm said, "We'll go back. It'll be daylight again before we reach the flying ship, and we can harvest some spear plants for Stutts, Birdcall, and Flash to eat. Once we're all together, we can repair the engine—" He regarded Kit gravely. "—with the iron that Kitiara and I wear on us. You gnomes can forge our arms and armor into the parts you need." Murmurs of approval rippled through the gnomes.

"Do you think I'd allow my sword, my mail, to be hammered into machine parts? With what will we defend ourselves? Scoops and beans?" Kitiara said furiously.

"All we've used our weapons for so far is chopping weeds," Sturm countered. "This could be our only way home."

Kitiara crossed her arms. "I don't like it."

"Nor do I, but what choice do we have? We can be well-armed and marooned, or unarmed and on our way home."

"Not a handsome choice," she had to admit.

"You needn't make up your mind right now. Whatever you decide, we should return to the ship first," said Sturm. No one disputed his decision. The gnomes prepared to break camp. Like their unpacking, this was a brisk procedure. Each gnome tossed an item into the righted cart. Sometimes they wrestled over the same item, and Rainspot and Cutwood even got carried away and threw Fitter in. Sturm pulled the littlest gnome out before he was buried.

With a clear sky and plenty of stars, the explorers were able to plot their way back to the plain of stones. Once they left the chain of hills, they beheld a lovely sight. On the southwestern horizon, a blue-white glow lit the sky. Within a few hundred yards' walk, the source of the glow was revealed to be the world of Krynn, rising into sight for the first time since their arrival on the red moon.

The party stopped to admire the great azure orb. "What are the fuzzy white parts?" asked Kitiara.

"Clouds," said Rainspot.

"And the blue is ocean, the brown, land?"

"Exactly right, lady."

Sturm stood apart from the rest, contemplating his home world. Kitiara peered through the gnome's spyglass, squinting one eye closed and bending far down to Sighter's level. When she was done, she went to where Sturm stood.

"Don't you want to take a look?" she asked.

Sturm rubbed his newly bearded chin. "I can see it fine." The bright white light of Krynn caught on his ring and glimmered. The emblem of the Knights of Solamnia's Order of the Rose caught his eye.

He inhaled smoke and coughed.

Not again! The vision was upon him without any warning. Sturm fought to stay calm. Something always happened to trigger the experience—first the moon's chill air, then the feel of his wolf fur cloak, and now the light reflecting off his ring, the only real relic of his Solamnic heritage. It wasn't his father's ring, but his mother's; Sturm wore it on his little finger.

A high, dark wall loomed over his back. Sturm was standing in the shadow of the wall, and it was night. Twenty yards away, a fire burned. He seemed to be in the courtyard of a castle. Two men in ragged cloaks stood hunched over the fire. A third lay on the ground, unmoving.

Sturm came nearer, and saw that the tallest man was his father. Sturm's heart raced. He held out his hands to Angriff Brightblade for the first time in thirteen years. The old warrior lifted his head and stared right past Sturm. They can't see me, Sturm thought. Was there a way he could make himself known?

"We should not have come here, my lord," said the other standing man. "It's dangerous!"

"The last place our enemies would look for us is in my own sacked castle," replied Lord Brightblade. "Besides, we had to get Marbred out of the wind. The fever has settled in his chest."

Father! Sturm tried to shout. He could not even hear himself.

Lord Brightblade squatted by the man on the ground. His breath had frozen on his beard, making it as white as Marbred's. "How do you feel, old friend?" Sturm's father asked.

Marbred wheezed, "Fit for any command of my lord." Angriff squeezed his old retainer's arm, stood, and turned his back on the sick man.

"He may not last the night," he said. "Tomorrow there may be only you and I, Bren."

"What shall we do, my lord?"

Lord Brightblade reached under the tattered layers of cloak and blankets that hung from his broad shoulders. He unbuckled his belt and brought out his sword and scabbard. "I will not allow this blade, forged by the first of my ancestors and borne with honor all these years, to fall into the hands of the enemy."

Bren grabbed Lord Brightblade's wrist. "My lord—you don't intend—you can't mean to destroy it!"

Angriff pulled six inches of the sword from its covering. The fitful firelight caught on the burnished steel and made it glitter. "No," he said. "As long as my son lives, the Brightblade line will continue. My sword and armor will be his."

Sturm felt as if his heart would burst. Then, suddenly, the pain caused by the scene was replaced by an odd lightness. It stole into Sturm's limbs and, though he tried to hold himself in the vision, to keep everything in sharp focus, the image faded. The fire, the men, his father, and the sword of the Brightblades wavered and dissolved. Sturm's fingers clenched into tight fists as he tried literally to grasp the scene. Sturm found himself clenching the nap of Kitiara's fur coat.

"I'm all right," Sturm said. His heart slowly resumed its normal rhythm.

"You were very quiet this time," she reported. "You stared into space as if you were watching a stage play in Solace."

"In a way, I was." He described his father's vigil. "It must be the present or the recent past," he reasoned. "The castle was in ruins, but my father did not look so old—perhaps fifty years. His beard had not grayed. He must be alive!"

Sturm became aware that he was lying on his back and moving. He sat up hastily and almost fell off the gnomes' cart. "How'd I get up here?" he asked.

"I put you there. You didn't look as if you could make it on your own," said Kitiara.

"You picked me up?"

"With one hand," said Wingover. Sturm looked down. All the gnomes but Sighter were on the poles pushing the cart along. He suddenly felt embarrassed to be such a burden to his companions, and jumped off the cart. Kitiara slid down, too.

"How long was I out?" Sturm asked.

"Better part of an hour," said Sighter, referring to the stars. "The visions are getting longer, aren't they?"

"Yes, but I think they're triggered when I'm reminded of something from the past," Sturm said. "If I concentrate on the present, perhaps I can avoid episodes like this."

"Sturm doesn't approve of the supernatural," Kitiara explained to the gnomes. "It's part of his knightly code."

Krynn was now high overhead, and the terrain around them was as bright as day. No plants grew in the brilliant light, however; all was cold and lifeless under the planet's clear glow. Sighter led his colleagues in another long discussion. Kitiara and Sturm were trailing behind the cart, so no one saw the ditch until the front wheels spilled into it. The gnomes on the front pole—Cutwood, Fitter, and Wingover—fell on their faces. Roperig, Rainspot, and Bellcrank struggled to keep the heavily laden wagon from turning over. Kitiara and Sturm rushed in and steadied the sides.

"Let it roll down," Kitiara said. "Let go."

Rainspot and Bellcrank stepped back, but Roperig did not. The cart bounded down the side of the ditch with the humans running alongside and Roperig bouncing painfully against the push-pole.

"What's the matter with you?" Bellcrank said, when the cart halted. "Why didn't you let go?"

"I-I can't," Roperig complained. "My hands are stuck!" He

wallowed to his feet. Dust poured from his pockets and cuffs. His stubby fingers were firmly attached to the push-pole. Rainspot tried prying his colleague's fingers free. "Ow, ow!" Roperig yelled. "You're tearing my fingers off!"

"Don't be such a crybaby," said Sighter.

"Cutwood, did you put glue on this end of the pole?" asked Rainspot.

"Absolutely not! By gears, I would never do that without telling him first." Cutwood's invocation of the sacred word 'gears' proved that he was telling the truth.

"Hmm." Kitiara drummed her fingers on the cart wheel. "Maybe it's more of this crazy Lunitari magic."

"You mean I'll be stuck to this cart forever?"

"Don't be distressed, master. I can saw this pole off," Fitter said. He patted his boss on the back consolingly.

"Rot," said Bellcrank. "If Master Brightblade will lend me his knife, I'll scrape your fingers off in no time."

Roperig blanched. "You will not!"

"Then we can saw very carefully around your fingers."

"No one's going to cut or saw anything," Kitiara said. "If this stickiness is related to my strength or Sturm's visions, then you ought to give some thought to how it works before you start hacking away on a fellow's fingers."

"Quite so," said Sighter. "Now, could it be more than coincidence that we acquire abilities connected to our life's work? Rainspot makes rain, Lady Kitiara grows mightier as a warrior—and Roperig, master of cords and knots finds himself bound by his own hands. It's as though some subtle, yet powerful, force were enhancing our natural attributes."

"Roperig can probably free himself if he wishes to," said Kitiara. "Just as Rainspot can wish for his rain."

"All I wanted to do was keep my grip when we slipped in the ditch," Roperig said glumly.

He screwed his eyes tightly shut and wished hard.

"Harder! Concentrate!" urged Sighter. Cutwood whipped out his magnifying glass and peered intently at Roperig's stuck hands. Slowly, with faint sucking sounds, his hands peeled off the cart pole.

"Ow, ow!" Roperig whimpered, waving his hands about. "That stings!"

The cart was shoved to the top of the gully rim. The gnomes passed a water bottle around. Fitter handed it to Kitiara, who had a short swig before offering it to Sturm. He held it a long time, staring at the ground and not drinking.

"Now what?" she said, taking the bottle back.

"This magic worries me. Couldn't we refuse it somehow, give it back?"

She pushed the plug back into the bottle. "Why should we? We ought to get used to it, learn to control the effect." Kitiara flexed a hand into a fist. She could feel the strength within her, like the warmth of sweet wine in her veins. It was intoxicating, that taste of power. She looked Sturm in the eye. "If we return to Krynn penniless, weaponless, and armorless, I hope our powers remain."

"It isn't right," he said stubbornly.

"Right? This is the only right that matters!" The water bottle exploded when she crushed it in her fingers.

Little Fitter stooped to get the glazed shards. "You broke the bottle, lady," he said. "Did you cut yourself?"

She showed him her undamaged hand. "A lot of things may get broken around here before I'm through," she said angrily.

By the hour Krynn had set on the northeast horizon, the explorers were more than halfway back to the *Cloudmaster*. There was nothing ahead but flat ground, rocks, and red dust. They trod on, the humans apart and silent, the gnomes once more chattering.

The pilot of the flying ship walked slower and slower, until finally he stopped.

"Move along, lad," said Sighter, pushing Wingover in the back. "Don't want to get left behind, do you?"

"It's gone," announced Wingover.

"What's gone?"

"The ship. The *Cloudmaster*."

"You're plain daft. We're a good eight miles away, how could you see from here?"

"I don't know, but I can see the spot clearly," said Wingover. He squinted into the distance. "There's a big rut, some skid marks, and a few broken crates lying around, but the ship is gone."

Sturm and Kitiara converged on the far-seeing gnome. "Are you sure, Wingover?" said Sturm.

"It's gone," the gnome insisted.

Sighter and the other gnomes were loudly skeptical, but Sturm ordered them to quicken their pace. The miles rolled aside, and still Wingover said the flying ship was missing from its landing place. He described in precise detail the jetsam left at the scene, and his certainty infected the party with apprehension. With barely a mile left to go, Kitiara could stand it no longer. She broke into a run and quickly left the rest behind.

Sturm and the gnomes plodded on. Kitiara came jogging back. "Wingover's right," she said. "The *Cloudmaster* is gone." The gnomes immediately surrounded Wingover and started poking his face and pulling at his eyelids. The gnome pilot slapped at the intruding fingers, while his colleagues, completely forgetting the news Kitiara had brought, tried to discover the cause of his remarkable eyesight.

"It's the Lunitari magic," Wingover said. "Leave me alone!"

"Could Stutts and company have repaired the ship themselves and flown away?" Sturm asked.

Kitiara loosened her fur collar to let the cool air in. "There are tracks all over—little circular imprints—I think the ship was carried off."

"Carried off?" said Fitter in awe.

"Do you know how much that ship weighs?" said Sighter.

She put out her chin and replied, "I don't care if it's heavier than Mt. Nevermind. Somebody or something picked it up and carried it away."

Sturm said, "Then 'they' are very strong, or very numerous."

"Or both," said Kitiara grimly.

Chapter 13

The Walking Trees

The sun shone over the field of stones where the *Cloudmaster* had first met Lunitari. The exploration party ringed the site, gazing helplessly at the empty furrow in the ground. As Wingover had seen from eight miles away, the flying ship and the three gnomes who remained on it were gone. The landing wheels that had broken off when they struck the moon were the only part of the ship left behind. Aside from the wheels, there were two empty crates, some bean sacks, and the remnants of a campfire.

"Who could have done this?" Bellcrank asked.

Cutwood crawled about with his lens, studying tracks. Sturm kicked through the pitiful remains of the camp and said, "At least there's no sign of bloodshed."

"Sixty," Cutwood proclaimed. He had dirt on his nose and

in his beard. "At least sixty people were here. They must've carried the *Cloudmaster* away on their shoulders, 'cause there are no marks of the hull being dragged."

"I don't believe it," said Sighter. "Sixty humans couldn't carry the *Cloudmaster* away on their shoulders."

"Even if they were as strong as Lady Kitiara?" asked Roperig. That gave them all pause.

Kitiara squatted by the trail of footprints. "No human feet made these," she said. "The impressions are round, almost like the hooves of unshod horses." She noted how closely spaced they were, too. "The clumsy fools must have been treading on each others' heels! We'll have to go after them. Track them down and get the ship back."

"No question about it," said Sturm. Kitiara fished the whetstone out of her belt pouch and sat down to hone the edges of her sword. Sturm gathered the gnomes together.

"We're going after your colleagues," he announced. The gnomes set up a cheer. Sturm waved for quiet. "Because we don't know how much of a head start they had, we have to move as fast as possible. That means," he saw the anticipation in their faces, "each of you can take along only what you can carry."

That threw the gnomes into a tumult of preparation and counter-preparation. Before Sturm's eyes, they tore the Four-Gnome-Power Exploratory Cart to pieces and began assembling Single-Gnome Exploration Packs, made of wooden slats and strips of canvas and blanket cloth. The packs strapped on like knapsacks, but they towered twice as high as the gnomes stood. This called for all kinds of supporting straps and cords and counter-load balancing. Soon each gnome staggered under a complex tent of wood and cloth, but in the end they didn't leave one bit of their beloved equipment behind.

Sturm looked them over and groaned inwardly. At this rate, they would never find the *Cloudmaster*, never get back to Krynn, and never find his father. He wanted to rail at the little men, but he knew it would do no good. Gnomes proceed at their own rate, awkwardly and haphazardly, but they do proceed.

Sighter waddled past, scribbling his notes under a creaking canopy of canvas. "I'm starting a new log," he said, swaying from side to side. The top of his exploration pack just missed Sturm's nose. "This is no longer the Lunitari Exploratory March." He walked on. Wingover puffed along behind him.

"Now we are the Lunitari Flying Ship Rescue Mission," Wingover said.

The trail was wide and plain, and as far as anyone could tell, no effort had been made to hide it. Either those who had captured the flying ship were not very smart, or else they thought Stutts, Birdcall, and Flash were the only crew on board.

Kitiara and Wingover moved out ahead of the rest. She tested his long-distance vision by having the gnome describe arrangements of rocks from as far away as six miles. Poor Wingover got a terrific headache, and his short legs were no match for Kitiara's long, powerful stride. She shouldered his exploratory pack (its straps were strained to the bursting point) and lifted him by the coat collar. Tucking Wingover under her arm, Kitiara took to sprinting far ahead, relying on the gnome's far-seeing to keep them from getting lost. The trail carried on in an unswerving line due west.

Sturm plodded along with the overburdened gnomes. They marched on both sides of the trail, arguing over the reasons for Wingover's gift of far-seeing. Sturm shaded his eyes from the sun and looked at the footprints. They were strikingly regular circular depressions in five distinct columns. He said to Bellcrank, "Don't these prints seem strange to you?"

"Undoubtedly, yes, Master Brightblade, as we've seen no animal life since arriving on the red moon," replied the gnome.

"Exactly! Have you noticed how very precise the footprints are? All of them are perfectly aligned."

"I don't follow."

"Even a gaited horse will have a little jog, a sideways motion now and then that distinguishes its track."

"A machine!" Bellcrank exclaimed. "Master Brightblade, you've done it!"Bellcrank grasped Roperig by his lapels. "Don't you see, what else could pick up the *Cloudmaster* and carry it off but another machine!"

"By Reorx, I hadn't thought of that," said Roperig. Fitter rattled to Rainspot and told him Bellcrank's theory. The idea then leaped the trail to where Cutwood and Sighter were walking. Sighter pooh-poohed the notion.

"That doesn't solve a thing!" he said. "Where there's a machine, there has to be a machine-maker, yes?"

Bellcrank opened his mouth to vent his opinion, but just then Kitiara and Wingover came running at them. The warrior woman carried the gnome under her arm like a loaf of bread. Wingover's head bounced and jiggled each time her heels struck the ground. In another situation, the image might have been comic.

Kitiara braced to a halt in front of Sturm. "There's a village up ahead," she said. She wasn't even out of breath.

"Village? What sort of village?" asked Roperig.

"A village village," said Wingover from under Kitiara's arm. "There's some kind of keep in the center of the place."

"Does the trail lead to this village?" asked Sturm.

Kitiara shook her head. "It veers off to the north, avoiding it completely."

"We ought to inspect this village," Cutwood called from thirty yards away. Sturm and the others looked at each other, then at Cutwood.

"Can you hear what we're saying?" said Wingover in a bare whisper.

"Well certainly! Do you think I'm deaf?" Cutwood yelled back. Sighter tapped him on the shoulder.

"I can't hear them," he said. He grabbed Cutwood by the ears and turned his head from side to side, peering into the carpenter's ears. "Everything looks normal," he said. "Does my voice sound loud to you?"

"It does when you yell from an inch away!"

Sighter took Cutwood by the hand to where the others stood. "It's happened again," he reported. "Cutwood can hear normal conversation from thirty yards away, maybe more."

"Really? This calls for some tests," said Rainspot. He lowered his pack to the ground and tried to disentangle himself from the cords and straps.

"Never mind!" Kitiara said. "What do we do about the village?"

"How close will we have to pass if we follow the trail?" Sturm queried.

"Spitting distance."

He squinted into the sky. "Half the day's gone. If we start now, we can be past the village before nightfall and not lose the trail." Sighter grumbled about the human's lack of scientific curiosity, but no gnome seriously considered going against Sturm's plan.

Sturm formed the party single file and sternly admonished the gnomes to keep quiet. "I feel trouble coming," he said. "A keep means a lord of some kind, and probably armed retainers. If," he added, "if this world is anything like Krynn."

Looking straight ahead, Kit said, "Are you afraid?"

"Afraid, no. Concerned, yes. Our stay here has never been more precarious. A pitched battle could destroy us even if we win."

"That's the difference between us, Sturm. You fight to preserve order and honor; I fight for myself. If trouble is brewing, the only thing to do is come out on top."

"No matter what happens to the rest of us?"

He scored a touch. Kitiara's eyes flashed. "I have never changed sides in a battle, nor betrayed a friend! The little men need our protection, and I'll shed my last drops of blood defending them. You've no right to imply otherwise!"

Sturm walked on silently for a moment, then said, "I'm sorry, Kit. It's becoming harder for me to know your mind. I think this magical strength you've gained has affected your outlook."

"My mind, you mean."

"Trust you to say it the most brutal way."

"Life is brutal, and so are facts."

At the rear of the column, Cutwood could hear everything, and he said, "I think they're mad at each other."

"Shows how much you know," Sighter replied. "Human males and females always act strangely toward each other. They never want their true feelings to show."

"Why is that?"

"Because they don't want to seem vulnerable. Humans have a lot of this attitude called 'pride,' which is sort of like the satisfaction you get when your machine performs correctly. Pride makes them act contrary to the way they really feel."

"That's silly!"

Sighter shrugged under his towering pack and almost fell down. "Unh! By Reorx! Of course it's silly, and these two humans have especially bad cases of pride, which means the fiercer they act and the louder they yell, the more they care about each other."

Cutwood was dazzled by his colleague's understanding of human behavior. "Where did you learn so much about humans?" he said.

"I listen and learn," said Sighter, very ungnomishly. Though he didn't yet realize it, that was the change wrought in Sighter by the magic of Lunitari. From an intuitive, impetuous gnome, he had become a logical, thoughtful, deductive gnome, a creature that had never before existed.

* * * * *

The field of stones was largely barren of plants, even by day, so the first sign the marchers had that they were near the village was when stands of scarlet-capped mushrooms seven feet tall appeared, growing in neat rows between two low stone walls. Roperig picked a section of wall apart to study; it was simply made of loose rocks stacked conveniently together. "Very primitive," was his disdainful verdict.

The mushroom orchard served to screen them from the village itself. Sturm, Kitiara, Wingover, and Cutwood crept through the rows of fungus to the very edge of the settlement.

By Krynnish standards, it wasn't much of a village. There weren't any houses at all, just a series of concentric stone walls about waist high, plus a few cribs filled with harvested food. The only full-scale structure was the keep, a squat, single-story, windowless block in the center of the village walls. A lone pole stuck up from the keep, and a dirty gray banner hung limply from it.

"Not exactly the golden halls of Silvanost, is it?" said Kitiara. To the gnomes, she said, "Can you hear or see anything stirring down there?" Wingover could see nothing moving. Cutwood squinted one eye shut and listened hard.

"I hear footsteps," he said uncertainly, "pretty faint. Someone's walking around inside the keep."

"Fine. Let's bypass this place," said Sturm.

The other gnomes waited patiently on the other side, chattering in whispers. When Wingover, Cutwood, and the humans returned, they shouldered their lofty packs and formed a single file again.

"The village looks deserted," Sturm said. "So we're going past it. Be quiet anyway."

The trail of the *Cloudmaster* bent away from the village just beyond the walls of the mushroom orchard. As they rounded the tall red stalks, Kitiara, who was leading, saw that the path was lined on either side by tall, leafless trees.

"Odd," she said. "Those weren't there before."

"Did they grow up suddenly, like the other plants?" asked Roperig. Kitiara shook her head and drew her sword.

The trees stood about seven feet high. Their trunks were graduated in bands of color, ranging from deep burgundy red at the base to the lightest of pinks at their rounded-off tops. All had branches that grew out and bent down.

"Ugliest trees I ever saw," said Cutwood. He left the line long enough to chip a piece of the flaky bark off with his Twenty Tool Pocket Kit. He was examining the fleshy gray wood when the tree's left branch flexed and swatted the specimen from his hand.

"Hey!" he said. "The tree hit me!"

The double row of trees launched into motion. They pulled their roots out of the ground and freed their limbs. Black dishlike eyes opened in the trunks, and ragged mouths split apart.

Sturm grabbed for his hilt. The gnomes bunched together between him and Kitiara.

"Suffering bloodstained gods! What are these things?" Kitiara exclaimed.

"Unless I'm gravely mistaken, these are our villagers. They were expecting us," Sturm replied, keeping the tip of his sword moving back and forth to discourage the tree-things.

The tree-folk emitted a series of deep hooting sounds, like a chorus of rams' horns. From recesses in their own bodies they produced an array of swords and spears—all made of clear red glass. The tree-folk closed the circle around the besieged band.

"Be ready," Kitiara said, her voice taut with anticipation. "When we break through them, everybody run."

"Run where?" asked Fitter tremulously.

One tree-man, the tallest of the lot, broke ranks with its fellows and advanced. It did not actually walk. Rather, the tangle of roots that made up its feet flexed and carried the creature forward. The tree-man raised its crude, hiltless glass sword in one bark-covered hand and hooted loudly.

"Yah!" Kitiara sprang forward and cut at the glass blade. She knocked it aside and swung again, this time striking the tree-man below its left arm. Her sword bit deeply into the soft wood-flesh—so deeply that it would not easily come out. Kitiara ducked the return cut by the tree-man's sword and let go of her own. She retreated a few steps, leaving her blade embedded in the foe. The tree-man did not appear too much discomforted by the yard of steel stuck in him.

"Sturm, lend me your sword," said Kitiara quickly.

"I will not," he replied. "Calm down, will you? That creature wasn't attacking, it was trying to speak."

The impaled tree-man regarded them with wide, unblinking eyes. In a raspy bass voice it said, "Men. Iron. Men?"

"Yes," said Sturm. "We are men."

"And we're gnomes," said Bellcrank. "Pleased to meet—"

"Iron?" The tree-man plucked Kitiara's sword from its flank, grasping it by the blade. He offered the hilt to Kitiara. "Iron, men—" She gingerly took the handle and let the point fall to the ground.

"Men, come," said the tree-man. His eyes and mouth vanished, only to reappear on the opposite side. "Men, come, iron king."

The tree-man reversed direction without turning around. The other tree-folk did likewise; their eyes closed up on one side of their heads and reopened on the other.

"Fascinating," said Cutwood. "Completely saves them the trouble of turning around."

"Do we go with them?" asked Rainspot.

Sturm looked away to the trail of the stolen flying ship. "For now," he said. "We should pay our respects to this iron king. Maybe he knows what could've taken our ship."

The tree-folk made straight for the village keep. Sturm, Kitiara, and the gnomes fell in behind them. Closer to the village, they saw signs of damage to the walls and gardens. Something had battered down a long section of wall, and a crib full of yellow fruit shaped like corkscrews had been plundered. Slippery pulp and seeds were splashed all over the place.

The tree-men's leader, the one Kitiara had cut, halted before the door of the keep. The gate consisted of overlapping slabs of red glass, hanging from hinges of the same material. The tree-man boomed, "King! Men, iron come." Without waiting for any reply, the tree-man leaned on the gate, and it swung in. The tree-man did not enter himself, but stood back, and with a sweep of his arm indicated that the visitors should go in.

Kitiara slipped in, her back pressed against the rough stone wall. With a practiced eye for danger, she surveyed the scene. The interior was well lit, as it had no roof. The walls rose ten feet and slanted in, but no thatch or shingles kept out the sun. The room she'd entered was actually a corridor, branching off to the left and right. The facing wall was blank, though smoothly plastered with gritty mortar painted white.

"It's clear," she reported. Her voice was taut and low. Sturm let the gnomes enter.

"Man." Sturm looked up at the impassive eyes of the tree-man. "Iron king. Him." It pointed left.

"I understand. Thank you." The tree-man tapped his long, jointed finger on the gate and Sturm pushed it shut.

"Our host will be found down the left corridor," he said. "Everyone, be on your guard!" Kitiara moved to the end of the line, steeled for signs of treachery. The hall turned right and widened. The high walls and lack of ceiling made Sturm feel as if he were in a maze.

They came upon an unexpectedly familiar artifact: a low, thick door made of oak and strapped with iron hinges. This relic leaned against the wall. Fitter peeked behind it.

"It doesn't lead anywhere," he said.

"There's something familiar about it," mused Cutwood.

"You silly loon, of course it's familiar. You've seen doors before!" said Bellcrank.

"No, it's the style that's familiar. I have it! This is a ship's door!" he announced.

"It's not from the *Cloudmaster*, is it?" Sturm said, alarmed.

"No, this door is oak, the *Cloudmaster*'s are pine."

"Now how would a ship's door get on the red moon?" Wingover asked rhetorically. Cutwood was composing an answer when Kitiara shooed him on.

They passed more debris from their world: empty kegs, clay pots and cups, tatters of canvas and scraps of leather, a rusty, broken cutlass. Some coils of rope were identified by an eager Roperig as ship's cordage made in southern Ergoth. Excitement mounted as more and more tantalizing things cropped up.

The corridor turned right again, this time into a wide room. There, standing by an overturned wooden chair, was a man. A genuine man, short and scrawny. He was dressed in a dirty tan vest and cut-off pants, rope sandals, and a peaked canvas cap. His face was dirty and his gray-streaked beard came down almost to his stomach.

"Heh, heh, heh," rasped the man. "Visitors at last. I've been wanting visitors for a long, long time!"

"Who are you?" asked Sturm.

"Me? Me? Why, I'm the King of Lunitari," proclaimed the tattered scarecrow.

Chapter 14

Rapaldo the First

"*You don't believe me*," said the self-proclaimed monarch.

"You hardly conform to the stereotypical archetype," said Sighter. The king of Lunitari cocked his head.

"What'd you say?" he asked.

"You don't look like a king," Sturm interpreted.

"Well I am! Rapaldo the First, mariner, shipwright, and absolute ruler of the red moon, that's me." He approached the band in a nervous, hesitant shuffle. "Who are you?"

The gnomes eagerly pushed themselves up to King Rapaldo, shaking hands in quick succession and rattling off the shorter versions of their impossibly long names. Rapaldo's eyes glazed over from the barrage.

Sturm cleared his throat and gently steered Fitter, the last gnome, away from the bewildered man. "Sturm Brightblade of Solamnia," he said of himself.

Kitiara stepped forward and pushed back her fur collar. Rapaldo gasped aloud. "Kitiara Uth Matar," she said.

"L-Lady," Rapaldo stammered. "I have not seen a real lady in many, many years."

"I'm not sure you're seeing one now," Kitiara said with a laugh. Rapaldo gently took her hand. He held it carefully, looking at the back and palm with embarrassing intentness. Kitiara's hands were not refined or delicate. They were the strong, supple hands of a warrior. Rapaldo's reverent interest amused her.

As if suddenly aware that he was being foolish, Rapaldo dropped Kitiara's hand and drew himself up to his full height—not much more than five and a half feet—and announced, "If you would follow me to the royal audience hall, I'll hear the story of your coming here, and tell the tale of my own shipwreck." He went back to his overturned chair and righted it. "This way," said the king of Lunitari.

They followed Rapaldo through a series of mostly empty rooms, all open to the sky. What furniture there was had a nautical cast to it, here a seaman's chest, there a railed captain's chair. Other bits of ship were hung on the wall. A brass hawse pipe liner, some loops of anchor chain, a lathe-turned rail studded with iron spikes.

Bellcrank tugged on Sturm's sleeve. "Metal," he whispered. "Lots of it."

"I see it," Sturm said calmly.

"This way. This way," Rapaldo said, gesturing.

The very center of the keep was the audience hall, a square room ten yards wide. When Rapaldo entered, a half dozen tree-men snapped glass spears to their nonexistent shoulders in salute. They hooted in unison three times, and dropped their spears to a ported position.

"My palace guard," Rapaldo said with pride.

"Are they intelligent?" asked Wingover.

"Not like you and I are. They learn things I teach them, remember orders, and such like, but they weren't civilized when I first came here."

At the far end of the room, a crude throne was set up, a

high-backed chair mounted on a thick rectangle of ruby glass. The chair had obviously been cobbled together from ship's timbers; the peg holes from the trenails were still visible.

Rapaldo hopped upon the glass pedestal and picked up his scepter from the seat of the chair. He turned around and sat down with a sigh, laying the emblem of his office in the crook of his arm. It was a broadhead axe.

"Hear ye, hear ye. The royal court of Lunitari may begin," Rapaldo recited in a high-pitched voice. He coughed once, and his skinny chest convulsed. "I, King Rapaldo the First, am present and speaking.

"In honor of the unexpected guests who have arrived today, I, King Rapaldo, will relate the marvelous tale of my coming to this place." Roperig and Fitter, sensing that a long story was beginning, sat down.

Rapaldo leaped to his feet. "You will stand in the presence of the king!" he shouted, punctuating the command with a sweep of his scepter-axe. The two gnomes stood with alacrity. Rapaldo shivered with fury. "Those who do not show respect will be removed by the Royal Guard!"

Sturm flashed Kitiara a knowing look. She bowed and said, "Forgive us, Your Majesty. We've not been in the presence of a king for quite some time."

Her intervention had an almost magical effect. Rapaldo relaxed and sat on his wooden throne again. There was a distinct clink as he did so. Sturm spied a glint of chain around his waist.

"Better, better. What's a king without subjects who pay him respect? A captain without a ship, a ship without a rudder? Ta-ra!" Rapaldo gripped the arms of his throne tightly for a moment. "It's been t-ten years since last I spoke to another human being," he said. "If I rattle and prattle, lay it to that fact."

He drew a deep breath. "I was born the son and grandson of sailors, on the island of Enstar, in the Sirrian Sea. My father was slain by Kernaffi pirates when I was but a lad, and the day the word came home, I ran away to sea. I learned to use the axe and adze."

Cutwood heard this and squirmed to comment. Sighter

and Wingover both put hands over his mouth.

"The trade of the shipwright built a man out of a boy, heh, heh, and as the summers passed, I stopped going to sea and stayed ashore on Enstar, making craft that plied the wide green ocean." The royal axe slid down to Rapaldo's lap. "Had I stayed a land-bound shipwright, though, I would not now be the royal person you see before you." A frayed sleeve slipped off his bony shoulder. Absently, Rapaldo replaced it. "I would not now be on this moon," he muttered. "A prosperous ship owner named Melvalyn hired me to sail with him to southern Ergoth. Melvalyn planned to buy timber to build a new fleet of merchant ships, and he wanted an expert along to grade the available wood. We were to depart from Enstar for Daltigoth on the third day of autumn, an ill-starred day. The soothsayer, Dirazo, the one I always consulted for times of good luck and bad, parleyed with the dark spirits and pronounced the sailing date as damned by the rise of Nuitari, the black moon. I tried to beg off, but Melvalyn insisted the voyage begin as planned. Heh, heh, old Melvalyn learned what it means to disregard the omens! Yes, he learned!

"Cold, contrary winds from the southeast blew us west of Ergoth. We tacked and tacked, but made little headway against the Kharolis Blow. Then, four days out to sea, the wind died. We were becalmed.

"There's not a more helpless feeling than being at sea with no wind. Melvalyn tried all the tricks, wetting the sails, kedging with the anchors, and such like, but we didn't move enough to measure. The sky sort of closed in on us, fish-eye gray, and then the father of all storms broke on us."

Rapaldo, caught up in his own monologue, stood abruptly. He made swift, jerky gestures to illustrate his story.

"The sea, it was running like this, and the wind, it was blowing like this—" His hands swung in from opposite directions and clashed in front of his face. "Rain was screeching over the deck flat sideways. The *Tarvolina*, that was our ship, lost her topmast and yards straight away. And then, and then, *it* came down and grabbed us." Rapaldo stepped upon his throne and crouched, his head ducked to protect himself from the memory.

"What was it?" Rainspot burst out unwittingly. Rapaldo, waiting for this cue, didn't get angry this time.

"A waterspout," he said, shivering. "A mighty, twisting column of water a hundred feet wide at the bottom! It sucked up the *Tarvolina* like a dry leaf, and we went right through the hollow middle of it, up and up and up! Some of the sailors got scared and jumped overboard. Those that jumped down the middle fell all the way back to the sea, miles and miles, but those that hit the wall of twisting water . . ." Rapaldo stamped his foot on the chair. All the gnomes jumped in fright. "They were ripped to pieces. Might as well have jumped into an ocean of knife blades." The metaphor seemed to please him, for he smiled. For all his scruffiness, the king of Lunitari had a fine set of straight white teeth. "The waterspout carried us so high that the blue went out of the sky. Only six men out of the full crew of twenty lived to the funnel's end. The waterspout turned inside out, and dropped the *Tarvolina* upside down, here on Lunitari."

King Rapaldo hopped down to the glass throne base. His shaggy eyebrows closed in over his dark brown eyes. "Three men survived the shipwreck: Melvalyn, Darnino, the navigator, and Rapaldo the First. Melvalyn had a broken leg, and died not long after. Darnino and I almost starved, until we learned to eat the plants that grow by day and drink the dew that collects in the red turf at night."

That's something we didn't know, Sturm thought.

"Darnino and I stayed together until we met the Oudouhai, the tree-people. The tree-folk had never seen men before, and they took us for their dread enemies—" Here Rapaldo paused. He peered at each member of the group in turn. "Anyway, there was a fight, and Darnino was killed. The Lunitarians were about to kill me, too, when I raised my axe." He suited the action to the words. "And they were so awestruck that they proclaimed me *oum-owa-oya*, supreme ruler of them all and wielder of the holy iron."

Rapaldo finished his story with a giggle. Unmindful of the guards standing nearby, he added, "The worthless savages had never seen metal before! They figured it must have come from the gods, and that I was a holy messenger sent to look after them."

"Have the Lunitarians no metal of their own?" asked Bell-crank.

"There's no metal on the whole bloody moon, as near as I can tell," said Rapaldo. He flopped into his throne and adjusted his ragged clothes with extreme care and dignity. "Now I would hear of your own coming," he said loftily. Wingover started to speak, but the king rapped the side of his axe on the throne. "Let the lady tell it."

Kitiara unhooked her sword belt and stood the weapon, in its sheath, before her. She leaned on the sword and told the tale of how she and Sturm had met the gnomes in the rainstorm, the flight to the red moon, their expedition, and the theft of the *Cloudmaster*.

"Heh, heh, heh," Rapaldo laughed. "You can't leave things lying about unguarded, not even on Lunitari. The Micones have taken your craft."

"Micones?"

"The enemies I spoke of. The Oud-ouhai have no predators to fear, as there are no animals on Lunitari, only plants. But the Micones, when directed, are a plague indeed."

"But what are they?" asked Kitiara.

"Ants."

"Ants?" said Sighter.

"Giant ants," said Rapaldo. "Six feet of solid rock crystal. The magic in this moon gives them the power to move and work, but they haven't got a single brain among them."

"Who—or what—directs these Micones?" asked Sturm.

The king of Lunitari shrank from the question. "I've never seen it," he said evasively, "though I once heard it speak."

Sturm saw Kitiara ball a fist in frustration. Rapaldo's quirky behavior was getting on her nerves. She relaxed her hand slowly and said as evenly as her temper would allow, "Who is their mastermind, Your Majesty?"

"The Voice in the Obelisk. Some ten miles from my palace sits a great stone obelisk five hundred feet or more high. It's hollow, and a demon dwells within. It speaks in a sweet voice to the Micones, who live in a burrow under the base. The demon never comes out of its tower, and I've never gone in to see it."

"And these Micones have taken our ship?" asked Sturm.

"Did I not say it?" Rapaldo answered sulkily. "Two nights ago, a host of crystal ants marched past in the dark. They tore down one of our walls to clear a path. Evil, I tell you—they could've walked around. It must have been your craft that they were carrying."

"Why didn't your warriors oppose them?"

"Because they are trees, after all! When the sun sets, they root themselves where they stand and feed all night long. Only with the coming of day can they shake off the dirt and walk about." Rapaldo popped up again. He directed a glare at Sturm. "Your manners are impertinent! I won't answer any more questions." The shrillness left his voice and he added, "We are tired. You may leave us now. If you follow the corridor to the right, you will find rooms you can sleep in."

Kitiara and Sturm bowed, the gnomes waved, and the group filed out of the audience hall. A tree-man led the way.

"What did you think of that!" Kitiara said in a loud whisper.

"Later," Sturm replied softly. The roofless walls were no guarantee of privacy.

Along the corridor that Rapaldo had mentioned, they found a series of niches. Some were filled with more wreckage of the lost *Tarvolina*, others were empty. The tree-man indicated that the empty niches were their "rooms," then departed.

The gnomes shrugged off their packs and set to work making as much noise and confusion as seven gnomes could make. Sturm pulled Kitiara aside.

"I fear that His Majesty is a bit out of the weather," Sturm whispered.

"He's as crazy as a bug chaser."

"That's another way to say it, yes. But Kit, we need him to take us to this obelisk, if that's where the giant ants have taken the *Cloudmaster*. So we'll have to humor his royal pose to keep his good will, at least till we leave."

"I'd like to give him a good shaking," she said. "That's what he needs."

"Use your head, Kit. There are probably hundreds of tree-men around, all loyal to King Rapaldo. How do we kill a tree? Even with your increased strength, all you did was cut a chunk out of one of them."

"You're right," she said. Her expression darkened. "I'll tell you something else: He's wearing mail under those rags. I heard it clink when he sat down. There are two reasons for people to wear mail—when they know they're going to be attacked, or when they think they're going to be attacked. Mad he may be, but old Rapaldo is afraid of something." She tapped a finger on Sturm's chest. "I say it's us."

"Why us?"

"'Cause we're human, and we've got metal of our own, which probably confuses the Lunitarians to death. Most of all, we're younger, bigger, and stronger than His Majesty."

"Oh, let him be king of the tree-men, if he wants. If Rapaldo's afraid of anything, it's this mysterious demon of the obelisk. Have any ideas about it?"

"On this crazy moon, it could be anything, but if the demon's got Stutts and the others with the flying ship, he'd better be prepared to give them over, or face a fight!"

Fitter appeared with two steaming bowls. "Dinner," said the gnome. "Pink spears and mushroom gills seasoned with puffball dust." Fitter handed over the bowls and returned to his colleagues.

They ate their food in silence for a while. Sturm said at last, "I've been thinking about when we get back to Krynn."

"Optimist," she said. "What were you thinking?"

"If my visions so far have been true, then the first thing I should do is go to my ancestral home. It may be that my father secreted his sword there somewhere. He may also have left me a clue as to where he was going."

Kitiara idly stirred her pink soup. "And what if you can't find it, or him? What then?"

"I shall keep searching," he said.

She set the bowl down on the ground between her feet. "How long, Sturm? Forever? Haven't you thought of any life beyond your family? I never faulted you for wanting to find your father—it seemed a worthy cause and a great adventure—but I see now that there's more to it than that. You're not out to restore just the Brightblade name and fortune; you want to restore the entire knightly order." Her tone was derisive.

Sturm's hands grew cold. "Is that such a terrible goal? The world could use a force for good again."

"These are modern times, Sturm! The knights are gone. The people cast them off because they couldn't change to meet the changing times. There's a new code among warriors: Power is the only truth."

He stared at her. "Am I to give up my quest, then?"

"Look beyond, will you? You're a good fighter and you're smart. Think of what we could do together, you and I. If we joined the right mercenary band, in a year's time we'd be the captains. Then the glory and power would be ours."

Sturm stood up and slung his sword belt over one shoulder. "I could never live like that, Kit."

"Hey!" she called to his retreating back. Sturm continued down the corridor. The heat of fury filled Kitiara's heart. It surged through her, and she felt an overwhelming need to smash something. How dare he be so righteous! What did he know of the world, the real world? Sentimental, boring, knightly rubbish—

"Ma'am?" Fitter stood before her, the stew pot in his hand. "Are you all right?"

The quickening heat in her limbs subsided rapidly. She blinked at the gnome and finally said, "Yes, what do you want?"

"You were pounding on the wall," said the gnome. "Sprockets! You've cracked it!"

Kitiara saw a spider's web of cracks radiating from a shallow hole in the soft sandy mortar. There was white dust on her knuckles. She didn't remember hitting the wall at all.

* * * * *

Rapaldo the First watched as his Royal Guard members slowed to rooted immobility and froze where they were. Their eyes and mouths closed, leaving not a trace in the ridged bark. Seeing them this way, no one would ever imagine that they could walk and talk.

Rapaldo walked over and kicked the nearest Lunitarian. It hurt his toe, and he hopped backward on one foot, cursing the entire pantheon of Enstar.

"Soon I'll be gone, and you'll have a new king," he said to the unheeding tree-man. "Flown away, that's what, in a flying ship built by gnomes! There's a neat trick! I had an accursed whirlwind lift me to this rotten moon, and they go and make wings and fly here on purpose! Ta-ra-ra! They can stay here, too. They'll stay behind, and I'll fly home."

He slipped an arm conspiratorially around the tree-man and whispered to him, "I could take the woman with me, yes? She is very beautiful, though a bit too tall. If the king commands it, she will go with me, yes? Yes, yes—how could she resist? I'll give the big fellow with the mustache to you. He can be the new king, Brightblade the First. I appoint him heir apparent, remember that. For all I care, you can make him a god. I shall fly, fly, fly away home."

The lengthening shadows crept across the royal audience hall. Rapaldo stared into the darkest corner and shivered. He grasped his axe and stalked to the middle of the room.

"I see you there, Darnino! Yes, it's you! You always come back to visit, don't you? Dead men should stay dead, Darnino! Especially when I kill them with my royal axe!" He charged into the shadows, throwing the axe from side to side. The heavy blade clinked off the rock walls, striking sparks. Rapaldo flailed away at the ghost in his mind for some time. Fatigue chased Darnino away more surely than any of the king's axe cuts.

"There's a lesson for you," he said, panting. "Trifle with Rapaldo the First, will you?"

He dragged his feet across the hall. By the throne, he stopped, ear cocked to the open sky. "Laughing? Who said you could laugh?" he said. The Lunitarians were still. "No one laughs at the king!" Rapaldo cried. He hurled himself at the nearest Lunitarian, chopping fiercely with his shipwright's axe. Chips of gray flew off the tree-man, who could not resist the unwarranted attack. Rapaldo yelled and cursed and chopped until the guard was a stump surrounded by scraps of broken wood-flesh.

The axe fell from his hand. Rapaldo staggered a few feet toward his throne and collapsed, sobbing.

Chapter 15

The King's Garden

Sturm awoke to a tapping on his nose. He cracked an eyelid and saw Rainspot standing over him, his stubby forefinger poised for another tap.

"What do you want?" he rumbled. The gnome withdrew his finger.

"We're having a secret meeting," whispered Rainspot. "I can't find the lady, but we want you to take part."

Sturm sat up. It was still night and he could hear hushed murmurs from the gnomes down the hall. Kitiara's place was empty, but he wasn't too concerned. Sturm knew that she could take care of herself quite well.

He tightened the lacings on his leggings and went down the hall with Rainspot. The gnomes flinched in unison when they appeared.

"I told you it was them," said the sharp-eared Cutwood.

"But you didn't say when they were coming," objected Bellcrank.

"You should learn to be more exact," said Roperig. There was general nodding of small pink heads.

Sturm rubbed his forehead. It was too soon after waking to jump into a gnomish conversation. "What's all this about?" he asked at normal volume.

"Shh!" seven gnomes said at once. Wingover waved for Sturm to come to their level, so he knelt beside Sighter.

"We're discussing plans to, uh, abscond with some of King Rapaldo's scrap metal," said Wingover. "We'd like to hear your ideas."

Sturm was surprised at such tactics coming from the gnomes.

"My idea is, don't steal from your host," he said bluntly.

"Don't misunderstand, Master Brightblade," said Bellcrank quickly. "We don't want to steal from the king, it's just that we haven't any gold or silver to pay him with."

"Then we must arrange some other method," Sturm said. "After all, we sorely need his help, and it will serve us ill to rob a potential benefactor."

"Suppose he won't give us any metal," said Wingover.

"We have no reason to be so suspicious."

"His Majesty seems rather unstable to me," Sighter said.

"He's completely off his gears," said Fitter.

"It's not our place to judge," said Sturm. "If the gods saw fit to take Rapaldo's wits, it's because he was so lonely here. Imagine being on this moon for ten years or more with no one but the tree-folk for company. You should feel pity for Rapaldo." Sturm looked over the gnomes' crestfallen faces. "Why not think of some way to win Rapaldo's gratitude? Then he would probably give us the metal we need."

The gnomes looked ashamedly at the ground. After a moment's silence, Wingover said, "Perhaps we could invent something to cheer His Majesty up."

Six gnome faces popped up, smiling. "Excellent, excellent! What shall it be?" asked Bellcrank.

"A musical instrument," said Roperig.

"Suppose he doesn't know how to play it?" countered

Sighter.

"We'll make one that plays itself," said Cutwood.

"We could give him a Personal Heating Apparatus—"

"An automatic bathing device—"

"—an instrument!"

Sturm stood and backed out of the newest wrangle. Let them figure it out, he thought. It'll keep them occupied. He decided to find Kit.

He wandered along the corridor. By night, the way was dim and confusing, and more than once he walked into a dead end. This place is a maze, he decided. He doubled back to what he believed was the main corridor and started again for the outside. There was a series of niches along the right again, but he didn't hear the gnomes. The niches were dusty and empty. It was not the same hall.

At the end, the passage turned left. Sturm swung into the black gap and immediately stumbled over some dry sticks on the floor. He fell hard on his chest and banged his head against something solid that skittered away when he hit it. The object bounced off the wall and rolled back to Sturm. He heaved himself up on his hands. A wedge of starlight fell across the open end of the niche. Sturm held up the object that he'd knocked his head on. It was a dry white human skull. The 'sticks' he'd tripped over were bones.

He went back out into the open passage and examined the skull. It was broad and well developed; certainly a man's. The most disturbing feature was the deep cleft in the bone of the forehead. The man had died by violence—as by an axe stroke.

Sturm carefully replaced the skull in the cul-de-sac. Out of reflex, he checked to see if his sword was hanging in its scabbard. The cold hilt was reassuring to his touch. He was worried. Where was Kitiara?

He bumped into Kitiara as she came skulking down the passage. She had a tousled, slightly wild look that made him think she'd been drinking. But no, ale was hard to come by on Lunitari.

"Kit, are you all right?"

"Yes. I am. I think."

He put an arm around her waist to support her and

steered her to a low stretch of wall, where they sat.

"What happened?" he asked.

"I went walking," she said. "Rapaldo's gardens take longer to vanish after dark than the wild plants we saw. There were some big toadstools, with pink spores coming out. They smelled good."

"They've affected you," he said, noting the light dusting of pink on her shoulders and hands. "How do you feel?"

"I feel—strong. Very strong." She gripped his free hand and squeezed his wrist. Pain raced up Sturm's arm.

"Careful!" he said, wincing. "You'll break my arm!"

Her grip didn't slacken. Sturm felt the blood pounding in his fingertips. In her present state, it wasn't prudent to struggle. She might crush his arm without realizing it.

"Kit," he said as evenly as the pain would allow, "you're hurting me. Let go."

Her hand snapped open, and Sturm's arm dropped out like a dead weight. He massaged the bruised arm back to life.

"You must've inhaled those spores," he said. "Why don't you go lie down? Do you remember the way?"

"I remember," she said dreamily. "I never get lost." She slipped away like a sleepwalker, making unerring turns and avoiding all the wrong passages. Sturm shook his head. Such uncontrolled strength was deadly. What was happening to her—to all of them?

Then, curious, he decided to see those mushrooms from a safe distance. He went along the path Kitiara had used until he reached the outside wall. The neatly boxed-in garden beds were empty. No trace of the mushrooms remained. He stepped over the low wall and dipped his hand into the ever-present scarlet dust. Had she indeed been walking in her sleep? Or had the mushrooms withered in the short time between her seeing them and his arrival? The stars and setting silver moon offered no clues.

Sturm noticed a dull light moving along the gallery on the north side of the palace. He cut across the gardens to intercept the light. It proved to be His Majesty, carrying a weakly burning oil lamp.

"Oh," said Rapaldo, "I remember you."

"Good evening, Your Majesty," said Sturm graciously. "I saw your lamp."

"Did you? It's a feeble thing, but the oil I make is not of the best quality, heh, heh."

"Your Majesty, I wonder if I might have a word with you."

"What word?"

Sturm fidgeted. This was as bad as trying to talk with the gnomes. "My friends were wondering, Sire, if we might be able to get some scrap metal from you to fix our flying ship, once we find it."

"You'll never get it back from the Micones," said Rapaldo.

"We must try, Sire. Could we get some metal from your supply?"

"What kind and how much?" asked the king sharply.

"Forty pounds of iron."

"Forty pounds! Ta-ra! That's a king's ransom, and I should know. I am the king!"

"Surely iron is not so precious—"

Rapaldo hopped backward, the wavering lamp throwing weird shadows behind him. "Iron is the most precious thing of all! It was the iron axe I carry that made me master of the red moon. Do you not see, Sir Knight, that there is no metal at all here? Why do you think my subjects bear swords of glass? Every scrap of iron is a buttress to my rule, and I will not part with any of it."

Sturm waited until Rapaldo's quivering hands had grown more steady. He said, slowly, "Sire, perhaps you would like to go with us when we leave on the gnomes' flying ship."

"Eh? Leave my kingdom?"

"If you so desire."

Rapaldo's eyes narrowed. "My subjects would never allow it. They won't even let me leave the town. I've tried. I've tried. I'm their link with the gods, you know, and they are very jealous of me. They won't let me go."

"What's to stop you from leaving at night, when the Lunitarians are rooted where they stand?"

"Heh, heh, heh! They would hunt me down by daylight! They move very fast when they want to, don't worry! And there's never been anyplace else to go. The ants have your craft and will not let you have it. The Voice has it now."

Sturm said firmly, "We intend to ask this Voice to return our ship."

"The Voice! Ta-ra-ra! Why not ask the High Lords of Heaven to bear you home on their backs, like birdies, tweet, tweet? The Voice is evil, Sir Knightblade; beware of it!"

Sturm felt as if he were swimming against a strong current. Rapaldo's mind could not follow the course of reason that Sturm had set out, but there were some nuggets of truth in what he said. The 'Voice,' if it existed, was a great unknown quantity. If it refused them, their hopes for getting home were destroyed.

Sturm made one last attempt to persuade Rapaldo. "Your Majesty, if my friends and I can convince the Voice to release our flying ship, would you then provide us with forty pounds of iron? In return, we'll carry you back to Krynn—to your home island, if you wish."

"Enstar?" said Rapaldo, blinking rapidly. Tears formed in his eyes. "Home?"

"To your very doorstep," Sturm promised.

Rapaldo set the lamp on the ground. His hand flashed to his hip, and came back gripping the broad shipwright's axe. Sturm tensed.

"Come!" said Rapaldo. "I will show you the obelisk."

He padded away, leaving the lamp flickering on the floor. Sturm looked at the lamp, shrugged, and followed the mad king of Lunitari. Rapaldo's skinny, rag-wrapped feet made only the faintest thumps as he scampered ahead of Sturm. "This way, Sir Brightsturm! I have a map, a chart, a diagram, heh, heh."

Sturm followed him around half a dozen twists and turns. When he faltered or felt uncertain, Rapaldo urged him on. "The obelisk is in a secret valley, very hard to find! You must have my map to locate it!" Then Rapaldo's tread abruptly ceased, as did his lunatic cackle.

"Your Majesty?" Sturm called quietly. No reply. Carefully, Sturm drew his sword, letting the blade slip through his fingers to deaden the scrape of metal. "King Rapaldo?" The passage ahead was violet shadows and silence. Sturm advanced into the darkness, sliding his feet along the floor to avoid being tripped.

Rapaldo leaped down from a recess in the wall and brought the axe down on Sturm's head. His helmet saved his skull from the fate of Darnino, but the blow drove the light from his mind and left him laid out cold on the floor.

"Well, well," said Rapaldo, breathing quickly. "A rude dint, I'm sure, and not at all fitting for the new king of Lunitari, eh? The tree-men would never allow their only king to fly away, fly! So I'll take the flying ship and lady, I will, and the trees will have their king. You! Ha, ha!" He giggled and picked up Sturm's helmet. The iron pot had taken the axe's edge with only a slight dent. Rapaldo tried the helmet on. It was far too large for him, and fell over his eyes. The monarch of the red moon stood over his victim, spinning the helmet around his head with his hands and laughing ceaselessly.

Chapter 16

The Royal Axe

The long night was almost spent when the gnomes dared wake Kitiara. She grunted with pain and got to her feet. "Suffering bloodstained gods," she muttered. "What happened? I feel like somebody's worked me over with a stick."

"Are you sore?" asked Rainspot.

She worked one shoulder around and grimaced. "Very."

"I have a liniment that may be of comfort to you." The gnome searched rapidly through his vest and pants pockets. He produced a small leather bag with a tight drawstring. "Here," said Rainspot.

Kitiara accepted the bag and sniffed the closed mouth. "What is it?" she said suspiciously.

"Dr. Finger's Efficacious Ointment. Also known as the

Self-Administered Massage Balm."

"Well, ah, thanks, Rainspot. I'll give it a try," she said, though she thought it more likely that the liniment would blister her skin than soothe her muscles. She tucked it away. "Where's Sturm?" Kitiara asked with sudden realization.

"We saw him several hours ago. He was looking for you," said Cutwood.

"Did he find me?"

"How should we know? He told us we couldn't take any of Rapaldo's iron without asking permission, then he went looking for you," said Bellcrank peevishly.

Kitiara rubbed her aching temples. "I remember I went for a walk, came back obviously, but outside of that my memory is dry." She coughed. "So's my throat. Is there any water?"

"Rainspot called down a batch this morning," said Sighter. He proffered a full bottle to Kitiara, and she drank deeply. The gnomes watched this process solemnly. When Kitiara at last lowered the water bottle, Wingover said, "Lady, we are unanimous in our resolve to be gone from here as quickly as possible. We think the king is dangerous; also, the trail of the Micones grows colder as we wait."

Kitiara surveyed the serious little faces. She'd never seen the gnomes so united and intent. "Very well, let's see if we can hunt down Sturm," she said.

Rapaldo was in his audience hall, flanked by twenty tall tree-men when Kitiara and the gnomes arrived. He was wearing Sturm's horned helmet, padded out with rags so that it wouldn't fall over his eyes. The axe lay nestled in his arms.

He regarded them idly. "I didn't send for you. Go away."

"Cut the lip wagging," Kitiara snapped. She recognized the helmet. "Where's Sturm?"

"Do all of the women of Abanasinia have such bad manners? That's what comes of letting them carry swords—"

She drew both weapons, sword and dagger, and took one step toward Rapaldo. The Lunitarians promptly raised their glass swords and spears and closed ranks around their divine, though mad, king.

"You'll never reach me," Rapaldo said, giggling. "It might

be fun to see you try."

"Your Majesty," said Sighter diplomatically, "what has become of our friend Sturm?"

Rapaldo leaned forward and waggled a bony finger at the gnome. "See? Now that's the proper way to ask a question." He slumped back in his high chair and pronounced, "He is resting. Shortly he will be the new king of Lunitari."

"New king? What's going to happen to the old one?" asked Kitiara with barely concealed fury.

"I'm abdicating. Ten years is long enough to rule, don't you think? I'm going back to Krynn and live among my own kind as an honored and respected shipwright." He licked his fingers to smooth back his lank gray hair. "After my subjects take back the aerial ship, you all shall remain here, except for whatever gnomes are needed to fly it." He cocked his head toward Kitiara. "I was going to take you with me, but I see now that you are completely unsuited. Heh, heh. Completely."

"We won't fly you anywhere," said Wingover defiantly.

"I think you will—if I order my faithful subjects to kill you off, one by one. I think you'll fall in with my plan."

"Never!" said Kitiara. The rage was rising in her.

Rapaldo looked up at the nearest tree-man and said, "Kill one of the gnomes. Start with the littlest one." The gnomes closed in a tight circle around Fitter.

The Lunitarian came at them straight on. Kitiara cried, "Run!" and moved to meet the tree-man. She parried his strong but clumsy cuts. Chips of glass flew each time her steel blade met the glass one, but the haft of the tree-man's weapon was so thick that she didn't think it would snap without a direct crosswise blow. The gibbering gnomes retreated in a body to the door. None of the other Lunitarians deigned to bother them.

She had managed to pin the tree-man's point to the floor and now she raised her foot and smashed the glass sword in two. The Lunitarian stepped back out of her reach.

Rapaldo applauded. "Ta-ra!" he crowed. "What a show!"

There were too many of them. Though she hated to do it, Kitiara backed out of the room with her blood boiling. Rapaldo laughed and whistled loudly.

Out in the passage, Kitiara halted, her face burning furiously with shame. To be whistled out of a room—what an insult! As if she were some juggler or painted fool!

"We're going back in there," she said tensely. "I'm going to get that lunatic woodcutter if I have to—"

"I have an idea," said Sighter, tugging vainly at her trouser leg.

"Suffering gods, we've got to find Sturm! We don't have time for a silly gnomish idea!"

The gnomes drew back with expressions of hurt. Kitiara hastily apologized, and Sighter went on. "As this place has no roof, why don't we climb the walls? We could walk along the top of the walls and peer down into every room."

Kitiara blinked. "Sighter, you—you're a genius."

He polished his nails on his vest and said, "Well, I am extremely intelligent."

She turned to the wall and ran a hand over the dry plaster. "I don't know if we can get enough purchase to climb up," she said.

"I can do it," said Roperig. He pressed his hands on the wall and muttered, "Strong grip. Strong grip." To everyone's delight, his palms stuck, and he proceeded to climb right up the wall like a spider. The gnomes cheered; Kitiara hushed them.

"It's all right," Roperig said from atop the wall. "It's just wide enough for me to walk on. Boost Fitter up, will you?" Kitiara hoisted Fitter up with one hand. Roperig caught his upstretched hands and pulled his apprentice up beside him. Cutwood and Wingover were next.

"That's enough," said Sighter. "We'll stay with the lady and divert the king's attention. You find Sturm."

The four gnomes on the wall set off. Kitiara went back to the entry of the audience hall, banging sword and dagger together for attention. Bellcrank and Sighter stood close behind her, filling the doorway.

"You're back. Happy, happy to see you!" exclaimed Rapaldo, who was still hooting from his roost.

"We want to negotiate," Kitiara said. It was galling, even if it was a lie.

"You touched me with your sword," Rapaldo said petulantly. "That's treason, impious blasphemy and treason. Throw your sword into the hall where I can see it."

"I won't give up my sword, not while I still live."

"Really? The king will see about that!" Rapaldo hooted some words in the Lunitarians' language. The guards in the room took up the message and repeated it again and again, louder and louder. Soon thousands outside were hooting the words.

Roperig and the others could hear the tree-men take up Rapaldo's chant as they fairly flew over the narrow wall tops, peeking into every room in the keep. Cutwood, of course, stopped to make notes of the contents of every room and passage, while Wingover kept probing the distant vistas instead of searching the nearer rooms below. Only Fitter took his task to heart. The little gnome raced along at blinding speed, running, leaping, searching. He doubled back to his panting boss.

"Where did you learn to run so fast?" Roperig gasped.

"I don't know. Haven't I always run this way?"

"No indeed!"

"Oh! The magic has gotten to me at last!" Fitter flashed along the wall, sidestepping Cutwood, who was in the midst of compiling his umpteenth catalog. Cutwood, startled by the speedy Fitter, lost his balance and fell.

"Oof!" said Sturm as the forty-pound gnome landed in his lap. "Cutwood! Where did you come from?"

"Sancrist." He called out to Roperig, and the other three gnomes quickly found them.

"My hands are bound," Sturm explained. He was sitting in an old chair, and his feet were tied to the chair legs. "Rapaldo took my knife."

"The lady has the dagger," said Roperig.

"I'll get it!" said Fitter, and in an instant he was gone.

Sturm blinked. "I know I've got the grandfather of all headaches, but our friend Fitter seems to me to have gotten awfully fast since last I saw him."

"Here it is!" called Fitter. He dropped the dagger, point first. Cutwood picked it up and started sawing away at Sturm's bonds. The dagger was made for thrusting, not cutting, and didn't have much of an edge.

"Hurry," said Fitter breathlessly. "The others are in *big* trouble."

"What are we in, a pleasant daydream?" Cutwood said sourly.

"Don't talk, cut," said Sturm.

'Trouble' was a mild word for what Kitiara and the two gnomes were facing. Scores of Lunitarians had filled the corridor behind them, and guards from the audience hall had seized each of them. Rapaldo strutted in front of them, tapping the back of the axe head against the palm of his hand.

"Treasonous piglets," he said imperiously. "You are all worthy of death. The question is, who shall feel the royal axe first?"

"Kill me, you witless scab; at least then I won't have to listen to you spout on like the gibbering swabby you are," Kitiara said. She was held by no fewer than seven tree-men. Their wooden limbs were wrapped around her so securely that only her face and feet showed. Rapaldo smirked and lifted her chin with the handle of his axe.

"Oh, no, pretty, I shall spare you, heh, heh. I would make you queen of Lunitari, if only for a day."

"I'd rather have my eyes put out!"

He shrugged and stepped in front of Sighter, held by a single guard. "Shall I kill this one?" said Rapaldo. "Or that?"

"Kill me," pleaded Bellcrank. "I'm only a metallurgist. Sighter is the navigator of our flying ship. Without him, you'll never reach Krynn."

"That's ridiculous," Sighter argued. "If you die, who will fix the damage to the *Cloudmaster*? No one can work iron like Bellcrank."

"They're just gnomes," said Kitiara. "Kill me, rotten Rapaldo, or I'll surely kill you!"

"Enough, enough! Heh, heh, I know what to do, I do. You try to fool me, but I am the king!" He strode away a pace or two and dropped his axe. The king of Lunitari pulled apart the tied ends of his decrepit tunic. Under his shirt, but over his woolens, Rapaldo wore chain. Not chain mail, but heavy, rusty chain, wound around his waist.

"You see, I know what it means to live on Lunitari," Rapaldo said. He let his shirt fall off and untwisted a bale of

wire that held the end of the chain in place. He unlooped
several turns of chain. As the links piled up on the floor,
Rapaldo's feet rose. Soon he was floating two feet in the air,
and the tree-folk were rapt in their devoted attention.

"I fly! Ta-ra! Who are you puny mortals to bandy words
with me? I float! If I didn't wear fifty pounds of chain, I'd
drift away. They won't let me have a ceiling, you know, the
tree-people. Shade makes them take root. Without this
chain, I'd fly away like a wisp of smoke." Rapaldo let
another loop of chain fall to the floor. He pivoted until his
feet were floating out behind him. "I am the king, you see!
The gods have given me this power!"

"No," Sighter tried to explain. "It must be a consequence
of the Lunitari magic—"

"Silence!" Rapaldo made clumsy swimming motions with
his hands and drifted over to Kitiara. "You wear armor, but
you can take it off when you want to. I can't! I have to wear
this chain every hour, every day." He shoved his dirty,
bearded face close to hers. "I renounce the power! I'm going
home, I am, and walk like a man again. The trees will not
miss me with Sir Sturmbright as king.

"Treason! Treason! You're all guilty!" Rapaldo somer-
saulted in the air, away from Kitiara. He scooped up his axe
and flung it at his chosen victim.

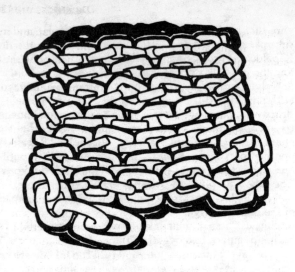

Chapter 17

Without Honor

The last loop of cord gave way, and Sturm's hands were free. He snatched the dagger from Cutwood and quickly worked through the ropes around his ankles. The hemp from the *Tarvolina* was old and quickly parted. Sturm leaped to his feet.

"Lead me back to the audience hall!" he said to the gnomes atop the wall. Fitter waved and ran all the way around the room before veering off for the king's audience chamber. Roperig and Wingover trotted behind him.

"Come on, Cutwood," Sturm shouted, hoisting the gnome on his shoulders.

The sun was going down. Sturm thanked Paladine for that. Without sunlight, the hordes of tree-men loyal to the mad Rapaldo would soon revert to rooted plants.

He passed through another opening in the wall and found himself facing a dozen armed tree-men. They presented a solid front, barring his progress. Sturm had only Kitiara's dagger to oppose their long glass swords.

"Hold on, Cutwood," he said. The gnome gripped Sturm's head tightly.

Flat shadows climbed the walls. The sun was sinking fast. Already the lower halves of the Lunitarians were in shade; soon their feet would fix where they stood. A tree-man thrust the forty-inch span of his scarlet glass sword at Sturm. Though the guard was slow, the blade flickered past Sturm's chin, far outreaching his twelve-inch dagger.

Woodenness began to claim the Lunitarians' lower bodies, and they took root. The edge of night was midway up their trunks now. The tree-men's arms wavered in slow motion, like weeds beneath the surface of a pond. The guard that Sturm faced snagged the tip of his sword on Sturm's fur hood and ripped through the hide and hair. That was the tree-man's last act. Bark closed over his eyes, leaving him and the others featureless and inert.

Wingover appeared atop the wall. "Master Brightblade! Come quickly! Something terrible has happened!" Before the human could ask what, the gnome ran back the way he'd come.

"He was weeping," Cutwood noted in astonishment. "Wingover never weeps."

Sturm thrust his arms and shoulder between the trunks of the tree-men and heaved himself through. Their bark scraped and pulled at him, but he struggled on until he broke out of the rear rank of guards. The passage ahead was clear.

Sturm and Cutwood burst into the audience hall. The knight looked first to Kitiara. Was it her? Was she hurt, dying, or dead? The woman and the two gnomes were locked tightly in the embrace of their now-immobile guards. Blood stained the knotty fingers of the one that held Bellcrank.

Bellcrank was dead. Rapaldo was nowhere to be seen.

"Kit! Are you all right?" Sturm called.

"Yes, and Sighter, too, but Bellcrank—"

"I see. Where's Rapaldo?"

"He's nearby. Be wary, Sturm, he's got that axe."

The room was thick with immobile tree-men. The gathering darkness made the audience hall a forest of shadows. Out of the uncertain dark came Rapaldo's snickering laugh.

"Who has a lamp to light you to bed? Who has a chopper to chop off your head?"

"Rapaldo! Face me and fight!" Sturm cried.

"Heh, heh, heh."

Something moved overhead. From the wall, Wingover shouted, "He's up there! Duck, Sturm!"

Sturm dropped to the floor just as the axe blade whisked through the place his head had been. "Kit, where's your sword? Rapaldo has mine!"

"On the floor in front of Sighter," she said.

Sturm scrambled forward on his belly as Rapaldo flitted through the tops of the tree-men. Kitiara called to Sturm, explaining the crazed king's ability to levitate.

"He's dropped part of his weights," Sighter added. "He's floating about six feet off the ground."

Sturm's hand closed over Kitiara's sword handle and was up in a flash. Her blade was light and keen, and seemed to slice the air with a will of its own. Sturm saw Rapaldo's tattered pants' legs and rope sandals stepping on the heads of the tree-men. Sturm slashed at him, but only succeeded in chipping off bits of the Lunitarian that Rapaldo was standing on. The king of Lunitari bounded away, giggling.

"I can't see him!" Sturm complained. "Wingover, where is he?"

"On your left—behind—" Sturm ducked the axe blow and cut at Rapaldo. He felt the tip of Kitiara's sword snag cloth and heard the cloth tear.

"Close, very close, Sir Sturmbright, but you're too heavy on your feet," Rapaldo said, chortling.

"Kit, I'd welcome any tactical suggestions you might want to make," Sturm said, his chest heaving in the chill night air.

"What you need is a crossbow," Kitiara hissed. She strained against the enfolded limbs of solid wood that held her. Because her arms were pinned at her sides, she could not get any leverage. Kitiara tried to twist her shoulders from side to side. The tree-man's arms groaned and cracked, but held firm.

Sturm shifted the dagger to his right hand and put the sword in his left. The hall was very quiet. The gnomes, who had been crying for their fallen colleague, ceased all noise. Sturm crouched low and moved to the ramshackle throne. He climbed up on the chair and stood erect. "Rapaldo! Rapaldo, I'm on your throne. I spit on it, Rapaldo! You're a petty, lunatic carpenter who dreams he is a king."

The clink of chain warned him—a split second later the axe bit deeply into the back of the chair and stuck there, wedged tightly by the tough oak of Krynn. Rapaldo tried frantically to free the axe, but his spindly arms and lack of leverage prevented him.

"Surrender!" Sturm demanded, presenting the point of the dagger to Rapaldo's throat.

"Ta-ra-ra!" cried the king, planting his feet on the back of the throne. He heaved the tall chair over backward, sending him, Sturm, bare sword, axe, and dagger down together in a heap. There was a mighty crash, a scream, and silence.

"Sturm!" called Kitiara.

He shook himself free of the shattered chair and stood. A gash in his cheek bled, but Sturm was otherwise unhurt. Rapaldo was pinned to the floor, the dagger through his heart. His legs and arms floated above aimlessly. Drops of blood flowed up the dagger's hilt and detached, drifting up into the air.

Sturm found the axe in the debris. Stolidly ignoring the fact that the trees would be living beings again by morning, he chopped Kitiara and Sighter free. The other gnomes descended from the wall and helped get Bellcrank out of the wooden bonds. They laid the stout gnome gently on the floor and covered his face with their kerchiefs. Fitter began to sob.

"What shall we do?" asked Wingover tearfully.

Kitiara said, "Bellcrank is avenged. What more is there to do?"

"Oughtn't we to bury him?" said Roperig heavily.

"Yes, of course," said Sturm. He gathered Bellcrank in his

arms and led the sorrowing band outside.

The gnomes stood together. The only sounds were sniffles and the scuffing of small shoes. Sighter brushed the wood chips from his clothes and strode off. The others fell in behind him. He went to the middle of the mushroom garden and stopped. Pointing to the red fluff, he declared that this was the spot.

The gnomes began to dig. Kitiara offered to help, but Cutwood politely declined. The gnomes knelt in a circle and dug the grave with their hands. When they were satisfied, Sturm stepped in and, with great feeling, laid the heroic Bellcrank in his final resting place.

Sighter spoke first. "Bellcrank was a fine technician and a good chemist. Now he is dead. The engine has ceased to run, the gears have seized and stopped." Sighter tossed a handful of pale crimson soil over his friend. "Farewell, farewell."

Wingover said, "He was a skilled metallurgist," and added another handful of dirt.

"An excellent arguer," noted Cutwood, choking back emotion.

"A dedicated experimenter," Rainspot said, sprinkling his portion.

"The finest of gear makers," said Roperig sorrowfully.

When Fitter's turn came, he was too upset to think of anything to say. "He-he was a hearty eater," the littlest gnome murmured at last. Roperig managed a fond smile and patted his apprentice on the back.

They mounded the dirt over their fallen friend. Wingover went back into the keep and returned with a piece of ironwork from Rapaldo's wrecked ship. It was a gear, part of the *Tarvolina*'s capstan. The gnomes set this on the grave, as a monument to their colleague.

Kitiara turned her back and headed for the keep. After a moment of respectful silence, Sturm hurried after her. "You might have found something to say to the gnomes," he chided.

"We have much to do before the sun rises again. We've got to gather our belongings and get as far from here as the night will let us," she said.

"Why the haste? Rapaldo is dead."

Kitiara swept an arm around. "His subjects are very much alive! How do you think they'll feel when they awaken and find their god-king dead?"

Sturm pondered this a moment, then said, "We can hide the body."

"No good," she said, crossing the outer wall. "The tree-men will assume the worst if we're gone and Rapaldo's missing." Kitiara paused at the door to the throne room. "All the more reason to get out of here and find the *Cloudmaster*."

She was right. Sturm found his dented helmet and put it on. Kitiara replaced her sword and wrenched the dagger out of the dead man's chest. Seeing Rapaldo bobbing like a cork gave her a macabre idea. She knelt on one knee and unwound the remaining chain from Rapaldo's waist. They could use it when they found the flying ship.

Kitiara gripped Rapaldo's bloody shirt and guided the body toward Sturm. "Here's my idea of a quick and easy funeral," she said, letting go. The lifeless body of Rapaldo the First rose slowly, turning slightly as it went. Within minutes, it was lost from sight in the violet vault of the sky. Sturm was aghast.

"It could just as easily have been me he killed, you know," she said flatly. "My only regret is that you got to him instead of me."

"He was a demented wretch. There was no honor in slaying such a person."

"Honor! One day you'll face a foe without your concept of honor, and that will be the end of Sturm Brightblade."

They went back to the mushroom garden. The gnomes were waiting. Their tall expedition packs were weighed down even further with bits of metal salvaged from Rapaldo's cache. Kitiara announced her intention to follow the path that the Micones had been on before their tracks were lost in the rocks. Sighter looked to Sturm.

"What do you say, Master Brightblade?"

"I have no better plan," he replied simply. A chill was growing in his heart. The woman who dealt so harshly with a dead foe was more and more like a stranger to him.

This was their darkest hour since leaving Krynn. One of

their own was dead, buried in the cold moon soil, and a poor, insane king spiraled ever upward, a weightless corpse with no place to land. It would be a long, unhappy night.

And yet, when the sun next shone over Rapaldo's garden, a giant mushroom grew out of the grave of Bellcrank. Unlike the scarlet fungi around it, this one was pure and shining white.

* * * * *

Sturm had another vision. It came to him while he walked, yet his step never faltered.

A horse neighed. Sturm saw four bony beasts tied to a charred post. It was day, but heavy shadows lay over everything. Sturm looked up and recognized the ruined battlements of his father's castle. Across the courtyard he saw a broken wagon lying with one wheel off. A man was lashed to the remaining wheel, his wrists cruelly bound to its rim. Sturm closed on this desperate figure. He prayed to Paladine that it was not his father.

The man lifted his eyes. Through the wild growth of beard and the bruises of a brutal beating Sturm recognized Bren, his father's companion in exile. As in Sturm's last vision, Bren looked right through Sturm. The younger Brightblade was a phantom, a thing of no substance.

Four men shuffled out of the shadows on Sturm's right. They were lean, rough-looking men of a type Sturm had often seen on the road. Vagabonds. Brigands. Killers.

"When is we moving on, Touk?" said one of the men. "This here castle is haunted, I tell you."

"You afraid of ghosts?" said the dirty-faced fellow with the brass earring.

"I'm afraid of anything I can't stick my billhook through."

"When are we leavin'?" asked the last brigand in line.

Dirty-Face laughed, showing yellow teeth. "When I'm sure there ain't no more swag here'bout, that's when." Touk spat in the dirt. "Let's have a word wi' our honored guest."

The bandit and two of his men stood over the prisoner. Touk grabbed Bren by his matted hair and lifted his head. Sturm ached to help him, but he could do nothing.

"Where's the treasure, old man?" asked Touk, flashing a wicked knife under the old soldier's chin.

"There's no treasure," Bren gasped. "The castle was sacked years ago."

"Come on! Do you take us for fools? There's always a few coins tucked away somewhere, eh? So where are they?" He pressed the tip of the blade into Bren's throat.

"I-I'll tell," he said weakly. "Below the great hall—a secret room. I can show you."

Touk removed the knife. "This better be a straight story."

"No tricks. I'll take you right to it."

They cut him loose and dragged him along. Sturm followed on their heels, close enough to smell the mingled stench of sweat, grime, fear, and greed.

Bren guided them to the cellar beneath the great hall. There, in a long corridor, he counted the torch sconces on the right side. At number eight, he said, "That's it, that's the one." One of the brigands lit the stump in the sconce with the brand he carried.

"The bracket turns," said Bren.

Touk seized the stout iron holder and shook it. It swung to the left and stayed there. A section of the tiled floor lifted with a loud grinding sound. Touk tossed his torch into the widening gap. It bounced down a steep stone staircase and came to rest, still burning, at the bottom. Something shiny gleamed in the torch light.

"Good work," Touk said, grinning. Without another word, he shoved his knife between Bren's ribs. Angriff Brightblade's loyal man groaned and slid down the wall. His head sagged as the dark stain spread over his chest.

"C'mon, lads, let's collect our reward!" Touk led his two cronies down the steps.

Sturm bent to see Bren's face. Though his skin had gone waxen, Bren's eyes still glittered with life. "Young master," he said. Blood flecked his lips.

Sturm recoiled. *Bren could see him!*

Slowly, with terrible effort, the old soldier gripped the rough stone wall and dragged himself to his feet. "Master Sturm—you've come back. I always knew you would." Bren reached out to Sturm, hand swaying. Sturm tried to clasp his hand, but of course he had no substance. Bren's fingers passed through him and closed on the sconce. As death claimed him, Bren fell, and his weight bore the bracket back to its original position.

The trap door lowered noisily. One robber gave a yell and dashed to safety. At the top of the steps, he stopped, riveted, staring at Sturm.

"Ahh!" he screamed. "Ghost!" He stumbled back, bowling over Touk and the other brigand. The slab of stone descended, cutting off their screams for help.

* * * * *

The world went red. Sturm shook his head, where the screams of Touk and the other robbers still rang. He was plodding across the plains of Lunitari as before.

"Back with us?" asked Kitiara. Sturm made inarticulate sounds. This had been his longest vision yet, and somehow near the end, the men on Krynn had been able to see him. He told his companions his tale.

"Hmm, it's said that dying men have second sight," Kitiara mused. "Bren and the thief were both facing death; maybe that's why they could see you."

"But I couldn't help them," Sturm complained. "I had to watch them die. Bren was a good man. He served my father well."

"Did you see or hear of your father at all?" asked Sighter.

Sturm shook his head. That very omission preyed on his mind. What had separated Bren from Lord Brightblade? Was his father well? Where was he?

Wingover let out a yell. "I see the tracks!" he cried. Where the slabs of wine-colored sandstone broke into fingers of rock, crimson sand had drifted in between. And there were the circular prints, as regular as clockwork. Kitiara's notion had been right—the Micones had come this way.

Chapter 18

The Valley of the Voice

At last Wingover spied the great obelisk. The band
had come to a place where the rocky ledges reared up as
low, jagged peaks. Kitiara and Wingover climbed this saw-
toothed barrier and reported that beyond lay a magnificent
bowl-shaped valley that stretched far beyond the limits of
the horizon. Kitiara could not see the obelisk, but Wingover
assured them that a single, tall spire stood forty miles away,
in the exact center of the valley.

The gnomes took heart from the news. They had been
uncommonly subdued on the trek from the village.

"Bellcrank's death has them hanging their heads," Kitiara
said privately to Sturm. "I guess the little fellows have never
faced death before."

Sturm agreed. What the gnomes needed was a problem,

to stimulate their imaginations. He called them together.
"Here's the situation," Sturm began. "Wingover estimates
the obelisk is forty miles away. Forty miles is a ten-hour
march, if we don't stop for food or rest. Fifteen hours is a
more reasonable estimate, but by then the sun will be up
and the Lunitarians can be on the move, too."

"If only we had some way to get down in a hurry," said
Kitiara. "Horses, oxen, anything."

"Or carts, for that matter," Sturm mused.

Kitiara shot him a knowing glance. "Yes, the slope down
from the saw-toothed ridge is steep but fairly smooth. We
could roll quite a ways."

The spirit of technical challenge was infectious, and
ideas—wild, gnomish ideas—began flashing about the little
group. The gnomes dumped their packs into one big heap
and went into a close huddle. Their rapid patter made no
sense to Sturm or Kitiara, but the humans saw it as a good
sign.

As suddenly as the gnomes had put their heads together,
they broke apart. Tools appeared, and the gnomes proceeded to knock their wooden backpacks to pieces.

"What are you making this time?" Sturm asked Cutwood.

"Sleds," was the simple reply.

"Did he say 'sleds'?" asked Kitiara.

Within half an hour, each gnome had constructed,
according to his lights, a sled—that is, a Single-Gnome Inertia Transport Device. "By these we expect to descend the
cliff slope at prodigious speed," announced Sighter.

"And break your reckless little necks," said Kitiara under
her breath.

"These are for you and Master Sturm," said Roperig. He
and Fitter pushed two flimsy sleds to the human's feet. Having only short slats of wood to work with, the gnomes held
their inventions together with nails, screws, glue, string,
wire, and, in Rainspot's case, his suspenders. Wingover had
designed his sled to let him ride on his belly; Sighter's
allowed the rider to gracefully recline. Because of their relative size, Sturm's and Kitiara's sleds allowed them only a
wide bit of plank for a seat.

"You can't be serious," Kitiara said dubiously. "Ride that

down there?"

"It will be fast," encouraged Sighter.

"And fun!" Fitter exclaimed.

"We've calculated all the available data on stress and strength of materials," Cutwood noted. He brandished his notebook as proof; there were five pages covered with tiny, closely spaced letters and numbers. "In all cases except yours, there'll be a safety factor of three."

"What do you mean, 'in all cases except yours'?" Kitiara felt obliged to ask.

Cutwood stowed his notebook in his vest pocket. "Being larger and heavier, you will naturally put more stress on the Single-Gnome Inertia Transport Devices. Your chances of reaching the bottom of the hill without crashing are no more than even."

Kitiara opened her mouth to protest, but Sturm forestalled her with a tolerant glance. "Those are better odds than the Lunitarians will give us," he had to admit. He boosted the flimsy sled to his shoulder. "Are you coming?"

She looked more than doubtful. "Why don't we stay here and break each others' necks? Then we'll at least save the trouble of tumbling and rolling."

"Are you afraid?"

He knew just how to provoke her. Kitiara flushed and took up her sled. "Want to wager who gets to the bottom first?" she said.

"Why not?" he replied. "I haven't any money."

"What good is money here? How about if the loser has to carry the winner's bedroll all the way to the obelisk?"

"It's a wager." They shook hands.

Wingover was giving his colleagues an impromptu course on steering and braking. "Mostly you steer by leaning in the direction you want to go," he advised. "For stopping, use the heels of your shoes, not the toes. The downhill momentum can turn your feet under and break your toes."

Rainspot and Cutwood flipped open their notebooks and scribbled furiously. "Given a maximum velocity of fifty-six miles per hour—"

"And feet approximately seven inches long—"

"One can expect to break three toes on the left foot—"

"And four on the right," said Rainspot. The gnomes applauded.

"Wingover just told us not to use our toes, so why in the name of the suffering gods do you calculate something no one in his right mind would try?" Kitiara asked.

"The principle of scientific inquiry should not be limited to merely the practical or the possible," explained Sighter. "Only by investigating the unlikely and the unthought-of is the sum total of knowledge advanced."

Sturm was looking at his feet. "What I don't understand is why more toes on the right foot would break than on the left."

"Don't encourage them!" Kitiara told Sturm. She dragged her shaky bundle of slats to the edge of the cliff. The glass-smooth slope plunged down at a breathtaking angle. Kitiara inhaled sharply and looked back. The gnomes crowded forward to the edge, quite unafraid.

"Obviously an example of vitreous concretion," observed Cutwood, running a hand over the smooth, bubbly surface.

"Do you think? Volcanic?" Wingover said.

"Hardly. I should say this entire valley constitutes a thermoflexic astrobleme," theorized Sighter.

Kitiara uttered an angry snort that cut off further gnomish theorizing. She dropped her sled and straddled it. When she let her weight down on it, the slats creaked ominously.

"You did say even odds?" she said to Cutwood. The gnome babbled something about "within two standard deviations," and Kitiara decided not to query further. She pulled herself forward by hands and heels until she teetered on the brink.

"C'mon, Sturm! Or do you want to pack my bedroll for the next forty miles?"

Sturm laid his sled on the ground. He told Wingover that he and Kit were going to race. Wingover replied, "Oh! Then you'll need someone at the bottom to see who wins! Wait, wait—I'll go down first, and when I'm in place, I'll call you."

"All right with you, Kit?" She waved a casual affirmative.

"All right, lads. Here I go!" said Wingover. "For science!" he proclaimed, and slid over. Immediately, the other gnomes lined up and went right after him.

Cutwood called, "For Sancrist!" and went over.

"For technology!" cried Rainspot, as he tipped over the edge.

"For the *Cloudmaster*!" was Roperig's toast.

"For raisin muffins!" Fitter followed close behind his boss.

Sighter, the last, pushed his sled forward and slipped into the seat. "For Bellcrank," he said softly.

The gnomes' sleds bounded down the hill, swaying and leaping over bumps in the glasslike rock. Wingover, lying prone on his mount, steered skillfully around the worst obstacles. He'd built a front yoke on his sled, and weaved a serpentine course down the slope. On his heels, Cutwood howled straight down, knees tight against his chin, his silky beard clamped firmly between them. Sturm and Kitiara heard his high-pitched "Woo-haa!" as he hit bump after bump.

Rainspot had a drag-brake on the tail of his sled, and he coasted along at a relatively mild rate. Roperig, who had designed his sled to be ridden in a standing crouch, whistled by the weather seer, frantically waving his outstretched arms in an effort to keep his balance. His apprentice was having all sorts of trouble. Fitter's mount was wider than it was long, and it tended to rotate as it slid. This made his progress somewhat slower than the others but the spinning threatened to turn his stomach. Sighter, cool and rational, proceeded under perfect control. He would touch his heels to the ground at specific points to correct the direction he was taking.

All was going fairly well until Wingover reached bottom, four hundred feet away. There the glass cliff face changed to dry red gravel, and Wingover's sled stopped dead on its runners. His stop was so sudden that the trailing gnomes piled right into him—Cutwood and Roperig immediately, Fitter and Rainspot a little later. Slats and tools and gnomes flew through the air after a series of hair-raising crashes. Sturm saw Sighter move unflinching toward the pile, but averted his eyes and missed Sighter's sharp turn, which left him two feet to the right of the scrambled group.

Kitiara burst out laughing. "Acres of slope, and they all have to stop on the same spot!"

Sturm frowned. "I hope no one's hurt."

Feet and legs and wreckage untangled into six shaky gnomes. Sighter helped them untangle themselves. Wingover finally waved to the humans.

"That means go!" Kitiara shouted, and pushed herself off. Sturm was caught off guard.

"Not fair!" he cried, but dug in his heels and tipped over the cliff lip in hot pursuit.

He immediately lost control. The sled careened sharply to the right, and Sturm leaned away from the turn. There was a sickening snap, and his seat sagged under him. Sturm lessened his lean, and the sled slowly corrected itself.

Kitiara barreled straight down the slope at full speed, her feet pressed together and her knees poking out on either side. "Ya-ha-ha-ha!" she crowed. She was far out in front of Sturm, who couldn't seem to get his sled to run in a straight line for more than a few feet at a time.

Kitiara hit a hump and bounced several inches off her seat. Instead of frightening her, the bump only increased her delight. A whole series of bumps approached, and she didn't slacken speed at all.

It wasn't until she hit the fourth bump that she realized she was in trouble. That bump slammed her hard against the flimsy seat struts. The left runner splintered along its length. Kitiara put her left boot down to slow herself. The hobnails in her shoe sole bit, and her left leg was yanked back. Mindful of what Cutwood had said about breaking toes, she didn't resist the pulling and was swept off the sled. She landed hard on her right shoulder and rolled over and over. Sturm didn't dare try to stop his sled, and coasted to the bottom. The second his runners stuck in the gravel, he was on his feet. Kitiara lay motionless on her stomach.

Sturm ran to her, closely followed by the gnomes. He dropped on one knee and gently turned her over. Her face was contorted, and she uttered a ferocious curse.

"Where does it hurt?" he said.

"My shoulder," she hissed through clenched teeth.

"Could be a broken collarbone," said Rainspot.

"Is there any way to tell for sure?"

"Ask her to touch her left shoulder with her right hand,"

suggested Roperig. "If she can, the bone must not be broken."

"Such anatomical ignorance!" said Sighter. "One must probe with one's fingers in order to find the ends of the separated bone—"

"Don't let them touch me," Kitiara whispered. "If they can't prove it any other way, they may decide to cut me open to examine my bones." Just then Sturm heard Cutwood saying something about "exploratory surgery."

Wingover, who was standing by Kitiara's feet, said, "No bones are broken."

"How do you know?" asked Cutwood.

"I can see them," he replied. "There don't even seem to be any cracks. It's probably a sprain."

"You can see through *flesh* now?" Sturm asked incredulously. Put so bluntly, Wingover suddenly realized what he was doing.

"By Reorx!" he said. "This is terrific! I wonder what else I can see through?" The gnomes crowded around him, Kitiara forgotten. They took turns having Wingover peer through their bodies and describing what he saw. Cries of "Hydrodynamics!" filled the air.

Kitiara tried to sit up, but the pain took her breath away.

"Keep still," Sturm cautioned. "I'll have to find something to bind up your shoulder."

He rummaged through his belongings and found his only change of shirt—a white linen blouse made by the best tailor in Solace. Regretfully, he tore it into inch-wide strips and tied their ends into one long bandage.

"You'll have to get your arm out of the sleeve," he said.

"Cut the seams," said Kitiara.

Sturm checked. "The seams are underneath. You'll still have to slip it off."

"All right. Help me up."

As easily as he could, Sturm helped Kitiara to sit up. Her face went pale, and as he tried to loosen the sleeve from her right arm, tears of pain trickled down her face.

"You know, I've never seen you cry before," he said in a low voice.

"Ah! Ah!—what's the matter, didn't you think I could?"

Sturm kept his mouth shut and turned her fur coat. The leather he could cut away, but underneath she still wore her mail shirt. "I'll have to bind you over the mail," he said.

"Yes, yes," she said. Pain made her impatient.

He sat down facing her and carefully lifted her right arm until she could rest it on his shoulder. Sturm wound the linen bandage over Kitiara's shoulder and under her arm.

"Tight enough?"

Gasp. "Yes."

"I'll leave enough cloth to make a sling," he said sympathetically.

"Whatever." She lowered her head into her left hand. Her face was flushed.

I thought she'd be stronger than this, Sturm thought, as he wrapped. Surely she's been wounded in battle worse than this! Aloud, he said, "With all your combat experience, you must be an old hand at field dressings. Am I doing this right?"

"I've never been wounded," Kitiara murmured through her hand. "A few cuts and scrapes, that's all."

"You've been lucky." Sturm was amazed.

"I don't let enemies get close enough to hurt me."

Sturm helped her stand. He draped the empty sleeve over Kitiara's shoulder. The gnomes were energetically debating the nature of Wingover's expanding talent.

"Obviously, he is seeing a subtle variety of light that normal eyes cannot detect," said Cutwood.

"Obvious to any fool," Sighter countered. "The method is this: Wingover is now emitting rays from his eyes that pierce flesh and clothing. The source of his sight must be his own eyes."

"Ahem!" interrupted Sturm, "Could you manage this argument while walking? We have a long way to go and a short night to do it in."

"How is the lady?" asked Roperig. "Can she walk?"

"I can run. How about you?" said Kitiara challengingly.

There wasn't much left to salvage from the smashed remains of the sleds. Sturm realized that for the first time the gnomes were going to have to travel light; they had no means left by which to carry their heavy, useless gear. They dithered over what to take and what to abandon. The gnomes were about to adopt Roperig's suggestion that they assign numerical values to each item and then choose a total value of items not to exceed two hundred points per gnome.

"I'm going," Kitiara said shortly. She tried to sling her and Sturm's bedrolls on her good shoulder. Sturm caught the straps and took both rolls away from her. "I lost the bet," she admitted.

"Don't be a fool," he said. "I'll carry them."

They walked about half a mile and stopped to let the gnomes catch up. How they rattled and jingled! Each gnome had a workshop's worth of tools dangling from his vest and belt.

"I hope we don't have to sneak up on anybody," muttered Kitiara. The weary but steadfast party formed again and set out for the great obelisk and the Voice that inhabited it.

* * * * *

Ten miles had passed beneath their feet when Cutwood started complaining of a pounding in his head. His colleagues made jokes at his expense until Sturm shushed them. Rainspot gave Cutwood a cursory examination.

"I see nothing out of the ordinary," he said.

"You needn't shout," Cutwood said, wincing.

Rainspot raised his wispy white eyebrows in surprise. "Who's shouting?" he asked mildly.

Sighter dropped back behind Cutwood, and when he was out of his sight, snapped his fingers. Cutwood ducked his head and put his hands up to ward off some unseen blow.

"Did you hear that crack of lightning?" he said, his voice wavering.

"Most interesting. Cutwood's hearing has intensified, just as Wingover's vision has," said Sighter.

"Does this mean we're getting more of the power?" wondered Rainspot.

"It would seem so," Sighter said gravely.

"Stop screaming!" begged Cutwood in a whisper.

Roperig quickly made a crude pair of earmuffs for Cutwood out of strips of rattan from his water bottle and a wad of old socks. Ears muffled, Cutwood smiled.

"The pounding is much less now, thank you!"

"Don't mention it," Roperig said in a slightly lower than normal voice. Cutwood beamed and clapped his colleague on the back.

"Do you feel any different?" Sturm asked Kitiara.

"My shoulder still hurts."

"You don't feel any new access of strength?"

She shook her head. "All I feel is a crying need for a mug of Otik's best ale."

Sturm had to smile. It seemed eons since they'd all sat at the inn and enjoyed Otik's brew. It felt as if it would be eons before they could do so again.

At the twelve-mile mark, the gnomes were trailing out in a long line behind Kitiara and Sturm. Their short legs simply couldn't maintain the humans' rapid pace. Reluctantly, Sturm called for a break. The gnomes dropped where they stood, as though felled by a shower of arrows.

The air stirred. Glimmers of roseate light showed in the east—the direction they'd decided was east. "Sunrise," Kitiara said flatly.

Westward, toward the center of the valley, an answering flicker of light greeted the sunrise. Sighter tried to get his spyglass trained on the source of this second dawn. Wingover moved over to him.

"It's the obelisk," he said. He squinted into the far distance. "I can see a glow surrounding the peak."

Brilliant white streaks—more shooting stars—sprayed across the heavens. A bright, steady glow in the east was soon mimicked in the west. The sun was coming up over the cliffs, yellow and warm; the glow from the obelisk was a stubborn and muddy scarlet.

The rim of the sun broke over the cliffs. There was a clap of thunder, and bolts of red fire snapped from the far-off obelisk toward the surrounding chain of hills. The explorers put their faces to the ground, and all felt a blast of burning as the red beams crackled overhead. Five times the scarlet lightning lashed out, and the resulting thunder pounded the sky with ringing blows. When the sun was fully above the valley walls, the strange storm ceased.

Sturm sat up. The ground around them steamed lightly. Kitiara struggled to her feet and surveyed the valley by daylight. Plants were beginning to emerge from the flaky soil. Wingover dusted himself off and looked back at the cliff they had sledded down.

"Now I understand how the sides got to be as hard and smooth as glass," he said. "The lightning must hit them every morning."

The gentlest gnome said shakily, "Those were not pluvial discharges." He tried to stand and failed. "The atmosphere is charged with another power."

"Magic." Sturm felt his face harden with distaste as he practically spat the word. Though hardly unexpected, the sudden onset of such enormous magical power left him feeling vulnerable, exposed—and tainted.

Chapter 19

Cupelix

The vegetation in the valley was much the same as elsewhere on Lunitari, but it grew less thickly and to greater size. The pink spears topped twelve feet in an hour's growth, and the toadstools towered twenty and thirty feet. One new species the explorers found was a five-foot-wide puffball. After seeing one such puffball explode, sending a shower of javelin-sharp spikes in all directions, the marchers gave them a very wide berth.

The sky seemed brighter, too, and a steady hum filled their ears. Cutwood complained constantly of a loud buzzing, despite his makeshift earmuffs. Wingover took to shielding his eyes with his hands, just to cut down on the intense glare he saw everywhere. The other gnomes found their special attributes becoming more and more onerous.

Roperig couldn't touch anything without his hands sticking. He once accidentally scratched his nose, and it took an hour to free his fingers. Fitter fidgeted about like a hovering hummingbird, moving with such speed that he seemed little more than a blur. He fell down a lot and continually bumped into other members of the party. Rainspot walked in a perpetual haze—a real fog that clung to his head and shoulders—his own private cloud. Moisture condensed on his face, and his ears and beard dripped nonstop.

Of all the gnomes, only Sighter exhibited no obvious ill effects. But Sturm noticed a subtle change in his expression; Sighter's usually incisive gaze had given way to a hard smirk, as if he were listening to some lurid tale being whispered in his ear. Sturm wasn't certain that the world was ready for a logical gnome.

Sturm worried about Kitiara, too. She kept ahead of the others, walking purposefully toward the waiting obelisk. Her right arm was still slung across her chest, but her left hand, firmly clenched in a fist, rose and fell with each determined step. Each strike of her heels left a deep notch in the ground. Sturm wondered how much power she could bear.

He lost sight of Kitiara for a time among the pink spears and spidersticks. "Hello?" he called. "Kit, wait for us." There was no answer but the hive-hum that surrounded them.

Sturm spied Kitiara standing under an enormous toadstool. Pink spores rained lightly over her. Her hand was at her throat, and she was looking at something.

"Kit?" he said, touching her shoulder.

She flinched. "Sturm! I just noticed this." It was Tirolan's gem, the amethyst arrowhead that had turned clear after Kit had used it to free herself from the spell of the goblin robbers. She held the crystal out for Sturm to see. It was blood red, like a heartsfire ruby.

"When did that happen?" he asked.

"At Rapaldo's palace, I saw that the gem was turning pale pink. The color has deepened since sunrise."

"Get rid of it, Kit. It's a receptacle of magic. It too may be affected by the atmosphere of Lunitari. Nothing good can come of it."

"No!" she said, slipping the gem back under her mail

shirt. I intend to keep it. Have you so soon forgotten how Tirolan helped us?"

"No, I haven't forgotten. But the gem may be filled with a different power now, a power you know nothing about. Drop it on the ground, Kit, please! If you don't, the consequences may be horrible."

"I will not!" she said, her dark eyes flashing. "You're a fool, Sturm Brightblade—a frightened little boy. I'm not afraid of power. I welcome it!"

Sturm was about to argue back, but the file of gnomes appeared. He was not willing to provoke a confrontation in front of the little people. There was a thinly veiled rage in Kitiara, and to push her at this juncture would lead nowhere.

"Wingover says the obelisk should soon be in view for all of us," said Roperig. His right hand was stuck to Fitter's back. The apprentice was running in place, his short legs nearly invisible with motion. Roperig saw Sturm's startled expression and added, "Fitter's having a hard time standing still. I'm the only one who can keep hold of him."

"How are the rest of you?" Sturm asked. Cutwood and Wingover, muffled and blindfolded respectively, gallantly waved their good spirits. Rainspot looked sodden and forlorn under his cloud, but avowed that he felt well.

Sighter cleared his throat and arched an eyebrow in a maddeningly superior way. "It is evident that the closer we get to the obelisk, the more intensely the neutral power of Lunitari infects us," he said.

"Let's push on," said Sturm.

They continued on for about an hour, when they came upon a path, cleared from the strange jungle. And where the cleared path met the horizon, there stood a tall spire—the mysterious obelisk of Lunitari. They were still some ten miles away, but the land sloped downward toward the obelisk at an easy grade. There were no other features to overshadow it.

"Looks like we're expected," said Sturm.

"The Voice?" Fitter wondered.

"Who else?" Sighter replied. He hooked his thumbs under his suspenders. "If I'm right, we're going to meet a very remarkable being. Someone who'll make all the other wonders of Lunitari seem like cheap carnival tricks."

The obelisk grew from a slim red line to a robust tower five hundred feet tall. It had a curiously striped appearance, caused by thin black bands that alternated with the red stone of its walls. The closer the explorers came, the higher the grand tower seemed to thrust into the sky.

Cutwood broke the long silence. He said, "Have you noticed how the plants lean toward the tower?" It was true. All of them, even the spiny puffballs, were bent so that they faced the great obelisk.

"Like lilies turned to the sun," surmised Kitiara.

They halted fifty yards from the base of the obelisk. The red marble sides were beautifully dressed and squared, unlike the crude masonry of the tree-men's village. The black bands between the courses of marble were mortar of some kind. On ground level, facing the explorers, was an open entrance, a notch cut in the smooth stone. Inside was only darkness. At regular intervals, the obelisk's walls were pierced by long, narrow windows.

"What do we do now?" asked Fitter in a very small voice.

Come closer!

Sturm and Kitiara stepped back, reaching for their weapons. "Who said that?" called Sturm.

I, the Keeper of the New Lives, said a soothing bass voice within their own heads.

"Where are you?" Kitiara demanded.

In the edifice before you. Come closer.

"We'll stay right here, thank you," said Cutwood.

Ah, you are afraid. Is mortal flesh so dear that you would ignore the opportunity to feast your eyes on a rare and wonderful sight, namely myself? That the humans would be afraid I did not doubt, but I expected better of you gnomes.

"We saw a colleague die not long ago, so you'll excuse us if we're a bit cautious," Wingover said.

You require proof of my good will? Behold.

A small shape stirred in the dim doorway. It emerged into the light of day, stopped and waved. It looked like Stutts.

"Gears and sprockets!" Fitter crowed, dashing forward. Of course, he dragged Roperig with him. Cutwood and

Wingover stumbled after them, while Rainspot wandered over in a fog, with Sighter chuckling at his side.

"Wait," said Sturm. "It could be an illusion!"

But it was not an illusion. The gnomes engulfed Stutts, yelling with unrestrained delight. Birdcall and Flash appeared in the door and leaped on the pile of happy gnomes. After a heartily bruising hello, Stutts extricated himself from the press and toddled to Sturm and Kitiara. He shook Sturm's hand solidly and expressed concern for Kitiara's bandaged shoulder.

"It *is* you," she said, pinching his ear.

"It is, and I am quite well, thank you. We've been waiting for you all for days."

"What happened to your stutter?" Sturm asked. Suspicion made him blunt.

"Oh, that! It's gone, you know, poof! The Keeper says it's due to the leveling effect of the magic forces present on Lunitari." Stutts peered behind the humans. "Where's Bellcrank?"

Sturm laid a hand on the gnome's shoulder. "I fear that we have grave news, my friend."

"Grave? How—?"

Are your fears alleviated? intruded the voice.

"For now," Kitiara said. "May we have our flying ship back, please?"

Don't be so hasty! We've not been properly introduced. Please come in, won't you?

"Explain later," Stutts said quickly. He took Kitiara's and Sturm's hands and led them to the door. "We've had the most tremendous adventure since you left to prospect for ore," he reported. "The Keeper has treated us marvelously."

"Who is this Keeper? Where is he?" asked Kitiara.

"Come and see for yourselves."

Stutts let go of their hands. Sturm and Kitiara stepped through the deep door-notch into the shadowed interior of the grand obelisk.

Sunlight filtered down from the slit windows higher up in the obelisk. In the center of the floor, illuminated by the sunlight, sat the flying ship *Cloudmaster*. The ethereal air bag had shrunk to half its previous size, just a soft lump in many folds of loose netting. The wings had been detached from the hull, no doubt to allow the craft to fit through the door in the obelisk. The leather wings were neatly folded and lying on the red marble floor beside the ship. Clicking in the darkness beyond the *Cloudmaster* proved the presence of Micones.

Inevitably, the warriors' gazes were lifted by the soaring hollowness of the interior. As Sturm and Kitiara raised their eyes, they saw a series of ledges and horizontal pillars set into the immensely thick walls. Perched about fifty feet above the floor was the occupant of the obelisk, the Keeper.

A dragon. Where blades of sunlight struck him, his scales shone greenish gold.

No dragon had been seen on Krynn in centuries, so long, in fact, that their actual existence was a sorely debated point among historians, clerics, and natural philosophers. Sturm believed from boyhood that there had been dragons, but face to face with a living example, he felt so much fear that he thought he'd faint.

Be a man, a knight! he admonished himself. Men had faced dragons before. Huma had done it. So while Sturm's head swam from this newest and greatest revelation, he kept his feet firmly under him.

Kitiara, too, was stunned. Her eyes were huge and white in the dim light. She recovered more quickly than Sturm, however, and said, "Are you the Keeper who spoke to us?"

Yes. "Or do you prefer spoken language?" asked the dragon. Its voice was not as booming as Sturm had expected it to be; considering its size (thirty-five feet from nose to tail) and the distance to it, it was quite soft-spoken.

"Spoken is best. That way I can be sure of what I'm hearing," answered Kitiara.

"As you wish. I do enjoy speaking, and I've gone such a long time without having anyone to speak to. The ants, you see, respond best to telepathy." The dragon shook its broad, angular head with a noise of clanging brass. It lifted its feet off the ledge and dropped to a lower perch with a single fluff of its wings. The breeze washed over the amazed explorers.

"Where are my manners? I am Cupelix Trisfendamir, Keeper of the New Lives and resident of this obelisk." The gnomes had retreated behind the humans when the dragon appeared. Now they spread out and began to bombard him with questions.

"Keeper of what new lives?"

"How much do you weigh?"

"How did you get here?"

"How long have you been here?"

"Do you have any raisins?"

The dragon was amused by this barrage, but he dismissed the gnomes with a wave of one giant foreclaw. "You are Kitiara Uth Matar and Sturm Brightblade, are you not?" he asked. The two nodded dumbly. "Your small friend, Stutts, speaks very highly of you both. Apparently, you have impressed him with many sterling qualities."

"Apparently?" said Kitiara dryly.

"I have only the evidence of Stutts's impressions. Be that as it may, I am very glad you are here. I followed your progress along the trail I had the Micones make—" Cupelix tilted his burnished head and peered at Sturm with dagger eyes. "Yes, Sir Knight, the trail was deliberate."

"You read minds," Sturm said uncomfortably.

"Not deeply. Only when a thought is so clearly on the tip of one's tongue."

Stutts introduced his colleagues to the dragon. Cupelix exchanged witty banter with each one, until Sighter's turn came.

"You are a bronze dragon?" questioned the gnome.

"Brass, if you must know. But enough of these trivialities! You have come a long way and labored hard to recover your flying craft. Now that you have found it and each other once more, enjoy a moment of repose at my expense."

"We'd rather be on our way," said Sturm.

"But I insist," said the dragon. He slid along the edge of his perch, his rear legs gripping the stone ledge and his wings flaring out for balance. Cupelix worked his way around to just over the door—the only way out.

Sturm didn't like what was happening. By instinct, his hand strayed to the pommel of his sword—which changed to a chicken drumstick when he touched it. The gnomes looked popeyed, and Kitiara's jaw fell open in surprise.

"Please excuse my little joke," said Cupelix. In the wink of an eye, the poultry leg was gone and the sword was back. "Your weapons are unnecessary here. That was just my way of showing you the truth of it. Men so often have to be shown the truth before they believe something.

"And now," said Cupelix, drawing himself erect. "Let there be victuals!" His eyes flashed with an inner light that seemed to leave bright sparkles in the air. The sparkles collected in the open space before the bow of the *Cloudmaster*. When they faded, they left behind a broad oak table groaning under the weight of food and drink.

"Eat, my friends. Drink, and we shall tell each other tales of great doings," intoned the dragon. The gnomes fell upon the table with squeals of delight. Kitiara eyed the pitchers of foaming ale and sauntered over. Though the spear plants could taste like any food she wished, Kitiara had missed the sight of real food. Only Sturm remained where he stood, his hands folded at his waist.

"You do not eat, Master Brightblade," said Cupelix.

"The fruits of magic are not fit victuals," Sturm said.

The reptilian nostrils twitched. "You have poor manners for one who styles himself a knight."

Sturm answered carefully. "There are higher directives than mere manners. The Measure tells us to reject magic in all its forms, for example." The brass jaws widened, revealing saber-sized teeth and a forked black tongue flecked with gold. For a second, Sturm's heart contracted to a tight knot in his chest, for he knew he could not withstand this monster's attack. Then, he realized Cupelix was grinning at him.

"Oh, how boring it has been these centuries past without creatures to dispute with! Bless your stiff neck, Sturm Brightblade! What pleasure you give me!" The jaws closed with a metallic clank. "But come now, surely you have heard of Huma the Lancer?"

"Of course."

"He got along quite well with some types of dragons, did he not?"

"So the histories say. I can only point out that while Huma was a brave warrior and a great hero, he was not a model knight."

Cupelix burst out laughing; it sounded like a chorus of mighty gongs. "Do as you please, then! I would not want to be responsible for undermining such formidable virtue!" With that, Cupelix sprang from his stand and, beating his wings furiously, flew up to the highest recesses of the hollow obelisk.

Sturm went to the sumptuous table. The gnomes were gorging themselves on baked apples, dove stuffed with bacon and chestnuts, wild rice with saffron, whole sweet onions glazed with honey, venison steaks, blood pudding, pickled eggs, breads, punch, wine, and ale.

Kitiara had taken her injured arm out of its sling and let it rest on the table. With her coat falling off one shoulder and the flush of new ale on her cheeks, she looked quite wanton. She sniffed when her eyes met Sturm's, and she popped a whole pickled egg in her mouth.

"You're missing a feast," she said after swallowing. "The old emperors of Ergoth never ate so well."

"I wonder what it's made from?" Sturm said, picking up a warm roll and letting it fall back into its tray. "Sand? Poisonous mushrooms?"

"Sometimes you are tiresome beyond belief," said Kitiara and quaffed a three-gulp swallow of ale. "If the dragon wanted to kill us, he could do it without resorting to the subtleties of poison."

"Actually," Cutwood said, leaning across the table and spewing bread crumbs with every syllable, "brass dragons traditionally are not aligned with evil."

"Have we nothing to fear from this creature?" Sturm asked the table at large. He glanced up at the darkness that held the dragon, and lowered his voice. "Our ancestors on Krynn fought long and hard to eliminate dragons from the world. Were they all wrong?"

"The situation here is completely different," said Stutts. "Lunitari is this dragon's home. He has taken a kindly interest in our plight. We shouldn't refuse his help because of ancient prejudices that have no application at the present time."

"What does he want from us?"

"He hasn't told us yet," Stutts admitted. "But he, ah,

won't let us leave."

"What do you mean?" Sturm said sharply.

"Birdcall, Flash, and I wanted to go searching for you. We rerouted the engine control sufficiently to make short ascents—hops, really—but Cupelix refused to allow us out of the obelisk. He claimed it wasn't safe, and that he was taking steps to bring you all here."

"Well, we're here now," said Kitiara, reaching for another broiled dove. "And we'll soon be on our way."

"Will we?" Sturm asked, craning his neck again to peer into the dim heights of the obelisk. "Now that he has us all, will he let us go?"

Chapter 20

A New Age

After Kitiara and the gnomes had their fill, they stole off to the *Cloudmaster* for a nap. Only Stutts remained with Sturm. The two of them strolled around the interior of the vast obelisk, and Sturm related the story of Bellcrank's death.

"It was pure chance that Bellcrank died instead of Kit or Sighter." They paused in their walk as Stutts plucked a handkerchief from his vest pocket and dabbed at his nose. Sturm told of Rapaldo's death, and how they placed Bellcrank in the middle of the mushroom garden.

"He and I were at gear-making school together, you know," Stutts said softly. "I'll miss him a great deal." They passed under the bow of the flying ship, and Sturm saw a smooth round hole, eight feet wide, bored in the hard marble floor. He asked Stutts what it was.

"The Micones live in a cavern below," Stutts said. "They enter and leave by these holes." He indicated two others not far away. Sturm stood on the lip of one of the holes and looked down. There was a feeble bluish glow below, and he could see the jagged shapes of stalagmites. A faintly bitter smell wafted up from the depths.

"Did the Micones build this place?" Sturm asked.

"Not as far as I can tell," Stutts replied, resuming his walk. "The Micones are a rather new addition to this place. Cupelix hints that he created them, but I don't believe he's that powerful. But to address your question: The obelisk was here even before the dragon."

"How do you know that?"

"By observing Cupelix. While a healthy adult specimen of a brass dragon, his features are in many ways molded by the fact that he grew up inside this obelisk. Notice, for example, his short wings and powerful legs; he spends all his time perching on the ledges rather than flying. He can jump tremendous distances, even straight up." Stutts stopped, seeing that Sturm was studying him. "What?" asked the gnome.

"You're so changed," said Sturm. "Not just the lack of a stutter; you seem so calm and collected."

Stutts blushed pink under his neatly trimmed beard. "I suppose we gnomes must appear awfully disorganized and impractical to you humans."

Sturm smiled. "Not at all."

Stutts returned the grin. He said, "Being on Lunitari has changed me—all of us. The flight of the *Cloudmaster*, while erratic, has been the first true success in my life. I spent years in the workshops of Mt. Nevermind, building flying machines. They all failed. It wasn't until I learned of Bellcrank's experiments with ethereal air that the *Cloudmaster* became possible." Mention of the lost chemist quelled conversation for a moment.

"Be at peace," Sturm finally said. "He was avenged."

They passed below the tail of the flying ship. A mixed chorus of snores issued from the open portholes. Stutts gestured toward the sound.

"They are a fine band of colleagues," he said. "They deserve to go home to the cheers of all Sancrist."

"Do you think we'll ever see Krynn again?" Sturm asked.

"That all depends on Cupelix and what he wants. I have a theory—"

A wind flowed over them. With a customary metallic ringing, the dragon alighted on the lowest sill, perhaps fifteen feet above Sturm and Stutts. The gnome sidled away from Cupelix.

"I trust you are satiated," Cupelix said to Stutts.

"The meal was excellent, as always," Stutts replied. He yawned. "It weighs a bit heavy on my stomach, though. I think I shall join my colleagues." With a polite nod, Stutts returned to the ship. Cupelix loomed over Sturm.

"So it is you and I, Master Brightblade. What shall we talk about? Let us debate our philosophies, knight to dragon. What do you say?"

"No magic?"

Cupelix laid a burnished claw on his breast. "Dragon's honor."

"How is it," Sturm wondered, "that you speak so fluently the Krynnish tongue?"

"Books," replied the dragon. "My nest on high is plentifully supplied with books by authors mortal and immortal. Now I shall ask a question: What is it you seek from life?"

"To live honorably and in the manner befitting an Oath-taken knight. My turn. Have you always lived inside this tower?"

"From the days when I was a dragonlet no larger than a gnome, I have been the Keeper. I have never seen outside these walls, save what I spy by the doors and windows." His broad pupils narrowed. "Do you ever question the tenets of the Knights' Oath or Measure? After all, the Order of Solamnus was not revived after the Cataclysm."

Sturm folded his arms across his chest. "If you are well read, then you know the Cataclysm was not caused by anything the knights did. They accepted the blame of the common people, as all preservers of order must do when that order breaks down. Where did the Micones come from?"

"They were created to serve me. The Lunitarian tree-folk did not prove reliable." Cupelix flicked out his tongue. "Are you in love with the woman, Kitiara?"

Cupelix's pointed query threw Sturm off guard. "I have

some affection for her, but I'm not in love with her, if you understand the difference." The dragon nodded, human-fashion. Sturm continued, "So the tree-men and the Micones were created in succession as your servants, the tree-men being a failed effort. Who created them?"

"Higher powers," replied Cupelix evasively. "This is wonderful! I wish people had come to Lunitari centuries ago! But hark now: If you're not in love with the woman, why is she so predominant in your thoughts? Behind many of your spoken thoughts is an image of her."

Drops of sweat broke out on Sturm's face. "I'm very concerned about her. The magical force that pervades this moon has invested her with enormous physical strength. Her temper has sharpened, too. I worry about the power getting control of her."

"Yes, magic can cause problems. I studied Stutts, Birdcall, and Flash as the power changed them. It was most interesting. So the woman has become very strong? That must complicate your feelings. I've never yet heard of a human male who relished a female being stronger than he."

"That's ridiculous! I don't care—" Sturm halted his outburst. Blast that sly dragon. He was deliberately probing for a sore point.

"My turn to ask something," Sturm said. "Why does a powerful, magic-using dragon like yourself need servants? What can they do that you can't?"

"I cannot leave the obelisk; isn't that obvious? The door and windows are far too small to permit me to pass through."

"Ah, but a skillful magic-user could overcome a problem of mere size."

Cupelix's tail swept back, thwack! against the marble wall. "I'm not allowed to leave. I cannot pass the windows or door, and have not been able to break, cut or bore through the walls, nor magic them aside. I am Keeper of the New Lives, and such is my lot until darkness claims me!"

"What new lives?"

"All in good time, Sir Knight. A more pressing matter engages my attention: the matter of my freedom."

"You need us to get you out," Sturm said.

A wisp of fine vapor trickled from the dragon's nostrils.

"Yes, I need you. Only clever machines can release me from this stifling prison. Tree-men could not do it. The Micones will not. The gnomes can. You shall have your flying ship when I am free."

The vaporous threads thickened until they enveloped Sturm. He felt the strength drain from his limbs. His eyelids drooped. . . . A sleeping mist! Sturm's legs buckled. He mumbled, "No magic, you said."

"Not magic, exactly," Cupelix said soothingly. "Merely a soporific vapor I have at my disposal. My dear fellow, you're so full of suspicions. This will help you. Sleep, and you will not remember this distressing conversation. Sleep, rest, dream. Sleep. Rest. Dream. Forget. . . ."

* * * * *

Kitiara woke up. She had that vaguely troubled feeling that often went with a sudden return to consciousness, as though she'd been having a bad dream that she couldn't remember. She was lying on the deck of the dining room aboard the *Cloudmaster*. Below, the gnomes snored with the regularity of a water-driven mill. Kitiara combed through her short curls with her fingers. Her skin was clammy, and her hair damp with sweat.

Outside, the air was cool. She inhaled deeply, but her breath caught when she saw Sturm lying crumpled on the stone floor some yards away. Kitiara hurried down the ramp and ran to where he lay. Sturm breathed, strong and steady, soundly asleep.

Kitiara became aware that she was being watched. She whirled and saw Cupelix lying on his side along the lower ledge. His neck was bowed and he held his tail off the stone. When he saw that she saw him, his tail came down and began to twitch from side to side in a very feline manner.

"When did this happen?" she asked, gesturing to Sturm.

"A short time ago. It's not a natural sleep," said the dragon.

"He's been having visions since coming to Lunitari. We've all been affected by the magic here."

"Truly? Visions of what?" Kitiara firmed her lips, unwilling to say. "Come, my dear. Master Brightblade has no secrets from you, does he? A man always tells his lover of his dreams."

"We are not lovers!"

"That sounds definite. I see I'm guilty of inferring too much. No matter. He has told you what he visualizes, hasn't he?"

She shrugged. "Scenes of home, on Krynn. His father, mostly, whom he hasn't seen in twelve years."

Cupelix let out a dragon-sized sigh that swirled dust in Kitiara's face. "Ah, Krynn! Where once thousands of my kind lived, to fly the broad skies in absolute freedom!"

"You've never been to Krynn?"

"Alas, never. My entire span of days has been spent within the stone walls of this structure. Sad, isn't it?"

"Confining, at any rate."

The tip of Cupelix's forked tongue flickered out. "You're not afraid of me, are you?"

Kitiara lifted her chin. "Should I be?"

"Most mortals would find me awesome."

"When you've been around as much as I have, you get used to new things. That, and the fact that those who can't adjust quickly die."

"You're a survivor," said Cupelix.

"I do what I can."

The black tongue protruded farther. "How did you hurt yourself?" asked the dragon. Kitiara described the sled ride down the cliff. "Ho, ho, I see! Very clever, those gnomes. I can heal your hurt."

"Can you really?"

"It's simply done. You'll have to remove the wrapping."

Why not? Kitiara thought. She fiddled with the knot that Sturm had tied, but couldn't untie it with her left hand. She pulled her dagger and slit the linen with a few deft strokes.

"The mail, too," said Cupelix.

She raised one eyebrow but put the point of the dagger under the rawhide lacing on her shoulder. The slightly rusty mail peeled back. Kitiara pulled her shirt off her injured shoulder, exposing a hideous purple-black bruise.

"Come closer," said Cupelix. She stepped forward once, and was prepared to go farther, when the dragon swung his head down on his long, supple neck. The black tongue lanced out, just barely touching the bruised area. A shock jolted through Kitiara. Cupelix flicked his tongue again, and a harder shock rocked her back on her heels.

Cupelix reared back. "Done," he said.

Kitiara ran her hand over the site of the sprain. Not a trace of discoloration or soreness remained. She worked her right arm around in a wide circle and felt no twinges.

"Wonderful!" she exclaimed. "Many thanks, dragon!"

"It was nothing. A simple healing spell," he said modestly.

Kitiara stretched luxuriously. "I feel like a new woman! I could best a hundred goblins in a fair fight!"

"I'm glad you are pleased," said Cupelix. "The time may soon come when you can repay the favor."

She stopped in mid arm-swing. "What is it you want?"

"Good company, some philosophy, and words with heat in them. Small things."

"So talk to me. I have time to spare."

"Ah, but the life of a mortal is a star falling from the heavens. I have lived twenty-nine hundred years in this tower. Can you converse for even half that time? A quarter? No, of course you can't. But there is a way to help me do these things to the end of my days."

Kitiara folded her arms. "And that is?"

"Free me from this obelisk. Set me loose, that I might fly to Krynn and live as a dragon should!"

"Men and elves would try to slay you."

Cupelix said, "It is a chance I would willingly take. There are great changes in the offing, deep stirrings in the tide of heaven. You have felt them yourself, haven't you? Even before you flew here, didn't you notice a new tide rising in the affairs of Krynn?"

Fragments of thought came back to Kitiara. Tirolan and his elves on the high seas, in direct defiance of their elders. Robbers and wicked clerics plundering the countryside. Strange bands of warriors—monstrous, inhuman warriors—crossing the land, intent on some mission. And a word muttered by the elvish seamen: Draconians.

"You see it, don't you?" asked Cupelix softly. "Our time is coming again. A new age of dragons is about to begin."

Chapter 21

Wood to Burn

As Kitiara pondered Cupelix's words, Wingover appeared, yawning, at the ship railing.

"G'morning! When's breckfiss?" he asked, thick-tongued.

"You ate not five hours ago," Kitiara chided. She slipped her shirt and mail back on her shoulder.

Roperig and Fitter stood in the hull door. Roperig's hand was still firmly fixed to his apprentice's back. "Hello, dragon!" he said heartily.

"Hello!" added Fitter.

"Did you sleep well, little friends?" asked Cupelix.

"Very well indeed, thank you. I—We thought we might go outside and take in a bit of fresh air," said Roperig.

"Stay close," Kitiara warned. "Every time one of you gnomes does something on his own, he ends up putting us to no end of trouble."

Roperig promised not to stray, and Fitter had no choice but to agree. They strolled to the door of the obelisk in hilarious misstep. Small cyclones of wind swirled through the hollow interior of the obelisk. Kitiara realized that this was Cupelix laughing. She couldn't resist; small chuckles burst out of her and changed to full-fledged guffaws.

* * * * *

Sturm braced himself on his arms and shook his head. He heard laughter. His head cleared, though his memory seemed adrift in fog. He got to his feet, turned to the sound of laughter, and was bowled down by Roperig and Fitter.

Kitiara hauled the gnomes off Sturm and held them up at arm's length. "What's the matter with you two? Didn't you see Sturm standing there?"

"But-but-but," stuttered Fitter.

She shook them. "Well, out with it!"

"It was an accident, Kit," said Sturm, getting to his feet once more. Poor Fitter was running in midair, his short legs churning. Kitiara set the gnomes on their feet.

"Tree-men!" Roperig exploded. "Outside!"

"What! How many?"

"See for yourself!"

They rushed to the door. Even as Sturm appeared in the outer opening, a red glass spear hit the pavement in front of him and shattered into a thousand razor-sharp slivers. Kitiara grabbed him by his sword belt and hauled him back with one hand.

"Better stay back," Kitiara suggested.

"I can keep myself out of harm's way." Sturm pressed close to the right wall and peered out. The valley floor around the obelisk was thick with tree-men—thousands, if not tens of thousands of them. They began to hoot, "*Ou-Stoom laud, Ou-Stoom laud.*"

"What are they saying?" Kitiara asked, behind him.

"How should I know? Rouse all the gnomes," he told Kitiara. "I'll speak to Cupelix." Kitiara got Roperig, Fitter, and Wingover to help her.

"Cupelix?" Sturm called, for the dragon had vanished into the top of the tower again. "Cupelix, come down! There's trouble outside!"

Trouble? I dare say, there is trouble!

A great rustle of brassy wings sounded, and the dragon alighted on one of the crossing pillars that ran from one side of the obelisk to the other. Cupelix's metallic claws closed over the marble pillar with a clack. He furled his wings and started preening himself along either wing.

"You don't seem very disturbed by this development," Sturm said, planting his fists on his hips.

"Should I be?" asked the dragon.

"Considering the tower is besieged, I would think yes."

"The Lunitarians are not very intelligent. They would never have come here if you hadn't killed that fool of a mortal they made their king."

"Rapaldo was mad. He killed one of the gnomes, and would've killed others if we hadn't resisted," said Sturm.

"You should feel flattered that they have come all this way to kill you. That uncouth phrase they keep repeating—do you know what it means? 'Sturm must die.'"

Sturm's hand tightened around his sword handle. "I am prepared to fight," he said grimly.

"Your kind is always ready to fight. Relax, my knightly friend; the tree-folk will not attack."

"Are you so certain?"

Cupelix yawned, exposing teeth green with verdigris. "I am the Keeper of the New Lives. Only a severe trauma would have compelled the Lunitarians to come here in the first place. However, they are not so bold as to trifle with me."

"We can't just let them blockade us!" Sturm insisted.

"Shortly, the sun will set, and the tree-folk will take root. The Micones will awaken and clear them away."

"The Micones come out only at night?"

"No, but they are practically blind in sunlight." Cupelix pricked up his ears when Kitiara returned, herding the gnomes ahead of her. The dragon reassured them all that they were in no danger from the Lunitarians.

"Perhaps we should prepare a barricade, just the same," said Stutts.

"I think our time would be better spent repairing the *Cloudmaster*," said Sighter. "With the scrap metal we brought from Rapaldo's keep, we ought to be able to make repairs in a few hours."

Birdcall whistled a sharp note. Stutts nodded, saying, "We haven't the fire needed to work iron."

"I may be able to help you there," Cupelix said smoothly. "How much wood will you need?"

"You're being awfully helpful," Sturm said. "Why?"

The beast's eyes narrowed to vertical slits. "Do you question my motives?" he asked. With his long ears laid back, Cupelix looked quite fierce.

"Frankly, yes."

The dragon relaxed. "Ho, ho! Very good! I blink first, Master Brightblade! I do have a favor to ask of you all, but first we shall see to the repair of your ingenious vessel."

Already the light in the obelisk had subsided to a dusty rose. The hooting of the tree-men, muffled by the thick walls, faded with the sunlight. It was soon quite dark inside the obelisk. Kitiara complained to Cupelix, while the gnomes ranged noisily through the *Cloudmaster* in search of tools.

"Oh, very well," said the dragon. "I forget your mortal eyes cannot pierce the simple veil of darkness." He spread his wings until the tips scraped the surrounding walls and bowed his neck in a swanlike curve.

"*Ab-biray solem!* Creatures of the dark!
Bring forth a fair and living spark
To light the tower bright as day.
Come, Micones! *Solem ab-biray!*"

The glassy clicking that they all associated with the giant ants arose from the holes in the obelisk floor. It grew quite loud, as though hundreds of the formidable creatures were stirring below their feet.

Something stroked Sturm's leg. He was near one of the large holes in the floor, and a Micone had poked its head out to touch Sturm with one of its antennae. He recoiled, and the giant ant emerged, to be followed immediately by another, and another. The floor rapidly filled with Micones, all clicking and gently waving their crystalline feelers.

"To your places, my pets," ordered Cupelix. The ants

nearest the walls climbed up to the lowest ledge and hung there, their broad, plum-shaped abdomens poised off the edge. When the entire interior was ringed with hanging ant bodies, the Micones began rubbing their bellies against the smooth marble shelf. As they did, their translucent abdomens glowed, first a dull red, then warmer and brighter. Like a mass of living lanterns, the ants gradually illuminated the whole lower half of the obelisk.

Sturm and Kitiara stared. No matter how jaded they thought they'd become to the strange wonders of the red moon, something new and startling was always happening.

"Better?" said Cupelix smugly.

"Tolerable," said Kitiara, sauntering away.

Sturm went to the door. The Lunitarians were a true forest now, still and tall in the starlight. This forest, though, was arranged in perfect concentric circles around the great obelisk that shielded the killers of their Iron King.

Cupelix withdrew to his lofty sanctum. Not long after he did, Sturm returned to the *Cloudmaster*, where the gnomes were up to their elbows in repair work.

When he descended to the engine room, he found to his shock that Flash, Birdcall, and Stutts had torn apart the entire engine, searching for defects. The deck was covered with cogs and gears, copper rods that Wingover called 'armatures,' and hundreds of other examples of gnomish technology. Sturm was afraid to enter, for fear of stepping on and crushing some delicate, vital component.

"Uh, how goes it?" he ventured.

"Oh, not to worry, not to worry!" Stutts said blithely. "All is in good order." He snatched a metal curlicue from Cutwood and snapped at Flash, "Stay away from the Indispensable Inductor Coil! It mustn't be magnetized!" Lunitari had finally bestowed its 'gift' upon Flash; he was intensely magnetic. Bits of iron and steel had begun to cling to him.

Flash meekly stepped away from the Indispensable Inductor Coil. "We're trying to find what parts were damaged by the lightning strike," Stutts went on, "so they can be fixed, too."

"Keep at it," Sturm said, trying not to smile. He knew the gnomes would find an answer of sorts—eventually.

He found Kitiara in the wheelhouse, sitting in Stutts's

chair. She had one leg cocked over the arm of the chair and was drinking from a tall clay tankard. "Dragon ale?" asked Sturm.

"Umm. Want some? No, of course you don't." She drank some more. "All the more for me then."

"The gnomes are hard at it," he said. "We could be on our way home in a day or two."

"Can't be too soon for me," she replied.

"Oh? Do you have plans?"

Kitiara cradled the tankard in her lap. "Do you really want to know?"

"I feel a bit useless with the gnomes working, and the Micones working, and us not doing anything."

She let her head fall back as she slouched lower in the small chair. "I was thinking how I would like to raise an army of my own and not be a mercenary any longer. My own troops, loyal to me."

"And what would you do with your own army?"

"Make myself a kingdom. Seize an existing one in a weakened state, or carve one out of a larger country." Kitiara looked Sturm in the eye. "What do you think of that?"

He sensed she was baiting him. He merely replied, "Do you think you're up to commanding an entire army?"

She made a fist. "I'm almost an army on my own. With my new strength and my old experience, yes, I'm up to it. Would you like a commission in my guard? You're pretty decent with a sword. If I could break you of your foolish notions of honor, you'd be even better."

"No, thank you, Kit," he spoke seriously. "I have a duty to my heritage. I know that one day in my lifetime, the Knights of Solamnia will recover from their disgrace. I shall be there when they do." He turned away to the wide windows. "And I have other obligations. There's still my father to find. He's alive, I've seen that. He has left a legacy for me at our castle, and I intend to claim it." His voice trailed off.

"Is that your final word?" she asked. Sturm nodded. "I don't understand you. Don't you ever think of yourself?"

"Of course I do. Entirely too much, sometimes."

Kitiara let the tankard dangle from her fingers. "Name an occasion. It can't have been since I've known you."

Sturm opened his mouth to speak, but before he could a shadow fell across the bow of the *Cloudmaster*. Kitiara jumped up. It was the shadow of the dragon.

Will you come out a moment, my friends? he thought at them. Kitiara and Sturm went down the ramp and descended to the obelisk floor.

"What is it?" asked Kitiara.

"I have set the Micones to building a rampart that will impede the tree-folk from entering the obelisk," Cupelix said. He preened himself with a foreclaw, as if proud of his ingenuity.

"I thought you said they didn't dare come in," Sturm said sharply. Cupelix stopped in midpreen.

"That was true of ordinary times, but you, dear fellow, have incited the Lunitarians to overcome their fear of me. Their presence here is proof of that. It does not take deep wisdom to deduce they may soon decide to go where they have never been."

"We can't have that," said Kitiara, folding her arms belligerently.

"No indeed. So I thought you might like to inspect my defenses, as it is your lives they will defend."

Sturm roused the gnomes from their current work, salvaging scraps of wood from the *Cloudmaster* to burn in the forge fire. Everyone trooped to the open door to see what Cupelix had set the Micones doing.

The giant ants were lined up in echelon, parallel to the door of the obelisk. At some invisible, inaudible signal, the Micones lowered their triangular heads to the ground. They pushed the red soil forward in a long heap, and repeated this process many times. Thus they created a trench around the obelisk. The dirt they piled into a high rampart.

"Satisfactory?" asked the dragon from his perch.

Kitiara shrugged and sauntered back to the ship. The gnomes followed in twos and threes as they grew bored with watching the mighty Micones shift the red earth. Soon only Sturm was left. He watched until all the gaps in the rampart were filled. The loose dirt spilled down from the top of the wall, burying the nearest tree-men until only their jagged tops protruded from the crimson soil.

Chapter 22

Keeper
of the New Lives

The forge fire's making showed the party yet
another of Cupelix's powers. With scavenged stones, they
erected a crude hearth. Kitiara, stripped to her shirt and
with her pants legs rolled up, stood by, sweating, as the last
of the stones was put in place.

"Now," she said, "who's got the flint?"

Stutts put his hand out to Wingover. Wingover stared at
the open palm. "Come, come, give me the flint," Stutts said.

"I haven't got the flint," his colleague replied.

"I gave it to you when you went off on your march."

"No, you didn't. Maybe you gave it to one of the others."
A quick poll of the remaining gnomes failed to turn up any
flint.

"This is ridiculous! Who made the fires while we were on our own?" asked Kitiara.

Fitter raised a hand timidly. "Bellcrank," he said.

Stutts clapped a hand to his head. "He had the flint!"

"I think so," said Wingover, looking at his dusty, worn-out shoes.

"Not to worry, little friends," said a voice from above. With amazing silence, Cupelix drifted down the shaft to alight on the nearest ledge. "Fire is what we dragons do best."

Kitiara and the gnomes took shelter in the far corner of the obelisk, after first taking the precaution of dragging the *Cloudmaster* aside as well. Cupelix raised his long, scaly neck and inhaled so sharply that the air shrieked into his nostrils. The gnomes flattened themselves against the wall. Cupelix raked his wing claws back and forth across his brass cheeks, throwing out cascades of sparks. Then Cupelix exhaled, hard, through the fountain of sparks. His breath caught fire with a dull 'whuffing' sound, and streamed down over the kindling. Thick smoke roiled out of the hearth, followed by lighter white smoke, then flame. His great convex chest almost inverted from the exhalation, Cupelix ceased his fire-making. Smoke drifted in the still air, rising to hidden heights of the tower.

"Come along," said Stutts. With a cheer, the gnomes hurried to their tools. They laid out all the scrap metal they'd liberated from Rapaldo's horde—copper tree nails and iron brackets, bronze chain and tin buckets. All of it was going under the hammer, to be recast and reforged into engine parts. The interior of the obelisk rang with the sound of steel and iron melding together. The firelight cast distorted, monstrous shapes on the marble walls. The monsters were the gnomes, toiling around the fire.

Kitiara slipped past the busy little men and went outside. The cool air washed over her like a splash of fresh water. Over the head-high wall that the Micones had built she could see the cold stars. Faint streaks of haze crossed the sky, lit by a distant light source. She walked slowly around the obelisk's massive base and found Sturm, gazing up at the blue-white splendor of Krynn.

"Rather pretty," she said, stopping behind him.

"Yes, it is," he said noncommittally.

"I keep wondering if we will ever get back there."

"We will. I feel it, here." Sturm tapped his chest. "And it is confirmed by these visions of mine. They seem to show the future."

Kitiara managed a mildly crooked grin. "You didn't happen to see me on Krynn while you were perusing the future, did you? I'd like to know that I'll make it back, too."

Sturm tried to summon up an image of Kit from his memory. All he got for his effort was a stabbing pain in the chest. He coughed and said, "I'm worried, Kit. Are we right to deal with this dragon? The gods and heroes of ancient times were wise—they knew men and dragons could not coexist. That's why the beasts were killed or banished."

Chill forgotten, Kitiara planted a foot in the rising bank of red soil. "You surprise me," she said. "You, who are educated and tolerant of most creatures, advocating hatred for all dragons, even one of good lineage, like Cupelix."

"I'm not advocating hatred. I just don't trust him. He wants something from us."

"Should he help us for nothing?"

Sturm tugged fitfully at the ends of his mustache. "You just don't see, Kit. Anyone with power, be he dragon, goblin, gnome or human, is not going to relinquish that power merely to help others. That's the evil of power, and anyone or anything who has it is tainted by it."

"You're wrong!" she said with verve. "Wrong! A cruel man is cruel no matter what his station in life; but many dragons skilled in magic were aligned with good. It is the heart and soul that are the seats of good or evil. Power is something else. To have power is to live. To lose it is to exist as something less than you are."

He listened to this short tirade in mute astonishment. Where was the Kit he once knew, the fun-loving, passionate woman who could laugh at danger? The Kit who carried herself with the pride of a queen, even when she had only a few coppers in her pocket?

"Where is she?" he said aloud. Kitiara asked him what he meant. "The Kit I knew in Solace. The good companion.

The friend."

Hurt and anger flowered in her eyes. "She is with you."

He could sense the anger radiating from her, like heat from a hearthstone. She turned and disappeared around the corner of the obelisk.

*　　*　　*　　*　　*

The gnomes forged a massive lever switch of iron and copper, and converted the rest of the scrap into huge couplings that could be clamped over the severed cables in the *Cloudmaster* and closed by great iron hooks. This work took most of the night, and when it was done, Rainspot precipitated a short shower inside the obelisk to quench the fire and dispel the pall of smoke that hung over everything. Cupelix watched it all from his perch, never questioning, hardly even moving for nine and a half hours. Afterward, the tired gnomes climbed the ramp into the ship for a rest, leaving Cupelix to admire their work.

Sturm looked over the metalwork, too, as he idly ate his supper of dried spear plant and cold beans. Cupelix teased him with magically produced haunches of roast pig and pitchers of sweet cream, but Sturm stolidly ignored the proffered treats.

"You're a stubborn fellow," said the dragon, as Sturm continued to munch his meager fare.

"Principles are not to be cast aside whenever they become inconvenient," he replied.

"Principles don't fill an empty belly."

"Nor does magic salve an empty heart."

"Very good!" exclaimed Cupelix. "Let us trade proverbs that contradict each other; that's a worthy entertainment."

"Some other time. I'm not in the mood for games," said Sturm with a sigh.

"Ah, I see the fair face of Mistress Kitiara in this," said the dragon with a mischievous lilt in his voice. "Do you pine for her, my boy? Shall I put in a good word for you?"

"No!" Sturm snapped. "You really are quite irritating sometimes."

"Inasmuch as I've had no one to talk to for nearly three

millennia, I admit my etiquette is sorely underdeveloped. "Still," said Cupelix, "this presents you with the opportunity to inform me. I would be as polite and genteel as a knight. Will you teach me?"

Sturm stifled a yawn. "It isn't manners or gentility taught by the fireside that makes a knight. It's long study and training, living by the Oath and the Measure. Such things cannot be taught in light conversation. Besides, I doubt that you genuinely want to learn anything; you're just looking for diversion."

"You're so untrusting," said Cupelix. "No, don't deny it! I can hear it in your mind before you speak. How can I convince you of my true good will, Sir Doubter?"

"Answer me this: Why are you, a fully grown brass dragon, permanently confined to this tower, on this strange and magic-ridden moon?"

"I am Keeper of the New Lives," said Cupelix.

"What does that mean?"

The dragon darted his snaky neck from side to side, as though looking for nonexistent eavesdroppers. "I guard the repository of my race." When Sturm continued to look blank, Cupelix said loudly, "Eggs, my dear, ignorant mortal! The eggs of dragons lie in caverns beneath this obelisk. It is my task to watch over them and protect them from insensate brutes like yourself." His great mouth widened in a grin. "No offense intended, of course."

"None taken."

Sturm looked at the floor, light red and veined with dark wine streaks. He tried to imagine the nest of dragon eggs below, but he could not grasp it.

"How do they come to be here? The eggs, I mean," he said.

"I do not know for certain. I was born here, you see, and grew from dragonlet to maturity within these walls. Out of eggs, mine was chosen to hatch and live as guardian, as the Keeper of the New Lives."

Sturm's mind boggled. He lowered himself to the floor. "Who deposited the eggs and built the tower?" he asked.

"I have a theory," said Cupelix, consciously mimicking the gnomes. "Three thousand years ago, when dragons were banished from Krynn, the evil ones were driven by Paladine to the Great Nullity, the negative plane, where they were to remain until doomsday. The dragons aligned with the forces of good left the lands of man as well. Paladine made a pact with Gilean, a neutral god who was sympathetic to our plight, and arranged for a number of good dragon eggs to be collected and deposited here, to serve as sentinels for when the evil ones returned. He caused the tower to be raised and hatched me."

"How many types of dragon eggs lie below?"

"Some of the brass, bronze, and copper clans, in the number of 496. It is the collected spirit of these unborn dragons that provides the magic that saturates Lunitari."

"Four—" Sturm shifted on his haunches, as if he could feel the movement of so many creatures below the thick marble slab. So many!

"When will they hatch?" asked Sturm.

"Tomorrow or never." Sturm pressed for a better answer, and Cupelix said, "A veil of dormancy laid down by Gilean lies over the entire cache. It will take a god, or a mighty spell, to lift the veil and cause the eggs to hatch. Now you know all about me," added Cupelix. "Do you trust me?"

"Almost. Could I see the eggs?"

Cupelix scratched his shiny chest with one of his foreclaws and Sturm winced at the screeching sound. "I don't know about that—"

"Don't you trust me?" asked Sturm.

"A true touch, mortal! You shall see them then, a sight no mortal eye has ever beheld. Hmm." The dragon lifted one tree-sized leg and flexed his birdlike toes. "I'll have to warn the Micones. They live in the caverns and keep the eggs clean, turning them every day so the yolks don't settle. They would certainly slay you if you ventured down there without my permission." Cupelix settled again and fluffed out his wings. "I will inform the Micones, but you must be sure not to touch the eggs. The protective instinct runs so deeply in them that not even my intervention would prevent the Micones from ripping you limb from limb if you touched an egg."

"I'll keep that in mind," said Sturm. He stood to go. "May I invite the others?"

"Why not? I'm sure the little men will be fascinated."

"Thank you, dragon."

Sturm nodded and made for the quiet ship. Once the human was inside, Cupelix spread his wings and telepathically ordered the illuminating ants to cease their glow. The light went out of their bodies, and one by one the Micones dropped off and scuttled back into their holes in the floor.

Kitiara re-entered the darkened obelisk. "Where is everybody?" she called out.

"In the flying machine," said Cupelix, unseen above her in the shadows. She flinched at the sound of his voice.

"You should give a person warning that you're there," she chided. "Is there anything left to eat?"

A table, set with candles, appeared before her. Delicate cutlets of veal, bread, and melted sweet butter awaited her. A tall, clear glass goblet brimmed with rich red wine. Kitiara pulled out the velvet-cushioned, high-backed chair and sat down.

"What's the occasion?" she asked.

"No occasion," replied the dragon from on high. "A gesture of friendship."

"Are we friends?" said Kitiara, forking up a slice of veal.

"Oh, yes, and I hope we shall be better friends still."

"A woman could do worse," she said, sipping the wine. It wasn't grape wine at all, but some sort of berry, tart and cleansing on the tongue. "Good," she said, not quite sure how else to characterize the wine.

"I'm glad you like it. It's pleasing to me to do things for you, Kitiara. May I call you Kitiara? You appreciate my little gifts. Unlike that Brightblade fellow. He's so stiff and proper, it's a wonder he doesn't chip himself when he shaves." Kitiara laughed at the dragon's very apt image.

"You have a very charming laugh," said Cupelix.

"Careful," she said. "If I were less mindful, I'd think you were trying to cozen me."

"I merely delight in your company." There was a heavy rustle as the dragon flew from one side of the obelisk to the other. The candle flames on Kitiara's table wavered in the disturbed air.

"Soon Master Brightblade and his gnomish companions

will make a descent into the caverns below the tower," Cupelix said, and further explained about the cache of dragon eggs. "While they are down there, I should like you to visit me in my private sanctum." The bulk of the brass dragon dropped from the darkness, landing with infinite grace and lightness in front of Kitiara's table.

"What for?" she said, not quite suppressing the catch in her throat.

Up close—at a range of no more than six feet—Cupelix's eyes were green orbs three hands wide. The vertical black pupils were cracks into the deepest abyss. His eyes narrowed as the dragon scrutinized the woman.

"I would hear of your life and philosophy, and you may pry into my secrets as well," he said. "Only don't tell the others. It would make them jealous."

"Not a word," Kitiara said. She winked at the dragon, and Cupelix flicked his tongue out. It touched her hand and a warm tingle spread up her arm.

"Until then." Cupelix spread his wings until they whisked the far walls. He sprang off the floor with one thrust of his powerful hind legs and vanished into the darkness above.

Kitiara's heartbeat slowly resumed its normal rhythm. The tingle in her arm slowly faded. Kitiara reached for her wine glass. To her surprise, her hand was shaking so much that she knocked the goblet off the table, and it shattered on the red marble floor.

"Damn!" she said, clenching her fist.

Chapter 23

Caverns Deep

The gnomes responded to Cupelix's invitation with characteristic enthusiasm. The new metal parts for the *Cloudmaster* had to cool a while longer before they could be fitted into place, and the proposed descent into the caverns suited them very well. They turned the ship upside down hunting for proper equipment: pens and paper, of course; rope and tape measures; and transits for surveying the layout of the caverns. Cutwood brought out a large balance scale to weigh representative specimens of dragon eggs.

"Oh, no," Sturm warned. "No one is to touch the eggs, not the least little bit."

"But why?" asked Rainspot, who was wearing his oilcloth slicker full-time now.

"The Micones are under orders to kill anyone who touches them," Sturm said. "Not even Cupelix can countermand that order." Cutwood reluctantly abandoned his scale.

Two hours before dawn, Sturm and the gnomes presented themselves before one of the large, round holes in the obelisk floor. Cupelix was poised on his ledge above them, and Kitiara lingered in the doorway, watching the comic marshaling of the gnome explorers. Some of them, particularly Fitter, were so laden with gear that they could scarcely stand. Sturm's only special item was a long hank of rope, secured at one shoulder and draped across his chest.

"I hope you don't intend to climb down," said the dragon mildly. "The way presents many difficulties."

"How else shall we get down there?" asked Stutts.

"By allowing the Micones to take you."

Sturm's eyes narrowed. "How will they do that?"

"It's very simple," said Cupelix. He shut his mouth and lowered his head, as he usually did when communicating telepathically with the ants. Hard, armored heads appeared in all the holes, and before Sturm could protest six Micones presented themselves to the exploration party. "The ants are quite capable of carrying two gnomes apiece, and the sixth will be Master Brightblade's mount."

Sturm turned to Kitiara. "Are you certain you won't change your mind and go with us?"

She shook her head. "I've explored enough of this moon, thank you."

The gnomes were already scrambling over their mounts, measuring, touching, and tapping the crystalline creatures from mandible to stinger. The glass-smooth ants presented no footholds or handholds for mounting and riding. After some discussion (cut short by Sturm's impatient sigh), the gnomes tied lengths of rope together into reasonable halters and bridles. The Micones stood stock-still through all this indignity. Even their restless antennae were motionless.

Flash bent down on his hands and knees and Stutts stepped on his back to reach his seat on the Micone. He was still too short to reach the ant's arched thorax. Sighter tried to boost Stutts up. He planted both hands and one shoulder in the seat of Stutts's pants and shoved with all his might. Stutts rose up the curving carapace of crystal, up and up—

and over. He slid headfirst over the ant's body and thumped down on the other side. Fortunately, something soft broke his fall. It was Birdcall.

Sturm made a stirrup loop in his rope and levered himself onto the creature's back. "It's like sitting on a statue," he said, wiggling to situate himself. "Cold and hard."

The gnomes emulated Sturm's rope stirrup, and with only a few minor bruises, managed to mount their ants. The pairs were Stutts and Flash, Birdcall and Sighter, Cutwood and Rainspot, Roperig and Fitter (naturally), with Wingover by himself.

"How do we steer these things?" Cutwood muttered. The makeshift halter ran around the giant ant's neck, but there was no way to control an animal that didn't breathe.

"There's no need for that," said the dragon. "I have told them to take you to the cavern, wait there, and bring you back. They will not deviate from my instructions, so don't try to get around them. Hold on and enjoy the ride."

"Ready, colleagues?" asked Stutts, with a wave.

"Ready!" "We're ready!" "Let's go!" were the replies. Sturm wrapped the rope around his clenched fist and nodded. The Micones were set in motion, and they were off.

The giant ant below Sturm was rock steady on its six spindly legs, though its side-to-side motion was a bit odd to him, who was used to the up-and-down gait of a four-footed horse. Sturm's feet were only a few inches off the floor, but the Micone bore him strongly to the nearest hole. He expected the ant to enter and descend like a man going down a spiral stair, but no. The creature entered the hole headfirst and kept bending, tipping Sturm farther and farther forward. He leaned down until his chest was pressed against the ant's domed back and clamped his arms and legs around its body. The Micone walked down the hole's vertical wall and emerged, upside down, in the vaulted cavern below, with the astonished Sturm hanging on for all he was worth.

The gnomes' mounts entered the same way, and the squeals of delight and terror that followed rang off the milky, china blue walls. Huge stalactites, thirty and forty feet long and ten feet wide at their bases, reached down to the floor. The pale blue formations shone with a dim light of their own. The walls and ceiling (which Sturm found himself staring at) were likewise encrusted with a coating of the hard blue-white crystal. It looked as smooth as ice, but the ants' barbed feet clung tenaciously to it and never slipped.

Sturm's mount followed a well-worn path amid the cold spires. The Micone walked thirty yards across the cavern's ceiling, then abruptly turned and descended straight down the wall. A hundred feet below, the ant righted itself and moved across the cavern floor, which was littered with what resembled large scraps of old parchment and red leather. This debris was kicked up around the ants' feet until they halted in a precise straight line, directly below the holes in the obelisk floor, now high above their heads. All around them the vaulted cavern glowed with faint luminescence. It was like Solinari in wane, but glowed from all directions and cast no shadows.

* * * * *

When Sturm and the gnomes had departed for the caverns, Kitiara waited nervously by the bow of the *Cloudmaster*. The gnomes' shrieks—half delight, half terror—faded as the ants carried them into the hollows below. Cupelix alighted on the floor beside the flying ship. "Well, my dear, are you ready?" asked the dragon.

Kitiara bit her lip and rubbed the palms of her hands on her sleeves. "Sure," she said. "How do I get up there?"

"The simplest way is for me to carry you."

She eyed him uncertainly. Cupelix's forelegs were small compared to his massive hind legs, which could easily crush an ox. Noting her hesitation, the dragon said, "If you climb upon my back and sit astride my neck, I'll fly very carefully to the top of the tower." So saying, he laid his chin on the cold floor. Kitiara threw one leg over the beast's long, sinewy neck. His scales were as cold and hard as she'd thought they would be. They were living flesh, but felt very much like true brass. Cupelix raised his head, and Kitiara felt taut muscles surge under the burnished scales. She leaned forward and grasped the edges of two scales to secure a grip, as Cupelix spread his wings and launched straight into the air.

The obelisk walls were square on its lowest third. Where one particularly heavy platform ringed the walls, they slanted inward, constricting the dragon's movement. Cupelix flared his wings and grabbed hold of the ledge with his powerful hind legs. He hopped sideways, sliding his four-toed feet along the sill, which was deeply worn by centuries of such movement. Kitiara looked over the dragon's shoulder and down. The *Cloudmaster* looked like a toy, and the holes that had so recently swallowed Sturm and the gnomes were mere ink blots on a crimson page.

Cupelix reached a horizontal pillar that crossed from the north ledge to the east side. He sidled on out onto this until he was almost centered in the shaft again. "Hold on!" he said, and leaped.

There was not enough room that high to allow him to fly, so he kept his wings furled. Cupelix leaped thirty yards up, to where the obelisk was very cramped indeed.

Kitiara opened her eyes. The floor, four hundred feet below, was a vague pink square. Above, the obelisk came to an abrupt end at a flat stone ceiling. She tightened her hold on the dragon's neck. A shiver ran through the great elephantine body.

"You're tickling me," he said, in a very undragonlike manner. A wickedly hooked claw set on the leading edge of Cupelix's right wing nudged against her. It scraped along the spot where Kitiara had held on, scratching the ticklish spot.

"Are you going to do any more jumping?" she asked, trying not to let her anxiety show in her voice.

"Oh, no, from here on it's all climbing."

By claw and muscular leg, the dragon climbed the remaining few yards with deft deliberation. He stopped when his horned head bumped the flat ceiling separating them from the obelisk's uppermost section. Kitiara expected him to utter some magic word that would open the way, but instead Cupelix planted his angular head against a stone slab and pushed. His neck bowed under the pressure, and Kitiara was pinned between the massive wing muscles. She was about to protest when a large section of the slab gave way grudgingly. Cupelix shoved it upward until it stood on edge. He lowered his neck, and Kitiara dismounted inside the dragon's inner sanctum. Her feet slipped on the marble, and for a second the distant floor below seemed ready to rush to her. Kitiara stepped farther away from the opening and breathed a silent sigh of relief.

"*Arryas shirak!*" said the dragon. A globe fully eight feet across, set in the very apex of the obelisk roof, blazed with light. The details of Cupelix's lair leaped out at her: heaps of old books and scrolls, candle stands, censers, braziers, and other magical apparatus all wrought in heavy gold; four tapestries covered the walls, tapestries so old that the lowest edges were crumbling to dust. One hanging, fifteen feet wide by fifteen feet high, showed Huma the Lancer astride a fire-breathing dragon, impaling a denizen of the Dark Queen's domain. The hero's armor was worked in gold and silver thread.

The second great tapestry was a map of Krynn. It showed not only the continent of Ansalon as Kitiara knew it, but other land masses to the north and west.

The third hanging showed a conclave of the gods. They were all there, the good, the neutral, and the evil, but the image that truly arrested her was that of the Dark Queen. Takhisis stood apart from the assembled gods of good and neutrality, regal and scornful. The weaver had made her not only beautiful, but also terrible, with scaly legs and a barbed tail. As Kitiara moved past the great figure, the expression on the Dark Queen's face was by turns cruel, contemptuous, bitter, and bewitching. Kitiara might have stood there forever staring at her, had not Cupelix levered the stone slab back into place, restoring it for a floor. The several tons of marble thunked down, and broke Kitiara's trance.

The last tapestry was the most enigmatic. It was a depiction of a balance, like the constellation Hiddukel, except that this scale was unbroken. In the right pan of the scales was an egg. On the left was the silhouette of a man. Cupelix clomped across the slab, his nails clicking on the stone.

"Do you understand the picture?" he asked.

"I'm not sure," Kitiara replied. "What sort of egg is that supposed to be?"

"What kind do you think it is?"

"Well, if it's a dragon egg, then I guess the picture represents the world in balance between humans and dragons—as long as the dragons are just eggs."

Cupelix said, "That's very good. It's also the most obvious interpretation. There are many others."

"Who made the hangings?"

"I don't know. The gods, perhaps. They were here before I was." The dragon went to the largest pile of books and lay back against them, drawing his tail around in front. Kitiara cast about for a convenient place to sit. She upended a black iron cauldron inlaid with silver runes and sat on that.

"So here I am," she said. "Why did you want to talk with me especially?"

"Because you are different from the others. The man Sturm, I enjoy debating, but one can talk to him for five minutes and know his entire mind. He is very plain-spoken and single-minded, isn't he?"

She shrugged. "He's a good fellow when he doesn't inflict his narrow values on others. It's hard to like him sometimes."

"And love?" asked the dragon slyly.

"Hardly! Oh, he's not bad looking, well made and all, but it'll take a different sort of woman from me to capture Sturm Brightblade's heart."

Cupelix cocked his head to one side. "In what way?"

"Innocent. Unworldly. Someone who fits his knightly version of purity."

"Ah," said the dragon. "A female untainted by lust."

Kitiara smiled crookedly. "Well, not completely."

"Ha!" Cupelix gave a hoot of laughter, thumping a six-foot stack of tomes. Dust puffed from between the yellowed vellum pages. "That's what I like about you, my dear; you're so frank, yet unpredictable. I've not yet been able to read your mind."

"But you've tried?"

"Oh, yes. It's important to know what dangerous mortals are thinking."

Kitiara laughed. "Am I dangerous?"

"Very. As I explained, Master Brightblade is an open book to me, and the gnomes' thoughts fly about like mad butterflies, but you—you, my dear Kitiara, bear much watching."

"The time has come for you to answer some questions

frankly, dragon," she said, planting her hands on her knees. "What is it you want from us? From me?"

"I told you," said Cupelix, twisting his neck from side to side. "I want to leave this tower and go to Krynn. I'm sick of being cooped up in here, with no one to talk to and nothing to eat but the leavings the Micones can scrounge for me."

"You feed us quite well," Kitiara objected.

"You do not understand the essential formula of magic. A small amount of matter can be changed by a large amount of energy—that is how it is done. What you consider a large meal would not be a snack for me."

"You're big and strong," she said. "Why don't you claw your way out?"

"And bring the stones down upon my head?" Cupelix preened his purplish cheeks. "That would hardly accomplish my purpose. Besides," his eyes narrowed vertically, "there is a *geas*, a magical prohibition against my damaging the structure. I have tried many times, using many formulae, to convince the Micones to demolish the tower, but they would not. There is a higher power at work here, which requires the attention of a third force to overcome. Your ingenious little friends are that third force, my dear. Their fertile little brains can conceive a hundred schemes for every one you or I may devise."

"And none of them practical."

"Really? You surprise me again, dear mortal girl. Did these same gnomes not get you to Lunitari in the first place?" She objected that that had been an accident.

"Accidents are only unexpected probabilities," said the dragon. "They can be encouraged."

When Cupelix said that, Kitiara looked over her left shoulder and saw the Dark Queen glaring down haughtily from her tapestry. "What," she began before taking her eyes off the mesmerizing visage, "will you do if we can get you out of here?"

"Fly to Krynn and take up residence there, of course. I am very keen to sample the mortal world with all its gaudy and vigorous life." She gave a derisive snort. "Why do you do that?" asked Cupelix.

"You think life on Krynn is strange! What do you call the

creatures who dwell around you?" she said.

"To me, they are normal. They are all I have known, you see, and they bore me. Have you ever tried to talk philosophy with a tree-man? One might as well talk to a stone. Did you know that the vegetable life that grows on Lunitari is so feeble and transient it has no magical aura of its own? It is only because of the pervasive force of my egg-bound compatriots that there is life here at all." Cupelix mustered a massive sigh. "I want to see oceans and forests and mountains. I want to converse with wise mortals of every race, and so increase my knowledge beyond the boundaries set by these ancient books."

Now she understood. "You want power," said Kitiara.

Cupelix clenched his foreclaw into a fist. "If knowledge is power, then the answer is yes. I ache to be free of this perfect prison. When my Micone scouts discovered the gnomes' flying ship, for the first time I hoped that I might escape."

Kitiara was silent for a moment. Choosing her words carefully, she said, "Do you fear retribution, should you escape?"

The dragon's head pulled back in surprise. "Retribution from whom?"

"Those who made the obelisk. If a prison stands, then there likely is a warden somewhere."

"The gods sleep. Gilean the Gray Voyager, Sirrion, and Reorx have laid down the reins of destiny. The way is clear for action. The very fact of your voyage to Lunitari bears this out. In the days of Huma, such a thing would not have been tolerated," Cupelix said.

The gods sleep, Kitiara mused. The way is clear for action! These thoughts stirred deep within her. It must be true; a dragon would know.

"Tell me your thoughts," Cupelix said. "I grow uneasy when you are so quiet."

A daring notion began to form in her head. "Have you considered what you will do once you reach Krynn?" she asked. "Your books are old. You could use a guide."

"Do you have anyone in mind, my dear?"

"Few know Ansalon as I do," Kitiara replied. "My travels have taken me far. Together we could tour the world and reap what benefits would come to us." She looked the dragon in the eye. "As partners."

Cupelix wheezed and whistled like a boiling teapot. He clapped his forearms against his sides. He really was quite good at parodying human gestures.

"Oh, my dear woman! You wound me with mirth! I am killed!" he exclaimed.

Kitiara frowned. "Why do you laugh?"

"You speak of partnership with a dragon as casually as I speak of my servants, the Micones. Do you imagine that you and I are equals? That is a rich jest indeed!" Cupelix rocked so hard with merriment that he banged his head sharply on the wall behind him. That calmed him, but Kitiara was already offended. She sprang to her feet.

"I wish to leave!" she exclaimed. "I see no reason to sit here and be laughed at!"

"Sit down," Cupelix said genially. When she struck a defiant pose, the dragon swept his tail in behind her, and down she went to the marble floor.

"Let us be clear about one thing, my dear girl: On the scale of life, I sit far higher than you. And I will have good manners from my guests, yes?" Kitiara rubbed her bruised posterior and said nothing. "Face-to-face with one of the greatest creatures that ever existed, you are insolent. What makes you so proud?

"I am what I have made myself," Kitiara said tersely. "In a world where most are ignorant peasants, I made myself a warrior. I take what I can and give when I like. I don't need you, dragon. I don't need anyone!"

"Not even Tanis?" Kitiara's face darkened dramatically. "Be at ease. Even your mortal friend Sturm could have heard your heart cry out his name just then. Who is this man, and why do you love him?"

"He's half-elf, not human, if you must know." Kitiara took a deep breath. "And I don't love him!"

"Indeed? Can my sense for such things be so wrong? I would hear the tale of Tanis," Cupelix said. He curled back his lips in a waggish imitation of a human smile. "Please?"

"You only want to hear so you can mock me."

"No, no! Human relationships fascinate me. I need to understand."

Kitiara slipped back onto the overturned cauldron. She gazed into space, marshaling images of her past. "I'd like to understand Tanis myself," she said. "Being a woman in a man's game—war—throws you in with all sorts of men. Most of them are a scurvy lot of bullies and cutthroats. In my younger days, I must have fought a hundred duels with men who tried to push me around, take advantage of me, until I became as hard and cold as the blade I carried." Kitiara fingered the hilt of her sword. "Then came Tanis.

"I was on my way back to Solace one autumn a few years back. The summer campaigning season was done, and I'd been paid off by my most recent commander. With a pocket full of silver, I rode south. In the forest, I was ambushed by a pack of goblins. An arrow took out my horse, and I was thrown down. The goblins came out of the brush with axes and clubs to finish me off, but I lay in wait for them. When they got close, I was on them before they could blink. I killed two right away and settled down to toy with the last pair. Goblins are startlingly bad thieves and even worse in stand-up combat. One of them tripped and managed to impale itself on its own weapon. I carved my mark on the last one, and it screamed its bloody head off. I was ready to finish the pest, when out of the bushes bounded this beautiful fellow with a bow. He scared me for a second. I thought he was with the goblins. Before I could move, he'd put a gray-goose shaft into the last goblin. It was then I realized he thought he was rescuing me."

She paused, and the ghost of a smile played about her lips. "It's funny, but at the time I was mad. That goblin was mine to kill, you see, and Tanis had taken that away from me. I went after him, but he stood me off long enough for the blood-anger to leave me. How we laughed after that! He made me feel good, Tanis did. No one had done that for a long, long time. Sure, we were lovers soon enough, but we were more than that. We rode and hunted and played pranks together. We lived, you understand? *We lived.*"

"Why did this love not continue?" asked Cupelix quietly.

"He wanted me to stay in Solace. I couldn't do that. I tried to get him to go on the road with me, but he wouldn't fight for pay. He's half-elf, as I said; some rogue mercenary molested his elf mother to conceive him, and he's ever had a cold place in his heart for soldiers." Kitiara made a fist. "If Tanis had fought by my side, I would never have left him till the last drop of blood spilled from my body."

She slapped her knee. "Tanis was great fun, and in that he was far better as a companion than Sturm, who's always serious, but the time came when I had to choose between his way of living and mine. I chose, and here I am."

"I'm glad," said Cupelix. "Will you help liberate me?"

"Back to that, are we? What is it worth to you?"

Cupelix raised his ears, making the veined webbing behind them stand up. "Don't you worry about your own safety?" he asked in a rumbling voice.

"Don't bluff me, dragon. If you were going to use threats, you'd have threatened Stutts, Birdcall, and Flash before we got here. You can't force us to help. You're not the sort of dragon to do it."

The dragon's threatening posture collapsed, and the theatrical menace left his voice. "True, true," Cupelix said. "You are a razor, Kit. You cut deep with little effort."

Kitiara flipped a hand in salute, mockingly. "I'm not new to the game of threat and bluff," she said, standing. A slim band of new light fell across her shoulder from a slit window in the obelisk wall. "Consider what I said about partnership, dragon. It needn't be for life, just a year or two. Do that for me, and I'll speak for you."

Sunlight brightened the room. The magic globe at the ceiling's apex dimmed and went out. By the natural light, Kitiara could see that the dragon's books and scrolls were more decayed than she thought. The tapestries were rotten, too. In the midst of this decay, the dragon's predicament was more obvious. Someday, Cupelix would have nothing to read or study but a heap of mildewed pulp.

"How many more centuries will you live?" Kitiara asked.

The dragon's eyes narrowed. "A great many."

"Well, maybe someone else will show up and help you escape. But think how lonely it will be. Soon no more books, no tapestries, no company."

"Partnership . . . one year?" said Cupelix.

"Two years," Kitiara said firmly. "A very short span in the

life of a dragon."

"True, true." Cupelix gave his word that he would travel with Kitiara for two years upon their return to Krynn.

She stretched, smiling expansively. Kitiara felt good. She would come out of this crazy voyage to the red moon with more than increased muscle power. A dragon, a living dragon, as her companion for two whole years!

"It'll be a great adventure," she said to him.

Cupelix snapped his jaws. "Indubitably."

Kitiara went to the window to take in the fresh air. Lightning crackled from the obelisk peak as the magic essence discharged into the red moon's sky. When the flashes ended, Kitiara looked down at the valley below.

"The Lunitarians are moving!" she exclaimed.

"Of course; it's day, their time to move," said Cupelix.

"But they're forming ranks! I think they're going to attack!"

* * * * *

The Micones showed no signs of moving, so Sturm announced that they'd best proceed on foot. The gnomes were already untied and sliding off the backs of their mounts. Sturm got down and patted the Micone on the head, a habit he'd always had since owning his first horse. The giant ant cocked its wedge-shaped head and clacked its mandibles together. A response of pleasure? Sturm wondered. It was hard to tell.

The rubbish around them was knee-deep to Sturm and chest-deep to the gnomes. Sturm found Sighter examining a piece of the red leather with his magnifying glass.

"Hm, doesn't look like vegetable material," said Sighter. Cutwood tried writing on the soft brown parchment-stuff, but it wouldn't take a pencil mark; it was too soft and supple. Sturm tried to tear a sheet of it in two, but couldn't do it.

"This would make admirable boot tops," he said. "I wonder what it is?"

"I would say it's some form of animal hide," said Sighter, snapping his glass back into its case.

"We haven't found any animals on Lunitari, except the

dragon," Stutts objected. "Even the Micones are more mineral than animal."

"Maybe," Wingover said slowly, "there are other kinds of animals in these caves. Animals we haven't seen before."

Rainspot swallowed audibly. "Gnome-eating animals?"

"Bosh," said Sighter. "The Micones wouldn't allow anything dangerous to live near the dragon eggs. Stop scaring yourselves."

Flash was off a little ways, touching the white crust on the walls. He plucked a tack hammer from his tool-laden belt and butted a cold steel chisel against the wall. Back swung the hammer.

Bong! The little hammer hit the chisel, and the whole cavern reverberated with the sound. So powerful were the vibrations, that the gnomes lost their footing and fell in the thick rubbish. Sturm braced himself against a squat stalagmite until the ringing ceased.

"Don't do that!" Cutwood said plaintively. With his augmented hearing, the tone had been enough to start his nose bleeding. All the Micones were clicking their mandibles and shaking their heads.

"Fascinating," said Stutts. "A perfect resonant chamber! Ah! It makes sense!"

"What does?" asked Roperig.

"This extraneous jetsam. It's padding, to deaden the ants' footsteps on the floor."

They waded though the rubbish toward the end of the oblong chamber. The ceiling level fell and the floor rose to form a tight circular opening. The rim of the opening had been notched with jagged spikes of quartz, probably by the Micones. Anything softer than a giant ant would be cut to pieces if it tried to walk or crawl over the spikes. The gnomes held back and proposed many solutions to the problem of the entrance. Sturm planted his fists on his hips and sighed. He turned back and gathered up an armful of the tough parchmentlike shreds, then laid them across the spikes. He put his hands on the parchment and pushed. The spikes poked through three or four layers, but the top layers remained unpierced.

"Allow me," said Sturm. He lifted Stutts and sat him on

the padding. Stutts slid through the opening to the chamber beyond. One by one, the other gnomes followed. Sturm went last. The gnomes plunged ahead in their bumbling, fearless way, and he had to catch up with them.

Sturm hurried down the narrow slit in the rock and into another large chamber. Here veins of wine red crystal oozed out of fissures in the rock. When the soft crystal touched the warmer, moister air of the cavern, it lightened to clear crimson and began to take more exact form. Around them were dozens of half-formed Micones; some only heads, some whole bodies but without legs, and some so complete that their antennae wiggled.

"So this is the ant hatchery," said Wingover.

"'Hatchery' isn't the right word for it," said Roperig.

"Living rock crystal," said Stutts breathlessly. "I wonder what influences it to take on an ant shape?"

"The dragon, I would think," said Sighter, turning a complete circle to see all the budding Micones. "Remember, he said he tried to make the tree-folk into servants but failed. He must have uncovered this living crystal and decided to use it to make perfectly obedient and hard-working slaves."

They walked in single file down the center of the high, narrow cavern. As before, bluish stalactites on the ceiling shed a weak light on the scene. Flash approached one of the nearly finished Micones and tried to measure the width of its head. The ant moved like lightning and clamped its powerful jaws on the gnome's arm. Flash let out a yell.

"Get back!" Sturm cried, drawing his sword. He tried to lever the jaws open, but the creature's grip was too strong. The cruel saw-toothed jaws could easily cut through flesh and bone—

Sturm noticed that Flash's arm wasn't bleeding. The gnome struggled, beating the stone-hard ant on the head with his flimsy folding rule.

"Has he got you by the arm?" Sturm asked.

"Uh! Agh! Yes! What do you think this is, my foot?"

Sturm eased his hand forward and felt Flash's arm. The Micone's jaws had missed the gnome's flesh. All it had was his jacket sleeve.

"Take your jacket off," Sturm said calmly.

"Uh! Argh! Eee! I can't!"

"I'll help you." Sturm reached in front of the gnome and undid the complex series of buttons and lacings on his jacket. He pulled Flash's left arm out, then his right. The empty jacket dangled in the Micone's jaws. The half-formed Micone did not move.

"My jacket!" Flash howled.

"Never mind! Just thank your gods that your arm didn't get caught in that thing's pincers," Sturm said.

"Thank you, Reorx," said the gnome. He looked longingly at the lost jacket. A big tear rolled down his cheek. "I designed that jacket myself. The One Size Fits All Windproof Jacket Mark III."

"You can make another," Wingover said consolingly. "An even better one. With detachable sleeves, in case you ever get in such a predicament again."

"Yes, yes! What a splendid notion, detachable sleeves!" Flash made a hasty sketch on his white shirt cuff.

Beyond the ant hatchery the cavern wound off in several directions, and there was no clear indication which way the explorers should go. Cutwood suggested that they split up and try all the tunnels, but Stutts vetoed that, and Sturm agreed.

"We've no idea how large this cave is, and if you go off on your own, you stand a good chance of getting lost forever. We also don't know how the Micones will react to us if we split up," Sturm said.

"They do seem very literal-minded," Sighter said. "Separate pairs may not mean the same thing to them as a band of ten." The sight of Flash's jacket locked in the unbreakable grip of the Micone's jaws was a powerful inducement to stay together. Nothing more was said about splitting up.

They chose the widest, straightest path onward. The floor sloped down from the Micones' birth chamber at such a steep angle that the gnomes gave up trying to walk down and instead sat down to slide. Sturm would have preferred to walk down, but the floor was slick with dew, so it didn't take him long to decide to do as the gnomes did.

Sturm slid gently into another, lower cavern. It was very much warmer and wetter here; the air was steamy. Water trickled down the walls and dripped from overhead. As he stood up, he saw the gnomes' dark shapes strolling through the wispy white clouds of steam.

"Stutts! Sighter! Where are all of you?" he called.

"Right here!" Sturm walked uncertainly into the mist. The cavern was well lit from above (from a large number of the glowing stalactites), and considerable heat radiated from the floor.

"Mind the magma," said Cutwood, appearing in the steam in front of him. The gnome pointed to a raised funnel of glazed rock in their path. A fiery halo hung over the wide mouth. Sturm bent over it and saw that the natural bowl was full of a bright orange liquid. A bubble burst wetly in its center.

"Molten rock," Cutwood explained. "That's why the cave is so warm."

Sturm had an almost irresistible urge to touch the bubbling stuff, but the glare of heat on his face told him quite plainly how hot the magma was. Another gnome, Wingover, appeared in the swirling steam.

"This way!" he cried.

They wended their way through a garden of seething cauldrons, each one emitting gurgles as the molten rock boiled. The air around them became sulfurous and hard to take in. Sturm coughed and held a kerchief to his face.

The vapors abated somewhat near the cavern wall. The remaining gnomes were clustered by a small hole in the wall. Sturm raised his head and saw that the hole was dark.

"Is that it?" Sturm wondered aloud.

"Must be," said Sighter. "Seems to be no other way out."

"Perhaps one of the other tunnels we missed," Roperig suggested. The black circle was not very inviting.

"The established path clearly leads here," said Stutts. "As senior colleague, it is up to me to go first—"

"No, you don't," Sturm said. "I'm armed. I'll go first to make sure it's safe."

"Oh, excellent idea!" said Rainspot.

"Well, if you insist—" said Stutts.

"You will need a light," said Flash. He unbuttoned one of the capacious pockets on the front of his trouser legs. "Give me a moment and I'll lend you my Collapsing Self-Igniting

Pocket Lamp Mark XVI." Flash unfolded a flattish box of tin and set it on the floor. From a separate wooden case he extracted a bit of gooey stuff that resembled axle grease. He put a dollop of this in the lamp. From a different pocket, Flash produced a slender glass vial, tightly stoppered. He broke the wax seal and popped the cork. A sharp, volatile aroma filled the cavern. Flash crouched down and extended his arm cautiously to the lamp. One eye clenched shut as a single drop of the fluid fell from the vial.

The droplet hit the plug of grease and went poof! The flash lit up the whole area, and the grease burned merrily. Sturm reached for it, and the lamp popped and sputtered, sending bits of flaming grease in all directions.

"Are you sure this is safe?" he asked.

"Well, after a few minutes, the tin will melt," Flash said. "But it should be all right until then."

"Wonderful." He picked up the violent little lamp by its slim metal ring and started through the hole. The gnomes clustered around the opening, their pink faces and white beards facing upward like so many daisies seeking the sun.

Sturm walked up a curving ramp and soon entered a chamber of profound silence. Even the lamp's sputtering declined to a fitful flicker. He stepped off the ramp and onto the roughly cleared stone floor and beheld a sight that no mortal had seen in millennia.

Dragon eggs. Row upon row of carved niches, each holding a single melon-sized egg. Row after row, tier upon tier, stretching far beyond the feeble range of light from the Collapsing Self-Igniting Pocket Lamp Mark XVI. The lips of each niche glittered with dew, formed when the steamy air below met the cooler air of this chamber.

A gnomish voice drifted to Sturm. "What do you see?"

"This is it," he called back, hand cupped to his mouth. "The great egg chamber!"

The gnomes scrambled up the ramp and spilled into the cavern, jostling past Sturm for a better view. They oohed and aahed and uttered fervent exclamations to their holy trio: Reorx, gears, and hydrodynamics.

"How many eggs do you suppose there are?" breathed Fitter. Sturm shot a glance at Sighter.

"In view, there are eight tiers," said Sighter. "And sixty-two per tier."

"For a total of—" Cutwood figured frantically.

"—496, said Sturm, recalling the figure that Cupelix had given him.

"That's right," said Stutts, totting up his numbers.

They walked forward with Sturm leading. Wingover hovered at the rear, since the lamp dazzled his piercing eyesight. He could see through the velvet darkness, so he was able to keep their entry hole in sight.

"Ow," Sturm muttered, shifting the lamp to his other hand. The ring was getting very hot.

"This way! Turn this way!" said Roperig suddenly. Sturm turned to his left.

"What was it?" he asked.

"Something moved over there. I didn't see it very clearly."

A jet black thing scuttled out of the niche behind the eggs and leaped into the air toward Sturm's light. He recoiled clumsily and dropped the lamp. Something small and furry-feeling brushed over his foot and was gone. The gnomes were all yelling and stamping their feet.

"Silence! Silence, I say!" Sturm roared. He found the lost lamp. Its fuel was almost extinguished. Only a faint corona of blue flame circled the lump of grease. Sturm sheltered the tiny fire with his hands and it grew brighter. He picked up the lamp and faced the gnomes.

They were not scared in the least. Wingover had bounded forward from his place in line and planted his foot on the thing that had burst from the egg niche. It squirmed under his toes, trying to get away. At first sight, it resembled a fat, hairy spider, but as Sturm brought the lamp nearer, they all recognized it.

"It's a glove!" said Stutts.

"One of Kit's gloves," said Sturm, recognizing the pattern of stitching on the back. "It's one of a pair she left behind on the *Cloudmaster* when we went off on our ore expedition."

"How'd it get here?" asked Rainspot. Birdcall twittered a question of his own.

"He says, 'Why is it alive?'" Stutts added.

Rainspot grasped the glove by its 'fingers' and told

Wingover to lift his foot. The weather seer brought the wriggling thing to eye level and grunted. "Strong little thing!"

Sighter glared through his ever-present lens. "This glove is made of cowhide and rabbit fur, but the seams have disappeared." He pressed a finger into the soft leather side. "It has a heartbeat."

"Ridiculous," Flash said. "Gloves don't come to life."

"On Lunitari?" said Stutts. "Why not?"

Sturm remembered Cupelix's remark about the cumulative life force of all the dragon eggs being responsible for the intense aura of magical power on Lunitari. He offered this bit of information to the gnomes.

"Ah," said Sighter with a sage expression. "The level of magical force must be particularly high in these caverns. I dare say, any animal or vegetable product left down here long enough might develop a life of its own."

Roperig looked down at his own pigskin boots. "You mean my shoes might take on life and run away with me?"

"We shan't be down here long enough for that to happen," Stutts assured him.

Rainspot put the glove down on its back and pinned it with his foot. Cutwood suggested that they dissect it to see what internal organs it had.

"Let it go. It's harmless," said Sturm. "We don't have time to fool around with it."

Rainspot raised his foot and the glove flipped over. It scampered into the recesses of the egg niches.

"I wonder," said Flash, "what a living glove eats?"

"Finger food," said Fitter. Roperig cuffed him lightly on the head and his hand promptly stuck there.

"Are you finished?" Sturm said impatiently. "There's more of the cave to see, and I don't think the lamp will last much longer." Indeed, even as he spoke, silver drops of molten tin dripped off the lamp's front end.

They hurried down the tunnel. Sounds of movement came to them and they halted. The rear legs and teardrop abdomen of a working Micone maneuvered out of the darkness. The Micone sensed their light and scuttled around to face the intruders. Its antennae almost straightened while it studied the man and gnomes. Sturm had a momentary flash of fear. If the Micone attacked, his lone sword would never prevail.

The Micone kinked its feelers again and turned away. Sturm and the gnomes let out a collective sigh of relief.

They inched past the giant, who was busy chipping away glassy 'dew' from the shelf below a row of eggs. A fragment of the clear encrustation landed at Rainspot's feet, and he pounced on it. He dropped it in a tiny silk bag and pulled the drawstring. "For later analysis," he said.

The caverns gave no sign of ending, and after penetrating a hundred yards or so into them, Sturm called a halt. The place they stopped was thick with Micones, and the giant ants swept past the explorers without any heed. Cupelix had told the ants to ignore them, and the ants obeyed, in their precise, unswerving way.

"We'd best go back before we get trampled," Sturm said, dodging a flurry of Micone legs.

Rainspot drifted away from the others to where the ants were engaged in cleaning the dragon eggs. As they chipped and anointed and turned the blockish eggs, the ants exposed the undersides of the eggs to the air. Some of the shells had a scabrous layer peeling off, and the ants scrupulously removed this dead layer. It was this cast-off shell that made the parchmentlike skin they'd found in the first chamber. Rainspot picked up a sheaf of cast-offs below the lowest egg shelf. A Micone turned sharply toward him and snatched the leathery shell fragment with its mandibles.

"No!" said Rainspot stubbornly. "It's mine, you threw it away!" The gnome dug in his toes and pulled. The shell wouldn't yield and neither would the ant. Rainspot got angry. His enveloping cloud thickened and lightning flashed within it.

"Rainspot, leave it. We'll take samples from the outer cave," said Wingover. But the Micone's implacable resistance made the usually mild gnome madder and madder. A cyclone four feet wide lashed at the ant, and miniature claps of thunder reverberated through the cave.

Sturm entered Rainspot's tiny tempest. To his surprise, the whirling rain was hot. "Rainspot!" he said, grabbing the little fellow by the shoulders. "Let go!"

A bolt of lightning, diminutive by nature's standards, yet still five feet long, struck the Micone in the center of its head. The strike knocked Sturm and Rainspot backward at least six feet. The gnome landed on Sturm, shook his head, and found that he was holding the scrap of eggshell.

"I have it!" he said triumphantly.

Sturm, flat on his back and not happy, said, "Do you mind?" Rainspot blushed and rolled off the man's stomach.

"Look at that," Cutwood said in awe. The gnomes ringed the lightning-struck ant.

The bolt had split the creature's head in half with the precision of a diamond cutter. The Micone's headless body collapsed, the thorax sagging to the floor. Immediately, two more Micones appeared and began to clean up. They nipped the shattered ant's carcass apart and carried each bit away.

"At least we know they can be killed," said Roperig.

"And our Rainspot did it!" said Fitter. The gentle weather seer was mortified.

"I've never lost my temper like that," he said. "I'm sorry! It was unforgivable. The poor myrmidon was only doing its appointed task, and I killed it."

"You very thoroughly killed it," Sturm said, impressed. "Remind me not to make you angry, Rainspot."

"I hope Cupelix won't be angry," Rainspot said worriedly.

"It wasn't intentional," said Roperig consolingly.

"I doubt any single ant is that important to him," Sturm said. "Now can we go back?"

The lamp failed before they were all up the ramp to the steam chamber. Wingover took the lead and each one held the hand of the person in front of and behind him. They avoided the budding giants in the birthing cave—though Flash cast a longing look at his jacket, still dangling from the Micone's jaws—and soon they were back in the rubbish-filled grand cavern. The six Micones who had brought them were just as they'd left them, unmoved by as much as an inch. Sturm and the gnomes mounted, and without a word or gesture needed, the giant ants lurched into motion.

Chapter 24

Little Fitter's Pants

The dragon, with Kitiara clinging to his neck, dropped like a stone from his lair, flaring out his wings to ease his landing. Kitiara discarded her cloak and reached the notch-shaped doorway just as the Micones bearing Sturm and the gnomes appeared.

"It's about time you got back!" she yelled. "Stand to arms, all of you—the Lunitarians are forming to attack!"

A barrage of glass javelins arced through the doorway to shatter on the marble floor. The gnomes, though curious, retreated under a shower of red glass splinters. The Lunitarians were hooting wildly.

"They mean to have you," Cupelix said. "They're calling for your blood."

"Surely they can't get in?" Rainspot said.

"The tree-men are beyond reason," the dragon replied.

"So they're coming," Sturm said grimly. He shucked off his outer garb and made ready his armor and helmet. Kitiara marched recklessly back and forth before the door, drawing the tree-men's attention.

"Shall we sting them a little?" she said to Sturm.

"It does seem necessary to discourage them," he admitted. To the dragon, he said, "Can you lend us some Micones? They would even the odds for us."

"They would be of little use," said Cupelix. A glass hatchet whistled in and thumped against his scaly belly. It bounced off harmlessly and broke on the floor. Cupelix regarded the ruined weapon idly. "The Micones are almost totally blind in daylight," he said. "If I unleashed them, they would as likely cut you two to pieces as any tree-man."

"Enough talk," Kitiara barked. She hitched her shield up on her forearm. "I'm going to swing some steel!"

Sturm cinched his sword belt tighter. "Kit, wait for me!" He was shieldless, but his mail was heavier than Kit's. He drew his sword and ran to the door.

The tree-men had scaled the earthen rampart turned up by the Micones and were using its height to gain velocity for their spear casts. Kitiara held her shield to her face as missile after missile crashed against it. "C'mon, you bark-covered devils!" she shouted. "Throw on! Kitiara Uth Matar is coming for you!"

She started up the slope. It was hard going, what with the steep angle and the loose soil. Sturm, more circumspect, worked his way around the obelisk to where the rampart was not so steep. He gained the top at nearly the same time Kitiara did, though there were forty yards and twenty-odd tree-men between them.

Sturm had to fence with the Lunitarians on the mound and dodge spears hurled from the ground below. The Lunitarians were hooting at the top of their voices, and it didn't take much imagination to see the anger distorting their simple faces.

Kitiara plowed into a trio of tree-men, all of whom towered over her. She did little more than inflict deep chips on them with her sword. She did catch one tree-man with his arm down, and lopped it off with a single stroke. The severed limb hit the ground and crawled about, seeking its former owner. It got tangled up in Kitiara's legs, and she tripped, falling backward amid a flurry of spear thrusts.

The tree-men converged on the fallen woman, and Sturm could only think that she'd been wounded. He roared at the foe and cut at their backs. Unable to strike through a heart and kill them, he concentrated on their stumpy legs. A glass blade swept over his face. The hot line it left dripped blood. He ignored it. Lunitarians toppled off the dirt wall, rolling down to bowl over their fellows on the ground.

There was a terrible tearing sensation in Sturm's right leg. He looked back and saw a spear embedded in the back of his thigh, blood welling around the already crimson shaft. He swung his sword back, snapping the spear shaft off and leaving the head in his leg. He couldn't see Kitiara at all. He went down, weak from the pain and loss of blood. He slid down the rampart on the side nearest the obelisk. Whooping tree-men skidded after him, shouting their version of his name.

Finished, he thought. This is how it ends—

The expected spear points did not descend on his unarmored face and neck. The sounds of battle raged over him, though he fancied that he heard high-pitched cries of delight and triumph. The gnomes? Surely they hadn't ventured forth. They'd be slaughtered!

The hooting of the berserk Lunitarians receded. Sturm lifted his head with great effort and tried to see what was happening. A tree-man stood atop the rampart, waving his sword before him, trying to ward off some unseen foe. A dark object whipped into view and hit the tree-man in the face, thunk! The Lunitarian disappeared over the rampart amid shouts of gnomish laughter.

Someone turned Sturm over. The red dirt was dusted from his eyes. Kitiara.

"Looks like you caught one," she said in a friendly way. Her face was scratched and her hands cut up, but she was otherwise unhurt.

"Are you well?" he asked weakly. Kitiara nodded and put the neck of her water bottle to his lips. The trickle of rainwater was the most delicious thing he'd ever tasted.

"Ho, Master Sturm! Mistress Kitiara! We have won!" Stutts declared. He stuck his thumbs under his suspenders and threw out his chest. "The Improvised Trouser Flail Mark I was a success!"

"The what?"

"Never mind," Kitiara said. "Let's get you inside." She scooped him up as easily as Sturm would pick up an infant and carried him into the obelisk.

The gnomes were pounding each other on the back and talking as fast and as loudly as they could. Sturm saw a weird contraption to one side of the passage: an upright collection of posts and gears, from which dangled three pairs of gnome-sized pants, stuffed tightly with something heavy, probably dirt. Cupelix was on his lowest perch, watching intently. When he saw that Sturm was wounded, he offered to help treat the injury.

"No magic," Sturm said stubbornly. His whole leg was achingly numb. It was cold, very cold. The dragon's broad brass face swooped down close to his.

"No magic, even if it means your life?" said the polished reptilian voice.

"No magic," Sturm insisted.

Rainspot turned Sturm's face away and put a bitter-tasting root in his mouth. The gnome said, "Chew, please." Confident that he was in the thoroughly non-magical care of the gnomes, Sturm did as he was told. Numbness spread through his body.

He didn't fall asleep. Sturm quite distinctly heard the gnomes consulting over his wound, heard rather than felt the glass spear tip being removed from his flesh, heard the dragon offering advice on how best to close the gaping hole. Then he was lying on his stomach, the numbness gone. Sturm's leg throbbed unmercifully. He lifted himself up on his hands.

"If you say 'where am I?' I'll hit you," said Kitiara genially.

"What happened?" he said.

"You were injured," said Sighter, who was squatting near Sturm's head.

"That I recall well. Who repelled the tree-folk?"

"I wish I could say that I did," Kitiara said.

"We did it," Stutts declared, coming up behind Sighter. Cupelix rumbled something that Sturm couldn't make out. Stutts blanched and said, "With help from the dragon, that is."

"We adapted a gnomeflinger design," Wingover said. He knelt alongside Stutts and peeked over Sighter's shoulder. "We used Cutwood's pants, filled with dirt, as a test subject for flinging. Birdcall suggested hurling the pants at the Lunitarians, but that would have sufficed for only one shot—"

"So me and Roperig gave up ours," said Fitter, who squirmed into view. His striped long johns were eloquent proof of the truth of his statement. "We filled 'em with dirt and tied 'em to the throwing arms—"

"—and used the gear system to pummel the enemy off the wall," Roperig finished for his apprentice.

"Very clever," Sturm admitted. "But why should fiercely angry tree-folk flee when thumped with a few pairs of pants? Why didn't they swarm all over you?"

"That was my doing," said Cupelix modestly. "I wove a spell of illusion over the gnomes and their machine. The Lunitarians saw a huge, flame-breathing red dragon attacking them, its terrible claws snatching them one by one from the rampart. The physical effect, combined with the vivid illusion, was quite effective. The tree-men have fled."

"What's to prevent them from recovering their nerve and coming back?" said Kitiara.

"At sunset, I shall send the Micones to harry them back to their village once and for all."

Their story told, the gnomes dispersed. Sturm called Stutts back to him.

"Yes?" said the senior gnome.

"Have you inspected the repairs on the *Cloudmaster*?"

"Not yet."

"Urge your colleagues forward, my friend. We must be off this world soon," said Sturm.

Stutts stroked his short, silky beard. "What's the hurry? The new engine components ought to be tested first."

Sturm lowered his voice. "The dragon may believe the tree-men will not come back, but I don't want to take the chance of being besieged in here again. Besides Cupelix will—" He closed his mouth when he saw Kitiara coming. "We'll speak later," Sturm finished. Stutts nodded and strolled back to the *Cloudmaster*, his thumbs hooked in his vest pockets. Kitiara paid no attention to his exaggerated nonchalance.

Kitiara dropped down beside Sturm. "Does it hurt much?"

"Only when I dance," he said uncharacteristically.

She snorted. "You'll live," she said. She poked around the bandaged area and added, "Probably won't even have a limp. What made you charge into those tree-men? You weren't carrying a shield or wearing leg armor."

"I saw you go down," he said. "I was going to help you."

Kitiara was silent for a moment. "Thank you."

Sturm gingerly eased himself onto his good side and sat up. "That's better! I was getting a headache lying like that."

"You know what the most unforgivable thing is, don't you? That you and I, two fighters soundly trained in the warrior arts, should fall to a bunch of savages and be saved by a band of nutty gnomes using pants full of dirt as flails!" Kitiara started to laugh. All the tensions and suspicions surfaced and flew away in her laughter. Tears welled in her eyes, and she couldn't stop.

"Little Fitter's pants," Sturm said, feeling the guffaws building deep inside. "Little Fitter's pants disguised as the claws of a red dragon!" Kitiara nodded helplessly, her face contorted with hysterical mirth. Great rolling laughs boomed out of Sturm. His shaking jounced painfully his tightly wrapped wound, but he couldn't stop. When he tried to speak, all he could gasp was "Trouser Flail!" before erupting into fresh gales.

Kitiara leaned against him, forcing herself to breathe in the too-short intervals between new merry convulsions. Her head rested on Sturm's shoulder; she draped an arm around his neck.

Above them, Cupelix perched in a shadowed corner of the tower, a shaft of amber sunlight falling across the enfolding tips of his leathery wings. Illuminated from behind, the brass dragon's skin shone like gold.

*　*　*　*　*

Despite his earlier protests, when Kitiara had brought Sturm a bowl of venison stew that Cupelix had made, he ate without a second glance. There was something more; he accepted her offer to make a backrest out of her fur cloak and blanket. Ordinarily, Sturm would have stoically rejected such treatment.

The gnomes ate heartily, as usual, under the gentle glow of the four Micones who remained behind when the bulk of them went out to chase the Lunitarians away. The ants hung overhead by their forelegs like grotesque paper lanterns, the ominous barbed stingers the only threatening aspect of their otherwise benign posture.

"The new parts showed no sign of cracking or fatigue," Flash said, ladling gravy over his roast. "If we can get a decent charge of lightning, I don't see why we couldn't fly home right away." He tried to set the metal ladle back in its bowl, but it clung to his magnetic hands. Cutwood plucked it off for him.

"You know," Sighter said, stirring his pudding idly, "with the proper angle of flight, we could very likely fly from here to one of the other moons." This option was greeted with thunderous silence. "Solinari or the dark moon. What do you think?"

Birdcall answered for all of them. He put two fingers to his lips and made a very rude noise.

Sighter grumbled, "No need to be insulting."

"The important thing is to return to Mt. Nevermind and announce our success," said Stutts. "Aerial navigation is now a fact, and the gnomish people must not delay in exploring all the possibilities it presents."

Sturm, reclining on the floor by the dinner table, spoke up: "What possibilities do you foresee?"

"Exploring and mapping can be done easily from the air. These would be a boon to navigation. All the heavy work of transport now done by ships could be more efficiently done in the skies. I can see a time when great aerial galleons, with six or eight pairs of wings, ply trade routes in the clouds, bringing goods to and from every corner of Krynn. . . ."

Stutts got quite lost in the grandness of his conception.

"Then there's war," said Sighter ominously.

"What war?" asked Kitiara.

"Any war. There's always a war someplace, isn't there? Can you see the cavalry of the clouds, swooping down to destroy field and farm, town, temple, and castle alike? It would be easy, yes, very easy to fling down fire and stone on the heads of the foe. In the workshops of Mt. Nevermind there are stranger things still. Weapons that require no magic power to destroy the entire world."

His morose vision quelled all conversation. Then, from above, Cupelix said, "It sounds as though you gnomes are planning to create your own race of dragons—mechanical dragons, completely obedient to their master's hand. All those things Master Sighter describes happened a thousand or more years ago, when dragons served in the great wars."

"Perhaps we shouldn't share the secret of aerial navigation," Fitter said hesitantly.

"Knowledge must be shared," Stutts declared. "There is no evil in pure knowledge. It's how it's put to use that determines what good or ill comes of it."

"Knowledge is power," said the dragon, catching Kitiara's eye. She buried her nose in her cup. When it was empty, she set it down on the table with a loud thump.

"We're forgetting one important thing," she said, wiping her lips on the back of her hand. "We owe a debt here. We oughtn't leave without paying it."

"Debt?" said Cutwood. "To whom?"

"Our host," Kitiara replied. "The excellent dragon, Cupelix." The gnomes broke into polite applause.

"Thank you, you're very kind," said the dragon.

"We would long ago have fallen into the hands of the Lunitarians, had it not been for the intervention of Cupelix," Kitiara went on. "Now we're safe, the flying ship is repaired, and we have a debt to pay. How shall we do it?"

"Would you care for some fresh water?" asked Rainspot.

"Kind, but unnecessary," said the dragon. "The Micones bring me water from the cavern depths."

"Do you have any machines to be repaired?" asked Flash thoughtfully.

"None whatsoever."

The remaining gnomes all tried suggestions, which the dragon politely dismissed as unneeded or inapplicable. "What can we do?" said Wingover, frustrated.

Cupelix launched into a compressed description of his situation inside the obelisk, and how he very much wanted to escape it. The gnomes just looked up at him and blinked.

"Is that all?" said Roperig.

"Nothing else?" added Birdcall by translation.

"Just this one simple task," answered the dragon.

Sturm pushed himself up to a seated position, mindful of the pressure this put on his injured leg. "Have you considered, dragon, that a higher power intended for you to live out your life within these walls? Would we be committing an act of impiety by releasing you?"

"The gods raised these walls and brought these many eggs here, but in all the thousands of years I've been resident in the obelisk, no god, demigod, or spirit has deigned to reveal any such divine plan to me," said Cupelix. He shifted from one massive foot to the other. "You seem to think my being kept here like a rooster in a coop is a good thing; can you not see it as I do, that I am in fact a prisoner? Is it an evil deed to free an innocent captive?"

"What will happen to all the dragon eggs if you leave?" asked Roperig.

"The Micones will tend them and guard the caverns forever. No egg will hatch without deliberate inducement. At this point, I am totally superfluous."

"I say we help him," said Kitiara with conviction. She leaned forward to the table and gave each gnome a piercing look. "Who can honestly say the dragon hasn't earned our help?"

All was silent until Sturm said, "I will agree if the dragon answers one question: What will he do once he is free?"

"Revel in my liberty, of course. I shall travel thereafter, wherever the winds of heaven carry me."

Sturm folded his arms. "To Krynn?" he said sharply.

"Why not? Is there a fairer land betwixt here and the stars?"

"Dragons were driven out of Krynn long ago because

their power was used to scheme and control the affairs of mortals. You cannot return to Krynn," Sturm said.

"Cupelix is not an evil dragon," Kitiara argued. "Do you think he could live so long on the moon of neutral magic and not be moderated by its influence?"

"And what if," Sturm said slowly, "Cupelix is no danger to Krynn. He is still a dragon. My ancestors fought and died to rid our world of dragons. How can I dishonor them by aiding a dragon—even a benign one—to return?"

Kitiara stood so suddenly that her chair fell over. "Suffering gods! Who do you think you are, Sturm Brightblade? My ancestors fought in the Dragon Wars, too. It was a different time and different circumstances." She turned to the gnomes. "I put it to you. Shall we repay the dragon's hospitality with indifference? Will we fill our bellies with his food and drink, fix the ship with his help, and depart without so much as attempting to help him be free?"

She had them now. All nine little faces, paler in the short, faint days of Lunitari, were rapt with attention. Kitiara raised her hand to the silent Cupelix, who contrived to look forlorn and desolate atop his marble perch. "Put yourself in his place," she said grandly.

"Which one of us?" asked Cutwood.

"It doesn't matter—any or all of you. Think of how you'd feel, spending all your life inside this tower, unable to even walk outdoors. And consider that a dragon's life is not fifty years, or two hundred years, but twenty times two hundred! How would you feel, imprisoned in a lonely tower, with no one to talk to and no tools either?"

Roperig and Fitter gasped. "No tools?"

"Yes, and no wood or metal to work with. No gears or valves or pulleys."

"Horrible!" said Flash. Birdcall seconded him with a steady descending note.

"And we—you—have the chance to correct this wrong. You have the inventive powers to devise some way to allow Cupelix to fly free. Will you do it?" she asked.

Wingover leaped to his feet. "We will! We will!" Rainspot and Fitter wept for the injustice inflicted on the dragon, while Stutts and Sighter were already bombarding each other with first schemes to open the obelisk. Wingover got up on his chair and then on the table, pointing dramatically to the wingless hull of the *Cloudmaster*.

"To the ship!" he cried. "We must make plans!"

"Yes, yes, the tools are there," said Cutwood.

"And parchment and pencils!"

"Chemicals and crucibles!"

"Rope and rigging!"

"Raisins!"

The gnomes surged away from the table, a tiny tide of boisterous idealism and ramshackle ingenuity. When the last gnome had disappeared up the ramp, Kitiara turned, smiling, to Sturm.

"Very clever," he said at last. "You did that well."

"Did what?" she replied guilelessly.

"We both know how impulsive the gnomes are. Between your passionate call for freedom and the prospect of a major engineering project, the obelisk hasn't got a chance."

"I hope you're right," said Cupelix. It was uncanny how easy it was to forget him when he stayed quiet above their line of sight. Sturm frowned. "Don't be so suspicious!" chided the dragon. "If my intentions were black, do you think I would have resorted to banquets and cajoling? My Micones could have held the ship indefinitely until you agreed to help, or I could have left you to the tree-men."

"No one ever said you were evil, Cupelix," Sturm persisted. "Subtle, you are, and very much concerned with getting your way. If you could have gotten out of your prison by sacrificing Kit, myself, or the gnomes, I don't think you would have dallied long in giving us up."

Cupelix spread his wings and coiled his legs to spring into the air. "Be at ease, Master Brightblade. No one need be sacrificed. We shall all see Krynn again, I promise."

Chapter 25

Gnomeplans

The gnomes divided into two groups. The first group, which consisted of Stutts, Flash, Wingover, Sighter, and Birdcall, was to study the problem of breaching the walls of the obelisk. The other four gnomes had as their task the safe removal of the contents of the tower, including Cupelix himself, the *Cloudmaster*, Sturm, and Kitiara.

The Micones returned with the night half gone, and on the dragon's orders, leveled out the dirt rampart they'd piled up some days before. Because there were more than fifty of the powerful giants at work, the land around the base of the obelisk was soon smooth and passable again. Kitiara and the Breaching Group (as they called themselves) went outside to survey the structure.

"The walls at ground level are marble no less than eleven

feet thick," Stutts reported, reading off his calculations. "With the best steel picks and mattocks, it would take a digging gang days and days to hack through all that rock."

"And furthermore," said Sighter, "my analysis of the stone shows it to be extremely hard, much harder, in fact, than regular marble. It's glazed."

"Glazed? Hmm." Kitiara looked to the obelisk's high pinnacle. A flickering red aura wavered about the top. She reminded the gnomes of the violent discharges they'd seen when the sun came up. "All that energy, must have hardened the stone," she said.

Stutts reached to touch the cold stone. Between the wide courses was a band of shiny black, colder even than the scarlet marble. "Metal," he mused. "Metal for mortar."

"Really?" said Flash. "What sort of metal is it?"

Stutts scraped at the six-inch-wide band with his thumbnail. The color did not scratch off. "It's soft," he said. "Lead, perhaps?"

Sighter and Birdcall examined the mortar, too. Birdcall confirmed with a twitter that the metal was indeed lead.

"Pretty solid," said Wingover, slapping the wall.

"I have an idea," Kitiara announced. The gnomes looked at her as if she'd said she was growing another head. "Well, I *do*. Here it is: I've seen lots of castle walls fall to besieging armies, and they are often as thick, if not as hard, as these walls. The besiegers brought them down by tunneling under the foundations and undermining the wall."

Consternation spread on the faces in the Breaching Party. "Why, that's bloody simple," Stutts declared.

"Why didn't we think of that?" asked Flash.

"All we have to do is dig away the sand!" said Wingover.

They fell on their knees and crimson dirt flew. Kitiara, shaking her head, went inside to the ship. Sturm was on his feet, leaning on a crutch that Cutwood had fashioned for him. He was keeping aloof from the preparations, but he asked what the gnomes had decided to do.

"We're digging now," Kitiara remarked. She appropriated a wrecking bar from the store of tools and returned to the frantic diggers. Sturm hobbled after her.

The gnomes carved out a crater deeper than their own

height in a very short time. Below grade, the foundation of the obelisk showed no alteration from the structure above—more massive marble blocks joined with lead. Kitiara cleared them out of the hole and swung the iron bar at the stone.

"Wait," said Wingover, "that's solid—"

She drew the bar back in a deep arc and struck the foundation with all her extra strength. There was a crack, like the breaking of a great tree branch, and a single chip of marble flew off. It landed at Sturm's feet, a lost petal from a stone rose. He stooped awkwardly to pick it up.

"Look at the bar!" said Flash.

Kitiara held up the inch-thick rod. The flat prying edge had mushroomed out from the blow, and the whole bar was bent in a graceful curve. Kitiara braced the bar against her knee and tried to straighten it, but only succeeded in bending it the opposite way. She tossed it aside in disgust.

"I tried to tell you," Wingover said as Kitiara climbed out of the hole. "The base of the tower rests on the roof of the cavern. It's solid stone."

"There are holes through it," said Sighter. "The Micones' holes. We went through them ourselves, to visit the egg chamber."

"Mining won't work," Stutts said sadly. "We're no more able to bore through the foundation than the upper walls."

Kitiara clambered out of the hole and dusted off her hands and leggings. Her breath showed white in the night air. "It's up to you gnomes now."

The little men faced each other for a few minutes and talked in their lightning patter. Finally, Stutts poked his face out and said, "We'll have to consult with our colleagues."

"Do you have a plan?" asked Sturm.

"The rudiments of one, but we need the wisdom of our fellows inside." The gnomes trooped off.

Sturm pushed the wrecking bar around with his toe. "That much strength is hard to control, isn't it?" When Kitiara didn't answer, he went on. "Are you getting stronger all the time, Kit? Is that why you move as if the world were made of glass?"

She snatched up the iron bar and, holding it in one hand,

steadily bent the rod into a right angle—using only her thumb! She dropped the bar and said, "Is that what you wanted to see?"

* * * * *

Cupelix and the humans sat attentively on one side of the obelisk—which is to say, Sturm and Kitiara sat on crates, while the dragon sat on his ledge above them. The gnomes sat on a bench facing them. Cutwood had rigged up an easel, which was shrouded with a loose cloth. Stutts stood by the easel, a long, pointed stick in his hand.

"Lady, gentleman, and beast," he began. The dragon's gusty sigh sent Stutts's beard whipping over his shoulder. "Lady, gentleman, and dragon," Stutts said smoothly, "may I present the Obelisk Escape Auger, Mark I." He whisked the cloth away, revealing a large sheet of parchment tacked to the easel. A fantastic-looking device was drawn in brown ink. Supported by a massive timber frame was an enormous helical auger, a grossly enlarged version of the tool used by carpenters to bore holes. According to the figures on the parchment, the bit alone was fifteen feet wide, the optimum diameter, Stutts said, to allow Cupelix to pass through.

"Very ingenious," said the dragon, eyeing the peculiar creation with evident skepticism. "How is it operated?"

"By this eccentric crank, here." The pointer tapped the drawing. "All eleven of us will man the crank. According to our best estimates, the auger will bore through the wall in sixty-seven hours of work."

"That's almost three days!" Kitiara said.

"On Lunitari, only two days and nights," said Sighter.

"Never mind that," Sturm said. "Where will the steel come from to make the bit? Where will you get the timber to build the frame?"

"Ah," said Cutwood. "Except for the bit blades and a few points of stress, such as the bearings, all parts of the Obelisk Escape Auger will be made of wood."

"What wood?"

"Why, the hull and frame of the *Cloudmaster*."

"Ai!" said Kitiara. She let her head fall forward into her

234

hands. Sturm sighed.

"If you dismantle the flying ship, how will we get home?" he said with as much patience as he could muster.

The gnomes looked from one to another, surprised. Very faintly, Fitter said something about putting the ship back together once the dragon was out.

"No!" said Kitiara. "You'll never get the timbers back together as a ship. You fellows must do better!"

"Not to worry!" Stutts rejoined. He whipped the elaborate drawing of the Obelisk Escape Auger off the easel. Beneath it was another, equally detailed diagram. "This, I am proud to say, is the Obelisk Arch Doorway Widener," said Stutts.

"Reasoning that the doorway represents a natural point of entry, we came up with this alternative scheme. These screw jacks—" Again the pointer flew to the diagram. "—will be fitted in the doorway. By tightening them with these turnbuckles here, here, and here, the rams will be forced apart, cracking the door wide open."

It took exactly one minute for Sturm and Kitiara to demolish the Arch Doorway Widener, mostly for the same reasons as the Obelisk Escape Auger: lack of quality materials. There was just no wood or metal to be had, except what the *Cloudmaster* and its crew had brought with them.

"It seems hopeless," said the dragon with a profound sigh.

"Never!" vowed Wingover. He pushed the bandages up from his face so that everyone could see his eyes. They had turned completely black. Wingover shielded them futilely with his hands.

"You see what has happened to me," he said. "I no longer can shut out anything. I have to sleep face down to the ground, where I count strata all the way down to the moon's core." He pointed with a thumb at Cutwood, next to him. "My good colleague hears every grain of sand rubbing against another. Roperig's hands are almost sealed together, aren't they, Roperig? Rainspot's clothes are beginning to rot from the constant damp. All the rest of us have problems, too, but we won't leave until we solve this problem."

Sturm heard these words carefully. He said, "As long as we are discussing our gifts, let me show you this." He tore the cloth bandage from his leg. Where two nights and a day before there had been an ugly, gaping wound, there was now only smooth, unscarred skin.

"The same magic that makes trees walk and fight has healed my wound. I did not ask for it to be done, but it has convinced me of one thing. This is no place for mortals. I'll lend my aid, dragon, for that reason alone. The longer we remain on Lunitari, the more the magic will affect us. Since my companions have resolved to help you, my resistance only impedes their progress."

"Welcome to the struggle," said Cupelix.

"Wingover," Kitiara said, "if you can see into the ground we stand on, can you see any deposits of iron or copper? Anything we can use?"

"Alas, lady, nothing. This entire moon seems made of sand, granite, and more sand."

"Sand," said Sighter, musing. He hopped down from the bench and strolled to the far wall and back. He traced a stubby finger along the lead seams where two marble courses lay on top of each other. "Sand!" he shouted. "Sand, sand, sand!"

"Look out," said Rainspot. "He's slipped his gears."

Sighter took a deep breath and strode to Stutts with grave dignity. "Sand," he said, "is the one thing this world provides in abundance, yes?"

"Uh, yes," said Stutts.

Sighter snapped his spyglass open and laid it across his colleague's palm. "What are lenses made of?"

"Glass," Roperig said promptly.

Sighter whirled, pointing to the adhesive gnome. "And what do the Lunitarians make their weapons out of?"

"Glass," said Sturm and Kitiara together.

"Yes! And what is glass made of?" Sighter cried.

No one said a word. Finally, Fitter said, "Sand, but—"

"Sand, glass, lenses! Don't you see? We can cast a giant lens, and with that concentrate the rays of the sun into a burning beam. The focal point of the rays will be far hotter than the melting point of lead, so—"

"The wall will come tumbling down," said Cupelix. "Do you think you can do it?"

"Nothing is for certain," Sighter said with ungnomish caution. "We'll need a continuous source of heat for the melting of the sand."

"What about the heat source we found in the caverns?" said Sturm. "Would that be hot enough for you?"

"Hmm, magma is more than hot enough to melt sand," said Flash.

"The Micones can gather any amount of sand you'll need," said Cupelix. "Shall I get them started?"

"We'd better push the *Cloudmaster* outside," Stutts said. "We'll need the floor space in here to work."

Cupelix summoned two ants, and the gnomes harnessed them to the bow of the flying ship. The Micones pulled the creaking craft through the doorway and out to the smoothed soil. The gnomes carried the detached wings and laid them in the shadow of the hull. Cupelix fell into a lengthy telepathic commune with his minions, and soon the Micones were mustered in the valley. They surrounded the obelisk on all sides, an army of mute, clicking creatures, intent on a voice no one heard but them. Without as much as a nod, the three score giant ants turned their backs to the tower and began to plow the soil with their heads. Furrows of dull red sand turned up to the starry sky, and other Micones pushed the sand into convenient mounds.

Sighter showed off his hasty design for a burning lens, twenty-two feet in diameter and five feet, seven inches thick in the center.

"Do you think it will work?" Kitiara said.

"If the lens can be cast in one piece, the polishing shouldn't take long. There's plenty of sand, after all," said Sighter. He rolled up his parchment drawing and tucked it under his arm. Outside, the Micones slaved on, the ground trembling against the force of their unyielding heads.

Chapter 26

The Lens

To refine the sand and eliminate any impurities, the gnomes resorted to washing it. Poor Rainspot was hauled up to the lowest of Cupelix's ledges and instructed to make it rain for several hours. The floor of the obelisk grew quite grimy with wet sand and sodden vegetable muck. The dragon descended from his sanctum with the news that clouds were forming up there, too. A gentle rain was falling 450 feet above Rainspot. Midget streaks of lightning flickered through the hollow shaft, glancing off the marble like minnows in a racing brook. Far from being annoyed, Cupelix was delighted with all this. He had read of the mysterious thing called 'weather,' but had never experienced it.

"It doesn't naturally occur indoors," Sturm said sourly. He was wet to the skin, as the gnomes had appropriated his oilcloth slicker to make buckets for the clean sand.

Micones were fitted with pairs of big buckets, which were draped like saddlebags on each side of their globular thoraxes. They scuttled down to the cavern with their loads, where Sighter, Birdcall, and Flash were preparing the vat in which the sand would be melted. This, like the mold in which the lens would be cast, was simply and roughly made from mud. The disintegrated plant fluff that coated the entire red moon, mixed with dry dirt, made an admirable clay. The gnomes in the cavern slapped together a wide tub of mud, reinforced with just a few laths 'borrowed' from the *Cloudmaster*. At about dawn, the vat was ready. With a Micone as a draft beast, the gnomes shifted the vat into place over one of the volcanic vents. Then they sat back and waited for the clay to harden.

Flash's head popped up through one of the holes in the floor. "We're ready for the sand!" he cried.

Roperig moved closer to the hole and said, "What's holding you up?"

"Nothing," said the mud-caked gnome. "I said, we're ready for the sand."

"He means, what's holding you up in the hole?" said Sturm.

"Oh! I'm standing on a Micone." The giant ant was clinging upside down under the opening, and Flash was standing on its belly.

The whole crew, save Kitiara and Rainspot, descended to the great cavern. There the train of Micones saddled with hoppers of sand stood in a line, like a cavalry troop on parade. Each time Birdcall poked his head through the toothed passage in the rock and whistled, an ant detached and followed him.

Farther in, past the Micones' birthing chamber, the gnomes labored over the glass vat. Sturm watched as they emptied bucket after bucket into the baked mud bowl, spreading the sand evenly across the bottom and sprinkling in various unnamed powders they'd brought down from the flying ship. The heat in the chamber was terrific. On Cupelix's orders, the Micones had broken open one of the magma flues, allowing more of the rock to well out of the ground.

The giant creatures seemed unaffected by the heat. The vat was precariously perched above the magma pool on piers of stones. The little men walked nonchalantly along the edge of the fiery pit, hardly noticing painful death could claim them if they slipped. Not for the first time, Sturm felt an admiration for the gnomes. They were foolish and trying at times, but in their element, they were indomitable.

The sand grew hot and steamed. In a process too sudden and subtle to see, the hard grains softened into a smooth mass, first bright orange and then nearly white as the heat rose to its highest level. The glare was too much for the gnomes and Sturm, and they drew back to the cooler end of the chamber.

"How will you get the melted glass up to the lens mold?" asked Sturm.

"We shan't," said Stutts, mopping his florid pink brow. "We're casting the rough lens down here."

Even as he said this, Micones laden with fresh mud clicked into the chamber. Birdcall, who seemed to have a particular rapport with the ants, directed them to dump their loads in a natural hollow in the cavern floor. Birdcall and Sighter fell to with trowels, sweeping the crimson mud about in smooth swirls, forming a round bowl.

When the mud was firm, though not entirely dry, Stutts and Sighter conferred. Everyone waited for the word—the gnomes, Sturm, the Micones, even Kitiara and Cupelix in the obelisk above. Stutts tapped his fingers together and talked far too fast for Sturm to follow. Sighter nodded.

Four Micones took up positions around the glass vat. Birdcall sat astride one ant, warbling and waving his hands to conduct the giants' efforts. The Micones clamped their pincer jaws on the studs the gnomes left poking through the mud walls, and lifted the vat easily off the magma furnace. Supported by twenty-four individual legs, the vat was maneuvered over the rocky floor to the mold.

"Are you ready?" Stutts called to Birdcall. The whistling gnome gave the high sign and Stutts called out, "You may pour now!"

Two ants lifted the vat up. White-hot molten glass slipped over the rim of the vat and splashed heavily into the mold.

Torrents of steam billowed out as the water was driven from the still-damp mud.

"Higher!" Stutts cried. "Tip the end up higher!"

Parts of the vat's outside began to crumble and break off. The molten mass of glass surged against the weakening walls. Cracks developed in the lip.

"Keep them back!" Sturm admonished Stutts. The gnomes, in their boundless urge to see everything, had crowded close to the lens mold. If the vat broke open, they would all be swamped with melted glass. Stutts pushed his colleagues to a safer distance.

The vat was vertical now, and the last gobs fell into the mold. There was more molten glass than the mold would hold, so it lapped over the edges. As the Micones lowered the vat to horizontal, the cracked sides fell to pieces.

"Phew!" said Stutts. His forehead was raw from constant wiping. "That was none too soon!"

The mold, being solidly bound by rock, was holding well. Already the edges of the lens were turning red, cooling from incandescent white. Bubbles popped in the center as steam forced its way out from the mud liner. Sighter frowned at the sight.

"Hadn't planned on that," he said. "Bubbles will distort the glass."

"It doesn't need to be of the first water," said Stutts.

"How long will it take to cool?" asked Sturm. The shimmering heat from the poured glass was mesmerizing.

"Fully cooled, twelve hours or more," said Sighter. "It'll be hard a lot sooner than that, but we can't crack the mold until we're sure the core is cooled."

"Maybe we could get Rainspot to sprinkle it with water," Cutwood suggested.

"No! It would shatter into a million pieces!"

With nothing else to do but wait, Sturm and all the gnomes but Sighter left the cavern. There was still some daylight left on the surface, and the gnomes wanted to get the *Cloudmaster* back into flying trim.

The flying ship posed proudly on the level valley floor, and once the wings were restored to the hull, it gained a majestic air. The obelisk's long shadow moved swiftly around with the rapidly setting sun.

"Ready for wing test?" Wingover hallooed in the voice pipe. A squawky, muffled "Yes" returned from the engine room. "Engage engine!"

Kitiara sensed a deep grinding vibration under her feet. The wing tips lifted, flexed and started down again, but balked. An agonizing shudder ran the length of the ship. The wings hung down where they were and quivered.

"No, no! Shut off!" Wingover yelled. The door of the dining room banged open, and Flash emerged, coughing.

Wingover stuck his head out the wheelhouse window. "What happened?" he said.

"That stupid Birdcall installed the armature switch upside down! When I fed lightning to the engine, it flashed back through the cable and burned out the storage jar! We have no power!" Flash exclaimed, close to tears.

Kitiara grabbed the gnome by the shoulder and spun him around. "No power?" she said. "What does that mean?"

"It means, we can't fly home!"

Chapter 27

The Invaders

Gloom settled in with the night. Birdcall was sound-
ly berated for his sloppy work, but once the reproaches
were finished, the gnomes went right back to their usual
good-natured camaraderie. Kitiara was furious, Sturm
resigned. The dragon tried to lighten their spirits.

"Be of stout heart!" he admonished. "If worse comes to
worst, I shall fly to Mt. Nevermind and notify the gnomish
authorities of your plight. They will, of course, mount a rescue expedition. Assuming I get clear of this tower, that is."

"Yes, assuming that," Sturm said. He went away to com-
miserate with the gnomes.

Kitiara sidled over to where Cupelix was perched. "Can
you hear me?" she said in the lowest of whispers.

Certainly. The dragon's telepathic voice caressed her

mind.

"When we get you out, I want you to take me with you she muttered.

And leave your friends behind?

"You said yourself the gnomes on Sancrist can be notifie It may take some months, but they'll try to reach their co leagues marooned on Lunitari." Since the ruin of the *Clou master*'s engine, Kitiara had begun to understand how th dragon felt, trapped on this moon. Also, once Cupelix w. free, she feared he would not linger on Lunitari while th gnomes struggled to repair the flying ship. Her dreams partnership would be over.

And what of Sturm?

"Someone has to look after the little fellows," she sai "Don't think me uncaring; I'm just eager to be gone fro here."

Fortunes to find, wars to win.

"Not to forget showing you around, too."

Yes, of course. Still, I wonder, dear Kit. If you could fl and I could not, would you leave me here also?

She grinned up at the huge creature. "You're far too b for me to carry," she said.

Supper was a subdued affair, and they all turned in soo after eating. Cupelix withdrew to his tower top, and th humans and gnomes slept scattered about the obelisk's now spacious floor.

Sturm was awake. He lay on his back, staring up into th tower's black recesses. It well matched his mood. Was th his ultimate fate, to be marooned on the red moon forever The dragon had said something about things never dyin here. Would he live on and on, bitter, lonely, forever denie his heritage as a knight?

The dark space above him closed in. The odd, displace sensation flooded over him yet again—

He sat up and heard crickets chirruping in the bushes. canopy of trees almost closed out the sky of Krynn. Stur could see the sculpted outline of a high wall in the distanc and knew that it was Castle Brightblade.

He drifted across the night-cloaked land to the castle main gate. To his surprise, torches flamed in the side brack ets, and two imposing figures in armor flanked the entrance. He moved in closer.

"Uh! What goes?" said the guard on Sturm's right. He leveled his poleaxe directly at Sturm.

He can see me! Sturm held up his hand and said, "I am Sturm Brightblade. This castle belongs to my father."

"Fool, nothing goes," said the other guard. "Put axe away."

"I say is." The right-hand guard took a torch down from its holder and stomped toward—and through—Sturm. By the blazing pine knot, Sturm saw the guard's face. It was not human, nor dwarven, elven, kender, or gnome. The protruding snout was green and scaly, and toothy horns sprouted from a wide mouth. His eyes were vertical slits, like Cupelix's.

Draconians! He was furious that these ugly brutes were in his ancestral home. Sturm pushed through the gate into the bailey. There were wagons and carts parked there, groaning with swords, spears, battle-axes, and sheafs of arrows. The draconians were turning Castle Brightblade into an arsenal, but for whom?

In the great hall he found a crackling fire built. Camp stools were set up before the hearth, and a trestle table was covered with scrolls. Sturm hovered by the table. The scrolls were maps, primarily of Solamnia and Abanasinia.

Steel rang on stone, and Sturm started, forgetting that he could not be seen. A tall, powerful figure strode out of the dark hall. He was helmetless, his face hard and expressionless. Long, smooth locks of white hair fell over his shoulders. The man crossed between the fire and the table and sat on one of the stools. He set his helmet down beside him. Sturm had never seen such a helmet before. Tusks protruded from the visor, and the whole form was shaped like the head of a predatory insect.

"Come and sit down," said the man, whom Sturm thought of as the general. A second figure stirred in the shadows. He—it?—did not come into the circle of firelight. A thin hand, sleeved in dark gray, reached out and dragged a camp chair into a dimmer corner of the hall.

"I forget you do not care for fire," said the general. "Pity.

Fire is such a useful force."

"Fire and light shall be my undoing some day," rasped th
robed figure. "I have seen my demise in flames. I am n
eager to meet my end just yet."

"Not with so much to do," replied the general. He peruse
the map of Solamnia. "When do you hear from your Mis
tress that Red Wing will be here? The arms grow rusty i
this damp old castle."

"Patience, Merinsaard. The Dark Queen has well gauge
the temper of the land, and she will set the armies in motio
when the auspices are most favorable."

The general snorted. "You speak of signs and portents as
they determined everything. It's the charge of the lance, th
shock of cavalry, that decides the fate of battles an
empires, Sorotin."

The hidden sorcerer chuckled, a moldering, decaye
sound that chilled Sturm. "Men of action always like t
think that their fate is in their hands. It comforts them an
makes them feel important."

Merinsaard said nothing. He leaned to the hearth
plucked out a burning brand, and thrust it toward his shad
owed compatriot. Sturm got a glimpse of a face that sur
prised him. It might've been handsome but for its deathl
paleness and the evil that emanated from burning eyes set i
it. The magic-user, Sorotin, groaned and shrank away from
the flame. Merinsaard tossed the burning twig after him.

"Mind your tongue," Merinsaard said. "And remember,
command here. If you displease me, or fail in your necro
mancy, I'll feed you to the fire myself."

The sorcerer panted raggedly with fear. "Be not too bold
my lord. For one is here now who watches and is no frien
to our cause." Sturm's heart skipped a beat.

"What?" said the general. He reached under the pile o
maps and pulled out a viciously curved dagger. A sticky
coating of greenish poison showed on the cutting edge
"Where is this intruder? Where?"

"Standing between us, great general." He did mea
Sturm!

Merinsaard slashed through the empty air. "You fool
There's no one there!"

"Not in the fleshly sense, my lord. He is a spirit from far away—very far, by the aura he emits. Perhaps as far as—Lunitari? That is far indeed."

"Get rid of it, whatever it is," said Merinsaard. "Kill the spy! No one must know of our plans!"

"Calm yourself, my lord. Our visitor is not here to spy. I sense that this was once his home."

"Dotard! No one has lived here for twenty years. The last lord of the castle was hounded out of the country."

"True enough, mighty Merinsaard," said Sorotin. "Shall I bring this spirit here in body, or bid him go back where he came?"

Sturm struggled with his feelings for a moment. He tried to will himself to solidity so that he might challenge these evil men. But he could sense no change in his state.

"Can he speak to the living of this world?" asked Merinsaard.

"I think not. He is too attenuated by the vast distance he has traveled. I sense no knowledge of magic in him."

"Then hurl him back to his wretched body and keep him there! I have no time for ghostly ambassadors."

Sturm saw a glint in the darkness. He heard a sweet chime. The sorcerer had struck the silver bell he carried.

"Hear me, O Spirit: As I ring this magic bell thrice, you will depart from this castle, this land, this world, never to return." The bell chimed once. "*Argon!*" Twice. "*H'rar!*" Three times. "In the name of the Dragonqueen!"

Every muscle in Sturm's body jolted at once. He literally felt as though he'd fallen from a height, but he was awake and in his body, in the obelisk on Lunitari. He sat up, breathing hard and shaking. The entire vision had passed without any new clue to his father's whereabouts. That was distressing enough, but the machinations of this Merinsaard and Sorotin—in Castle Brightblade—filled him with outrage. Someone must be told! The alarm must be given!

He roused Sighter from his blanket. "Wake up!" he said. "Let's have a look at that lens of yours."

"Now?" said the gnome through a jaw-cracking yawn.

"Yes, why not? It's been hours."

A Micone was standing by, as per orders, and it allowed

Sturm and Sighter to mount for a ride down to the casting chamber. The whole cavern was filled with dripping patches of mist. The giant ant didn't like the dampness at all. Once or twice, its barbed feet slipped on the vitreous wall, making Sturm cling tightly to the rope harness and causing Sighter to cling even more tightly to Sturm.

The lens was still ruby red, but very little heat radiated from it.

Sturm tapped his fingers lightly on the edge of the mold. The fourth tap broke loose a chunk of mud, now dry and brittle. The inward sloping side of the lens was exposed. Sighter stood on his toes to examine the glass.

"No," he muttered. Out came the magnifying glass. He peered into the scarlet casting. "Broken gears and slipped pulleys!" he exclaimed. "The lens is worthless!"

"What?"

"The glass, the glass! It's nearly opaque!"

"It can't be," Sturm said. Sighter handed him his magnifying glass. Sturm peered into the lens. All he could see were millions of tiny white bubbles trapped in the solidified glass. That, and the dark red color, made it obvious that the lens would be useless for focusing the sun's rays into a burning beam.

"Perhaps when it's polished," Sturm said hopefully.

"Never!" Sighter sputtered. "You'd have more chance trying to focus sunbeams through a cedar tree!" He threw his pocket glass on the rocks and stamped it until it shattered.

"What's the matter?" asked a voice. Stutts and the others had also come to inspect the giant lens. Sighter bitterly explained that their work had been for nothing. The crestfallen gnomes ringed the mold and stared down at the lens in disbelief.

"Worthless," said Fitter.

"Useless," said Roperig.

"A waste of time and effort," Cutwood added.

"Now what do we do?" asked Rainspot.

"Try to explain it to the dragon," said the crushed Sighter.

*   *   *   *   *

No one said much about the lens failure except Cupelix. The otherwise genial, well-mannered dragon had a dragon-sized tantrum.

"Thundering incompetents! Witless—inept!" A tremendous telepathic *FOOLS!* made them all flinch.

"Do be still," Kitiara said severely. "A dragon your age, carrying on like a spoiled child! Do you think the little fellows guarantee success?"

Sturm watched the effect of Kitiara's chiding on the beast. Cupelix's ears, which had been flattened on his head, slowly lifted, and the jets of acrid vapor stopped puffing from his nostrils.

"I had such hopes!" Cupelix allowed.

"Well, it looks like we're going to be here a long while," Kitiara said. "So we shall have plenty of time to think up new ways to get you out of this marble cell."

Mollified, the dragon prepared them a cold repast and retired to his high sanctum to meditate on his problems. Sturm, Kitiara, and the gnomes went outside and stared at the *Cloudmaster*. Poor, lifeless hulk, an immobile derelict gracing the red turf of Lunitari.

Sturm put a hand to his chin and pondered what he understood from Wingover's explanation of how the *Cloudmaster* flew. The wings were useless without lightning to turn the engine. All that remained was the half-empty bag of ethereal air. He said, "What about the ethereal air?"

"What about it?" asked Wingover.

Sturm, rather abashed to be making technical arguments to the gnomes, said, "Bellcrank used to say that when full, the ethereal air bag was sufficient to lift the ship."

"With all due respect to our late colleague, the lifting power of the bag is much less than the total weight of the hull of the ship," Stutts said. They lapsed into silence once again. Sturm thought some more. Kitiara's eyes narrowed as she, too, concentrated.

"What if we lightened the ship?" said Fitter.

"What?" said Sturm.

"What?" said Stutts, Wingover, Sighter, Rainspot, and Flash.

"What!" said Cutwood, Roperig, and (translated) Birdcall.

Kitiara grinned her off-center grin, something she did all too rarely these days. "Lighten the ship!" she declared. "Now that's something I can understand!" She picked little Fitter up and shook him so hard that his teeth rattled. Then she boosted him up to the rail. The gnome went below deck and opened the side boarding ramp. The other gnomes swarmed aboard, fired with the zeal of desperation. Before Sturm and Kitiara had even mounted the ramp, loud crashes and splintering creaks sounded within the ship.

"They may rip everything out," Sturm said wryly. "Deck, ceiling, planks, and posts."

The gnomes formed a chain from the lowest deck to the top rail and began flinging everything they could lay their hands on over the side. They ransacked their cabins and brought forth all their personal belongings. Sturm was astounded by the mass and variety of it: blankets, books, tools, clothing, barrels, pots, plates, rope, cord, twine, sail-cloth, a crate of ink, pens, bars of soap, two harmonicas, a fiddle, a flute, sixteen pairs of boots (all sized too big for Sturm, much less any gnome that ever lived), gloves, belts, and a stuffed billy goat that Cutwood kept in his cabin.

Some items couldn't be manhandled to the upper deck. Kitiara found Roperig and Fitter lying prostrate beside a large keg. "We can't budge it," Roperig panted.

"I'll do it." She turned the keg around to see if there was a bung attached. Liquid sloshed inside, and a single word in gnomish block letters was stenciled on the staves. Kitiara said, "What's in this, anyway?"

Fitter squinted at the label. "Oil of Vitriol. Must have been Bellcrank's," he said. A slight quiver invaded his chin.

"Vitriol, eh?" She recalled the mess that the acid had made of Bellcrank's Excellent Mouthless Siphon back on Krynn. "Why hasn't it eaten through the keg?"

"Oh, it's probably lined with some resistant coating," said Roperig. He wiped the back of his neck with his hand, and it promptly stuck there. "Oh, dry rot!"

Kitiara drummed her fingers on the barrel head. "Hmm, that's worth knowing. So this stuff dissolves some things but not others?"

"Yes." Roperig tried to free his hand and succeeded in sticking his other hand to his own arm. "Double dry rot!"

"Will oil of vitriol dissolve marble?" she asked.

"Maybe. It doesn't affect many glassy substances."

"What about lead?"

"Yes, definitely. Fitter, stop fidgeting and help me!"

She left the two gnomes locked in a struggle against Roperig's adhesive palms. The gnome she sought, Stutts, was outside the ship, sorting through the heap of goods that the gnomes had discarded. Kitiara pulled Stutts free of a pile of clothing and said, "I know how to get the dragon out!"

"What?" said the gnome. "How?"

"Bellcrank's vitriol." She gestured vaguely back toward the ship. "There's a whole barrelful of it on board. If we let it eat up the mortar in the lowest course of the obelisk, the walls are bound to collapse, aren't they?"

Understanding gradually lightened Stutts's face. Then it hit him full force. "Hydrodynamics! It will work!"

The gnomes heard Stutts's cry and rallied around. With extravagant hand motions and frequent compliments to Kitiara, Stutts explained her idea. The gnomes positively exploded with excitement. It was so simple! So elegant! They'd been fixated on a mechanical solution, and here the human woman had come up with a chemical answer!

Sturm heard the commotion and hustled down the ramp. He agreed that the plan was a good one, but saw one important consideration. "What happens to Cupelix when the tower falls?" he asked. "Not even a brass dragon can withstand tons of marble masonry falling on him."

"There has to be a way around that," said Kitiara.

"Why don't we ask the dragon?" said Sturm.

That's what they did. At first, the dragon was sulky and refused to come down from his aerie. Kitiara scolded him for his petulance, and still there was no response. Then she alone heard: *I don't wish to be disappointed again.*

"We're not making any promises," she proclaimed loudly. "We have a new scheme that we're pretty sure will work, but it has an awkward problem. Freeing you may kill you."

A unique solution. I would not be a prisoner any longer.

"Oh, shut up! If you can't come down and talk to us like a

reasonable dragon, we'll just bring the obelisk down around you." Kitiara jerked her head to the others. "Let's go."

"We're not really going to use the vitriol with him still up there, are we, ma'am?" said Fitter.

"Why not? You want to see if it'll work, don't you?" she replied.

"But the dragon will get hurt."

Cutwood chewed thoughtfully on the tip of his pencil. "I wonder," he mused, "what the tensile strength of dragon hide and flesh is?" Sighter produced some vellum.

"We can do a calculation!"

Chapter 28

Breakthrough

The Cloudmaster, freed of several hundred pounds of useless weight, buoyed a bit off the ground. Wingover had a fine time 'lifting' the big ship up with his hands. Roperig advised staking the hull to the ground, so wooden stakes were pounded into the turf and the flying ship was secured.

"Besides stacks of food and water, there isn't a scrap of anything left on board," Stutts reported. "Most of the interior partitions have been torn out, too."

"What about the engine?" asked Sturm. "It must weigh as much as the rest of the hull put together."

"It does," said Flash, not without pride.

"Then we must dump it."

"Not our beautiful engine! There isn't another machine

253

like it anywhere!"

Sturm could make no headway, so he went to where Kitiara, Cutwood, and Sighter were studying the matter of dissolving the obelisk's lead mortar.

"We'll need ladders to reach those higher courses," Kitiara
was saying.

"Scaffolding would be better," Sighter argued. "There's
some scrap lumber from the ship."

"How will we get the vitriol up there?" asked Cutwood.

"Glass vials and beakers," said Sighter. "That stuff will eat
through anything else."

Sturm cleared his throat loudly. Kitiara said impatiently,
"Speak up, Sturm."

"The ship is almost light enough to float, but Birdcall and
Flash won't agree to discard the useless engine," he reported.

"So what? Take a hammer and knock it to pieces," she
said. "That's the way to get things done." Cutwood and
Sighter looked at her in some surprise, and Sturm prudently
refrained from commenting. Instead, he asked if they'd
heard from Cupelix.

"Not a peep. He's being very stubborn."

Sturm went inside. The vast open floor was deserted. The
ship, the gnomes, and their gear had all been removed. Only
the three gaping holes for the Micones were the same.

"Cupelix?" he called. "Cupelix, I know you can hear me.
Come down." His voice echoed through the empty space.
"Kitiara is going ahead with this vitriol scheme of hers.
She'll bring this tower down about your ears, just to prove
she can do it." He felt the faint but distinct touch of the
dragon's mental voice.

I trust you, Brightblade. You tell the truth.

"A man's truthfulness is his duty to the Measure," Sturm
replied.

*I made a bargain with dear Kit: If she would advocate my
cause to the gnomes, I would accompany her for two years
upon our return to Krynn.*

Sturm frowned. "For what purpose?"

*I know not. But it was important enough that she was
willing to abandon you and your friends to reach Krynn.*

"You must be jesting! Kitiara wouldn't do that!"

I am very serious, Brightblade. When she believed the ship ruined, she pressed me to take her away when I left.

"Why are you telling me this?"

Her ambition worries me. Every living thing has an aura; have you heard this? It is true. The aura reveals the spark of life that animates the body without. Yours, for example, is a golden yellow, strong, radiant, and unvarying. But Kitiara's is fiery red and streaked with black. The black is growing in her.

Sturm waved dismissively. "I don't know what you're talking about. Kit is strong-willed and impetuous, that's all."

You are wrong, my virtuous friend.

"Come down, dragon, and help us with your release. That's all I have to say." Sturm marched out.

The gnomes had the lowest stages of a scaffold lashed together. Sturm noted the brightening sky. "Sunrise," he said. "Better come inside till after the tower discharges."

There was a rumble overhead. The sun peeked over the valley wall, and the early rays hit the marble tower. The rumble deepened. The first crackles of lightning were arcing from the obelisk's peak. The whole valley shook with the force. Another brief day began on Lunitari.

You don't have to shake the tower so! I intend to join in.

The group broke into relieved laughter. "Gives us a lot of credit, doesn't he?" Kitiara said. They streamed back to the unfinished scaffold.

Stutts explained, in great detail, the vitriol plan to Cupelix. The dragon was not sanguine about it. He was more interested in taking the top off the tower, but there was not enough wood to erect a scaffold five hundred feet high.

"It's too bad you can't go down to the cavern," said Wingover. "You'd be safe there."

"Who says I can't?" the dragon answered.

"The holes in the floor aren't big enough to let you pass," the gnome objected.

"Then we shall make them bigger. Will this corrosive of yours eat through marble?"

"Ah, we're not certain," said Stutts. "I wish I'd studied alchemy more closely! Then I could tell you."

"Why don't we try a more direct approach? Let's apply

vitriol to the floor stones," offered Cupelix.

The flying ship's erstwhile china milk pitcher was pressed into service as a vitriol vessel. They breached the keg head and dipped the pitcher in until it was full.

"Careful!" said Stutts. Kitiara nodded, tight-lipped, as drops fell from the pitcher's lip and landed, sizzling, on the ground, leaving black, smoking scorch marks.

Kitiara walked very slowly to the obelisk, gnomes dancing attendance on each side, prattling on with useless but well-intended advice. Sturm hurried ahead to clear the way.

Cupelix had come all the way down to the floor to be as close as possible to the experiment. Holding the pitcher at arm's length, Kitiara dribbled a thin stream of vitriol on the rim of one of the Micones' holes. The corrosive hissed and sizzled villainously, and after a few minutes, the bubbling stopped.

"Whew!" said Kitiara. "This stuff stinks!"

Wingover tapped the doused area with a slender mineral hammer. "The stone has definitely decayed," he announced, "though not by much. It would take gallons and gallons of oil of vitriol to eat through this thick marble."

"We haven't got an endless supply," Kitiara reminded him. "Fifty gallons; that's as much as we have."

"Then it's picks and mattocks," said Sturm. "Hand work. I knew it would come down to sweat and blisters eventually."

The gnomes returned outside to work on extending the scaffolding around three sides of the obelisk. Kitiara and Sturm found the heaviest digging tools the gnomes had and set to work. It was hard going. The floor was tough, and the tools were small. What amounted to a full-sized pick for a gnome was little bigger than a hand adze to a human.

It was hot inside the tower, as they chipped away at the marble. Kitiara stripped off her cloak and mail shirt and worked in her light blouse. Sturm set aside his armor and quilted tunic, too. Cupelix did what he could to make their labor easier. He fanned them with his broad wings and flushed the chips and dust out of their way. He told clever stories that he'd garnered from his reading.

Sturm discovered that Cupelix was a devotee of the elven bard, Quivalen Soth. The dragon knew the "Song of Huma" by heart. Even more interesting was a lost cycle of songs by Quivalen about Huma and the Silver Dragon. Kitiara had not heard the tale of Huma's love for the Silver Dragon, and was fascinated.

"A true tragedy," said Cupelix, fanning a breeze over them. "That a dragon should descend from its noble natural form to that of a mortal. Tsk, tsk."

Sturm traded his small pick for an equally small sledgehammer. It hit the floor with a crack that stung his hands. "You think dragons are better than people?" he asked.

"Without a doubt. Dragons are bigger, stronger, have more abilities and powers, live longer, do more, and have unequaled mental qualities," said Cupelix. "What can humans do that dragons can't?"

"Walk out of here," said Kitiara, leaning on her pick. The fanning wings missed a beat, then started up again.

"Too bad you can't change into a man, even briefly," Sturm said. "Then all this digging would be unnecessary."

"Alas, shape-shifting has never been a talent known among brass dragons. There are texts on the matter, that of the elf wizard Dromondothalas being the most famous. But my library is completely lacking in such books."

Kitiara kicked a wide wedge of stone loose. It slipped through the hole. Seconds later, a distant thud revealed that it had landed in the cavern below. She said, "Where did your books come from?"

"What books I have I had from the beginning. The maker of the obelisk provided them, I believe, so that the Keeper of the New Lives would have some knowledge of the wider worlds beyond Lunitari. There are tomes of history, geography, letters, medicine, alchemy—"

"And magic," said Sturm, bringing the hammer down.

"Half the scrolls are related to magic," agreed Cupelix.

In two hours' work, the humans succeeded in widening the hole by several inches all around. Cupelix expressed satisfaction with their progress, but Kitiara was disgusted.

"At this rate, we'll be too old to lift the tools by the time we cut a hole big enough for you," she said to the dragon.

"I think we're going about this the hard way," Sturm said. His arms and back ached, and his head pounded from the strain of working so hard in the thin air. "I remember the masons at the castle cleaving stones as thick as this floor with one or two blows. Let me have some cool water, and I'll think about it a while." He took the water bottle from Kitiara and slumped by the near wall.

Kitiara went out. To her unconcealed surprise, the gnomes had already wrapped their rickety platform around three sides of the obelisk to a height of six feet. Boards, posts, tool handles and beams were pegged and lashed together wherever space allowed.

"How goes it?" she said, turning away and almost bowling over Stutts.

"We're ratcheting right along," he said. "Are you making any progress on the floor?"

"Very little, I'm afraid." She fingered her left biceps. "All this extra muscle power is going to waste. If I swing too hard, I'll only break the tool."

"I see." Stutts squinted at the midday sun. "Only two and a half hours of light left. Let's have a look at your progress."

They entered and found Sturm kneeling on the floor, staring at the water pitcher. He looked from it to one of the areas where they'd scarred away the polished surface. Then he stared once more at the water pitcher. Cupelix had hopped back up to his perch.

"What are you doing?" Kitiara asked Sturm.

"I remember how they did it," Sturm replied. "The masons at Castle Brightblade used to quarry out enormous blocks of granite with just four men."

"How did they do it?" asked Stutts.

"They bored holes along the block they wanted to free and drove in thick wooden pegs. Then they soaked the pegs in water. The swelling wood cracked the stone."

Stutts looked at Sturm and blinked. "That's ingenious."

Kitiara said, "But can we bore holes in the marble?"

"We have some steel augers," said the gnome. "With your strength and the right approach—yes, easily!"

Stutts ran back to the pile of goods discarded from the flying ship and returned with a large brace and bit. He explained quickly how, when boring stone, it was important to keep the bit cool and lubricated. Sturm would trickle water around the bit while Kit turned the brace.

They tried it, and bored through the twenty-inch-thick floor in thirty minutes. Flushed with success, they bored more holes, connecting the first Micone hole with the second, about twelve feet away. Using this line as the base of a triangle, Sturm and Kitiara angled out into the main floor space. They were well into the triangle's second arm, when the sun went down and the gnomes came streaming in. Flash announced that the scaffold was done.

"Then find a bit and join in," Kitiara said. "More water, Sturm! The handle feels hot!"

It was well past midnight when they finished, thirty-six holes in all. Cupelix worked up an especially bracing repast with thick soup and lots of bread. They had ruined four bits, and Kitiara's hands were blistered.

Rainspot offered her some soothing salve, but she declined. "Let's get on with it," she said. "Get the pegs."

The gnomes did the peg work. They cut lengths from the remaining scrap wood, and Sturm banged these home with the sledge. Everyone cleared out of the triangle area formed by the bored holes. Kitiara filled a canvas bucket with water and handed it to Sturm.

"Your honor," she said. "Your idea."

He took the handle. "This is for the good yeoman of Castle Brightblade," he answered, dousing each peg in turn, refilling the bucket, and dousing them all again.

Nothing happened.

"Well?" said Kitiara, bracing one hand on her hip.

"It takes a while," said Sturm. "The pegs have to swell. We'd better have some more water."

Sturm poured water on the pegs three more times. The tops of the pegs clearly swelled above the level of the floor, but little else appeared to happen.

"Wonderful," Kitiara said sarcastically. She loped out, snorting with ill-concealed contempt. One by one, the gnomes gave up, and went outside. Sturm shook his head.

"It worked for my father's masons," he said.

"Masonry is an arcane art," Cupelix said. "Its secrets are not easily adapted by the untrained."

Then the floor went *crack*.

Near the hole that Sturm and Kitiara had so laboriously enlarged, a hairline crack reached from the first peg, across the marble, to the peg on the other side of the hole. Sturm laid the sledge on his shoulder and hurried to the scene. He was about to smite the splitting stone, when he heard another crack, and a fissure slowly zigzagged from the triangle's far point to its base. Sturm raised the hammer.

"No, wait," said the fascinated dragon.

The line between the Micone holes jumped apart, and Sturm started backward. A section of stone, larger than any they'd released by hand, broke free and plunged into the cavern below. That opened the floodgates, and the entire triangle collapsed into the cavern with a rush. The obelisk rang with the concussion as a ton of marble hit the resonant floor a hundred feet down.

Kitiara burst in, the gnomes at her heels. "Great suffering gods! What was that?" she cried.

Sturm dusted his hands and pointed dramatically to the gaping hole in the floor. "The way is clear for Cupelix to descend!" he said.

The gnomes were all for going on and bringing the obelisk down that very night, but Sturm and Kitiara were both exhausted and begged off. Cupelix supported them, saying that he had many items he wished to save from destruction before the tower was demolished. He flew up to his private aerie and left the mortals to take their ease.

The gnomes quieted after the initial rush of success wore off. They burrowed into the *Cloudmaster*'s jetsam and slept, their tinny snores sounding like an operatic war between bullfrogs and crickets. Sturm stretched out on a blanket surrounded by stacked crates. The sky was brilliantly clear as usual, and he counted stars to make himself drowsy.

Kitiara sauntered around the crates. "Asleep?" she asked.

"Huh? No, not yet."

She slipped down opposite him, her back braced by a box. "This may be our last night on Lunitari."

"Sounds good to me."

"You know, I've been trying to figure out how long we've been here. In local terms, we've seen about forty-four days and forty-five nights. How long does that make it back home?"

"I don't know," he admitted.

"Suppose we get back to Krynn and find that years have passed?"

He almost laughed at the idea, but stopped himself. Sturm couldn't prove that years hadn't elapsed while they were on the red moon.

"There are so many old tales about humans who went off to elf realms and returned in what they thought were a few months to find their children grown and their friends dead of old age," Kitiara said. Sturm thought she was just musing over possibilities, but then he realized that she was seriously concerned.

"What are you afraid of, Kit?" he asked gently.

"The five-year reunion. It's important that I not miss it."

"And Tanis?"

"Yes."

"Do you intend to go back to him?"

Kitiara shifted uncomfortably. "No, that's not it. We didn't part on the best of terms, and I want to patch things up, before—" She started to say something but stopped.

"Before what?" Sturm prompted.

"Before I begin my travels with Cupelix."

So, she was owning up to it. "Are you giving up trying to find your father and his people?"

"My father always said his family had disowned him and his forever," she said. "Much as I'd love to ride up to their front door and spit in their faces, partnership with a dragon promises to be more exciting." She shrugged. "I say, to the Abyss with the Uth Matars."

The quiet interval grew long, and Sturm felt his eyelids droop with sleep. He was about to nod off when Kitiara said, "Sturm, if you see Tanis before I do, will you tell him I'm sorry, and that he was right?" Sturm was too much of a gentleman to inquire what she had to be sorry about. He promised upon his honor as a Brightblade to bear her message back to Tanis Half-Elven.

Chapter 29

The Obelisk Falls

The dragon called to them, rousing them from their slumber. The gnomes bounced up, eager to be about their business. Sturm rubbed his eyes and looked about. Kitiara was not in sight.

He stretched and hunted around for a drink of water. As he was gulping a cool drink, Kitiara appeared. She tossed aside a handsaw and said, "What's the beast yelling about? I couldn't quite make it out."

"He wants us to get on with the demolition," said Sturm.

"Fine. I'm ready."

All the glass and porcelain jars and cups they had were to be used to pour vitriol on the lead mortar seams. The gnomes lined up like soldiers, mugs and cream pitchers in hand like swords. Kitiara gave them a mocking salute and told them to bide their time.

Inside, Cupelix was nervously hopping from one massive leg to the other. "All my books and manuscripts are safe," he said. "The Micones have transferred everything to a safe place in the cave." There was no longer reason to delay. Cupelix put his three-toed feet into the hole and curled his tail up close to his chest. It would be a tight fit.

"Get your wings in," Sturm said. "Closer! That's it."

"Good thing I am a svelte example of my race," Cupelix said. His massive body was in the hole. Only his head showed inside the obelisk.

"I believe I shall miss this place," he said.

"Go on!" Kitiara shouted. Cupelix's head disappeared. He fell forty feet before getting his wings open. He hit the cavern floor with enough force to rock the tower on its foundations, but to the dragon it was a minor tumble. He telepathed his good health and told the mortals to proceed.

"Cupelix is safely in the cavern," Sturm said to Stutts when they were outside.

Stutts put two fingers to his mouth and blew a shrieking whistle. "Begin pouring!" he cried.

The gnomes, spaced around the three sides of the obelisk, applied vitriol to the lead. Wisps of noxious vapor coiled off the walls, choking all the gnomes but Roperig and Fitter, who had invented Caustic Smoke Filters for Noses and Mouths (Mark II). Keen observers would have recognized the filters as being made of old bandannas and suspenders.

"Right! Now clear off the top level and pour on the second!" Stutts called. Convenient beakers of vitriol were positioned on the lower platforms of the scaffold.

Flash climbed down the spindly collection of poles and planks. He swung to the second level and promptly kicked over his beaker. Oil of vitriol streamed down the scaffold, eating away the wood and rope lashing with as much vigor as it consumed the lead.

"Look out!" said Sturm. The poles under Flash sagged and came apart. The gnome wavered back and forth on his toes and toppled from the planking.

Kitiara gauged his fall and stepped below him. She held up her arms and caught the plummeting gnome.

"Thank you so much," he said.

"Certainly," she asked.

The walls of the obelisk steamed with vitriol vapor Streaks of black showed on the flawless red marble wher the liquified lead ran down. The corrosive fluid ate into th joints between the courses of stone with alacrity, and half a hour after starting, the gnomes were down to the fourtl level of their scaffold.

"It looks like it's weeping," Sturm observed of the struc ture. "But I don't think it's suffering much damage."

"The effect should be cumulative," said Stutts. "Withou the lead support, each course will sag under the weight o the upper blocks. By the time we get down to ground level the whole structure may be leaning as much as three feet ou of plumb. The remaining fourth wall cannot support sucl an imbalance, and the obelisk will collapse."

The wine-purple sky segued into claret red. Sturn frowned. "Sunrise," he said. "Will the discharges affect th process?"

"How can they not?" Kitiara replied. "They may bring th whole thing down on our heads." She went to the foot of th scaffold and yelled, "Get a move on! Dawn is coming!"

There were accidents, gnomes being gnomes, with th imminent sunrise pressing on them. Vitriol burns, falls, an sprained ankles multiplied. The stars faded from view as th heavens changed from claret to rose. The usual streak o meteors ricocheted from one horizon to another, and th intense stillness was broken by a stirring in the air that Kiti ara felt, though Sturm could not.

"Hurry!"

The gnomes tumbled off the scaffold like mice from burning building. The platform groaned and curled uj wherever the vitriol dropped on it, and the lower third o the obelisk was coated with sickly gray steam.

"Run!" Sturm said. "Run as far and as fast as you can!"

He grabbed Cutwood, who was slow, and dragged hin off his feet. Kitiara scooped up Roperig and Flash, the las ones off the scaffold. And they ran, past the point at whicl they'd left *Cloudmaster*, on the unscarred side of the tower as far as where the valley began to rise in elevation. A hor rendous grinding noise filled the valley, overpowering even the first crackle of the morning discharge.

From under Kitiara's arm, Flash twisted around to see. "The blocks are giving way!" he cheered.

The grinding sound arrested their mad flight. Everyone stopped, turned, and stared.

Bolts of blue lightning sizzled from the obelisk's peak, not to the distant cliffs that defined the valley, but into the dry red soil a hundred yards from the monument's base. The obelisk leaned appreciably, and whole courses of stained marble tumbled to the ground. It seemed for a moment that the tower might withstand the loss of those blocks, but the weight of the upper reaches was too much for the undermined base. The five-hundred-foot obelisk slowly, gracefully, leaned over. Stones shattered under the unbearable pressure. The top broke apart in midfall, the stones separating with the tumult of a hundred thunderstorms. Blocks twelve feet long, six feet high, and three feet thick hurtled to the ground, gouging out deep craters in the soft turf. The obelisk lay down like a falling tree, pieces weighing several tons bounced off each other, breaking, crushing, and coming to rest at last, as though too tired to leap any farther. The great pyramid capstone crashed with blue and white sparkles dancing around it. Will-o'-the-wisps rose above the swelling cloud of dust and vanished, silent witnesses to the mighty structure's fall.

There was silence. The rumble died away.

"My," said Stutts solemnly.

"It worked," said Wingover.

"Did it ever work," said Rainspot.

Suddenly, Kitiara gave out a loud, long whoop of triumph. "Yaaahaaah!" she cried, leaping up into the air. "We did it! We did it!"

Sturm found himself grinning from ear to ear, but as the members of the little party moved slowly toward the fallen giant, an awed silence settled over them. Large blocks stood upright, buried to a third of their length. Sturm looked on and marveled. The shape of the obelisk proper could still be recognized as a heavier concentration of broken masonry.

Sturm climbed to a pile of blocks near the erstwhile base

of the obelisk. The dust thrown up by the collapse had risen
making a dull red ring in the sky. He had an odd thought
Would stargazers on Krynn be able to see the ring of dust?
was miles and miles across, and darker than the surface soi
Would the astronomers see it, theorize about it, mak
learned discourses on the cause and meaning of it?

Everyone gathered at the base. A dome of blocks ha
fallen over the hole in the obelisk floor, and only a ver
small person could wriggle through the resulting gap. Kit
ara called for Fitter.

"Go in and call to the dragon," she said. "See if he's a
right. I can't get him to answer."

"Yes, ma'am." Fitter scampered into the arch of stone. I
answer to his call, they all heard a telepathic *Success!*

"He's alive," Stutts said.

"We'll have to clear these stones away," Sturm said.

Get clear, little Fitter; I'm coming out!

Fitter crawled out, and the mortals drew back. The mas
of blocks flew apart, and Cupelix emerged. His massive fac
was split by a wide smile. Huge teeth gleamed dully in th
light as he flung back his head and expanded his chest.

"Rejoice, mortal friends! I am free!" he cried.

"You had no trouble shifting those blocks," Kitiara said

"None at all, my dear Kit. When the structure was bro
ken, so was its protective spell." Cupelix inhaled deepl∣
sucking in the tepid air in dragon-sized gulps. "It is sweet, :
it not, the first breath of freedom?"

No one was sure what to do next. "I suppose," said Stutt
reflectively, "we ought to prepare to depart ourselves." H
folded his hands over his round belly. "That is, assuming th
Cloudmaster can rise on its ethereal air alone."

"I'm confident," Kitiara said. Sturm shot her a questior
ing look. She winked and smiled just like the old Kit, the∣
moved away, toward the top end of the wreckage.

Without warning, Cupelix unfurled his wings to the∣
fullest extent. Never in the close confines of the obelisk ha
he been able to spread his wings in all their glory. Now h
groaned with pleasure at the stretching of his leather
wings. Cupelix launched himself in the air with one spring
and flapped leisurely, luxuriously, gaining height with eac

pass over the site of his deliverance. He rolled, stalled, hovered, wings bellying full and emptying in rapid sweeps. He climbed so high that he was a golden dot in the sky, and dived with such wild abandon that it seemed certain he would crash into the obelisk's ruins.

Sturm turned his gaze from the joyous dragon and realized that everyone had left him. Kitiara had nearly reached the top of the ruins and the gnomes were scattered throughout the debris, measuring, arguing, and enjoying their triumph immensely.

Kitiara found, amidst the rubble, the wonderful tapestries she had seen in Cupelix's private aerie. They were torn to shreds, but here and there whole portions were identifiable. Cupelix hadn't bothered to save the moldering tapestries, and she wondered why. She found a patch from the Assembly of the Gods tapestry, the patch with the face of the Dark Queen on it. The woven face was nearly as wide as Kitiara was tall, but she rolled the fragment up and tied it around her waist as a belt. She felt she had to save it.

"Care for a ride?" said Cupelix.

Kitiara looked up. The dragon hovered above her, the sweep of his wings sending dust swirling around the ruins.

Kitiara thought a brief moment, then said warily, "Yes. But no acrobatics."

"Certainly not." Cupelix's mouth was wide in one of his unnerving grins.

He landed and Kitiara mounted his neck. She took hold of the brass plates and said, "Ready."

He launched them straight up, and Kitiara felt the breath snatched from her body. With slow, lazy sweeps of his wings, Cupelix circled the ruins and the flying ship. Kitiara again felt the exhilaration she'd experienced those first few minutes on the *Cloudmaster*, when the whole of Krynn had been spread out below her. With the wind whipping her short hair, Kitiara grinned down at Sturm's astonished face. "Hai, Sturm Brightblade! Hai-yah!" She waved one hand at him. "You should try this!"

The gnomes set up a cheer as Cupelix banked into a steep climb. Sturm watched the dragon soar away with Kitiara. He felt a strange uneasiness. He wasn't afraid for Kit. There

was something about the image of a human riding on t
back of a dragon that chilled him deep inside.

"Well, I'm glad they're enjoying themselves," Sighter sa
sourly. "But can we get underway, ourselves?"

Sturm waved to Kitiara and called for her to come dow
After several mock diving attacks at the rubble, the gnome
and Sturm, Cupelix landed and Kitiara jumped to t
ground.

"Thank you, dragon," she said. Her face was flushed. S
pounded Sturm on the shoulder and said, "Well, let's g
going. No need to stand around here all day."

The humans and the gnomes trekked to the tethered fl
ing ship. In a moment of creative vandalism, Flash and Bir
call had agreed to sever the useless wings and tail, so t
ship presented an austere, clipped appearance. Kitiara w
smiling and humming a marching song.

"Pick up your feet, soldier," she said, linking an arm
Sturm's.

"What are you so pleased about?" he said. "The ship m.
not take flight."

"Believe that we will fly, and we will."

"I'll think lightheaded if it will help." She laughed at h
morose tone.

The ship was reloaded with what food and water t
gnomes collected, and a few items for emergency use
spare lumber, tools, nails, and so forth. Sturm bent dov
and saw that the keel was firmly set in the red dirt.

The gnomes filed up the ramp. Sturm and Kitiara pause
each with one foot at the ramp, the other on the soil of t
red moon.

"Will anyone ever believe we were here?" he asked, ta
ing in the panorama. "It all seems like a wild dream."

"What difference does it make?" Kitiara replied. "V
know what we've done and where we've been; even if v
never tell another soul, we'll know."

They walked up the ramp and hauled it up behind ther
When the hatch was secure, Sturm went up to the ma
deck. Kitiara disappeared into the hold.

Cupelix swooped in, beat his wings hard and alight
gently beside the *Cloudmaster*. "Glorious, my friends! I a

reborn—no, born for the first time! Freed of the stone sarcophagus in which I dwelt, I am a new dragon.

"Henceforth, I am no longer Cupelix, but Pteriol, the Flyer!"

"Pleased to meet you, Pteriol," said Fitter.

"We'd best be off," interrupted Sturm. "While it's still light."

"Yes, yes," said Stutts. "Listen, all of you; each fellow is to stand by the mooring ropes. When I give the word, slip the knots and let us rise."

"Tell them to pull in the ropes. They're all we've got," advised Roperig.

"And pull in the ropes!" Stutts said. "Everyone ready?" The gnomes piped their readiness. "Very good. All hands, slip your ropes!"

They managed to get most of the lines loose at the same time, though Rainspot at the stern had a hard knot and lagged behind. The ship rolled sideways, the hull planks groaning.

"We're too heavy!" Wingover shouted.

The distinct sound of splitting wood erupted below their feet. The starboard side rose, throwing everyone to port. Sturm banged the back of his head against the deck house. Then, with an ear-piercing crack, the *Cloudmaster* righted itself and lifted into the air.

"Halloo!" called Pteriol. "You've lost something!"

Sturm and the gnomes filled the rail. They were rising very slowly, but from a height of fifty feet, they could see a wide section of the hull planking and a mass of dark metal on the ground.

"The engine!" Flash cried. Birdcall uttered a hawkish scream of dismay.

They rushed from the ladder down to the hold. Near the deck hatch, Flash fell into the arms of Kitiara. She was whistling a Solacian dance tune.

"Quickly!" said the excited gnome. "We've lost the engine! We must go back and get it!"

Kitiara stopped whistling. "No," she said.

"No? No?"

"I don't know anything about aerial navigation, but I do

know this ship was too heavy to get off the ground. So
arranged for the extra weight to stay behind."

"How'd you do that?" Sturm asked.

"Sawed through the hull around the engine," she said.

"It's not fair! It's not right!" Flash said, blinking throug
angry tears. Birdcall made similar noises.

Sturm patted the two on their shoulders. "It may not b
fair, but it was the only thing to do," he said gently. "You ca
always build another engine once you get back to Sancris

Stutts and Wingover squeezed past Kitiara and starte
down the ladder. "We'd better inspect the hole," said Stutt
"The hull may be seriously weakened. Not to mentic
drafty."

Drafty was an understatement. A yawning hole, twel
feet by eight feet, showed where the lightning-powere
engine had been.

"My," said Stutts, peering down at the receding groun
They were already a hundred feet up. "This is rather inte
esting. We should have built a window into the bottom
the ship from the first."

"Keep that in mind," Sturm said, who kept well back fro
the hole. "We'll have to patch this somehow, if only to ke
ourselves from tumbling out." He wasn't too surprised b
Kitiara's deed. It was typical of her: quick, direct, and a b
ruthless. Still, they were off the ground at last.

Pteriol's brass scales glistened as he passed under the shi
The dragon circled in a rising spiral, wings flapping slow
The *Cloudmaster* moved very slowly westward, away fro
the fallen obelisk.

Wingover stepped forward until his toes were off the ed
of the hull timbers. He pushed back the swath of bandag
that shrouded his head. His disturbing black eyes focus
on something far below.

"What is that?" he asked, pointing at the distant groun

"I can't see anything," Stutts said.

"There's someone down there walking."

"A tree-man?" suggested Sturm. "It is daylight."

"Too small. It walks differently, more like—" Wingov
scrubbed his eyes with his small fists. "No! It can't be!"

"What, what?"

"It looks like a gnome—like Bellcrank!"

Sturm frowned. "Bellcrank is dead."

"I know! I know! But it looks just like him. His ears have this funny shape." Wingover brushed his own ears. "But now he's red all over!"

There was a shout from the upper deck. Sighter had spotted the walking figure with his spyglass. Sturm, Stutts, and Wingover hurried up. The astronomer gnome identified the figure as Bellcrank, too.

Fitter shivered. "Is it a ghost?" he asked plaintively.

"Hardly," Sighter responded. "It just stumbled on the turf."

"Then he's alive!" said Cutwood. "We have to go back for him!" Flash, Roperig, and Birdcall all seconded this notion. Stutts cleared his throat to get their attention.

"We can't go back," he said sadly. "We've no control over direction or altitude." Rainspot began to sniffle, and Cutwood dabbed his eyes on his sleeve.

"Isn't there anything we can do?" Sturm asked.

Just then, Pteriol flashed by the port side, banked steeply, and rolled over the top of the bag. Everyone on the *Cloudmaster* felt his telepathic whoops of delight.

"The dragon! The dragon can fetch him!" said Rainspot.

"He might," said Kitiara.

"You're his favorite. You ask him," said Cutwood.

The brass form arrowed past the starboard rail, the wind from his wings stirring the drifting ship into a slow eddy. "Hai, dragon. Cupelix! Suffering gods, I mean Pteriol!" Kitiara yelled. The dragon swept under the stern and raced along the underside of the ship.

"He can't hear me," she said, peeved. "Big, dumb brute!"

"He's drunk with freedom," Sturm said. "Can't blame him, after all the centuries he spent in that obelisk."

"We're losing Bellcrank!" Fitter cried as the ship floated over the valley cliff walls.

The tiny red figure shrank from even Wingover's powerful sight and was lost in the scarlet terrain. The gnomes watched, wordless, as the *Cloudmaster* drew away from their lost friend. Amid quiet weeping, Cutwood broke away and went below deck. He returned shortly with a hammer, a saw, and a pair of pliers. He threw these items overboard.

"Why did you do that?" Sturm said.

Cutwood turned his round pink face up to the taller man. "Bellcrank will need tools," he said.

Sighter, Stutts, and Wingover left the rail. Flash and Bird-call lingered a while longer, then they, too, departed. Roperig pulled Fitter away. Rainspot and Cutwood stayed, even as the valley fell farther and farther behind.

"It's so hard to believe," Rainspot said. "Bellcrank was dead. We buried him."

"Perhaps there's some truth to what the dragon said," Kiti-ara offered. Cutwood asked what she meant. "He said nothing ever died on Lunitari."

"You mean that wasn't Bellcrank down there, just something that looked like him?"

"I don't know, I'm no cleric or philosopher," she said. "The dead have been known to walk, even on Krynn. With all the magic rampant on Lunitari, it doesn't seem too strange that Bellcrank should return."

No one could answer her. Kitiara turned up the collar of her cloak and went below, leaving Rainspot and Cutwood alone at the rail.

* * * * *

They flew over many of the places they'd crossed on foot—the field of stones (alive with growth by daylight) and the oreless range of hills. From above, the short-lived jungle had a disquieting appearance. The plants writhed and undu-lated, like swells in a wind-tossed sea. Even that grew boring after a while, and Sturm went below to see what was being done to the hole in the ship's belly.

He almost choked when he saw what the gnomes were doing. Cutwood and Fitter were lying on their bellies on thin lengths of planking stretched across the gap. Less-than-inch-thick wood was all that stood between them and a long, long fall. Rainspot and Flash passed them other, short-er pieces of wood to nail crosswise. In this knockabout, trial-and-error style, the gnomes were repairing the hole.

From the stern, Kitiara looked down at the red moon.

Three hours aloft, and the land had fallen away far enough to lose its surface features. Now it was just a rolling bolt of red velvet, no more real than the permanent black of the sky. Cupelix (for Kitiara scoffed at the dragon's new name) was behind and slightly below them. The continuous effort of flying was tiring him out, and he no longer swooped and danced through the air. Now it was long, slow, steady work.

How do you do it?

"How do I do what?" said Kitiara.

How do you in the ship fly so effortlessly?

"The ethereal air holds us up," she said. "That's all I know. Shall I fetch Stutts, so he can explain?"

No. Gnomish explanations give me a headache.

She laughed. "Me, too." A thin veil fell between the ship and the flying dragon. "Clouds," said Kitiara. "We're getting pretty high."

My chest aches. I am not used to so much exertion.

"It's a long way to Krynn."

How long?

"Many days, at this rate. Maybe weeks. Did you think Krynn was just over the horizon?"

There is not much sympathy in your tone, my dear.

"You're not master of your own world anymore. Take this as a lesson in discipline."

You are a hard woman.

"Life's hard," said Kitiara. She turned away from the rail. The air was growing steadily colder and thinner, and she needed to don her gloves. In the former dining room (now without table or benches) Kitiara slipped into her boots. She did up her leggings and drew the string tight around her calves. The old knot passed by in the drawstring. She'd lost weight. No matter, she thought; I've traded ten pounds for the strength of ten men.

Kitiara tied a bow in the drawstring. Distracted, she pulled too hard and one end fell out, making a hard knot. She stared at the result, puzzled—not for mistying the bow, but because she hadn't snapped the string like a cobweb.

No one was around. Kitiara grasped the woven silk cord in both hands and pulled harder. It did not break.

Chapter 30

Little Red Man

ON hIGh the aIr was as clear and sharp as an elven sword. Without the constant beating of wings, there was no sensation of movement aboard the *Cloudmaster*. Quite to the contrary, it seemed as if the sun, stars, and Lunitari itself were moving, while the ship stood anchored in the sky. The effect of this mode of flight was curiously timeless. Only the wind-up clock in the wheelhouse showed that time was passing at all.

After they had been airborne almost five hours, Lunitari was far enough below them to resemble a sphere again. Of Krynn there was no sign, and that worried the travelers.

Sighter assured them that their home world would appear as Lunitari turned on its course through the heavens. "We have a better than even chance of reaching Krynn," he said severely. "As the largest body in the heavens, it naturally has the greatest attraction for us, just as it attracts a greater amount of sunlight than Lunitari. Still, we must be wary and release the proper amount of ethereal air when the propitious moment comes, so that we can descend homeward."

The strange, motionless flight bothered Sturm, so he kept below deck. There the hull and deck creaked as a proper ship should, and it comforted him. He'd always been fond of sailing ships.

The patch over the hole in the hull was finished, but it was not the finest example of the shipwright's art. Planks and laths and blocks of wood were nailed and mortised over the gap wherever they could fit. The gnomes strolled across the patch without a care, but Sturm did not trust it to support his weight. He prowled on past the patch to the forward end of the ship, which at sea would have been the forecastle. The hull there was barren of gear, and all the interior partitions had long since been ripped away. There was nothing forward at all but beams and planking. It was like being inside the skeleton of some great beast, all bones and no flesh.

Sturm ascended the fore ladder into the wheelhouse. There was no wheel, for there was no tail to be turned by a wheel. All the finely wrought brass fixtures had been ripped out for scrap or merely to lighten the ship. Only Stutts's chair remained, though its plump velvet cushions were gone.

Kitiara was there, sitting on the deck, gazing out the windows at nothing.

"Are you ill, Kit?"

"Do I look ill?"

"No." Sturm sat down on the deck opposite her.

Kitiara looked away, toying with the drawstring of her leggings. "Sturm, are you still having visions?"

"No, not for some time."

"Do you remember them?" she asked.

"Of course I do."

"What was the first one?"

"Why, it was the—when I saw—" A perplexed look came over Sturm's face. "Something about my father?" His high forehead became a mass of wrinkles as he tried to recall what he'd seen.

"What about the last one?" Kitiara asked.

He shook his head. "There was a sorcerer—I think."

"We've lost it," Kitiara said softly. "The effect the natural magic of Lunitari had on each of us. You've forgotten the substance of your visions. I'm losing my strength. Here, look." She took out her dagger and planted her thumbs on the back of the blade. Fingers knotting, Kitiara slowly bent the slim steel blade to a blunt angle.

"You seem very strong to me," said Sturm.

"Yesterday I could've folded this blade in half with two fingers." She tossed the bent dagger aside.

"We're better off without the powers," Sturm said.

"That's easy for you to say! I like being strong—powerful!"

"Mighty fighters live and die in every generation, the past ones forgotten by the present, the present destined to vanish in the memories of the future. Virtue, not ferocity or cunning, are what make a fighter a hero, Kit."

Kitiara straightened her stooped shoulders and said resolutely, "You're wrong, Sturm. Only success is remembered. Nothing else matters but success."

He opened his mouth to reply, but the wheelhouse door flew open and a blast of icy air rushed in. Cutwood, swathed to the top of his pink bald head in flannel rags and quilting, posed dramatically in the doorway, one stubby arm flung out, pointing astern.

"The dragon!" he said. "Cupelix is faltering!"

The whole crew was assembled aft. When Sturm and Kitiara joined them, the concentration of weight made the ship tip steeply back. Stutts said, "Spread out! We can't all stand in the same p-p-place!"

Wingover shook his head. "You stuttered," he said.

"Never mind that now," said Kitiara.

Cupelix was far back and nearly fifty feet below the rising *Cloudmaster*. He was holding his wings out in glide position, flapping only once every few seconds. His long neck was arched down, his head low. The dragon's large hind legs, normally held tightly against his belly when in flight, likewise dangled limply.

"Cupelix! Cupelix, can you hear me?" Kitiara called through cupped hands.

Yes, my dear.

"You can make it, beast. Do you hear me? You can make it!"

No. Done in . . . too weak. The dragon's tail dropped, making him waver.

"Flap, damn you! Don't give up. Remember, you're a brass dragon!" she cried. "This is your chance, Cupelix! Your chance to come to Krynn."

Can't fly . . . not meant to be, dear Kit.

Sturm called, "Is there anything we can do?"

Tell others, I live. Tell others to visit Lunitari.

"We will," shouted Rainspot.

*Bring books. Bring philosophers. Bring—*His thought trailed off. Cupelix was flapping weakly now.

Kitiara grabbed Wingover by his collar. "Why can't he fly? Why does he keep going down?" she demanded.

"The air is too thin. His wings aren't big enough to support him this high," said the wide-eyed gnome. Sturm broke her grip and put Wingover back on his feet. The gnome exhaled gustily. "*Cloudmaster* was able to stay aloft because we had two sets of wings and the ethereal air bag to hold us up. The dragon has neither."

Farewell.

Kitiara flung herself at the rail. The crimson orb of Lunitari looked no bigger than a dinner plate. Against the light-colored moon, the dark figure of the dragon moved, an agonized silhouette. Cupelix, the ill-named Pteriol, was going down. Wingover gave his colleagues a running commentary on the dragon's failing flight. The massive muscles in the dragon's back writhed in ferocious cramps. His wings spasmed, sending him into a heart-stopping plummet. With great effort and much obvious pain, he regained his balance and slowed his descent. Trailing behind him in the wind was a steady swirl of brass scales, torn off by his terrible exertions.

"Cupelix! Don't leave me! Our bargain!" Kitiara cried desperately. "My strength is fading, do you hear? I need you—our plans—" Sturm took hold of her shoulders and pulled her firmly away from the rail. Her fingers clutched at the smooth wood.

Farewell, dear Kit, was all they heard, and the tickling touch of the dragon's telepathic voice was gone. Sighter climbed up on the rail and scanned the moon with his spy glass. He could see nothing. "Good-bye, dragon!" he said. Sighter snapped his telescope shut and slipped back to the deck. The little men quietly dispersed.

Kitiara sobbed against Sturm's chest. "I'm sorry," he said. Her tears unsettled him more than Cupelix's tragic failure.

She pushed him away suddenly and snapped, "Stupid beast! He and I had a deal! Our plans, our great plans!" Suddenly ashamed, Kitiara scrubbed the tears from her cheeks and sniffed loudly. "Everyone leaves me. There's no one can rely on."

Sturm felt his sympathy for Kit drain away. "No one you can rely on?" he said coldly. "No one at all?" When she didn't answer, Sturm turned his back and left Kitiara alone.

* * * * *

Cupelix, defeated by the heights he had hoped to conquer, glided down in a wide spiral to the moon that had been, and always would be, his home. His flying muscles burned with fatigue, and the invidious cold of the upper air numbed his heart and soul. He skimmed over familiar landscapes, now cloaked in night, until the cliffs of his valley dropped away beneath his hanging feet. Striking heavily, Cupelix's horned head plowed into the red dust.

He raised his head and sneezed. A voice said, "Bless you!"

"Thank you," replied the dragon weakly. "Wait—who said that?"

A diminutive figure appeared from behind a pile of goods left behind by the gnomes. It resembled a gnome itself except that it was as hairless as an egg and colored red—skin, eyes, clothes, everything.

"I said it," said the little red creature. "It's a common wish to express when someone sneezes."

"I know that," said the dragon peevishly. He was far too

tired to play gnomish games. "Who are you?"

"I was hoping you might know," said the little red fellow. "I woke up a day ago, and I've been wandering since."

Cupelix raised himself on his hind legs and carefully furled his wings. The bending of his joints caused him considerable pain, and he hissed louder than a hundred snakes.

"Does it hurt?" asked the red man.

"Very much!"

"I saw a bottle of liniment over there. Perhaps that would help." A small red hand went to the dark red lips. "Though I'm not sure what liniment is."

"Never mind, Little Red Man," said Cupelix. "Fetch it, if you would."

"Is that my name?"

"If you like it, it is."

"Seems to fit, doesn't it?" The Little Red Man trotted off to find the bottle of Dr. Finger's Efficacious Ointment. He stopped and called back, "What's your name?"

"Cupelix," said the dragon. He was here to stay, all right, but at least he had someone to talk to. All things considered, it wasn't too bad a state of affairs.

"Little Red Man," Cupelix called across the valley, "would you like something to eat?"

Chapter 31

Highgold

The second voyage of the Cloudmaster was very different from the first. The engine's incessant turning, and the great wings' wafting had given those on board a sense of passage, of activity. The silent drift of the ship, now supported only by the ethereal air, was not like that. A pervasive lethargy invaded everyone on board. There was little to do in the way of managing the ship, and the less there was to do, the less anyone cared to do.

The gnomes quarreled, too. In the past, they had traded scoffing remarks and mild blows with equanimity; ten seconds afterward, no one remembered or cared. But now, cooped up in the bare hull of the *Cloudmaster*, the gnomes lost their generous natures. Roperig and Fitter squabbled over the correct way to store the small supply of rope they

had left. Cutwood grew deafer and deafer as he adjusted to his normal level of hearing. Flash yelled at him all the time, and Sighter yelled at Flash for yelling. Wingover had a slapping match with Birdcall that left red welts on both their faces for hours. And Rainspot, poor gentle Rainspot, sat in the 'tween decks and wept.

Stutts sought out Sturm. "Things are s-seriously wrong," he said. "My c-colleagues are behaving like a band of gully dwarves. They are b-bored. Now there's no great task to be accomplished, l-like toppling the obelisk."

"What can I do about it?" asked Sturm.

"We m-must give them a task, something that will t-take their minds off the slowness of our p-passage."

"What sort of task?"

Stutts said, "P-Perhaps Sighter could enlist their help in n-naming all the stars?"

"They would only argue," Sturm replied.

"Hmm, we c-could make a batch of m-muffins."

"No flour," Sturm reminded him. "Try again."

"Well, you c-could get seriously ill."

"Oh, no, your good colleagues would want to cut me open and find out what was wrong. Try again."

The gnome's shoulders sagged in defeat. "That was m-my last idea."

This is serious, Sturm thought. Who ever heard of a gnome out of ideas? "You know," he said, smoothing out his mustache, "perhaps there is some way to make this ship move faster."

"Without an en-engine?"

"Ships girdle the world without engines," Sturm observed. "How do they do it?"

"Let's s-see." Stutts twined his fingers together and thought hard. "Oars, s-sails, draft animals on shore, magic—" Here he traded a disapproving look with Sturm. "—muscle-turned p-paddle wheels, towing by whales or sea s-serpents—" A light kindled in his pale blue eyes. "Excuse me. I m-must confer with my colleagues."

"Good man," said Sturm. He watched the gnome hurry away, almost skipping with delight.

A cheer penetrated the deck from below as Stutts

explained his notion to the other gnomes. Thumps and squeaks told only too well that the gnomes' idleness had vanished. Sturm smiled.

He went looking for Kitiara. She was not in the dining room, so he went below. The gnomes were gathered in the berth deck's aft cabin. He peeked in the doorless doorway, to see Flash and Wingover sketching madly on the deck planks with lumps of charcoal.

"No, no," Sighter was saying, "you must increase the degree of camber, relative to the angle of incidence."

"What a lot of goat cheese! Any fool knows you have to decrease the planar surface," argued Flash, rapping his fist on the deck.

"Yes, any fool!"

Sturm withdrew. The gnomes were happy again.

He descended the short ladder to the hold. It was bitterly cold down there, since the flimsy patch in the hull scarcely kept out the wind, much less the cold. It was there that Sturm found Kitiara, perched on one of the stout hull ribs, sipping from her water bottle.

"You look comfortable," he said.

"Oh, I am. Care for some?" said Kitiara. She handed Sturm the bottle. He raised it to his lips, but before taking a swallow smelled the sweet tang of wine.

He lowered the bottle. "Where did you get this?"

"Cupelix made it for me. Wine of Ergoth."

Sturm took the smallest sip. It was extremely sweet, and as the few drops flowed down his throat, they burned strongly. His face must have reddened, for Kitiara chuckled at him.

"Deceptive, isn't it? Tastes like syrup at first, then it kicks like a bee-stung mule."

He gave the bottle back to her. "I thought you preferred ale," he said.

Kitiara drank. "Ale is for good times, good meals, and good company. Sweet wine of Ergoth is for melancholy hours, loneliness, and funerals."

Sturm knelt beside her. "You shouldn't be melancholy," he said. "We're on our way home, at last."

Kitiara leaned back against the curving rib. "Sometimes

envy you your patience. Other times, it sets my teeth on edge." She closed her eyes. "Do you ever wonder what the rest of your life will be like?" she asked.

"Only in a very basic way," Sturm replied. "Part of knighthood is acceptance of the fate the gods mete out."

"I could never think that way. I want to make it happen. That's what hurts so much about lost opportunities. I had strength, and now it's fading; I had a dragon for an ally, and now he's gone, too."

"And Tanis?"

Kitiara shot him a cold look. "Yes, damn your honesty. Tanis is gone, too. And my father." She swirled the bottle around. It was almost empty. "I'm tired," Kitiara said. "I'll make a resolution, Sturm, and you can be my witness. From now on, I shall contemplate, plan, reason, and calculate; whatever serves my purpose will be good and whatever impedes me will be evil. I'll not rely on anyone but myself; not share with anyone except my most loyal comrades in arms. I'll be queen of my own realm, this," she patted herself on the leg, "and not fear anything but failure." She turned her rather bleary eyes to him. "What do you think of my resolution?"

"I think you've had too much wine." He rose to go, but she called for him to stop.

"It's cold down here," she complained.

"So come up to the berth deck."

Kitiara held out her arms and tried to stand. She didn't get very far before sagging back to the hull rib. "I'm better off not trying," she said. "Come here."

Sturm stood over her. She grabbed hold of his sleeve. Still quite strong, Kitiara easily pulled Sturm down to her level. He tried to protest, but she pushed him back against the curving planks and nestled in close. "Just stay here a while," she said, eyes closed, "to keep me warm."

So Sturm found himself lying very still in the coldest part of the ship, Kitiara nestled under his left arm. Her breathing grew soft and regular. He studied the face showing under her fur-trimmed hood. Kitiara's tan had lightened over the past weeks, but her dark lashes and curls seemed out of place on so rugged a warrior. Her dark lips were parted slightly and her breath smelled of sweet wine.

* * * * *

The gnomes presented their grand design for improving the drifting *Cloudmaster*'s speed a few hours later in the former dining room. Birdcall had drawn the whole plan on the wall in chalk and charcoal. Sturm sat on the floor, listening attentively. Kitiara leaned on the wall several feet away, tight-lipped. She was experiencing ill effects from the wine.

"As you can see," Wingover began, "our plan calls for rigging the *Cloudmaster* with sails on each side of the ethereal air bag. That, and trimming the hull with the excess of weight well in the bow, should increase our speed by, ah— how much did you estimate, Sighter?"

The astronomer gnome studied the scribbles on his shirt cuff. "Sixty percent, or to about twelve knots."

"What will you make the sails out of?" asked Sturm.

"What clothing we can spare. You and Mistress Kitiara will have to contribute what you have as well."

"Ahem, well, if there are no more questions—"

"What about spars and masts and rigging?" Sturm said.

Cutwood waved his hand to be recognized. Wingover relinquished the floor. "I thought of an answer to that," the gnome said importantly. "With chisels and planes, we'll be able to slice off long pieces from the beams and rails of the ships. These lashed together will serve as spars."

"Let me tell about the rigging," said Roperig.

"I know about it, too," Cutwood complained.

"Let Roperig tell it!" ordered Fitter. Cutwood flopped down in a snit.

"We have some store of rope already," Roperig said. "And some cord, twine, string, thread—"

"Get on with it," said Wingover.

"Silly know-it-all," muttered Cutwood.

"These can be braided into whatever thickness of rope we need." Roperig snapped his fingers and sat down. Only Fitter applauded his report.

"Shall we get to it?" Sturm asked, bracing himself to rise.

They formed the *Cloudmaster* sewing circle on the dining room floor. A fair-sized heap of clothes grew up in the center, around which everyone sat. It was not an easy process.

Sturm could not sew and Kitiara steadfastly refused to even attempt it, confining her contribution to slitting the seams of the sacrificed clothes with her bent-bladed dagger. Of the gnomes, only Roperig and Fitter, not too surprisingly, proved to be adept sewers. They were so adept, in fact, that they sewed the clothes they were wearing into the sail, which then had to be cut apart again.

After a break for food and rest, the work resumed. Some hours later (it was hard to judge time in the constant night) the ragged, flimsy sails were done. Cutwood and Flash had by this time chiseled out spars from the largest beams in the ship. It was time then to rig the *Cloudmaster* for sail.

They tied the ends of the spars to the air bag's rigging and the sails stretched between them. The sails were simple rectangles that overlapped the deck rail by several feet. Once they were set, the flying ship did come slowly about in a new direction.

"How do we steer this thing?" Kitiara asked. Ordinary ships had rudders. The *Cloudmaster* had none.

"We'll have to manage by trimming the sails," Sturm said. He was cheered by the sight of wind filling the funny patchwork sails.

They shifted all their loose baggage forward and the flying ship surged ahead with noticeable vigor. It was possible to feel the wind now out on deck, and the ship rolled fore and aft like a rocking horse. Kitiara was a bit green from the motion. The rigging creaked and stretched. The stars and moons coursed by at an increasing rate.

Clouds loomed ahead, and the ship quickly overtook them. Streams of warm mist flowed over the ship, thawing the frost that coated the windows and ports and made the upper deck treacherous. They sailed through the clouds for only a short time. When they burst through the wall of white, a glorious sight greeted them.

The brilliant blue globe of Krynn hung before them, a bauble of silver and glass. It looked so small and fragile this far away, a marble in a child's hand. Other cloud banks towered around them, but by luffing the sails, the *Cloudmaster*'s crew weaved the ship through them. Some of the banks flickered with lightning. Rainspot eyed these with longing. He hadn't experienced any real weather in months. Unlike Kitiara, he was genuinely pleased to have lost his gift. No one should always walk about in a rainstorm, he had decided.

An odd thing happened as they steered cautiously through the maze of storm and cloud. Faint echoes of thunder rolled by, and in the dying claps Sturm heard another sound, a distant bleat, like the call of a trumpet.

"Did you hear that?" he said to Flash, who was by his elbow.

"No," said the gnome. "What was it?"

The noise sounded again, louder and nearer. "That's it!" said Sturm.

"Funny, it sounds like a—" Before Flash could finish, a green and gold mallard hurtled into the sail above their heads. "A duck!" Flash said hastily.

The mallard was a good-sized bird, and it half-tore the flimsy sail from the twig spars. Duck and spar tangled, and fell to the deck at Flash's feet. "Halloo! We've caught a duck!" he shouted.

"What did he say?" Roperig asked.

"He said to duck," Fitter replied, face down on the deck.

"No, by Reorx, he's snared a duck!" cried Wingover.

Flash folded the sail back and the mallard poked its head out. Its beady black eyes regarded the *Cloudmaster*'s crew with pure hostility.

"Wonder where it came from," said Rainspot.

"An egg, dumbhead," said Cutwood.

"Hold on to it," said Kitiara. "Ducks are good eating." Just as her strength had faded as they left the influence of Lunitari, so too had the spear plants lost their magical variety of flavors. They had become rubbery, tasteless. Kitiara smacked her lips at the thought of crisply browned duck meat.

"Not much meat for eleven," Sturm said. "If only there were more."

"Ducks ahoy!" Roperig sang out. Over the starboard rail, black against the gray clouds, came a great flock of ducks.

"Bring us about!" Sturm shouted. "They'll wreck us if they hit us!"

Gnomes scampered into the jury-rigging, collapsing the

sails on the port side. The ship heeled away from the flock, swinging under the air bag like a pendulum. Some of the mallards hit the hull and bounced off. A few swept across the deck, squawking loudly. They veered and banked in panic, thudding on the sides of the deckhouse. Fortunately, none hit the air bag or the sails.

"This is crazy," Kitiara declared. "What are ducks doing so far from home?"

Flash stood up from behind the railing. The first duck was still firmly under his arm. "Maybe this is where ducks go when they migrate," he posited.

"Interesting theory," Sighter said. "Do they just fly around for three months, or do they have a destination?"

Kitiara hobbled the duck with a loop of twine around its feet and pinioned its wings with a length of cord. Fitter watched her every move.

Unnerved, she said, "Would you rather do this?"

"No, I just don't want you to hurt it."

"Hurt it! I plan to eat it."

"Oh, no! It's so pretty. Those green and gold feathers—"

"Yes, and it'll look even better roasting on a spit," she said.

The ducks who'd been lying senseless on deck chose that moment to rouse and take wing, quacking loudly. In seconds, they were all gone, save for the mallard that Kitiara had trussed up. It honked forlornly at its departing comrades.

Fitter stared at the mallard in his hands. With two large tears rolling down his face, he held the duck out to Kitiara.

Kitiara's hands closed on the duck and a loud sob came from Fitter. "Suffering gods!" she exclaimed. "Keep it, Fitter. Enjoy it yourself."

"Oh! I will!" Fitter dashed to the deckhouse door. "I've already named him Highgold, because he flew so high and has gold feathers." The door banged shut behind him.

"So, instead of a duck dinner, we have another mouth to feed," said Kitiara.

"Don't worry," Sturm said. "The duck is one of us, flying too high and too far from home."

Chapter 32

The Lost Caravel

It was hard to say just when the change occurred. It came on slowly, with no dramatic oscillations or warnings. Somewhere in the billowing white clouds, the *Cloudmaster* stopped rising toward Krynn and began falling toward it. Sturm asked Sighter just how this worked, but the astronomer mumbled something about "density of matter in relation to air" and left it at that. Sighter plainly didn't understand the effect himself.

Nevertheless, the blue face of Krynn moved from over their heads to under their feet. The closer they got to their home world, the livelier the winds grew, and the faster they flew.

"We can't land too soon for me," Kitiara commented. "If I have to eat pink spears and drink water much longer, toadstools will sprout from my ears!" Fitter heard this and kept Highgold discreetly out of Kitiara's sight.

The air grew warmer and wetter. While the warmth was appreciated, the denser, moister air proved a hardship for them all after being used to Lunitari's thin air. The weightiness oppressed them. For a time, it was hard to do anything strenuous.

"By the gods," Sturm remarked, panting as he helped Cutwood and Flash trim the port sails, "I haven't been this winded since Flint and I had to flee the forest dwarves, after Tasslehoff 'borrowed' some of their silver."

Day and night fell into a more even rhythm again, and Sturm found himself sleeping longer and more soundly as the days slipped by. Sighter recorded that the *Cloudmaster* had been airborne for nineteen days and estimated that it would make landfall in two more days.

The sky changed from black to blue, and the horizon filled with clouds. Through puffy gaps they could see forests, fields, mountains, and seas below. They were still high, but at least they had a sense of solid ground beneath them again.

The morning of what was to be their last day aloft dawned sultry and wet. The sails hung from their spars, and dew stood in puddles on deck. A clinging mist held to the flying ship, and nothing was visible ten feet beyond the rail.

"Halloo!" Wingover shouted. "Halloo!"

"Can't see a thing," Kitiara reported, squinting hard.

"I can't even tell how high we are," Sturm said. The *Cloudmaster* seemed to be adrift in a box of wet fleece. Stutts appeared with the rope and grapnel.

"We should d-drop this over the side," he advised. "It m-may hook a tree and d-drag us to a stop."

He lowered the grapnel from the bowsprit and tied it off. When he returned amidships Kitiara asked him when they ought to open the bag and release the ethereal air.

"Only when w-we're certain we're about to l-land."

She stared at the wallowing bag overhead. The dirty canvas sack had shrunk steadily as it got warmer. Now it hung against the rope netting, rolling about furtively like a caged beast trying to escape. Kitiara fingered the hilt of her bent dagger. No more nonsense, she thought. When conditions look good, I'll open the bag myself!

Wingover, still entwined in the rigging, pointed off the starboard bow. "Fire!" he cried.

Sighter clicked open his telescope and swung it toward the orange glow far off in the mist. His mouth dropped open for a second, then he lowered his glass and shut it.

"You dolt!" he said to Wingover. "Haven't you ever seen a sunrise before?"

"What?"

"Sunrise?" said Kitiara. A sunrise could only mean they were low enough to the ground for the sun to appear as the ball of fire they remembered, and not as the yellow disk it looked like from between the red moon and Krynn.

The sun waxed hotter and brighter, and the fog dispersed. A thousand feet below lay only ocean—as far as every eye could see, nothing but oily green sea. The salty smell rose to greet them as the sun heated up the water.

A north wind pushed them along at an idle six knots. As the day wore on, the humidity rose and all the furs and cold weather gear came off. The gnomes stripped down to suspenders and trousers. The deck thumped with nine pairs of bare pink feet. As protection from sunburn, Fitter made them all bandannas from their shirts and soon the gnomes looked like a band of pirates shrunk to half size.

Kitiara joyously discarded her heavy clothes, keeping only her riding breeches and a leather vest. Sturm alone refused to shed his long-sleeved tunic and boots. Kitiara noted the dark sweat stains on his chest and arms. Dignity, she decided, could be an uncomfortable burden.

By angling the sails, they were able to drive the ship down closer to the sea. The grapnel dipped and leaped from wave crest to wave crest, slinging back from the impacts.

Sighter worked hard with his astrolabe to determine their location. Without a compass and accurate charts, he could make only a rough estimate, but he tried. The deck, from the door of the wheelhouse aft to the stern post, was covered with his figures. Sweat collected in his bushy brows and dripped annoyingly from the tip of his nose.

Kitiara and Sturm surveyed the vast calculations, and

finally Kit asked, "Well?"

"We're on Krynn," said Sighter. Kitiara counted to twenty, silently. "My best guess is, we're somewhere in the Sirion Sea, either four hundred, eight hundred, or twelve hundred miles from Sancrist."

"Four, eight, or twelve hundred?" Sturm said.

"Lacking a compass, it's very hard to be precise." Sighter flicked off a drop of sweat that had stubbornly clung to his nose. "I'm certain it's one of those multiples of four hundred."

Kitiara threw up her hands. "Wonderful! We may cruise into Thalan Bay in four days, or we may starve to death trying to reach an island a thousand miles away."

"I don't think we'll starve," said Wingover.

"Oh? What makes you so certain?"

"There's a ship," he said quietly, pointing out to sea.

Sighter's precious figures were trampled in the rush to the rail. Off the port they saw bow masts and snowy sails poking above the horizon. Out came the telescope. Kitiara plucked it from Sighter's grasp.

"What!" he said, but she already had the glass to her eye.

The ship was a two-masted caravel of uncertain origin. There was no figurehead or name scribed on the forecastle. The mastheads were bare of pennants or flags, though the deck was clean and the brightwork shined.

"Can you make out where she's from?" asked Sturm.

"No," Kitiara said. "Can't see any crew."

"Try in the rigging. They're running with the wind, so there's bound to be somebody aloft."

"I looked. There's nobody to be seen."

The *Cloudmaster* slowed as it entered a lower stratum of air. The direction changed, and the patchwork sails luffed and flapped impotently. While Sturm and four gnomes saw to resetting them, Kitiara studied the unidentified ship.

"Pirate, maybe? Or smuggler?" she mused. There were plenty of reasons to hide a ship's name, few legitimate.

"Sturm? Sturm?" she called.

"What is it?"

"Could we catch that ship and board it?"

He came to the edge of the deckhouse and shaded his eyes to look down at her. "Why?"

"They might have food and fresh water."

It was a powerful argument. Sturm was as sick of beans and Lunitarian fungi as the rest of them. "I suppose we could," he said. "The grappling hook is still out. We'll have to be careful not to snarl their rigging or rip their sails."

The unknown ship drove on with all sails set. There was no one on deck, and as the *Cloudmaster* flew around to the ship's port beam, Kitiara could see that the caravel's wheel was lashed. The sterncastle lights were shuttered, and all the hull ports were closed. On a hot, still day like this, the 'tween decks must be stifling, she thought.

"Let them out now," Sturm said. Birdcall and Roperig let the sails unfurl, and the flying ship spurted ahead. The swinging grapnel snagged the chain stays of the mainmast, and the *Cloudmaster* jerked to a stop. They pivoted with the drag and found themselves flying tail-first into the wind, towed by the far heavier caravel.

"Now what?" said Wingover, leaning over the side.

"Someone has to go down and tie us off," suggested Sturm. "I would go, but the grapnel rope is too thin for me."

"Don't look my way," Kitiara said. "I've had all the rope climbing I care for on this trip."

Fitter agreed to go, since he was small and nimble. He shinnied down the rope to the masthead. Standing on the crosstree, he waved up to his friends.

"Find a heavier line and tie us off!" Sturm bawled. Fitter nodded and slipped down the rigging to the ship's deck. A fat hawser line lay coiled behind the foremast. Fitter shouldered this burden and climbed back to the *Cloudmaster*.

"That's my apprentice," said Roperig proudly.

"Did you see any signs of life down there?" asked Kitiara.

Fitter dumped the hawser off his shoulder. "No, ma'am. Everything's neat as can be, but there isn't a soul around."

Sturm went down into the deckhouse and returned with his sword. He draped the belt over his shoulder and threw one leg over the rail. "I'd better be first to look around."

"I'll come behind you," said Kitiara.

"Me, too," volunteered Fitter. The other gnomes chimed in in quick succession.

"Someone has to stay on board," Sturm said. "You

gnomes work it out, but don't all of you come."

A hundred feet is a long way to climb down a rope. The heat was so bad that Sturm got dizzy halfway along and had to stop to mop the sweat from his eyes. How will I ever climb back up? he wondered. It was a relief when the dark, varnished oak of the yardarm touched his feet. Kitiara wrapped her bare legs around the hawser and started down.

Deck level was just as Fitter had described: tidy and ship-shape. Sturm had a bad feeling about it. Sailors did not abandon a well-founded vessel without good reason.

Kitiara dropped down to the deck. Sturm whirled, sword coming out with a whisk of steel.

"Easy!" she said. "I'm on your side, remember?"

"Sorry. This ship has me spooked. Go up the starboard side to the bow. I'll take port."

They met at the bow, finding nothing amiss except the complete lack of visible crew. There was a hatch behind the bowsprit. Kitiara suggested they go below deck.

"Not yet," said Sturm. "Let's check aft."

Sighter and Stutts arrived on deck. Sighter carried a carpenter's square and Stutts a hammer. These were the only 'weapons' they could find. More than ever they resembled diminutive pirates, boarding an unlucky ship from above.

"F-find anything?" said Stutts.

"Nothing."

The ship's wheel was firmly tied. It creaked an inch or two left and right as the wind and waves fought against the rudder. Sturm was trying to tell how long the wheel had been fixed when Kitiara drew in her breath sharply.

"Look here," she said.

Nailed to the wall of the sterncastle was a crow. A stuffed, dead crow with its tail and wings spread.

"I've seen these before. Someone has cast a spell over this ship, and to ward off the evil magic someone put this crow here," said Kitiara. "We've got to get out of here!"

"Take it easy," Sturm said quietly. "We've seen no signs of magic at work. Let's go inside and see if we can at least identify this vessel."

The louvered door creaked back on bright brass hinges. Within the sterncastle it was hot and dim. Slivers of light cast weird shadows across the room.

"Stutts, open the shutters, will you?" The gnome made for the row of shades on his right. There was a rustle as he wrestled with the latch. The shutters fell open, flooding the cabin with light.

"So, here's the captain," said Kitiara grimly.

The master of the caravel still sat at his table, gazing sightlessly through ivory eye sockets. His skull was clean and dry, and the skeletal fingers lying on the tabletop were still joined together. The captain wore a richly made coat of blue brocade, embellished with gold tassels and braid. A final macabre touch was the skeleton of his last meal still on the plate before him. Stutts poked through the tiny bones.

"Chicken," he announced. "A h-hen, I should say."

Sturm sniffed the pewter goblet by the dead man's right hand. There was no obvious trace of poison in the empty cup. He put it down and noticed a slim silver ring around one of the bony fingers. Gently he lifted the skeleton's hand. Despite his care, the bones fell apart at his touch. Sturm held the ring up to the light, trying to find an inscription or maker's mark. It was a simple, beaded silver band, slightly grimy. It could have been made anywhere by anyone.

Kitiara looked under the table. "Ho!" she said. "What's this?" She stood up with a second skull in her hands. "This was between Captain Bones's feet." She flipped the skull around. "Someone chopped this fellow's head off. You can see the axe mark, there." She set the gruesome relic on the table and bent over again. "Nice boots," she reported. "Silver buckles, deerskin tops. He was a dandy."

"I wonder who he was," Sturm said.

"M-my!" Stutts was over near the stern lights. He'd found a large leather-bound chest and sprung the simple lock. Inside were gold coins and scattered jewels. Kitiara whistled and fished out an especially fine emerald.

"Now I understand," she said. "This must be a pirate ship."

"Are you so certain?" said Sighter.

"You don't lay in swag like this trading fish and dry goods!" She threw open a second chest. It was filled to the brim with small wooden boxes. She pried the lid off one and leaned in to see what treasure it contained. Kitiara screwed up her face and gave a mighty sneeze.

"M-mercy!" said Stutts. "What is it?"

"Spice—pepper!" she wheezed, snapping the lid back on. Sturm peered over her shoulder.

"Spices are rarer than gold," he said. "This chest is probably more valuable than the other."

"Just the same, when we divvy it up, I'll take my share in gold and jewels," Kitiara said.

"Divvy? I thought you were concerned about the curse."

"With enough gold in my pocket, I'll face up to all the curses in the world." Suiting action to her words, she began to fill her pockets with gems and gold.

The cabin door flew open and they all jumped. It was only Rainspot.

"I thought I ought to come down and warn you," he said. "There's a storm brewing. It feels like a strong cyclone."

"Just enough time for a little salvage," said Kitiara. She leaned against the treasure chest and tried to shift it toward the door. It squeaked a scant inch out of place. "Don't just stand there, help me!"

"We don't have time for treasure," Sturm said. "We've got to get back to the *Cloudmaster.*"

She stopped shoving and stood up. "Do we?" she said.

"Do we what?"

"Have to go back to the flying ship. Why can't we stay on board this one?"

"We don't know anything about it," Sturm protested. "For all we know, it could founder in the first squall we hit."

"So could the *Cloudmaster.*"

Stutts fidgeted as the two humans argued. "P-please! I am returning n-now." He hurried out the door.

Sighter shrugged. "I'd like to explore this vessel some more, but my place is with my colleagues." He bowed and pushed Rainspot out the door ahead of him.

Alone with Kitiara, Sturm said with annoyance, "Are you going or staying?"

She crossed her arms stubbornly. "Staying."

"Then you're staying by yourself." Sturm went out on deck. A cool wind was blowing in from the south, and the caravel was heeled under sail to the north. Purple-black clouds closed to sea level and charged with the wind. In minutes, both ships would be engulfed.

Sighter and Stutts shinnied up the rope with little trouble. By the time Sturm had reached the top of the mainmast, they were climbing over the flying ship's rail. The *Cloudmaster* was whipping about like a fish on a hook, and Sturm watched the bouncing rope with trepidation. He took hold.

Rain, light and warm, puffed ahead of the storm. Sturm shook it out of his face. The gnomes had sheeted in all the *Cloudmaster*'s sails, but the air bag itself caught the wind, dragging the flying ship behind it. Sturm hauled himself hand over hand toward the bobbing craft, trying not to think about the tossing waves eighty feet below.

The first blow of rain hit like a wall, soaking Sturm to the skin in a second. He continued to inch higher, but the *Cloudmaster* scarcely grew closer the longer he climbed.

"Halloo, Sturm! Halloo!"

"Wingover, is that you?" he shouted in reply.

"Sturm, can you hear me? The rope is wet and stretching under your weight! The strain is too much!" cried the unseen gnome.

"I'll go back!"

Sturm could barely see the *Cloudmaster*'s gray outline. "We'll try to come back for you!" Then faintly, "May Reorx guard you well!" Wingover cried.

Sturm all but slid down the hawser to the waving mast. The stout oak yard swung into him, hitting him hard in the ribs. His breath rushed out, and he lost his grip on the rope. Sturm landed against the sail and clamped on as hard as he could. The powdery soft canvas gave way under his grip, and tore slowly down to the deck. Sturm landed, blind, wet, and breathless, in the caravel's waist.

The gnomes cut the rope at their end. The *Cloudmaster* soared into the driving clouds and was lost from sight.

Kitiara rolled Sturm over. "Can you stand? Can you walk?" she cried above the howling wind. He nodded dumbly. She dragged him to his feet, and together they staggered aft to the sterncastle. Sturm collapsed on the deck by the captain's table to collect his breath. Kitiara circled the room, closing the shutters and cranking the louvers tight.

"You all right?" she asked out of the darkness.

"Yes."

"Are the gnomes gone?"

"They—had to cut loose to save the ship." He coughed painfully.

Kitiara struck sparks from the sea captain's flint and lit a fat candle on the table. The wavering flame threw weird highlights on the dead captain's skull. Sturm wrung out his kerchief and draped it over the skull.

"He does tend to stare at you, doesn't he?" said Kitiara. She put out a hand to steady herself. The deck was rising and falling with the regularity of a water wheel.

"We'll have to trim the sails," Sturm said. "If the right gust hits us, we'll capsize."

"I'm not going up any rigging in that blow," she replied.

Out came his sword. "You won't have to. I'll cut all the stays on the lowest sails. They'll blow away, and that should do it." He went to the cabin door.

"Wait," she said. She found a painter line in the captain's locker and brought it over. "Hold your arms up." He did, and Kitiara reached around his chest and tied the line. "Don't do any swimming while you're gone," she said.

He lowered his arms. "I'll try not to."

Sturm threw open the door and received the storm's full blast. He staggered to the mainmast and slashed the lines to the mainsail. The torn canvas flopped like a live thing, crackling out from the main yard. He ducked under it and pushed on to the foremast, likewise hacking away the stays there. With only topsails and spritsail set, the going was easier. Sturm made it back to the sterncastle.

"It is steadier," Kitiara said.

"What do we do now?" asked Sturm as water dripped from his clothes and hair.

"Let's explore below," Kit suggested.

"Have you forgotten the curse?"

Her amusement evaporated. "I haven't forgotten. But if this is a sample of what's on board, I'm not much worried." She patted the captain's kerchief-covered skull. The head toppled off the neck bones and hit the table with a thump. It lay, eyes up, staring at the mortal intruders on its ship.

Chapter 33

The Wizard's Seal

A NARROW hatch covered a ladder that led down into the caravel's dark bowels. Kitiara lay flat on her belly and poked the candle into the hole. Warm stagnant air wafted out, but no obvious danger loomed. She climbed down and Sturm followed, hand on the pommel of his sword.

They'd entered nothing more interesting than the ship's rope locker. It contained only rope, sailcloth, and chain. Kitiara poked around, looking for more treasure. All she found were dead rats. Like everything else dead on the ship, the rats were a mere jumble of bones.

"Isn't it strange," Sturm whispered, "that all we ever find are bones?"

They passed through a light wooden partition into a larger space, a cargo area. Here Kitiara's candle shone on something more sinister than rope and cloth. They had found an armory, replete with swords, spears, shields, bronze breast-plates, shirts of mail, lances, bows, blocks of lead for sling pellets—enough to equip a small army.

"These are dwarf-forged shields," Sturm said, pushing a round buckler aside with his toe. "See, they have the mark of the Thorbardin Armorers' Guild. That breastplate bears the mark of the Thanes of Zhaman." He picked up the breastplate. The cold iron was polished to a finish like mir-rored silver, and though fully a third of an inch thick, it was remarkably light.

"These are first-quality arms. Why would pirates need so many weapons?" he said.

"Maybe they are captured stocks."

"Maybe, but space is precious aboard a ship. They might keep good items for their own use, but not this many."

"What's through there?" Kitiara hissed, pointing forward.

"Forecastle. Where the crew sleeps."

They stepped over the door sill and beheld a terrible sight. The forecastle was full of skeletons.

Row upon row of clean white bones lay huddled on either side of the ship. Some were stretched out, others knotted with the agony they had borne until death. Not all the bones were human. Some, by their shape and size, belonged to dwarves. Others, smaller bones, may have been kender or gnomes. There was one thing the skeletons had in common: They were all chained together at the ankles.

"I don't like this. There has been great evil here," Sturm hissed. "Come." He backed out.

"What's up front of that room?" Kitiara wondered.

"The bury of the bowsprit. Where the anchors are kept."

In the center of the armory was a large square hatch, which Sturm said led to the hold. Removing the hatch was not easy. Someone had secured it to the deck with a dozen large iron bolts. Sturm tried to figure out the best way to remove them, but Kitiara simply took a battle axe from the cache of weapons and bashed the heads off several bolts.

"Stop!" he demanded. "Did you ever think that hatch might be fastened down to keep something in?"

She paused in midswing. "No," she said and brought the

axe down on the next bolt. "The way I see it, those poor devils died of plague or something. You and I are the first living
souls on board in months, maybe, so what we find is ours
by right of salvage." She decapitated the last bolt. "If you
want a share, you'd better help me."

Reluctantly, Sturm got his fingers under the hatch's
flange, and together they lifted it off. The stout lid of oak
and copper fell aside, landing on a pile of armor. The ringing
boom echoed through the caravel.

Kitiara thrust her candle into the opening. A cold draft
flowed out, so she shielded the flame with her hand. The
weak amber globe of light fell over the open hold.

It was empty.

A wide set of plank steps led down. Kitiara lowered a foot
to the first step.

"Don't," warned Sturm.

"What's the matter with you? A few skulls and bones, and
suddenly you're afraid of your own shadow. Where's your
curiosity? Where's your knightly valor?"

"Alive and well, thank you."

She dropped down a few more steps. "Coming, then?"
Sturm held up one finger and went to the pile of shields. He
found a buckler of good dwarven make and slipped it over
his arm. Thus reinforced, he followed Kitiara into the hold.

"It's very black in here," she said. A post at the foot of the
steps proved to be coated with a greasy black powder.
"Soot?" she said.

"Hmm, yes." Sturm went down on one knee. The deck
was charred. "There was a fire down here." He brushed off
his fingertips. "This ship's lucky to be afloat." Fire at sea was
one of the worst fates a ship could face.

"Is there anything below this floor?" Kitiara asked.

"Just the bilge." Something caught the candlelight. Sturm
waved her to him. "Bring the light here," he whispered.

"What is it?" On the deck a few feet to the right of the
steps were four long scratches, so deep that they scored
through the charred wood's surface to the lighter, unburned
wood beneath. The scratches were three inches apart and
almost a foot long.

"What do you make of that?" Sturm asked.

Kitiara drew her sword. "Claw marks," she said grimly.

Toward the bow, a massive half cylinder descending from the ceiling divided the bulkhead in two. This was the lower end of the mainmast. On each side of the mast were doors. Both had been hastily but solidly blocked with boards. The barricade on the right of the mast was intact; the one on the left was burst asunder—from the other side.

"Whatever it was, it came through here," said Kitiara.

"'It'?"

She didn't answer, but stepped carefully through the shattered barrier into the forward hold. Sturm couldn't fit through the hole, so he broke out a few more boards. The charred planks split loudly.

The forward hold was even colder than the aft one. It was not sooted by fire. They found more bones, broken swords and cutlasses, and smashed helmets—the remnants of a fierce fight. Kitiara almost tripped over another form, this one still clad in a moldering brown robe. Where she had disturbed the robe there was a glint of gold.

"This was a cleric," Sturm said. "The robe, the amulets, are the kind a holy man would wear." He groped in the folds of the robe and pulled out a necklace wrought in copper. He held it to the candle. "A rose. The symbol of Majere. At least he served a good god." He laid the necklace down reverently on the dusky cloth.

Kitiara moved on to the facing wall. A ladder was set in the wall, going up to the forecastle. Halfway up, someone had sawed the rungs off. The stout base of the foremast intruded into the hold here, too, and beside it was another boarded-up door. This one was intact.

"Sturm, come here!" He stepped over the cleric's skeleton. Kitiara thrust her candle to the battened door. Scarlet threads were woven back and forth across the rough barrier and gathered in a knot in the center of the door. A blob of sealing wax held the threads together, and in the wax was the impression of a ring seal.

"Can you read it?" she asked.

Sturm squinted at the image. "'Majere protect us' and 'Obey the will of Novantumus'." He looked back at the cleric's remains. "He must have been Novantumus."

Kitiara put the point of her sword to the wax seal. "What do you think you're doing?" he said.

"There's something valuable on the other side of this door," she said. "I want to see what it is."

"It could be what killed all these men!"

She rapped on the door. "Hello, any monsters in there?" The only sounds were the steady, muffled roar of the storm outside and the creaking of the ship's timbers. "See, no danger."

Sturm pulled her roughly away. "I won't let you tamper with it!"

"You won't—!" She snatched her arm free of his grasp. "Since when do you give me orders, Sturm Brightblade?"

"I won't let you break that seal. It could mean our deaths."

Kitiara cut at the door. Sturm flung the shield out and deflected the blow. Kitiara uttered an angry snort. She set the candle down and assumed fighting stance. "Out of my way!" she declared.

"Will you think what you're doing? Do you want to fight, just to open that door? Look around, Kit. Do you think plague smashed up these armed men?"

"So they killed each other fighting over the treasure. Out of the way!"

Sturm started to reply, but Kitiara lunged at him. He backed away, unwilling to use his own sword. Sturm kept the shield up, fending off her cuts. This went on until Kitiara grew frustrated. She aimed a wild overhand slash at his head. Her blade hit the shield a glancing blow and skidded off. The arc of her cut ended against the door and shattered the brittle wax seal.

"Now you've done it," he said, panting.

Kitiara flung herself, sword and all, at the door. Sturm stared in amazement as she pressed herself against the wood. "At last," she said. "At last!"

There was a split second of silence, then a tremendous crash. Kitiara's sword was knocked from her hand as she flew backward and landed with a clatter among the bones. The center board was bowed outward and cracked. Sturm tossed the shield aside and went to help Kitiara stand. From inside there came another crash, and the board above the first one flexed out.

"What is it?" Kitiara cried.

"I don't know, but it's coming out of there. Let's go!"

They fled in such haste that they forgot the candle. Through the sooty midnight of the aft hold they ran and stumbled up the stairs to the armory. Kitiara made for the rope locker. Sturm called her back. "Help me with the hatch," he said.

They wrestled the heavy hatch into place and dropped it. Then it was through the rope locker and up the ladder to the captain's cabin. Kitiara dragged some heavy chests over to block the ladder well. Rain drummed on the poop deck above them, and wind whistled around the louvered shutters. They stood close together in the dark, breathing hard and listening.

The deck trembled beneath their feet and they heard wood breaking. The thing, whatever it was, was smashing its way out.

"I lost my sword," she said, deeply ashamed. She, a seasoned warrior, had lost her only weapon when she fell among the skeletons.

"It doesn't matter," Sturm said. "Swords didn't save the crew of this ship."

"Thanks," she said wryly. "You're a comfort."

Metal rang and rattled. 'It' was in the armory. Sturm flexed his damp hand around the handle of his sword. The uproar below got worse as the thing expended its anger on the store of weapons. From the crash and clang, it sounded like every item in the cache was being battered, twisted, and crushed. Then, abruptly, all the noise ceased.

Sturm and Kitiara, by some common impulse, drew closer together. Their arms touched in the dark.

"Can you hear anything?" he whispered.

"Just you. Shh." They strained to catch any stray sound.

The cabin door blew open with a bang. Rain poured in. Sturm struggled to close the door against the press of wind. By the greenish gray light that filtered in through the cyclone, he saw that the main hatch cover, forward of the mainmast, was blasted off.

"It's gone out on deck!" he shouted above the wind. "It

could be anywhere!"

"We'll have to close that hatch," she said. "Or the ship will flood, yes?" He nodded. Sturm felt exhausted. At that moment, he wondered what silliness the gnomes were up to, and fervently wished he was with them to see it.

"Ready?" said Kitiara. She threw the bolt back, and they plunged out onto the storm-swept deck.

They were soaked with sea water before they took two steps. The heel of the ship with the waves was more noticeable on deck. Mountains of green water rose and fell and the horizon swung from below eye level to nearly the masthead. Holding hands, Sturm and Kitiara staggered to the mainmast. The hatch cover was not just thrown open; gaping rents were torn in it. Sturm lost his footing twice as foaming sea swept over him. Finally, on their knees, they managed to get the hatch back over its coaming.

High above the rumble of the churning sea, a shrill cackle reached them. Sturm looked left and right for the source of the sound; Kitiara looked up and down. She spied the thing clinging to the rigging high over their heads.

It was a horrid-looking thing, ghastly white and gaunt. Except for its abnormal size, it might have been a man, starved and sallow. But this creature was seven feet tall. Its protruding eyes were like red burning coals, and its hands were clawed with silver nails two inches long. The head was round and hairless, the ears tall and pointed. The creature threw back its head and howled, showing long yellow fangs and a pointed black tongue.

"Suffering gods! What is it?"

"I don't know. Look out!" The creature sprang from the rigging to the stays hanging from the foremast. It swung under the spar and flipped over until its feet were on top of the yard. There it howled at them again.

They backed cautiously across the wet deck, ignoring the lashing rain and pounding sea. Once inside the cabin, they slammed the door and bolted it.

Kitiara turned. A strange white glow filled the rear of the cabin. They were no longer alone there, either.

Chapter 34

Pyrthis's Tale

The cold white light collected into a human form six feet tall. Kitiara pointed her sadly bent dagger at the apparition, but Sturm pushed the weapon down.

"In the name of Paladine and all the Gods of Good, depart in peace, spirit," he said.

The cabin filled with a deep, long sigh. "Would that I could depart," said a low voice. "For I am tired beyond measure and desire rest."

"Who are you?" asked Kitiara.

"In life I was master of this vessel. My name is Pyrthis."

"He doesn't seem dangerous," Kitiara muttered to Sturm, "but let's find a safer spot from that creature outside."

"The Gharm will not enter this cabin," the ghost said, "as long as I am here." Outside, the hellish thing shrieked, acknowledging the truth of the dead captain's words.

"What is the Gharm?" asked Sturm.

The indistinct figure drew closer and became more defined. Its legs did not move, and its arms stayed firmly by its sides. The ghost glided forward until Sturm and Kit could see deep, hollow eyes and a jaw that hung open, as slack as the face of a corpse. The voice issued from the mouth without the lips moving at all.

"Once he was my friend, and then a curse laid us all low. He became the Gharm, I, a walking spirit, and the crew of the *Werival* died in torment."

"Spirits walk for two reasons: to right an unavenged wrong, and to give warning to the living. Which is it, Captain? Why do you remain on this mortal plane?" asked Sturm.

Another mournful sigh. "Know, my friends, that I bargained with the forces of evil and lost." The ghost came closer still, enough for Kitiara to see its dead white eyes and corpse pallor.

"I was a merchant captain, bold and enterprising, who never turned down a cargo for money. I plied the Sirrion Sea and traded north and east to the Blood Sea maelstrom. In my time, I carried all goods—from spices to slaves."

Sturm frowned. "You trafficked in misery," he said flatly.

"Aye, I did. Thank your gods that you still live and can make amends for any evil deeds you have committed! I am past saving now."

The poop deck overhead resounded with the tramp of feet. Kitiara listened nervously as the Gharm stamped on the boards. "What is that thing?" she demanded.

"Once my first mate and friend, Drott, who I trained in all the wily ways I knew. Our coffers grew fat and heavy with gold, and I grew satisfied, as men in their waning years are wont to do. But Drott was young and keen and always searching for the richest commission to be made. It was a fateful day when he fell in with the scaled warriors."

Sturm had a glimmer of recognition. "Do you mean draconians?" he asked.

"Aye, some have called them thus." Pyrthis's ghost loomed over Sturm. Though seemingly benign, its presence was oppressive, and Sturm began to sweat.

"The dragonmen had a rich proposition: that we carry a shipment of weapons and money for them from Nordmaar to Coastlund, there to rendezvous with other dragonmen arriving from the northern seas. Drott accepted their commission and their money, thus damning us all." The ghost made a horrible rasping sound. "I am so weary . . ." The dead man's left arm came loose from his shoulder and fell silently to the floor. Kitiara flinched at the sight, more from surprise than disgust. She bent to pick up the gently glowing limb, but her hand passed right through it.

"We loaded sixty hundredweight of arms, and weighed anchor for Coastlund. We had a fair wind and made a swift passage. On the way, Drott schemed and plotted. He drew me into his plan, which was this: Since the dragonmen were barbarians and invaders, why should we not hold them up for as much gold as we could? They would pay doubly or triply for their swords, and we would have nothing to fear. Who could they complain to? Their purpose was even more illicit than ours.

"I fell in with Drott's scheme. In truth, I despised the scaly killers and feared them greatly. To cheat them seemed both just and profitable."

The ghost paused and the silence grew long. Sturm finally said, "What happened when you reached Coastlund?"

Rasp. "A dragonship was there, waiting. The leader of the dragonmen came aboard to accept transfer of the weapons. Drott laid out his demand for more money. The leader must have expected such a ploy, for he readily offered to pay half again the original price. Drott insisted on double the amount. The lizard resisted for a time, then conceded. He departed for his ship and returned with a second chest of treasure. This time a human came with him, a dark cleric wearing a metal mask that mimicked a dragon's face. This one frightened me very much. He stood by, watching and saying nothing. Drott laughed and joked as the second box of money came on board. He was drunk with success, and when I ordered the crew to begin transferring the cargo to the dragonship, he drew me aside and whispered another wicked design in my ear. 'Shall we not keep some part of the cargo ourselves?' he said. 'Could we not wring a bit more silver from these flush pigeons?'"

"That was pretty stupid," Kitiara said, "with a boatload of draconians alongside."

"We did not fear their force, for our crew was numerous and skilled in the use of saber and pike. We did not sail the pirate-infested seas unprepared."

"But the dark cleric—that was someone you weren't able to counter," said Sturm.

"Indeed, mortal man." The ghost's right arm dropped off. Part of the unreal flesh touched Sturm's booted foot. He withdrew it hastily and shivered. The ghost's touch was more frigid than the wind off the Ice Wall.

"We held back five hundredweight of arms. The dragonmen's leader discovered the shortage and complained. Drott jeered at him from the rail, saying there was a tax on illegal weapons and the dragonfolk had yet to pay. The dragonman threatened to storm the *Werival* and slaughter us all. The crew manned the rail with bare blades and taunted them to try. The dragonmen, less than a third our number, began to arm. I wanted to weigh anchor and be off, but Drott said we should stay and fight. After we killed the scaly folk, he said, we could take back all the weapons we'd sold them and sell them again.

"There was no battle. The dark cleric came from his place on the stern of the dragonship and threw his arms wide. 'Go, greedy vermin, and take away your dishonored gold. I curse you and yours forever! Those who lust for gold shall lust for the flesh of their fellows, those who jeer at the minions of the Dark Queen shall know her wrath! They shall hear her mocking laughter forever!' he said.

"It was a terrible curse, and the full weight of it did not fall on us for some weeks. We left the shores of Coastlund for Sancrist, but never saw land again. Strange, circular winds blew us farther and farther from land. The crew began to hear voices—a woman laughing—and they slowly went mad. The few healthy sailors that remained chained the mad ones below decks. Food and water dwindled, but try as we might, we could not bring the *Werival* to shore.

"Drott changed. He had always been a vain man, proud

of his quick mind and good looks. Now he ceased to care for himself, allowing his beard to grow and his clothes to fall to tatters. The meat shrank on his bones and his skin whitened to a ghastly color. As the days passed, my first mate and friend perished as the hideous curse worked upon his wretched body. Drott prowled below, snaring rats in his hands and eating them alive. Soon rats were not enough for him. He had become a Gharm, a ravenous ghoul that feeds on the flesh of men."

"Why didn't you kill him?" Kitiara said sharply. The drumming of feet had stopped, but they could still hear the Gharm's cackle as the monster capered madly in the rigging.

"I could not, for as much as his new form disgusted me, I pitied my lost friend. The crew, poor wretches, learned to keep him at bay by giving him those who died of madness and starvation. When there were only five sound men left, they decided to try to put an end to the Gharm. Our young cleric, Novantumus, wove a temporary protective spell. The sailors armed themselves and drove the Gharm to the fore end of the ship with fire and sword. Novantumus meant to imprison the fiend in the anchor locker, and he fashioned a magic seal to keep it in. The Gharm attacked the men savagely and killed them one by one. With his life's blood spilling on the deck, the brave Novantumus succeeded in compelling the Gharm into the locker. I alone lived, and here at my table I died of hunger, thirst, and despair."

The ghost had shrunk throughout his telling, and the cold glare that it cast had diminished to a firefly's sparkle. Sturm was deeply sorry for the captain.

"One question," said Kitiara. She picked up the skull that had been set between the captain's feet. "Who is this?"

"That was Drott's head. One of the sailors cut it off before the Gharm killed him."

"But that thing out there has a head!"

"A new one it grew afterward."

Sturm said, "Can the Gharm be killed?"

The ghost shriveled to a slender coil of white mist. "Not by steel, iron, or bronze," it said, a tiny, far-off voice. "Only purifying fire will make this ship clean." With those final words, the ghost vanished.

"This is wonderful," Kitiara said bitterly. "A monster we can't kill unless we burn up the ship that's keeping us out of the water!"

"What we must do is stay alive until the storm ends," Sturm said. "The gnomes will be looking for us and we'll be able to leave this cursed ship —" A splintering sound halted Sturm in midsentence. The Gharm had rammed one bony, clawed arm through the thin, louvered panel of the cabin door.

"Something tells me our moment of immunity is over!" Kitiara said. Sturm leaped up from the table, drawing his sword in one smooth motion. He brought the keen blade down hard on the grasping talons. The Gharm roared in pain and withdrew the stump of its left arm.

"Suffering gods!" Kitiara kicked the severed arm away. The limb rapidly decayed to bone, and then to dust. The Gharm put one of its baleful eyes to the hole that it had made and glared at them. Sturm raised his sword again and the monster backpedaled.

Kitiara went to the cabin's rear and started tearing through the captain's bunk.

"Kit, what are you doing?" he called.

"Don't worry, just keep that damned thing away a minute longer!" He heard wood being split behind him, then felt heat on the back of his neck.

Sturm turned and saw that Kitiara had made a torch from a bunk slat and a strip of ticking. Doused with oil from the captain's lamp and ignited by flint, it blazed furiously.

"Ha! Try this, ghoul!" she shouted, brandishing the flame before the door. The Gharm howled and hissed, its fangs dripping saliva. "I'll give you something to chew on." Kitiara kicked the smashed door frame open. The rain had almost stopped, but a fierce wind still raged across the open deck. Kitiara dashed out, whipping the torch to and fro like a fencing blade. The Gharm crouched back on its rail-thin haunches, spitting and hissing.

"Kit, be careful!"

"It's my fault this thing is out. I intend to kill it!"

She moved on the ghoul again, forcing it to retreat up the rigging. It hung twenty feet above the deck, giggling in an obscene parody of humanity. Kitiara paced below it, waving the torch to keep it bright and hot.

Sturm closed behind her. "Don't let it drop down on you," he counseled.

"If it does, it'll go back up a lot faster than it came down."

The ceiling of black clouds scattered into streams of dirty white as the blue of clear sky shone through. The wind had died down but did not cease. They were in the eye of the cyclone, the calm center of a miles-wide storm.

The Gharm swung over to the port side rigging. Kitiara followed across the deck. She was so intent on keeping the fiend in view that she missed the end of the mainsail Sturm had cut free. The heavy, flapping canvas was soaked with rain, and one corner of it whipped around and slapped Kitiara between the eyes. She fell backward and lost the torch. As the sail struck her, the Gharm pounced.

"No!" Sturm cried. He was on the fiend's back in a flash, slashing at its pale, leathery hide. The ghoul had one set of talons deep in Kitiara's shoulder, but Sturm's attack made it let go. He inflicted wounds that would have killed a mortal foe, but the Gharm wasn't slowed. A detached part of Sturm's mind noted that the ghoul already had grown back the arm that he'd chopped off.

Kitiara pushed herself away from the duel between Sturm and the Gharm. Her shoulder wound burned like Bellcrank's vitriol. She crawled to where the torch lay charring the deck. In her pants' pocket she still had the tin can of oil from the captain's storm lamp. At the right moment, when Sturm gave ground to the monster, she flung the oil over the Gharm, and with it the torch.

It was scarcely a cupful of oil, but it burned rapidly, and the Gharm yowled in unimaginable pain. It threw itself on the deck and rolled to put out the flames. Failing that, it leaped up and ran forward, burning as it went, and tore off the hatch cover. The Gharm disappeared below, trailing a thin plume of putrid smoke.

Sturm knelt and put an arm around Kitiara. Her teeth chattered. She had been poisoned by the ghoul's vile talons.

"Kit! Kit!" Her eyes were almost completely white, they had rolled so far back in her head. "Kit, listen to me! Don't give up! Fight it! Fight it!"

Her hand came trembling to her throat. There, under the thin fabric of her blouse was the amethyst arrowhead pendant that Tirolan Ambrodel had given her so many weeks before. Drained of color before they met the gnomes, the crystal's magic had been restored by the days they'd spent on Lunitari for it now was a rich, royal purple. The stone had not surrendered its power upon its return to Krynn.

Kitiara's fingers would not grasp the amethyst. They were already stiff and cold. Sturm gently lifted the magic crystal. Was there enough power in it to save Kit's life? Did he, a sworn opponent of magic, dare use it to heal her?

Her breath came short, in hard, ragged gasps. Death had Kitiara in its grasp. There was no time to debate. Sturm closed the amethyst in his fist and placed his other hand on Kitiara's injured shoulder.

"Forgive me, father," he whispered. "This is for her life."

The stone was hot for the merest second, but not enough to burn him. Kitiara gave a sharp cry and then went limp in his arms. He thought he was too late, that she was dead. Sturm opened his fingers, to see that the amethyst was clear again. He peeled back the bloody cloth over Kit's wound and saw that it was healed.

Smoke from the hatch was getting thicker. Sturm put an arm under Kitiara's legs and staggered to his feet. Muffled screams filtering through the open hatch proved that the Gharm hadn't yet overcome the fire.

The smoke got so bad that Sturm retreated to the poop deck, carrying Kitiara. The wind switched from port to starboard, never allowing the ship to drive clear of the fumes. When the first tongues of flame licked out of the hold, Sturm felt real fear. How could they escape if the ship was on fire? The *Werival*'s longboat was missing.

At that moment, the wall of rain off the starboard bow parted, and out came the brown hull of the *Cloudmaster*. The flying ship was skimming over the waves so low that a few high swells lapped the bottom of her hull. Sturm saw the gnomes at the bow, waving white handkerchiefs.

A great shout of triumph escaped his throat. "Kit, wake up!" he cried. "Kit, the gnomes are coming! We're saved!"

Fire blasted out of the fore hatch, and with it, the figure of the Gharm. Blazing from head to toe, the hideous ghoul bounced from bulwark to bulwark, shrieking its cursed life away. Unable to bear the burning any longer, the ghoul finally dived into the churning waves.

The bows were burning now, and the foremast was beginning to smolder. The *Cloudmaster* drifted past the stern. Sturm left Kitiara lying on the deck and grabbed a boat hook from the rail. As the gnome ship coasted slowly along the port side, Sturm hooked it and drew it tightly to the caravel.

The gnomes clutched the *Werival*'s sides as Sturm lifted the limp Kitiara over his shoulder. He sprinted for the rail and leaped, one foot kicking the rail top as he went. The gnomes let go, and the *Cloudmaster* sank toward the sea.

"Too much weight!" Wingover cried. "Out ballast!" Amidships, Sighter, Cutwood, and Birdcall threw doors, window glass, and other loose objects over the side. The ship rose again into the low clouds.

"W-welcome aboard!" Stutts said heartily.

"Glad to be here," Sturm said with genuine relief. He lay sprawled on the deck.

"What happened down there?" asked Wingover.

"It's a long story."

"Is the lady well? She seems unconscious," said Sighter. He lifted one of her arms and let it fall.

"She'll be all right," Sturm said. The *Cloudmaster* broke through the top of the clouds. Below, the cyclone's whirling mass spread out in all its glory. The gnomes set the sails and put the setting sun to their backs.

"It was very clever of you to start a signal fire," Wingover said. "But it got out of hand, didn't it? I mean, you might have destroyed the whole ship before we ever arrived."

Sturm felt a crazy desire to laugh. Instead, he said, "That's not the way things went." He paused to yawn prodigiously.

"Did you find anything useful on that vessel?" Sighter asked. But by then Sturm was already fast asleep.

Chapter 35

The Road to Garnet

STURM SMELLED LAND: WET SOIL AND FLOWERS AND FRESH-
ly turned fields. The sun was in his eyes. He sat up. He was
in the wheelhouse, alone. The windows and doors were
gone, as was most of the roof. He went out on deck. At the
bow was Sighter, surveying the ground below with his telescope. Aft, by the former tail post, sat Kitiara, Stutts, Fitter,
and Rainspot. Kitiara was talking rapidly and making wild
gestures with her hands.

"—and then Sturm stepped in and chopped the monster's
arm off!" The gnomes all went *Ohh*, and Kitiara described
how the arm had withered before their very eyes.

Stutts saw Sturm approach. "Ah, Master B-Brightblade!
You're awake. We are just hearing about your t-tremendous
adventure on board the cursed c-caravel."

314

Sturm grunted something noncommittal and looked at Kitiara. "How do you feel?" he asked.

"Fit as can be. How're you?"

"Rested," he said. "How long have I been asleep?"

"T-two nights and a day," said Stutts.

"Two nights!"

"And a day," added Fitter.

"I came to about an hour ago," Kitiara said. "I slept like a dead woman, but now I feel better than I have in ten summers."

"You almost were a dead woman." Sturm explained how the Gharm had poisoned her and told her that the elven pendant had saved her once again. Kitiara brought the amethyst out of her blouse. Not only was it clear once more, but it was seamed with hundreds of tiny cracks.

"I don't remember using it," she said, puzzled.

"You didn't. I did," said Sturm. Kitiara's eyes widened in surprise.

He turned and went into the dining room. There the water barrel sat, almost empty. Sturm downed a dipper of tepid water.

Outside, Wingover said, "I thought men of his order would not use magic under any circumstance."

"They're not supposed to," Kitiara said. She began to tuck the pendant back under her blouse, but as she did, it crumbled into dust. She stared sadly at the flakes on her tunic; Cirolan Ambrodel's gift was no more. Then, brushing them away, she rose and said to the gnomes, "Excuse me, fellows. I need to have a word with Sturm."

Kitiara found Sturm standing by the port rail, staring at the green land below.

"Northern Ergoth," she said. "Wingover spotted a flock of terns and followed them. The birds led them to land." Sturm stared on, saying nothing. "Not very scientific, I thought, but Wingover says, 'Anything that yields good results is scientific.'"

"I am tainted," Sturm said quietly.

"In what way?"

"I used magic. Such a thing is forbidden. How am I ever going to become a knight?"

"That's ridiculous! You used magic on Lunitari when you had those visions," she said.

"Those were inflicted on me; I had no choice. On the ship, I used the power of the pendant to heal your wound."

"I call that a right proper thing to do! Are you sorry you didn't let me die?" she asked sarcastically.

"Of course not."

"But you're 'tainted' nevertheless?"

"I am."

"Then you are a fool, Sturm Brightblade, a hidebound fool! Do you honestly believe that an ancient set of rules for knightly conduct is more important than a comrade's life? My life?" He did not answer. "There's something twisted about such thinking, Sturm."

Sturm shook his head vigorously. "No, Kit. I would have given my life to save yours, but it is a cruel turning of fate that made me break the Measure."

Her jaw clenched in anger and she said stiffly, "I never realized how little value you place on friendship. You want me to believe in your dusty old code. Just like Tanis. He tried to make me into something I wasn't. He couldn't control me, and neither can you!" She stamped the deck, barely containing her fury.

Sturm folded his hands and regarded them carefully. "Virtue is a hard master, Kit. The Measure and the Oath were never meant to be easy burdens to bear. A knight carries them like ponderous stones on his back, and their weight makes him strong and upright." He lifted his gaze until their eyes met. "You will never understand, because all you want from life is to give your burden over to someone else. A lover, a servant, even a brass dragon. As long as someone else can bear the burden of honor for you, you don't have to feel guilt, or face the consequences of your acts."

Color drained from her face. No one had ever spoken to her like that, not even Tanis. "Then this is the end," she said coldly. "From the moment this soap bubble touches the ground, we're finished."

Kitiara left him watching the canopy of trees unroll. They did not speak to each other again.

* * * * *

"Careful! Careful! Watch those branches!"

The *Cloudmaster* pushed into a forest clearing. Elm, ash, and birch branches clawed at them. Wingover was atop the deckhouse, trying to direct the landing. Flash and Birdcall had opened the neck of the ethereal air bag, letting some of the lifting power out. The flying ship had scraped over a few bald hills before the wind carried it down. Sturm stood at the bow, fending off dangerous limbs with the boat hook from the *Werival*—his only souvenir of the perilous hours on the cursed ship. They had no anchor, no grapnel to fix them in place, only timing and control of the air bag. Flash and Birdcall clung to the rope that held the half-empty bag shut.

Branches scraped the length of the deck, snapping when the gaping windows of the deckhouse caught them. Birds fled, chirping, when the ship disturbed their treetop homes.

"Clearing ahead!" Sturm called.

"Get ready!" Wingover cried.

The bow dipped once the trees were out of the way. The keel gently touched the meadow's grass, dragged a few yards, and stopped. Sturm jammed the boat hook into the ground and swung over the rail. He landed on the soil of Krynn with both feet.

"Praise Paladine!" he said. "Solid ground at last!"

The boarding ramp fell, and seven gnomes boiled out. Wingover was inhaling deep breaths and patting himself on the chest when he heard Birdcall whistle questioningly.

"Can we open the bag now?" asked Flash.

"Yes, yes, we're landed!"

The two gnomes pulled the zigzag stitching loose. A gust of sulfurous air fled the bag, and the exhausted craft settled, finally and heavily.

Kitiara descended the ramp and dumped what belongings she had left on the ground. In spite of the bitterness of their parting, Sturm couldn't stop his eyes from following her. She paid no one the slightest heed, but stood a ways off, hanging her water bottle and leather pouch on opposite hips to balance the load. She slung her bedroll over one shoulder by its strap. Sturm had an urge to speak, to say something conciliatory, but her hard expression forestalled him.

"Well, Wingover, it's been a long, strange voyage," Kitiara said, shaking the little man's hand. "I'll never forget it."

"We couldn't have made it without you, lady."

She moved on to Cutwood, Sighter, Birdcall, and Flash. "Keep thinking up new ideas," she said amiably, "That way the world will never get dull." She turned to Roperig and Fitter and chucked the littlest gnome under the chin. "So long, boys. Stick together—you make a good team."

"We will," said the two in unison.

Finally, she approached Rainspot and Stutts. "You're a very lucky fellow, Stutts," she said warmly. "Not many people get to realize their life's dream as completely as you have. Keep flying, old fellow. I hope you will have many more adventures."

"My," said Stutts. "It d-doesn't seem likely. I have so many reports to write and s-so many lectures to give. After all, the Gnomish Patent Office must be satisfied that we have d-done what we have done." He bowed formally. "Farewell, Mistress. You were a t-tower of strength."

"I was, wasn't I?"

"Where are you off to?" Wingover asked.

"Wherever the trail takes me," she replied.

Kitiara's crooked smile almost appeared. She squinted into the sky. It was not yet noon. The sun warmed her face.

Sturm stood apart from her leave-taking. He felt the weight of his own resolve and knew that what Kitiara had said was true. They were finished. And yet, he knew he would miss the old Kit, the brash, fun-loving companion.

Kitiara crossed the warm meadow briskly and did not look back. Sunlight burnished her black curls as she cut a swath through the high grass. Sturm bent over to shoulder his own gear. When he straightened again, Kitiara had vanished among the closely growing elms and birches at the field's far end.

"Aren't you going after her?" said Fitter.

"Why should I do that?" Sturm said. He tied a thready piece of twine around his bedroll and tucked it under his arm. "She can take care of herself. It's what she does best."

"I don't understand," Fitter said, scratching his nose. "I thought you two were going to get married one day."

Sturm dropped his cooking kit at that remark. The clay pot banged him smartly on the toe. "Where in the world did you get an idea like that?" he asked, flabbergasted.

"We've always heard how human men and women fight and yell at each other, but always end up married and, you know—" Fitter blushed. "Having babies."

Sturm picked up the spilled contents of his kit. "It will take a man with more riches and power than I'll ever have to claim her hand." He hung the kit bag around his neck. "The man who wins Kitiara Uth Matar had better have the patience of Paladine and the wisdom of Majere to keep her."

The gnomes gathered around him as he adjusted the last of his equipment. "Where will you go?" asked Wingover.

"Solamnia, as before. There are things I must investigate. The visions I had on the red moon have faded from my memory, but I know my father's trail begins at my ancestral home, Castle Brightblade. That is my destination."

Small hands patted him on the back. "We wish you every bit of luck, Master Brightblade," said Cutwood. "You're very smart, for a human."

"That means a lot, coming from you," Sturm answered wryly.

"W-we would offer to fly you on t-to Solamnia," Stutts said, "but we are on f-foot now ourselves."

That hadn't occurred to him. Sturm said, "Would you like me to escort you home to Sancrist?" It seemed the least he could do.

"No, no, we've delayed you long enough," said Sighter. "We'll get to Gwynned, all right. There'll be ships there for Sancrist."

"I shall miss you," said Rainspot fondly. He held out his small hand. With great solemnity, Sturm shook Rainspot's hand and each of the other gnomes' hands in succession. Then he hitched up his gear and started out.

Funny, he thought; to have traveled so far and walked so little. His feet were more tender now than before he went to Lunitari. Walking will be good penance, he decided. He could shed some of the stain of magic by walking and con-

319

templating his transgression. Perhaps he could also come to grips with the difficult choices he faced as he tried to live by the Code and the Measure.

"Good-bye! Good-bye!" called the gnomes. Sturm snapped out of his reverie and waved to them. They were good fellows indeed. He hoped they would not have any more trouble, but, being gnomes, they probably would.

He entered the humid forest and plunged through thicket after thicket of dense greenery. It cheered him to see vines and bushes with honest green leaves, plants that didn't bleed or cry when he tramped over them. Lunitari was such an unnatural world.

Two miles of woods later, he found a clear creek and filled his bottle. The water was cold, and had a mineral taste. It was a welcome change after weeks of drinking soft rain water. Sturm paralleled the creek bank for four miles, until he came to an arched stone bridge. He climbed the bank to the road that wended away north and south. A road marker was fixed to the corner of the bridge. On its south face, it read, 'Caergoth—20 Leagues', and on its east face, 'Garnet—6 Leagues'.

Sturm laughed until tears came. The gnomes had landed in Solamnia, not twenty miles from where they'd left in the first place! And he laughed for other reasons. To be home again, not merely on Krynn (though that was good), but in Solamnia. He felt light and free, without the gnomes to worry about, without the constant apprehension of what strange things might be around the next corner—and free of his curious relationship with Kitiara. Their separation was like the pulling of an aching tooth; a definite feeling of relief, yet tinged with an underlying sense of loss, of a void in himself.

Sturm took the road for Garnet. The roads in this province converged on the city, so it was the best way to get to the northern plains. He set himself a good pace. With his light burden and no dependents to herd, he ought to make Garnet by the next morning, he thought. As he marched, he took in the sights and sounds and smells of his native land. The scrub pastures and rolling hills. Peasants ranging through the dales, chasing cattle and driving them with sticks to tumble-down pens made of fieldstone. Once the Brightblade family had owned a vast herd of cattle, but those had been quickly lost in the upheavals that toppled the great, knightly estates throughout the country. Who knew but that the scrawny, ill-tended beasts that Sturm now saw shuffling over the hills were offspring of the prime Brightblade herd?

It wasn't cattle or land that bothered Sturm about the fall of the Solamnic Knights. Such things were not the true measure of a knight's worth. It was the injustice of it. The common folk blamed the Cataclysm and the troubles that followed on the arrogant pride of the knights, as if the Knights of Solamnia could turn the whole world on its ear and split the land asunder!

Sturm stopped in his tracks. His hands were clenched into fists so tight that his knuckles were blanched white. He let go of his anger and slowly opened his fists. Patience, he admonished himself. A knight must have self-control, or he is no better than a barbarian berserker.

*　*　*　*　*

From the time Sturm gained the road at the stone bridge to late afternoon of the following day, he met no other travelers. This struck him as ominous, especially as he got nearer to Garnet. Drovers and merchant caravans always moved from town to town, timing their arrivals to the local market day. An empty road indicated that something, or someone, was keeping the travelers at home.

The road began to rise and wind as the hills of Garnet grew out of the plain. Here he found signs of traffic: hoof prints, wheel tracks, and marks of bare and booted feet. The prints multiplied until it seemed a small army had marched through not long before.

Sturm saw smoke rising from around a bend. He shifted the pommel of his sword forward to be convenient to his hand.

He could smell the smoke now. Slowly the scene came into view. Several heavy wagons were overturned and burning in the road. From the extent of the damage already done, the fire must have started hours before.

Crows and other carrion birds stirred at his approach. Between two gutted wagons, Sturm found bodies. One, thick-waisted and richly dressed, obviously was a successful merchant. He had two arrows in his chest. Beside him was a younger man with the stump of a broken mace still clutched in his hand.

A groan brought Sturm running. A few yards away, a big, well-muscled man sat with his back against a scrub pine. He was a warrior. His body bled from a dozen wounds and arrayed at the warrior's feet were six dead goblins.

"Water," moaned the fighter. Sturm put a hand behind the warrior's head and raised his bottle to the man's parched lips.

"What happened here?" asked Sturm.

"Bandits. Attacked wagons. We fought—" The big man coughed. "Too many."

Sturm examined the fighter's wounds. He didn't have to be a healer to know the warrior was doomed, and because the man was a warrior, Sturm told him so.

"Thank you," he said. Sturm asked if he could do anything to make the man more comfortable. "No, but Paladine bless you for your mercy."

Something rustled behind the pine. Sturm reached for his sword, then saw the broad brown muzzle of a horse poke through the branches. The dying warrior called the animal by name. "Brumbar," he said. "Good fellow." The horse pushed through the scrub. He was an enormous animal, as black as coal. Brumbar dropped his nose to nuzzle his master's face.

"I see that you are a man of arms," rasped the warrior to Sturm. "I beg you, take Brumbar as your mount when I am dead."

"I will," Sturm said gently. "Is there anyone in Garnet I can tell about your fate?"

The man slowly closed his eyes. "No one. But do not go to Garnet, if you value your life." His chin fell to his chest.

"But why?" Sturm asked. "Why shouldn't I go to the city?"

"Loosen my breastplate . . ."

Sturm undid the sraps and pulled the steel cuirass aside. Beneath the armor, the man wore a quilted shirt. Embroidered over his heart was a small red rose. Sturm stared. The dying man was a knight of the Order's highest rank, the Order of the Rose! Only Solamnic Knights of noble lineage could enter that exalted brotherhood.

"The forces that destroyed the knights control Garnet," the man said. His breath came in ragged gasps. "I know you are one of us. It would not be safe for you there . . . assassins . . . "

"Who are you? What is your name?" Sturm asked frantically, but the Knight of the Rose would never again speak.

Sturm gave the brave fighter an honorable burial. It was well after sundown when he finished. He collected Brumbar and went through the saddlebags thrown across the horse's rump. There were dried rations in one bag, and in the other, surprisingly, were hundreds of coins, all of them small copper pieces. Sturm understood. The dead knight was living incognito because of the widespread hatred of the Order. He'd adopted the guise of a guard for hire, and took his wages in copper. No one would ever expect a Knight of the Rose to live so humbly.

Sturm left the Garnet road. He chose another trail through the highlands, one not frequented by traders, or (he hoped) bandits. Garnet he passed in the night. He saw the glow of its street lamps in the distance. Reining in Brumbar, he listened. Wind whirled around the mountain passes. A wolf gave voice, far away.

Chapter 36

Solamnia

His new horse was a steady, plodding beast. Brumbar, in Old Dwarvish, meant 'Black Bear.' Black he was, and bearishly stolid. Sturm didn't mind. The kind of traveling he was doing now was better suited to a steady animal, rather than some excitable, fragile charger. Brumbar had a back so broad that Sturm imagined he could put his feet up on the animal's nodding neck and take a nap. Festooned with Sturm's pack and other belongings, Brumbar kept a jingling pace all day long.

The Lemish forest thinned out to a few spindly pines, growing weakly amid the grassy undergrowth. It was hot on the plain, and very dry. Sturm began to ration his water when the streams and springs started getting fewer and farther between.

Being off the road, he saw few people. This southernmost finger of the Solamnic Plain, thrust between the Garnet Mountains and the Lemish forest, was too dry for cattle and farming. There were no robbers here, either; there was nothing to steal.

Alone, Sturm took time to reflect on things. Since he and Kitiara had left Solace so many weeks ago, he'd come to realize that there was danger on the horizon everywhere. The strange lizardlike mercenaries he had heard called draconians had been seen in port cities. Caches of weapons being moved about. Large numbers of brigands infesting the roads of the northern countries. Dark magic at work. Goblins led by a human magician. What was the common thread in all this? he wondered.

War. Invasion. Evil magic.

Sturm gave Brumbar a kick, and the big horse shuffled into a trot. A welter of vague impressions and shrouded memories surfaced in his mind. The visions he'd had on Lunitari were lost to him in detail, but shadows of them remained, dimly. The strongest of these was that his father was alive somewhere. There was something about the old castle, too, and death that was somehow linked to lingering impressions of Kitiara's.

Oh, Kit. Where are you now?

The day's shimmering heat built towers of black clouds in the sky. Lightning danced far away, and peals of thunder crossed the grassland long after the flashes of lightning were gone. The smell of rain pulled Brumbar toward the storm, and Sturm let him go. He was thirsty, too.

The storm seemed to retreat from them even as they rode to meet it. Brumbar splashed through gullies running fast with rainwater. The air was wet, oppressive, yet the edge of the rain receded from Sturm's approach. The lightning played about a stand of pines to the east. Sturm reined away from the dangerous display, but Brumbar had other ideas. Puffing hard through his dry throat, the horse headed straight for the trees.

Light, steamy drops of rain began to hit them. Brumbar cantered heavily through the widely spaced trees. The rain fell harder. Ahead, Sturm saw a dark shape flit between the pines. He blotted water from his eyes and looked again.

A rider in a flowing cape was weaving among the trees. Now and then, the pale oval of a face turned back, as if the rider were peering over his shoulder at Sturm. He seemed to have a long mustache much like Sturm's own.

Brumbar slowed by a shallow pool of water, but Sturm spurred him on; he was curious about the other rider and wanted to catch up to him.

"Hello!" called Sturm. "Could I talk to you?"

A bolt from the churning sky struck the ground a score of yards away, leaving a smoking crater in the grass. The rider didn't respond to Sturm's call, but continued to weave around the pines. Sturm slapped the reins across his horse's neck, and Brumbar launched into a jarring gallop. They were closing on the stranger.

The rider's dark hair was slicked down by the driving rain. He did indeed have a long mustache, symbol of the Knights of Solamnia.

The stranger's horse was light and agile, but it must have been running hard too long. Brumbar closed rapidly. Only the passing of a tree between them kept Sturm from reaching out to grab the other man's lashing cape.

"Wait!" Sturm shouted. "Stop, I want to talk to you!"

The stranger's horse went hard to the left, circling around Sturm. The man drew up and stopped thirty yards away. Brumbar shuddered to a halt. The wind was up and blowing rain into Sturm's face, so he turned his horse around. The stranger was waiting for him.

"I didn't mean to chase you," Sturm called out, "but—"

He never heard the stroke of lightning that hit the ground between him and the stranger. Nor did he feel it. In one instant, he was talking and in the next, he was lying on the muddy grass with rain pattering on his face. His arms and legs were leaden and weak.

A dark form loomed over him. For a second, he was afraid. Lying there, helpless, Sturm was easy prey for a thief or assassin.

The stranger, still horsed, towered over him. Against the gray sky, with the rain in his eyes, all Sturm could see of him was dark hair, high forehead and drooping mustache. The cape was close about the man's shoulders, which were wide and powerful.

The stranger sat in the saddle, looking down at Sturm and saying nothing. Sturm managed to gasp, "Who are you?"

The man parted the cape, revealing the hilt of a large sword. Sturm made out the shape of the pommel and some of the filigree work. With a start, he realized that he knew that sword. It was his father's.

"Beware of Merinsaard," said the man, in a voice Sturm didn't recognize.

With tremendous effort, Sturm got to his knees. "Who are you?" He reached out a muddy hand to the stranger. Where he should have touched the leg of the man's horse, he met nothing. Horse and rider vanished, silently and completely.

Sturm staggered to his feet. The rain was over. Already the sun was poking through the tattered clouds. Brumbar was several yards away, drinking from a puddle. Nearby, a pine tree had been blasted to smoking splinters by lightning.

Sturm put his face in his hands. Had he seen what he thought he'd seen? Who was the phantom rider? And what was Merinsaard? A person, a place?

Wearily he mounted Brumbar. The big horse shifted under Sturm's weight, and his broad hooves squelched in the mud. Sturm looked around. There were no other hoof prints in sight besides Brumbar's.

*   *   *   *   *

Though described as a plain, the country of Solamnia was not perfectly flat, as were, say, the Plains of Dust. There were ridges and gullies, dry creek beds and small stands of trees that grew like islands in the midst of the grassy steppe land. Sturm rode north at an easy pace, eating wild pears off the trees and filling his water bottle from the herders' wells.

He soon found himself moving among small herds of cattle, tended and guarded by hard-looking peasants with mauls and bows. They watched him closely as he rode by. Raiders were common, and in their eyes he might have been a scout for a larger band of rustlers. Also, Sturm wore the mustache and horned helmet of a Solamnic Knight—items not calculated to make him popular among the people who had overthrown the Order. Sturm didn't care. He rode proudly, sword turned out to show that he was ready for trouble. At night, he took special care with polishing his helmet, boots, and sword, to make them shine.

He decided to avoid the city of Solanthus. After the overthrow, Solanthus had proclaimed itself a free city, not subordinate to anyone but its own Guildmasters. Sturm had heard of several knights, friends and compatriots of his father, who had been imprisoned and executed in Solanthus. While he was willing to proclaim his heritage in open country, he saw no reason to walk into the city and put his head into a noose.

The country beyond Solanthus sloped gently down to the Vingaard River. It was rich land. The clods turned up by Brumbar's iron-shod hooves were black and fertile.

The herds were thicker the closer to the river he got. He spent an entire day guiding Brumbar through ranks of rusty brown cows and calves. The heat and dust were so bad that he traded his helmet for a cloth bandanna, like the herd riders wore.

The herds converged on the Ford of Kerdu, an artificial shallows created centuries before by the Solamnic Knights (another benefit that the common folk had forgotten). Thousands of small stones were dumped into the Vingaard River to make a fording place. As the river slowly scoured the stones away, each new generation on the river banks had to renew the ford with its own gathering of stones. A sort of winter festival had developed around the collecting and dumping of rocks in the river.

It soon became too congested for Sturm to ride, so he got off Brumbar and led the horse by his bridle. Here, by the river, the day's heat rapidly dispersed after sunset. Sturm walked down to the river bank where a hundred campfires blazed. The herders were settling for the night.

A half-dozen sun-browned faces turned up as Sturm approached the nearest camp. He raised his palm and said, "My hands are open," the traditional herders' greeting.

"Sit," said the herd leader, identified by the carved steer

horn that he wore on a thong around his neck. Sturm tied Brumbar to a small tree and joined the men.

"Sturm," he said, sitting.

"Onthar," said the leader. He pointed to the other men in turn. "Rorin, Frijje, Ostimar, and Belingen." Sturm nodded to each one.

"Share the pot?" said Onthar. A black kettle hung over the fire. Each man had to provide some ingredient in order to share the common meal. Herder's stew—an expression known throughout Krynn as meaning 'a little bit of everything.'

Sturm lifted the flap of his pack and saw the last of his provisions: an inch-thick slab of salt pork, two carrots, and a stoppered gourd half full of rye flour. He squatted by the kettle, took out his knife, and started slicing the meat.

"Been a good season?" he asked politely.

"Dry," said Onthar. "Too dry. Fodder on the lower plain is blowing away."

"No sickness, though," observed Frijje, whose straw-colored hair hung in two long braids. "We haven't lost a single calf to screwfoot or blue blister."

Shoving wispy red hair from his eyes, Rorin said, "Lot of raiders." He whetted a wicked-looking axe on a smooth gray stone. "Men and goblins together, in the same gang."

"I've seen that, too," Sturm said. "Farther south in Caergoth and Garnet."

Onthar regarded him with one thin brown eyebrow raised. "You're not from around here, are you?"

Sturm finished the salt pork and started slicing the carrots. "I was born in Solamnia, but grew up in Solace."

"Raise a lot of pigs down there, I hear," Ostimar said. His voice was deep and resonant, seemingly at odds with his small height and skinny body.

"Yes, quite a lot."

"Where you headed, Sturm?" asked Onthar.

"North."

"Looking for work?"

He stopped cutting. Why not? "If I can get some," he said.

"Ever drive cattle before?"

"No. But I can ride."

Ostimar and Belingen snorted derisively, but Onthar said, "We lost a man to goblin raiders two weeks ago, and that left us with a hole in our drag line. All you have to do is keep the beasts going ahead. We'll be crossing the Vingaard tomorrow, heading for the keep."

"The keep? But it's been deserted for years," Sturm said.

"Buyer there."

"Sounds fine. What's the pay?"

"Four coppers a day, payable when you leave us."

Sturm knew he was supposed to haggle, so he said, "I couldn't do it for less than eight coppers a day."

"Eight!" exclaimed Frijje. "And him a show rider!"

"Five might be possible," said Onthar.

Sturm shook the gourd to break up the lumps of flour. "Six?"

Onthar grinned, showing several missing teeth. "Six it is. Not too much flour now—we're cooking stew, not baking bread." Sturm stirred in a handful of gray rye flour. Rorin gave him a copper bowl and spoon. The stew was dished up, and the men ate quickly and silently. Then they passed a skin around. Sturm took a swig. He almost choked; the bag held a potent, fermented cider. He swallowed and passed the skin on.

"Who's buying cattle at the keep?" he said, after everyone had eaten and drunk.

"Don't know," Onthar admitted. "Men have been coming back from Vingaard Keep for weeks with tales of gold, saying there is a buyer up there paying top coin for good beasts. So the keep is where we're going."

The fire died down. Frijje produced a hand-whittled flute and began to blow lonely, lilting notes. The herders curled up on their single blankets and went to sleep. Sturm unsaddled Brumbar and curried him. He led the horse to the river for a drink and returned him to the sapling. That done, he made a bed with his blanket and the saddle.

The sky was clear. The silver moon was low in the south, while Lunitari was climbing toward its zenith. Sturm gazed at the distant red globe.

Had he really trod its crimson soil? Had he really fought tree-men, seen (and ridden) giant ants, and freed a chatterbox dragon from an obelisk of red marble? Here, on Krynn, among the simple, direct herdsmen, such memories were like a mad dream, fevered images now banished by the more practical concerns of Sturm's life.

The young knight slept, and dreamed that he was galloping through Solace, pursuing a caped man who carried his father's sword. He never gained on the stranger. The vallenwood trees were bathed in a red glow, and all around Sturm felt the cold air echo with the sound of a woman's laughter.

Chapter 37

The Ford of Kerdu

Sturm was roughly shaken awake before the sun was up. All along the river's south bank the herders were stirring, packing their meager possessions on their horses, and preparing for another day's move. Sturm had no time for anything other than a brief cup of water. Frijje thrust some jerky in his hand and told him to mount up.

Belingen galloped to him and tossed him a light wooden pole with a bronze leaf-shaped head. This was his herd goad. When the cows were balky or wanted to wander in the wrong direction, he was to poke them with the goad to set them straight.

"And woe to you if you cut the hide," Belingen said. "Onthar prides himself on his herd not being scarred." With an arrogant toss of his head, Belingen spurred his horse back to the front of the herd.

The cattle, more than nine hundred head, sensed the rise in activity and surged from side to side against the fringe riders. Two other herds had right-of-way over Onthar's, so the men had to bide their time as the other two swarms of cattle forded the river ahead of them. The Kerdu passage was a quarter-mile wide and more than half a mile across to the other bank. The ford's edges fell away sharply, and Ostimar warned Sturm not to stray off the stones.

"I've seen men and horses drop off the edge and never come up," he cautioned. "Nothing ever found but their goads and bandannas, floating on the water."

"I'll keep that in mind," Sturm replied.

The herd settled into a standard oval formation. Sturm couched his goad under his left arm. The bar was eight feet long, and he could easily touch the ground with it, even from as high a perch as Brumbar's back. Indeed, Sturm's own height, placed on the broad back of the Garnet horse, made him taller than any other rider in the group. He could see far across the tight mass of cows, their dusty coats and long horns always shifting, always moving, even when the herd itself was not in forward motion.

A horn blasted from the far shore, signaling that the previous herd had cleared the ford. Onthar stood in his stirrups and whipped his goad back and forth (there was a black pennant fixed to the tip). The riders whistled and shouted to stir the beasts forward. A wall of beef surged toward Sturm, but he yelled and waved the goad before the cows' faces. The animals turned away to follow those in front.

The track down to the river was a morass. Thousands of cattle and horses had churned it up, and under the rising sun the mud stank. Onthar and the front riders splashed into the Vingaard with the herd bulls. The steers and cows came after, and the rear riders were last of all. The stench and biting flies over the river were ferocious.

Brumbar put his heavy feet into the water. His iron shoes, suited to paved roads, did not provide a very sure grip on the round, wet rocks. Despite the uncertain footing, Brumbar went on, unperturbed. And then, perhaps twenty yards into the river, Sturm's horse slid sideways off the rocky ford.

Water rushed over Sturm's head. He immediately kicked free of the stirrups and thrust up for the surface. His head burst into the air, and he took a deep breath. Brumbar was out in the stream, swimming steadily for the south shore.

Frijje reined up and shouted, "You all right, Sturm?"

"Yes, the stupid horse slid off the ford!" He swam a few strokes toward the herdsman. Frijje extended the butt of this goad for Sturm to grab and hauled the soaked knight to the ford's sloping edge. Sturm stood up. Atop the stones, the water was only knee-deep.

"Can you ride me across, Frijje?" he asked.

"Can't leave the herd," was the reply. "You'll just have to catch up." Frijje rode on, long braids bouncing on his back. Sturm slogged through the muddy water back to the south bank, where Brumbar had climbed out and was drying off in the morning sun.

"Come here, you ignorant brute," Sturm said, then smiled. An ignorant brute Brumbar might be, but the horse stood quietly after his watery ordeal, calmly awaiting his rider's pleasure. Sturm swung into the saddle and twisted Brumbar's head. Onthar's herd was almost to the other shore. Sturm had lost his goad, and his pride had taken a beating, too, but he wasn't finished.

"Heyah!" he cried, snapping the reins on Brumbar's neck. The horse took off, big feet pounding down the bank and into the river. Straight down the center of the ford they went, Brumbar kicking up an impressive froth as he galloped. They gained the north side just as the last herder, Rorin, was leaving the water.

"Have a good swim?" Rorin asked, grinning.

"Not too bad," Sturm responded sheepishly. "Lend me a goad, will you? I've got to get back to my place." Rorin yanked an extra pole from a boot on his horse's neck and tossed it to Sturm. Sturm caught it neatly.

The cattle churned over the sandy flood plain on the Vingaard's north side. Here, at last, Brumbar's shoes proved their worth. While the herders' unshod ponies floundered in the loose sand, Sturm and Brumbar headed off a dangerous side movement by the rear third of the herd. Like some huge living tapestry, the herd and its riders climbed the bank to the drier, grass-covered plain of northern Solamnia. Once they were well clear of the river crossing, Onthar led them into a wide gully and halted the herd.

"Keep your place," he said as he rode up to Sturm. Onthar scanned the river for stragglers. "I hear you fell in," he added.

"Iron horseshoes and wet rocks don't make for a firm grip," Sturm said.

"Uh-huh. You lose the goad I gave you?"

"Yes, Onthar," Sturm said. "Rorin lent me another."

"Lost goad costs two coppers. I'll deduct it from your pay." Onthar swung around and rode on to speak with Rorin.

The more Sturm thought about it, the angrier he got with Onthar. To charge for the lost goad seemed downright petty. Then the teachings of the Measure reminded Sturm to see the situation from Onthar's point of view. Maybe they hadn't known Brumbar was shod. Ostimar did advise him to stay away from the ford's edge. Onthar had originally paid for the goad he'd lost. Given the scarcity of hard money in a life like herding, charging two coppers for a lost stick wasn't petty. It was absolutely necessary.

Sturm pulled off his bandanna and wrung it out. His clothes would dry rapidly in the sun, and there was a long day's ride still to go. He straightened in the saddle and thought of himself as being on a war foray. Alert yet relaxed. That's the way his old friend, Soren, had practiced soldiering, as sergeant of the castle guard for Sturm's father. A braver, more devoted man had never lived.

Onthar circumnavigated the herd, and when he was satisfied that all was in order, he returned to the head and signaled to resume the drive. The bawling calves and cows slowly came about as Onthar led them north and east toward Vingaard Keep, some sixty miles away.

* * * * *

It was a long, hard day, and the herders spent every minute of it in the saddle. Sturm had always thought of himself as an accomplished long-distance rider, but compared to Onthar's men, he was a tenderfoot after all. Except that it wasn't his feet that grew tender.

The herders rotated positions, moving slowly counterclockwise around the herd. The midday meal, such as it was, was eaten when a man reached the front. Then there were no cows to watch, only the lay of the land ahead. Saddle food was jerky and cheese and raw onions, all washed down with bitter cider.

The sun was still well up when Onthar called a halt. Sturm estimated that they'd covered twenty-five miles since crossing the river. Frijje, Belingen, and Rorin pushed the herd into a shallow ravine in the middle of the grassland. Judging by the trampled grass and scoured ground, this pit had been used by previous herds on their way north. Ostimar and Onthar took Sturm on a circuit of the pit and showed him how to set up the fence that would keep the animals from wandering in the night.

"Fence?" Sturm said. He hadn't seen anyone carrying anything as bulky as a fence.

Onthar pulled a wooden stake about two feet long with a fork at the top from a canvas satchel and stuck it in the ground. He tied the end of a length of rope to the fork and stretched it out eight or ten feet, where Ostimar set another stake. On and on this went, until the whole herd was surrounded by a single thickness of rope.

"And this flimsy barrier will keep them in?" asked Sturm.

"Cows and steers aren't real wise," Ostimar explained. "They'll think they can't push through the rope, so they won't try. 'Course, if a real panic set in, a stone wall wouldn't stop 'em."

"What would frighten them that much?"

"Wolves," noted Ostimar. "Or men."

The herders camped on the highest ground overlooking the pit. Rorin and Frijje scythed down sheafs of tall grass for cattle fodder, but the herd would get no water until the next day, when they reached Brantha's Pond.

Onthar built a fire from wind-blown twigs gleaned from the grass. The fire drew the other herders in. The common kettle was brought out and hung from its peg over the flames. Each man stooped over the pot and added something—water, cheese, flour, bits of meat, vegetables, and fruit. When the pot was full, Frijje knelt by the fire and stirred it.

"Not a bad day," said Rorin.

"Hot," Ostimar pointed out. "Should rain."

"Some of us don't mind taking a swim instead of working," Belingen cracked. Sturm sensed a challenge in his eyes.

"Some of us ought to get wet more often," he parried. "It would help to cut the smell."

Frijje stopped stirring the pot. The herders looked at Sturm intently. Belingen said coldly, "Only a city fool would ride a shod horse across a river ford."

"True enough," Sturm countered. "How many times did you do it, Belingen, before you thought to remove your horse's shoes?" He saw the Estwilder close one hand into a fist. Sturm knew that the only way he could keep the respect of these rough, simple men was to match Belingen insult for insult. If he showed any softness, real or imagined, they would let Belingen treat Sturm any way he liked.

The next thing Sturm knew, Onthar was on his feet, shouting. "Get up! Get up, you idiots! Raiders! Raiders are after the herd!"

A rumble of massed hooves and screams proved that Onthar was telling the truth. "I'll get my sword," Sturm said, running to find Brumbar.

The herders vaulted onto their short ponies and pulled their goads out of the ground. Sturm climbed heavily onto Brumbar. Drawing his sword, he spurred after his comrades.

In the twilight, he could see that the attackers outnumbered Onthar and his men—perhaps a dozen. The raiders wore fantastic masks with glaring, painted eyes and horns, tusks, and garish frills made of wildly painted leather. They were armed with sabers and short bows. Several steers were already down, lying on their sides with arrows sticking out.

Onthar charged into the pack of yelling thieves. His goad took one raider in the chest, but the slim shaft snapped. The cattle thief toppled off his horse with thirty inches of goad buried in his chest. Onthar shouted to Rorin, who slapped a new weapon into his leader's hand.

Sturm angled to the other side of the raider band. Brumbar burst through the ranks of the raiders' lighter beasts, overturning two of them. Sturm cut down one bow-armed thief wearing a horrible, leering mask. Another took his place, slashing hard with a crudely forged saber. Sturm turned the thin, curved blade and thrust home through the raider's throat. The thief's body fell forward but was caught in the stirrups; the horse galloped away from the fight, the dead man dragging behind.

The mounted thieves seemed to be getting the worst of it, until Sturm realized that there were foes on foot as well. Masked figures stole out of the grass and fell on the arrow-shot animals. As the battle raged around them, they swiftly skinned and butchered the steers. The raiders left hide and carcass, but carried away whole sides of beef. Frijje cut off one pair's escape by spearing one and trampling the other. It was a brutal, nasty fight.

Sturm felt a sharp blow on his back. As he pivoted Brumbar, he felt a short arrow sticking from his back. The raider who had loosed it was only a few yards away. The popeyed face on the leather mask reflected its wearer's obvious surprise that Sturm hadn't fallen. The raider couldn't know that Sturm still wore his mail shirt under his riding tunic.

Sturm flew at the archer. The raider turned to flee, but Brumbar's long legs rapidly outgained the thief's short-legged pony. Some instinct for mercy made Sturm turn away his sword edge, and he brought the flat of the tempered blade down on the raider's head. The thief threw up his hands and slid sideways off his pony.

The other raiders were in hot flight. Onthar's men chased them some way, but quickly returned to guard the rest of the herd. Sturm dismounted and dragged the unconscious raider to Brumbar. He threw the light body across the horse and led them back to Onthar.

"Filthy dirt-eating swine," Onthar said, spitting. "They got four. The robbers eat well tonight!"

"Not all of them," Sturm said. At least four of the raiders were dead. "I caught one." The herders clustered around. Frijje grabbed the raider by his characteristic ponytail and jerked his head back. Still out cold. Frijje tore the painted mask away.

"Haw! It's a girl!" he grunted.

It was indeed, a girl of maybe fifteen or sixteen years. Her blond hair was greasy and limp, and her face was smeared with paint from the mask.

"Phew!" said Rorin. "She stinks!" Sturm hadn't noticed—the herders themselves were rather pungent.

"Slit her throat and leave her on the steppe for the others to find," Belingen advised. "They'll learn not to steal from Onthar's herd."

"No," said Sturm, interposing himself between the unconscious girl and the others.

"She's a thief!" Ostimar protested.

"She's unarmed and unconscious," Sturm insisted.

"He's right," Onthar said after a moment's reflection. "She's worth more to us alive anyway."

"How so, Onthar?" asked Rorin.

"Hostage. Keep the others of her band away, maybe."

"Too much trouble," Belingen grumbled. "I say just kill her and be done with it."

"It's not for you to say," Onthar replied. "Sturm caught her, she's his now. He can do whatever he wants with her."

Sturm flushed slightly when Rorin and Frijje laughed, but he said, "I shall follow your advice, Onthar. We'll keep her as a hostage."

The herd leader nodded. "She's your problem then. You are responsible for anything she does. And what she eats comes out of your pay."

He'd expected that. "Agreed," said Sturm.

The girl groaned. Rorin grabbed her by the back of her hairy hide chaps and dragged her off Brumbar. He held her up by the scruff of the neck. The girl shook her head and opened her eyes.

"*Ma'troya!*" she cried, upon seeing her captors. She tried to run, but Rorin held her feet off the ground. She kicked him on the shin until he threw her to the ground. Her hand flashed to her waist and came up with a short, double-edged knife. Sturm clamped his strong hand over hers and plucked the little skinning knife away. "*Ma'troya!*" the girl repeated helplessly.

"What is she saying?" Sturm asked.

"That's an eastern dialect," Onthar said. "But I'll wager she speaks our tongue. Don't you, girl?" The girl's dark blue eyes flickered with recognition. "Yes, I see you do."

Sturm lifted the girl gently to her feet. "What's your name?" he said quietly.

"Tervy." She pronounced this with a 'ch' sound, like Tchair-vee.

"Well, Tervy, you're going to be staying with the herd a lot longer than you expected."

"You kill me now!"

"I don't think so," Sturm said dryly.

"They want kill me," gasped the girl, her eyes darting at the herders.

"Be still," Sturm said. "No one will hurt you if you do as you're told."

Onthar dislodged the arrow from Sturm's tunic and handed it to the young knight. "A souvenir," he said.

Tervy regarded the arrow quizzically, then looked up at Sturm. "I shoot you, you not bleed, not die. Why so?"

He pulled up his tunic and showed her the hip-length shirt of mail he wore. Tervy had never seen armor before. She hesitantly put out a dirty hand to touch the metal mesh.

"Iron skin," she uttered with awe.

"Yes, iron skin. It stops arrows and most swords. Now I've captured you, and you're going to stay with me. If you behave, I'll feed and take care of you. If you're wicked, I'll hobble you and make you walk behind the cattle."

"I do as you say, Ironskin."

Thus Sturm acquired a prisoner, a hostage, a servant— and a nickname. From that time on, the herders called him Ironskin.

Chapter 38

Tervy and Ironskin

By the time the herders returned from repulsing
the raiders, dinner was congealed. It was too dark to hunt
for more kindling, so Onthar ordered Frijje to collect some
chips from the cattle pit.

"Faw!" he grumbled. "That's a dirty job. I know! Make
the girl do it." Onthar deferred to Sturm.

"I doubt she could get much filthier," Sturm admitted. "I'll
go with her."

Tervy showed no sign of displeasure when Sturm
explained what she was to do. She plunged into the herd,
shoving aside yearling calves and cows. She filled a bandanna with the few pats that were dry enough, and came back
out. Showing them to Sturm, she said, "Enough?"

"Enough. Take them to Frijje."

The coals were stirred and the fire blazed up again. The stew was dished out. Tervy watched expectantly, licking her lips. Sturm asked for another bowl.

"There are none," Ostimar said sullenly. "Not for raider scum."

Sturm ate only a third of his portion and gave the rest to Tervy. She ate wolfishly, slapping gobs of thick stew into her mouth with her dirty fingers. Even Rorin, the least clean of the herders, was disgusted.

When it was time to bed down, Sturm asked, "Should someone stay awake, in case the raiders return?"

"They won't come back," Onthar assured him.

"Some other band might."

"Not at night," grunted Rorin, hunkering down on his blanket.

"And why is that?"

"Raiders don't move at night," Ostimar explained. "Wolves'll get 'em in the dark." He pulled his horsehair blanket up to his chin and slipped his rolled bandanna down over his eyes.

Wolves? The herdsmen didn't seem worried about wolves. Sturm mentioned as much to Frijje, the last one awake.

"Onthar has a charm against wolves," he said. "He hasn't lost a beast to wolves in three years. G'night."

Soon the circle around the campfire was filled with soft snores and wheezes. Sturm watched Tervy, sitting with her knees tucked under her chin, staring at the dying fire.

"Do I have to tie you up?" he said to her. "Or will you behave?"

"I not run," Tervy replied. "Out there is *tyinsk*. Wolves."

He smiled at her. "How old are you, Tervy?"

"Say?"

"How many years have you lived?"

She looked back over her shoulder, her brow furrowed with incomprehension. "How long ago were you born?" Sturm said.

"Baby doesn't know when born." Maybe her people were too primitive to count the years. Or perhaps it wasn't important; probably few of them survived to middle years.

"Do you have a family? Mother? Brothers and sisters?"

"Only uncle. He dead, out there. You cut, here to here," she said, running a finger across her throat. He felt a twinge of shame.

"I'm sorry," Sturm said regretfully. "I didn't know." She shrugged indifferently.

He kicked his bedroll so that it opened feet to the fire. Sturm lay down. "Don't worry, Tervy; I'll look after you. You're my responsibility." But for how long? he wondered.

"Ironskin keep Tervy. Tervy not run away."

Sturm pillowed his head on his arm and dropped off to sleep. Hours later, the sharp howl of a wolf roused him from slumber. He tried to sit up but found that a weight held him down. It was Tervy. She had crawled atop Sturm and gone to sleep, her arms draped over him.

Sturm eased the girl to one side. She fought sleepily, saying, "If charm fail, wolves come, have to get me before get you. Protection."

Smiling, he ordered her in hushed tones to do as he said. "I can protect myself," he assured her. Tervy curled up on a narrow strip of his blanket and returned to sleep.

*   *   *   *   *

Tervy spent half the morning trotting alongside Sturm and Brumbar. He had offered to let her ride, but she insisted on keeping pace on foot. However, as the northern plain's summer sun took its toll, Tervy relented and hopped on Brumbar's rump, behind Sturm.

"This the biggest horse in the world!" she declared.

He laughed. "No, not very likely." Her conclusion wasn't difficult to understand, considering that Brumbar was half again as tall and twice as heavy as the average plains pony.

At midday, the herd caught wind of Brantha's Pond. The pond had been built by Brantha of Kallimar, yet another Solamnic Knight, 150 years before. The pool was two hundred yards across, a perfect circle whose shore was paved with blocks of granite from the Vingaard Mountains.

The thirsty cattle quickened their pace. The herders had to concentrate at the head of the moving mass to discourage the animals from breaking into a dangerous stampede. At first, Sturm was mystified by their haste, but Tervy sniffed the air and informed him that she, too, could smell the water.

Within an hour, the silver-blue disk of Brantha's Pond came into view. Another herd, far larger than Onthar's, was being driven away. Horses, wagons, carts, and their occupants clustered around the pond's edge.

Sturm's own interest quickened, stimulated by the impending contact with new people. The herdsmen were good fellows (well, there was Belingen), but they were taciturn and rather dull in conversation. Sturm had actually begun to miss the distracting talk of the gnomes.

The travelers abandoned the pond's edge when they heard the massed mooing of Onthar's herd. The cattle broke ranks and lined the shore, burying their peeling pink noses in the green water. Sturm pulled Brumbar up short. Tervy threw a leg over and dropped off. She ran toward the pond.

"Hey! What are you doing?" Sturm called. Before his eyes, the girl stripped off her collection of skins and vaulted onto the back of a drinking cow. She stood up and walked across the hind ends of two more beasts, then dived into the water. Sturm urged Brumbar down to the granite paving. The girl swam in short, quick strokes to the center of the pond and disappeared. Sturm watched the green surface. No bubbles. No turbulence other than that created by the drinking cattle. Then Tervy burst out of the water not ten feet from Sturm, scattering the cows who were drinking there.

"Give hand," she said, and Sturm leaned down to pull her out of the water. "I not stink now, hey?"

"Not as much," he admitted. He handed her clothes to her and tried not to let his embarrassment show. "Did you jump in because we said you smelled?"

"I not care what they speak," Tervy said, tossing her shoulder at Onthar and his men. "I not want Ironskin to smell me bad."

He was touched by her gesture. Sturm turned Brumbar around and rode out of the congested pond bank. He tethered his horse with Onthar's ponies and saw the herders squatted on the ground, eating whatever they could scrounge from their rucksacks. Tervy was hungry, too. She snitched a flake of jerky from Belingen's bag. He caught her at it, and boxed her ears. She promptly put a thumb in his eye. Belingen howled with rage and groped for his skinning knife.

"Put it away," said Sturm. Belingen found himself staring up thirty-four inches of polished steel.

"That raider wench nearly put my eye out!" he snarled.

"You punched her pretty good. That should satisfy you— or are you fighting with girls now?"

Sturm decided to take the girl to the caravan wagons and see what he could buy to eat. Tervy's ponytail dripped water down her back as she eagerly trotted along beside him.

"Ironskin will truly buy food with money?" she said, incredulous.

"Of course. I don't steal," Sturm said.

"You have much money?"

"Not so much," he said. "I'm not rich."

"That I figure. Rich man always steal," Tervy said. Sturm had to smile at the blunt wisdom of her statement. He was smiling a lot lately, he suddenly realized.

Sturm found an Abanasinian group that was journeying to Palanthas. Besides the hired driver, there was a mercenary, a woman soothsayer, and an elderly tanner and his apprentice. Sturm swapped stories of Solace with them for a while, then came away with slices of dried apple beaded on a string, some pressed raisins, and a whole smoked chicken. For the fine victuals, he dipped into the purse that the Knight of the Rose had given him and paid twenty coppers, well more than his total wages as a herdsman.

Tervy danced around him, fairly bursting to get at the food. The apples didn't interest her, but she devoured most of the chicken, down to some of the small bones. Sturm untied the cheesecloth bundle that held the raisins.

"What that?" Tervy said, chicken grease smeared across her face.

"Raisins," Sturm said. "Dried grapes. Try some."

She grabbed a handful and stuffed them into her mouth. "Umm, sweet." Spilling raisins all around, she finished the first handful and reached for another. Sturm swatted her hand.

"You eat all those?" she said, wide-eyed.

"No," he said. "You can eat them if you do it in a civilized manner. Like this." He picked up four raisins, put them in the palm of his left hand, and ate them one by one with his right. Open-mouthed with curiosity, Tervy duplicated his actions precisely, except when it came to getting the raisins from her hand to her mouth one at a time.

"Too slow!" she declared, and crammed them all in at once. Sturm pulled her wrist down.

"People will stop treating you like a savage when you stop acting like one," he said. "Now do it the way I showed you." This time she did it just right.

"You eat like this all time?" asked Tervy.

"I do," said Sturm.

"Ah," she exclaimed knowingly. "You big man. Nobody steal your food. I little, eat fast so nobody steal my food."

"No one's going to take food away from you here. Take your time and enjoy it." When they had finished their meal, they strolled back to the herders' camp. Tervy gazed at Sturm with a mixture of awe and amusement.

Onthar announced that it would take only two more days to reach Vingaard Keep. Once the cattle were sold, each man would be paid his wages and could sign on for another drive, if he so desired.

Sturm was the only one to decline. "I have other business in the north," he stated. Frijje asked him what. "I'm looking for my father."

"Oh? What's his name?" asked Onthar.

"Angriff Brightblade." None of the herders responded to this disclosure. However, behind Sturm, Belingen stiffened. His mouth dropped open to speak, but he closed it without saying a word.

"Well, I hope you find him," Onthar said. "You're a fair hand with cattle and good with that sword. These others, they don't know a sword from a sharpened stick."

"Thank you, Onthar," Sturm said. "Traveling companions help shorten the journey."

Frijje played his pipe a while. Tervy, who had been sitting

by Sturm's side, arms wrapped around her shins, was wonderstruck by the funny noises that the young herdsman was making. Seeing her interest, Frijje handed her the flute. Tervy blew in the end as Frijje had done, but could only make a faint, unmusical rasp. She flung the pipe back to Frijje.

"Magic," she stated flatly.

"No, my girl. It's all skill." He dusted the dirt from the mouthpiece and trilled a fast scale.

"You move fingers like a cleverman," she pointed out.

"Believe what you want." Frijje lay back and played a slow ballad. Sturm put his head down, but Tervy continued to watch Frijje as long as he played.

In the days that followed, Tervy's command of language increased dramatically. She told Sturm that among her people no one spoke without leave from the head man, so that by habit they all spoke in clipped, short sentences. She had learned the Common tongue in order to be a scout. Tervy's raider band had stalked Onthar's herd for more than eight hours before striking.

"We didn't know you had a sword," she said. "If we know—if we had known, we'd have used another plan."

"Such as?"

She grinned. "Would've jumped you first."

These conversations took place while Sturm worked the herd and Tervy rode behind him. The resilient Tervy wasn't the least bit worn from riding the hard pillion all day. And in the evening, when the communal stew pot came out, she earned her portion of Sturm's meal by cleaning and oiling his boots, his sword, and sword belt.

"You've picked up a squire," Belingen said, as Tervy diligently buffed Sturm's boots with a piece of sheepskin.

"Um, and in a year or two she'll be a fine companion on cold nights," Ostimar added with a wicked grin.

"Why wait so long?" Rorin said. The herders laughed roughly.

"What do they mean?" Tervy asked.

"Never mind," Sturm said. For all her toughness, Tervy was completely innocent, and Sturm saw no reason for her to change.

Chapter 39

The Trader
at Vingaard Keep

The squat fortifications of Vingaard Keep loomed over the low-lying plain with a presence that far exceeded its modest height. Onthar led the herd up out of a flood-cut gully and the keep stood out like a mountain peak, though they were still miles away. Sturm was near the front position then, and the sight of the ancient knightly fortress filled him with excitement and longing. From Vingaard, Castle Brightblade was only a day's ride.

"Why do people build such places?" Tervy asked from behind him.

"A keep is a stronghold, to live in and defend against attacks," Sturm said.

"Lived in by other ironskins."

"Yes, and their families."

"Ironskins have families?"

"Well, of course, where do you think little ironski— knights come from?" he asked, amused.

A haze hung over the old keep, which was little more than a ruin these days. After the Cataclysm, marauders had burned the keep. The walls still stood, but the tower was an empty shell.

Closer in, the haze proved to be dust and smoke from tramping feet and campfires. A sizable body of troops was encamped around the outer wall. No banners flew. Sturm could not tell whose troops they were, but their presence explained the need for large numbers of cattle. Such an army needed huge amounts of food.

Riders slipped in on both sides, observing the oncoming herd. Sturm scrutinized them in return. Their armor was plain, undistinguished as to origin or age. The cavalry men wore barred visors on their helmets and carried long lances. Their proportions appeared human, but they kept to such a distance that it was impossible to be sure.

Tervy was intrigued. "More ironskins," she breathed.

Sturm corrected her. "Not all men in armor are knights," he said. "You be very careful around them. They may be evil." He felt her thin arms tighten a little around his waist. Whatever her failings in education, Tervy knew evil.

The keep grew larger as the day wore on, and the outriders thickened on the herd's flanks. Sturm rode past Onthar while making his circuit. "What do you make of those men?" asked Sturm.

"Cavalry," Onthar said. He chewed a long blade of grass. "Glad to see 'em. Won't be any raiders about with them out there."

Onthar halted at midday for a word with his men. "I do the talking, and I do the dealing. Any man speaks out of turn at a parley like this loses his head. I don't know if these are mercenaries, or some warlord's new army, but I don't want any trouble. So keep your mouths closed and your hands empty."

Half a mile from the keep, a column of horsemen galloped out to meet the herd. Sturm was on the right edge of the formation then, and he saw the men ride out. Onthar met them, and the cattle milled to a stop and fell to cropping the grass.

Sturm couldn't hear what was being said, but Tervy mumbled something. He said, "What did you say?"

"I'm catching their words," she replied.

"You're what?"

"Catching their words. If you watch their mouths move, you can catch the words they speak, even if you're too far away to hear them."

Sturm turned sharply to her. "You're jesting with me!"

"Cut my heart out if I lie, Ironskin. The man, Onthar, said he has brought his animals because he heard a great lord was buying cattle for top coin. And the man in the iron hat said, yes, they can use all the fresh meat they can get."

"Can you really tell what they are saying?"

"I can, if you let me look." Sturm wheeled Brumbar around so that Tervy had the best view of the parley.

"Onthar says he will bargain with the great lord himself, no one else. Iron Hat says, 'I speak for the great lord in small things.' 'Listen to me,' Onthar says, 'my herd is not a small thing. Either the great lord speaks to me, or I will drive the cattle over the mountains to Palanthas, where beef always commands a high price.' Iron Hat is angry, but he says, 'I will go and speak to the great lord; wait and I will return with his tidings.'" She smiled at Sturm. "How was that?"

The cavalry officer did in fact bring his horse around and gallop back to the keep. Sturm asked, "Where did you learn such a trick?"

"An old man in our band practiced this art. He was the best scout on the plain. He could catch words true from a bowshot away. He taught me before he died."

"Where did he learn it?"

"From a kender, he said."

They waited in the broiling sun until the cavalryman returned. His fine mount pranced out to where Onthar sat slouched on his stubby pony. Tervy squinted into the glare and caught their words again.

"He says to drive the herd into the baney, the bailey—?"

"Bailey," Sturm said. "The courtyard inside the keep."

"Yes, and 'the great lord will treat with you personally.' Onthar agrees."

With many whistles and pricks of the goad, the herders got the cattle moving again. The nine hundred beasts funneled into the keep's gate. The bailey easily accommodated the animals. When the last calves were spanked, bawling, into the gate, soldiers drew the bars shut.

There were clusters of tents all along the outer wall. Onthar and his men tethered their horses on a picket line and followed a plumed soldier along the tent line.

"Are these all the men you have?" said the soldier. His face was hidden by his visor. "I would have thought such a large herd would require more handlers."

"Not if the men are good," Onthar said.

Sturm was counting tents. Four men per tent, sixty tents so far—he had an uncomfortable feeling about this.

They came upon a very large tent, trimmed with dark blue brocade and golden fringe. Guards snapped to attention and crossed halberds at their approach. The visored soldier spoke to them, presenting Onthar and his company. The guards resumed normal positions. The plumed officer extended his hand, and the herders went in alone.

The interior was sumptuous. Carpets covered the ground, and tapestries, hanging from the ridge poles, gave the illusion of being in a solid building. While the others were gawking at the richness of their surroundings, Sturm was staring at the designs of the rugs and wall hangings. The recurring motif was that of a rampant red dragon, clutching a sheaf of spears in one claw and a crown in the other.

"Ironskin," Tervy said, too loudly.

"Not now."

A curtain of shimmering red beads closed the corridor. Onthar feigned disinterest and swept the curtain aside. Sturm thought the red 'beads' looked very much like rubies.

Two halberds swung down to bar Onthar's progress. He regarded the guards idly, as if he'd seen such beings many times and they bored him. Beyond the guards, a large, powerfully built man sat at a three-legged table that was draped with a golden cloth. He wore scale armor enameled in red and blue, and a fearsome helmet sat facing outward on the gold-topped table.

The man looked up. His hair was white, though he was by no means elderly. It swept back from his massive brow to fall around his shoulders. His skin was pale.

"Come in. You are Onthar the Herdsman, are you not?" said the man.

"I am, my lord. May I ask what I shall call you?"

"I am Merinsaard, Lord of Bayarn."

Sturm clenched his fists tightly at his sides. Merinsaard! The name spoken by Sturm's storm phantom! Sturm concentrated on the hard face and long white hair. Danger emanated from this man. Sturm tried to catch Onthar's eye, but could not.

There were no chairs for Onthar and his men. Ordinary folk did not sit in the presence of the great lord.

Merinsaard stated, "I am pleased that you chose to drive your fine cattle here. It was been some weeks since our last supply of fresh meat was consumed. How many head did you bring?"

"Nine hundred, more or less. Six hundred steers, two hundred cows, and one hundred yearling calves. What bulls we brought we will drive back with us," Onthar said. He crossed his hands at his waist and did not appear at all excited.

The great lord took out a ledger book and opened it. With a sharp quill, he made a notation. "And how much are you asking, Master Onthar?"

"Twelve coppers per calf, fifteen per steer, and one silver piece per cow," he said firmly.

"A high price, but fair considering the quality of the beasts in the bailey." Onthar permitted himself a smile.

Merinsaard snapped his fingers, and two more soldiers entered from a door in the wall behind his table. They carried a chest into the room and set it down. "Your payment," said the great lord.

Onthar reached out with steady hands. This was a fortune! His household would celebrate for days when he returned with such a bounty. He lifted the lid and let it fall back on its hinges.

The chest was empty.

"What?" Onthar said. Sturm snapped his sword out.

"Take them!" Merinsaard barked. Soldiers poured into the room from two sides.

"Treachery! Treachery!" The herders scattered. Sturm gathered Tervy to him.

"Stay behind me!" he said. A soldier thrust the point of his halberd at Sturm, but the knight parried the heavy steel head away. The herders, with only their flimsy goads, were quickly subdued by the soldiers.

"Ironskin!" Tervy shouted. "At your back!" Sturm whirled in time to dodge a savage cut by another halberd. He stabbed home, hitting the fellow below his breastplate. Bleeding heavily, the man fell. Tervy rolled the body over and snatched a small axe from the man's belt. "*Hai! Tirima!*" she yelled.

"Tervy, no!" Too late, Sturm saw her scamper through the press of struggling men and jump upon Merinsaard's golden table. By Paladine, she was brave! The great lord stood back from the table as the girl threatened him with the hatchet. He donned his helmet and raised his hands over his head.

He shouted at Tervy to get out, but she didn't. Instead, she whipped her arm back and hurled the hatchet at the great lord.

The puny weapon struck his armored chest and glanced off. Merinsaard's voice filled the tent with a booming incantation. The air seemed to solidify around Sturm's limbs, and his sword grew impossibly heavy to lift. Then, with a single silent burst, a white light dazzled him completely. Sturm sagged to his knees. The sword was torn from his hand, and the enemy soldiers bore him, immobile, to the richly carpeted floor.

* * * * *

Someone was groaning.

Sturm opened his eyes and found that he still couldn't see anything. There was no blindfold around his head; the effect of the dazzling light spell was lingering.

"Oh, I'm blind!" someone groaned.

"Shut up," Sturm said. "Be quiet, all of you. Who's here?"

"Onthar is here," said the herd leader.

"And Frijje."

"I'm here." Sturm asked who 'I' was. "Ostimar," was the sheepish reply. They were all present except Tervy. All of them were sitting on the ground in a circle, hands tied behind their backs to a stout wooden post.

Frijje said, "She hit the lord with an axe."

"Did she really?" Rorin asked.

"Yes, right on the wishbone. Didn't even scratch him."

"Quiet," Sturm said. "The light spell is beginning to wear off. I can see my legs."

Within a few minutes, they could all see again. Onthar apologized in his blunt, clipped way for getting them into this fix.

"It's not your fault," Sturm said. "Merinsaard must have lured other herds here after starting those rumors about a rich buyer at the keep."

"What does he need all those cattle for?" asked Frijje. "He doesn't have more than a couple hundred men."

"He's no mere cattle thief," said Sturm. "I think he's procuring food for a much larger army."

"What army?" asked Onthar.

"Well, I think—" The wall flap turned in and Merinsaard walked in, wearing his fearsome dragonlike helmet. It had just the effect he wanted.

"Please, don't kill us!" Belingen whined. "We're poor men! We have no ransom to pay!"

"Be silent!" The tusked face circled the room, studying each man in turn. "Which of you is the one the girl calls Ironskin?"

No one said anything. Merinsaard drew a dagger and tapped the flat of the blade against his palm. He circled around, stopping by Belingen. He pushed the tip of his dagger against Belingen's chest. "There is a simple way to find out which of you wears mail," he said. "I shall run this dagger through each of your chests." Merinsaard leaned on the dagger. Belingen inhaled sharply.

"No! Don't do it! I'll tell!"

"Shut your mouth, fool!" Onthar yelled. Merinsaard

went to the herd leader and struck him on the head with the butt of his dagger. Onthar slumped forward.

"The next man to speak will die," said Merinsaard. "Except you, my friend." Belingen managed a sweaty smile.

"It's him, the mustached one. Yes, him!" Sturm stared at the floor. Merinsaard's thigh-high boots moved into his line of sight. The lord called for his guards, and a squad of halberdiers cut Sturm loose from the post.

"That man, too," Merinsaard said, indicating Belingen. The guards marched Sturm and Belingen through the courtyard.

"Where's Tervy?" Sturm said at last.

"She is safe," the great lord said. "I have not harmed her."

"You can kill her, my lord; she's only a raider brat," Belingen said. Sturm shot him a fierce look.

Without sparing him a glance, Merinsaard replied, "She has considerable wit and courage, which is more than I can say for you."

They entered the rear of the same room they'd fought in an unknown time before. Tervy was sitting on the rug in front of the table. She saw Sturm and jumped to her feet. A clank announced that she was fettered to a table leg.

"Ironskin! I knew you'd come for me!" she said.

"Things are not so simple," said Merinsaard. The guards brought Sturm and Belingen in and forced them to kneel before the great lord's gold-decked table. The soldiers stood at their backs with halberds leveled, and Merinsaard sat in his chair.

"There is a problem," he said, removing his dragon mask. "Among a group of simple herdsmen I find a young stalwart, a swordsman and warrior, who wears mail and rides a Garnet-bred warhorse. Now I ask, why would such a man be here tending cows?"

"It's a living," said Sturm sullenly.

"I know who he is, master," said Belingen.

Merinsaard leaned forward on his elbows. "Yes?"

"His name is Sturm Brightblade. He's a knight."

The great lord didn't blink. "How do you know this?"

"I heard him tell his name was Brightblade. And I remembered that name from my younger days when I helped sack his father's castle."

Sturm leaped up. "You did what?" A guard struck him smartly on the back of his knees, and Sturm collapsed on the carpet.

"I see. Is there anything else you can tell me?"

"He's looking for his father, but his father's dead. I was with the band that breached the inner keep. We set fire to it, and all the knights threw themselves from the battlement rather than burn up." Sturm's face paled and Belingen grinned. "They was scared of a little fire."

"Thank you, ah, what is your name?"

"Belingen, master. Your devoted slave."

"Yes." Merinsaard nodded and the soldier standing behind Belingen raised his halberd. Down went the axe blade, and off came Belingen's astonished head. It rolled to Tervy's feet, and she kicked it away, spitting, "*Chu'yest!*" Sturm needed no translation. He grimaced at the severed head with regret and disgust. Belingen might have been a worthless fool, but he might also have had further information about Sturm's father.

"Remove the debris," declared Merinsaard. Two soldiers dragged the body out by the heels. "A man so easily persuaded to betray his comrades is of no use to anyone," said Merinsaard. He stood. "So you are Sturm Brightblade, of the House of Brightblade?"

"I am," he said defiantly.

Merinsaard signaled again, and a stool was brought in for Sturm to sit on. The soldiers withdrew, leaving Sturm and Tervy with the great lord.

"I would very much like for you to join my company of men," said Merinsaard. "I can use a young, trained warrior like you. Too many of the scum I pick up are no better than the fool I just shortened by a head." He folded his hands across his flat stomach and looked Sturm in the eye. "In a very short time, you could have your own command of picked troops, cavalry or infantry. What do you say?"

The blood was still fresh on the floor, so Sturm considered his reply. "I have never worked as a mercenary before," he said equivocally. He pointed to Tervy and said, "Will you release the girl?"

"If she behaves." Merinsaard placed a key on the table. Sturm picked it up and unlocked the fetter that enclosed Tervy's slender ankle.

"Before I commit myself, may I ask a question?" said Sturm. Merinsaard inclined his head affirmatively. "In this army, to whom would I be responsible?"

"To me and no one else."

"And from whom do you take your orders?"

"I am supreme," rumbled Merinsaard.

Sturm glanced at Tervy. The chain lay by her foot. She ran a hand over the crudely forged iron fetter. "I don't believe you," Sturm said, calmly.

Merinsaard bolted to his feet. "You question me?" he roared.

"Supreme commanders do not sit in lonely keeps, confiscating cattle like skulking freebooters," said Sturm.

Rage purpled the great lord's face. Sturm wondered if he'd gone too far. In his next breath, would Merinsaard order both their deaths? No, the color slowly left his face, and Merinsaard leaned on the table.

"You are wise for a young man," he said at last. "I have been given the task of collecting food and arms for a great host that will invade northern Ansalon soon. It is a task I undertake with total devotion. As to my leader, she—" He paused, conscious of revealing an important fact. "—she leaves all the handling of mundane affairs to me."

"I see," Sturm said. What now? "Ah, what would be the terms of my service?"

"Terms? I cannot offer you a contract, if that is what you mean. But know this, Master Brightblade, join with us and all manner of power and glory shall be yours. You will command and conquer. Among men you will be as a king."

Merinsaard sat down. Sturm looked to Tervy, which put his face away from the warlord's. Their eyes met. Tervy gave a very slight nod.

Merinsaard looked expectant, so Sturm said, "This is my answer. . . ." The great lord leaned forward. "Now!"

Tervy stood and pulled the chain as hard as she could. The folding table leg popped loose and the heavy tabletop collapsed on Merinsaard's legs. Sturm sprang over the fallen table, knocking Merinsaard down and pinning his hands. There would be no blinding incantation this time.

Tervy grabbed the shiny helmet from the floor and scampered behind the struggling men. She whacked Merinsaard on the head, and the big man howled under Sturm's clenching hand. Tervy smote him again and again.

"That's enough," Sturm said. "He's out."

"Shall we kill him?" she said.

"By the gods, you're a bloodthirsty child! No, we're not going to kill him. We're not assassins." The sight of the unconscious Merinsaard gave Sturm a dangerous idea. "Help me get his armor off."

"Oh, you want to skin him!" Tervy said. Sturm rolled his eyes and hurried to untie the lacings of the warlord's armor.

* * * * * *

The great lord Merinsaard threw back the wall flap. Guards in the corridor stiffened to attention. The fierce Dragon Highlord mask turned to them.

"I have immobilized Brightblade," he said. "He will remain here until I return. No one is to enter that room before me, do you understand? The paralysis spell will be broken if anyone does. Is that clear?"

"Yes, lord!" the guards shouted in unison.

"Very good." Merinsaard beckoned to Tervy. "Come along, girl." Tervy walked toward him, looking miserable. Chain dragged between her feet. She was hobbled with heavy iron fetters.

"When you prove your loyalty, I will remove them," Merinsaard said loftily.

"Oh, thank you, great lord!" Tervy replied.

The masked man swept on with the girl close on his heels. In the corridor, beyond earshot of the guards, Sturm said softly, "You did that very well."

"Oh, thank you, great lord!"

"You can stop now."

In the maze of silk walls, Sturm found the flap leading to the room where Onthar and his men were kept. He burst in. Ostimar raised his sagging head, and when he saw the dragon mask, his expression ran from fear to hatred.

"What now?" Onthar said.

"I'm going to let you go," said Sturm. He handed Merinsaard's dagger to Tervy, who busied herself freeing the astonished herders.

"Where are Sturm and Belingen?" said Frijje.

"Belingen betrayed his honor and died for it." Sturm removed the stifling helmet. "And Sturm is with you."

It was all Sturm could do to restrain the herders from cheering. Even the normally taciturn Onthar grinned and thumped Sturm on the back.

"There's no time for celebration," Sturm said hastily. "You must get to your horses and get out of here."

Rorin said, "You're not riding with us?"

"I can't. My destiny lies farther north. Besides, the only chance you fellows have is if Merinsaard wants to avenge himself on me rather than recapture all of you."

The realization of what this meant quickly sank in. Onthar grasped Sturm's arms. "We'll face the hordes of Takhisis if you say so, Ironskin."

"You may have that opportunity," Sturm said grimly. "So go. Warn all your people about Merinsaard. Make sure that no one else brings him cattle, or sheep, or other supplies. They would meet with the same treatment you did."

"I will spread the word across the plains," Onthar vowed. "Not even a partridge will get to Merinsaard's stores."

The herders gathered up their few belongings and started for the exit. Sturm added, "There's just one other thing."

"What?" asked Onthar.

Sturm paused. "I want you to take Tervy with you."

"No!" she said loudly. "I stay with you!"

"You can't do that. I've got to travel fast and light, and it will be too dangerous for you to remain with me," Sturm said solemnly.

"It wasn't too dangerous in Merinsaard's room, when I spilled the table and thumped him on the head."

Sturm laid a hand on the girl's shoulder. "You're braver than ten men, Tervy, but there's going to be more than just swords or arrows coming at me. There is evil magic abroad in the land, and the full weight of it may fall on me in the coming days."

Her lips quivered. "I don't care."

"I do. You're a fine girl, Tervy. You deserve a long and happy life." He turned to Frijje. "You'll look after her, won't you?"

The herder, still amazed to hear that the girl had subdued the mighty Merinsaard, replied, "I think she'll end up looking after me!"

It was agreed then, though not without some tears. Sturm hesitated a moment, then kissed her smudged forehead and sent her way with the herders. The pang of regret he felt was like a fresh wound, but Sturm knew that in the coming days his own odds of survival would be slim.

The guards tensed when Onthar and his party walked into view. Sturm, mask in place, ordered the soldiers to let them pass. "These men are to return with more provender," he boomed.

The herders' ponies were brought out, and they mounted. Frijje hauled Tervy up behind him. "You will bring the next herd to this same spot," Sturm said loudly.

"Aye, my lord," Onthar replied. "A thousand head, I promise."

Onthar swung his pony southward and kicked its dusty hide. He galloped away with the others strung out behind. Frijje and Tervy were last. The girl looked back until they were lost from sight. She held her right fist clenched to her chest; the temptation to wave farewell was strong.

Hands clasped behind his back, Sturm strode down the center passage, acting like a general at inspection. He glanced into several rooms until he found what he wanted: Merinsaard's wardrobe.

Quickly he shed the armor. Merinsaard was thicker through the chest and waist than Sturm, but otherwise they were nearly the same size. He donned a woolen tunic, scarf, and gloves. Though it was warm on the plain, in the higher elevations it would be cold at night. Sturm retained the dragon mask, and threw an ankle-length cloak around his shoulders. The hood hid his dark hair. There was no time to search for the sword that had been taken from him, so he 'borrowed' one of Merinsaard's. Tas would be proud of him, he thought ruefully. The simple-hilted weapon was plated with mirror-finished silver, and fitted with a black leather scabbard. Sturm buckled the sword belt under the cloak.

At the entrance of the grand tent, he shouted, "My horse!" A soldier ran to the picket line and returned with a magnificent white charger.

"The apothecary reports the poultice has healed Mai-tat's hoof," the soldier said in a rapid, breathless voice. "The man begs your lordship to spare him."

Why not? "I give him his life," Sturm said in what he hoped was a convincingly arrogant manner. He put a foot in the stirrup and swung onto Mai-tat. The spirited charger pranced in a half-circle, causing the soldier to retreat.

Sturm opened his mouth to explain his departure, then quickly realized that Merinsaard would likely do no such thing. "I shall return before morning," he said.

"The usual guard postings remain?" said the man who'd brought the horse.

"Yes." Sturm tightened the reins to quell the nervous animal. "Let there be no mistakes, or it will be your head!" he said.

He spurred lightly and galloped north, toward Castle Brightblade. Sturm regretted not having time to scatter the cattle inside the old keep. But there was no time for such diversions; the moment the real Merinsaard awoke and freed himself from his bonds, the hunt for Sturm Brightblade would begin.

Chapter 40

The Secret
Of Brightblade Castle

Mai-tat was as fleet as he was beautiful, and in a very short time the dark hump of Vingaard Keep sank below the southern horizon. With the stars to guide him, Sturm bore northwest. A tributary of the Vingaard River lay due north and the Verkhas Hills to the west. In the fertile pocket of land between the two lay Castle Brightblade.

The white stallion's hooves drummed a solo song on the plain. Several times Sturm halted his headlong flight to listen for sounds of pursuit. Aside from the whirring of crickets in the tall grass, the plain was silent.

A few hours before dawn, Sturm slowed Mai-tat as they closed upon a shadowy ruin. It was an old hut and a land marker, now demolished. The stump of the marker still bore the lower half of its carved name plaque. The lower petals of a rose showed, and beneath that a sun and a naked sword. Bright Blade. Sturm had come to the southern limits of his ancestral holdings.

He clucked his tongue and urged the horse forward. The fields beyond the marker that he remembered as rich grazing land and bountiful orchards were overgrown and wild. The neat rows of apple and pear trees were little more than a thicket now. Vines had long since reclaimed the road. Sturm rode on, tight-lipped, ducking now and then to clear the sagging tree branches.

The orchard was split by a creek, he remembered, and so it was still. He steered Mai-tat into the shallow stream. The creek ran a mile or so to the very base of the walls of Castle Brightblade. Mai-tat trotted through the cool water.

The east was brightening to amber when the gray walls appeared over the treetops. The profile of the battlements and towers brought a lump to his throat. But it was not the same as when he left; creepers scaled the walls in thick mats, blocks of stone had toppled, and the towers were naked to the sky, their roofs burned off years ago.

"Come on," Sturm said to the horse, tapping him gently with his heels. Mai-tat cantered through the creek, kicking up founts with every step. He climbed the bank on the west side and plowed through the hedges. On the castle's west face was the main gate. Sturm clattered up the grass-spotted, cobblestone road to the entrance. Shaded from the rising sun, the walls looked black.

The narrow moat was little more than a muddy ditch now; without the dam to divert the creek, it would never keep water. Sturm slowed Mai-tat once they hit the bridge. Belingen's cruel remarks about knights jumping into the moat echoed in Sturm's mind. The ditch was nothing but a dark, swampy morass.

The gate was gone. Only the blackened hinges remained, spiked to the stone walls with iron nails a foot long. The courtyard was thick with blown leaves and charred wood. Sturm looked up at the donjon rising before him. The windows gaped blankly, their sills displaying tongues of soot where fire had raged through. He wanted to call out, to yell,

Father, Father, I've come home!

But no one would hear. No one but ghosts.

The bailey had been used recently to house animals. Sturm found the tracks of massed cattle, and realized that Merinsaard's camp at Vingaard Keep was not the only site where the invaders were marshaling provisions. A deep anger welled in him at the thought of the low purpose for which the noble edifice of Castle Brightblade had been used.

He rounded the corner of the donjon and entered the north courtyard. There was the little postern gate that his mother and he had fled through that last time he had seen his father. He saw again his father embrace his mother for the last time, as snow fell around them. Lady Ilys Brightblade never recovered from the chill of that parting. To the end of her life, she was cold, rigid, and bitter.

Then he saw the body.

Sturm dismounted and led Mai-tat by the reins. He walked up to the body lying face down in the leaves and rolled it over. It was a man, and he'd not been dead long—a day perhaps, or two. He'd been neatly run through from behind. The corpse still clutched a cloth bag in his fist. Sturm pried open the fingers and found that the bag held petty valuables—silver coins, crude jewelry, and some semiprecious stones. Whoever had killed this man had not done so to rob him. In fact, by the dagger and picklock tucked in his belt, the dead man appeared to be a thief himself.

Sturm walked on. He discovered the remains of a campfire and some bedding, all trampled and tangled. Under a blue horsehair blanket he found another body. This one had died by sword as well. The usual sort of camp items were scattered about. Copper pan, clay pots, waterskins—more silver coins and a bolt of fine silk. Had the thieves had a falling out over their spoils? If so, why hadn't the winner taken everything with him?

An empty doorway yawned nearby. To the kitchens, Sturm mused. He used a broken tent pole for a stake and tied Mai-tat.

Sunlight streamed into the shattered donjon, but many halls were still pitch black. Sturm went back to the spoiled robber camp and made a torch with a stick and some rags.

As he worked, he heard a stirring in the doorway. He whirled, sword ready. There was nothing there.

The dead men had changed Sturm's perception of the castle. He'd been expecting a mournful tour of his old home, and a search for understanding to his father's fate. Now a more sinister air clung to the stones. No place was free of the probing fingers of evil, not even the former castle of a Solamnic Knight.

The kitchens were picked clean, plundered long ago, even of their fire brick and andirons. Cobwebs clung to every beam and doorway. He came to the great hall, where his father had often dined with great lords, such as Gunthar Uth Wistan, Dorman Hammerhand, and Drustan Sparfeld of Garnet. The great oak table was gone. The brass candleholders on the walls were ripped out. The fireplace, with its carved symbols of the Order of the Rose, had been deliberately defaced.

There was that noise again! Sturm was sure that it was footfalls. "Who are you? Come out and show yourself!" He waved the torch toward the vaulted ceiling. The stone arches were cloaked in a tightly nestled layer of bats. Disgusted, Sturm crossed the hall to the steps. One set led up to the private rooms, while another led down to the cellars. Sturm put a foot on the lowest of the rising steps.

"Hello. . . ." sighed a voice. Sturm froze. Under the hood his hair prickled.

"Who is there?" he called.

"This way. . . ." The voice came from below. Sword in his right hand, torch in his left, Sturm descended the steps.

It was cold down there. The torch flickered in the breeze rising through the stairwell. The corridor curved away on either side, following the foundation of the very ancient citadel that Castle Brightblade had been built on.

"Which way?" Sturm called boldly.

"This way. . . ." whispered the voice. It seemed oddly familiar as it sighed down the hall like the last gasp of a dying man. Sturm followed it to his left.

He had not gone fifty yards when he stumbled upon a third dead man. This one was different; he was no robber. He was older, his beard untrimmed and his face worn by wind and sun. The dead man sat slumped against the wall, a dagger buried in his ribs. Oddly, his right arm was bent and resting atop his head, a finger stiffly pointing down. Sturm studied the face. It was familiar—in a rush, he recognized the man as Bren, one of his father's old retainers. If he were here, could Sturm's father be far away?

"What are you pointing at, old fellow?" Sturm asked the dead man urgently. He opened the man's coat to see if Bren carried any clues to the fate of Sturm's father. When he did, the dead man's right arm slid out of position and came to rest pointing straight up, overhead. Sturm raised the torch. There was nothing above him but an iron wall sconce—

—which was crooked. Sturm looked more closely and saw a light mark scored on the wall block. The bracket pivoted, scratching this mark. Sturm grasped the lower end of the sconce and pushed. It turned, following the scratched path in the wall.

The floor trembled, and a tremendous grinding sound filled the tunnel. A section of floor rose in front of Sturm, revealing a dark cavity below. In all his life in the castle, he'd never known of such a secret room.

"Go down. . . . Go down. . . ." rasped the phantom voice. Sturm felt for the first time a presence to go with the voice. He turned sharply and saw the apparition behind him. It was a dim red figure, dressed in what looked like furs. Sturm stepped forward with the torch. He couldn't make out the face, but he caught a glimpse of a dark, drooping mustache. The man he'd seen in the thunderstorm!

"Come forward, you!" he shouted, and thrust the torch into the specter's face.

The face was his own. Sturm dropped the brand.

"Great Paladine!" he sputtered, backing away. His heel slipped off the top step into the secret vault. "What does this mean?"

"Go down. . . ." repeated the phantom Sturm. Its lips did not move, but the voice was distinct. "Go. . . ."

"Why are you here?" Sturm said. He reached for the torch with trembling hands. "Where did you come from?"

"Far away. . . ."

Sturm's eyes widened. The phantom repeatedly urged

him to descend into the secret chamber.

"I will," Sturm assured. "I will." With that, the red figure vanished.

Sturm turned to the steps, but could see nothing beyond the sphere of ruddy light cast by the torch. He took a deep breath and went down.

It was cold in the secret vault, and he was glad to be wearing Merinsaard's thick tunic. At the bottom of the steps, some eight feet beneath the level of the corridor, he found two more corpses. They were unmarked, but their faces told too well how they had met their fate. The trap door had sealed them in, and in the ensuing hours the men had suffocated.

Sturm turned from the dead robbers. As he did, his torchlight gleamed on something metallic. He walked into the velvet darkness, his breath pluming out before him. The glow of the torch fell over a suit of armor.

Sturm swallowed hard, trying to force down the lump in his throat. With one shaking hand, he reached out to brush the dust from the etched steel. It was. It was his. Sturm had found his father's suit of armor. Breast- and backplate, greaves, schildrons, and helmet were all there. The superlative war armor etched with the rose motif. The helmet had high horns on the forehead, making Sturm's old headgear, still dented from Rapaldo's axe, seem like a cheap imitation.

The armor was hung on a wooden frame. As Sturm ran his hands over the cherished suit, he felt the soft, cold links of a chain mail shirt under the breastplate. And hanging from the waist by a single thickness of scarlet ribbon was a slip of yellow parchment. Inscribed in Angriff Brightblade's forceful hand were the words, *For My Son.*

Sturm was filled with such joy at that moment, he could scarcely breathe. The mortal shell of a man could weaken and die, but the virtues that made him a leader among men, a Knight of Solamnia, were embodied in the imperishable metal. Sturm's life was half complete. All that remained was to know of his father's fate.

He threw off Merinsaard's clothes and, dusty or not, began to put on the armor. It fit well, almost perfectly. The shoulders were a bit roomy, but Sturm would grow into them. He finished tying the cops to his boots and lifted the breastplate off the crossbar. Beneath it, hanging from a single peg, was the sword.

The hilt curved toward the point in a graceful arc, the steel as clean and shiny as when it had come from the forge. The long handle was wrapped in rough wire, to ensure a tight grip even when soaked with blood. The almond-shaped pommel was hard brass, engraved with the symbol of the rose.

Sturm could bear it no longer. He felt the tears flow over his cheeks and made no move to wipe them away. He had not cried like this since the night he'd left his father behind, twelve years ago.

The sword came lightly off its peg. The balance was perfect, and the handle fit Sturm's hand as though it had been made for him. He drew Merinsaard's silver-handled weapon and tossed it, clanging, to the cold stone floor. Sturm slipped his father's sword into the black scabbard and hurriedly fit the breastplate and backplate over his head. He was still closing the buckles under his arms when he heard a strange humming.

Merinsaard's sword was glowing. The hum emanated from it. Sturm shoved the stand over on top of the glowing blade, and he watched, open-mouthed, as the sword rose into the air, flipping the heavy wooden crosstree over effortlessly. Merinsaard's sword drifted toward the stairs, and Sturm hastily snatched up his father's helmet and followed. The silver sword slanted upward, out of the vault.

The floating blade moved unerringly across the great hall to the despoiled kitchen and out the door. There stood Mai-tat, unmoving, like a statue of alabaster. The nervous stallion had never been so quiet. The sword came on, point first. The blade slowly circled the horse, its point barely touching Mai-tat's neck. The glow reached out to engulf the horse. The charger began to writhe and shrink within its white aura. He stepped forward, ready to cut the suffering animal down, but the fierce heat radiating from the sword stopped him. The glow intensified to searing level. There was a flash of blinding light and a great clap of thunder. Sturm was hurled back against the wall, the breath driven from his body.

A deep-throated laugh filled the courtyard. The hair on Sturm's neck prickled. He coughed and rubbed his eyes. Where Mai-tat had been, there now was Merinsaard, fully armed and full of rage.

"So, Brightblade! This is the treasure you traveled so far to find! Is it worth dying for?" he roared.

Sturm fell back a pace, his head throbbing from the shock of Merinsaard's appearance. Finding his voice, he replied, "The relics of a noble past are always worth having. But I don't expect to die just yet."

Sturm brought the Brightblade sword on guard. Merinsaard cut wide circles in the air with his own blade, but he didn't come forward to fence. He raised the silver sword high and declaimed, "Do you know what it was you so carelessly carried forth from my camp, impudent fool? This sword is the key to all the negative planes. It is Thresholder, the pathway to power! I allowed you to escape, worm; five seconds after you left me bound and gagged, I was free and plotting how best to follow you. Was it not convenient that you should impersonate me, and ride me in my equine form all the way here?"

An unnatural wind sprang up, blowing hot in Sturm's face. "It's a pity you did not stay a horse!" he said boldly. "In that form, at least you were a useful creature!"

A ball of silver fire flew out from Thresholder's tip. It spiraled up to the donjon's roof and burst there, shattering the tiles asunder. Sturm ducked inside the kitchen as broken rock rained down where he'd been standing.

Merinsaard laughed. "Flee, little man! Only now do you realize with whom you have trifled!"

Merinsaard smashed through the wall. He whipped his silver blade to and fro, leaving arcs of crackling-hot light behind. Sturm dodged into the great hall just ahead of a sizzling tongue of fire that scored molten ruts in the slate floor. Merinsaard was toying with him. He could bring the whole castle down on Sturm if he desired.

Sturm wanted to stand and fight, but only on ground of his own choosing. There would be less debris to fling at him on the open battlements, so Sturm led the maniacal warlord

to the second floor and down the narrow corridor wher
Sturm's bedroom used to be. Sturm cleared the end of th
corridor just as Merinsaard entered it. The warrior-wizar
sent white fire blasting down the empty passage, opening
hole through a wall two feet thick. Sturm ran on, past th
third and fourth floors, to the roof.

"Come back, young Brightblade! You can't hide forever!"
Merinsaard taunted him. A miasma of anger and evil settle
over the entire castle. Sturm came to a section of wall wher
the wooden boarding had been burned away. He teetere
along a charred beam, thinking the heavier Merinsaar
could not follow, then crouched behind the rubble from
fallen tower and tried to plan an attack.

When he came to the burned area, Merinsaard folded hi
arms across his chest and muttered a spell in an ancient, gut
tural tongue. Black clouds collected around the hoarding
and Merinsaard simply walked across on the vapor, chuck
ling fiercely as he came. Sturm pushed over a section of bro
ken wall in a desperate attempt to impede the wizard'
approach. Thresholder swept back and forth, shattering th
tumbling blocks into gravel.

"Where will you go next?" chortled Merinsaard. "You ar
running out of castle, Brightblade. What a disappointmen
you would have been to your father. He was a true warrior
ten times the man you'll ever be. My men pursued him fo
months after they sacked the castle. He survived them all
even the Trackers of Leereach."

"What was he to you?" Sturm shouted. "Why should yo
want his death?"

"He was a Knight and a battle lord. My mistress could no
allow him to live if our plan for conquest was to go for
ward." A blast from the silver sword shaved off the top o
the battered tower. "What an irony it is that you will di
wearing his armor. What a supreme moment for my Dark
Queen!"

He's right, Sturm thought. I've run out of castle, and I'm
not the man my father was. A curved wall of the towe
closed in behind him. Sturm looked up. There was no place
to go—no place but down.

Tiny droplets of fire burst around Sturm's feet. He

hopped aside, perilously close to the edge. "Jump, boy. Cheat my revenge, why don't you? It will be easier than the death I have in mind for you," Merinsaard said, a scant five yards away. Sturm looked down. It was a long, long fall.

"Take the step. Jump. For you it can be over quickly," hissed the wizard.

There was no hope. This was the end. Sturm would never again see his friends or solve the mystery of his father. For him, there was only a choice of deaths. A single step, and oblivion. Didn't every man want an easy death when his time came? But you're not every man! his mind screamed. You're the son and grandson of Solamnic Knights! his mind screamed. This knowledge helped melt the icy fear that gripped his heart.

He squared his shoulders and faced Merinsaard. The Brightblade sword pointed at the warlord's heart. "I do not do your evil bidding," Sturm stated. "If you claim to be a warrior and a lord, let your blade test mine, and we will see who acquits himself with honor."

Merinsaard smiled, showing white teeth. The blinding glow faded from Thresholder, and Sturm assumed a fighting stance. The wizard extended his blade at Sturm, and with no warning at all, a blast of fire lashed out from the tip. It struck Sturm in the chest and slammed him into the tower wall.

"As you see," said Merinsaard. "I am not an honorable man." He raised Thresholder for the final, mortal strike, and his eyes got very wide and white. Sturm struggled to bring the tip of his father's sword waveringly into the air.

Suddenly, Merinsaard made a gagging sound and staggered to the battlement. Sturm was astonished to see an arrow buried in his back. Some distance away, silhouetted against the morning sky, was a figure with a bow.

Sturm got to his feet. Merinsaard grasped the battlement with his mailed hands, but the iron links found no purchase, and the warrior-wizard toppled through a crenelation to the courtyard below. There was a scream, a heavy, ringing thud, and silence.

Sturm raced for the steps. The mysterious archer was nowhere in sight. He found Merinsaard dead, his sightless eyes staring into the mossy flagstones. Thresholder lay just beyond his lifeless fingers. As Sturm watched, the sword flared and vanished with a loud crack. Where it had lain, the stones were scorched.

Sturm wavered and braced himself against the donjon wall. As he tried to make sense of what had happened, another arrow struck the ground at his feet. The gray goose-feather fletching on the long black arrow quivered from the impact.

Sturm jerked around and saw the unknown archer atop the outer wall. The bowman raised a hand in salute, then ducked into an empty watchtower and was gone.

He stooped to examine the arrow. Tied to the shaft just behind the head was a slip of paper. Sturm freed it and read:

Dear S

I knew you'd come here and here I find you in a losing fight with a wizard. My new friends don't choose to play fair but I decided to even the odds in memory of our past friendship. Next time you might not be so lucky!

K

PS: You were a sucker to let him point the magic blade at you.

"Kitiara!" Sturm called to the sky and stones. "Kitiara, where are you?" But he knew she was gone, lost to him forever.

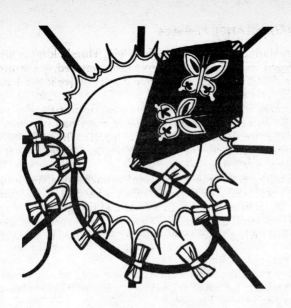

Chapter 41

Palanthas

It took some time, but a message dispatched by Sturm from Palanthas to Sancrist was answered. Stutts, inventor of the practical (well, mostly practical) flying ship, sent Sturm a reply that took up sixteen sheets of foolscap, front and back. It seems that he, Wingover, Sighter, and the rest made it back to Mt. Nevermind eventually, using the hull of the *Cloudmaster* as a conventional sailing ship. The massive report the gnomes submitted to the High Council of Gnomish Technology ran into thirty volumes.

"The irony is," Stutts wrote to Sturm, "in all the time we spent on Lunitari we didn't manage to bring back a single sample of soil, air, rock, or plant life. All our copious sample collection was abandoned trying to lighten the ship for takeoff. With only our notes, the High Council rendered a verdict of 'Not Proved' about our expedition. Sighter was pretty mad, but I'm not too disturbed. As I write this, the hull of the *Cloudmaster Mark II* is taking shape on the slopes of Mt. Nevermind. It will have four sets of wings and two bags for ethereal air, and carry . . ."

Sturm flipped through the letter with a smile. All the rest of the pages were a catalog of the things the gnomes planned to take with them on their next voyage. Only the last lines were of interest: "If you and Mistress Kitiara would like to accompany us again, please make your way to Sancrist by ten days before the winter solstice. That's when we're taking off for Lunitari. Cutwood wants to go to Solinari, but he was overruled. We still have a lot to learn about the red moon. Plus, there is some hope we might find evidence of Bellcrank. . . ." The letter was signed with several lines of Stutts's gnomish name.

Sturm set the pages aside. "Safe voyage," he said aloud. The maid in the inn where he was staying in Palanthas heard him and came to his table.

"Something you require?" she asked. Her name was Zerla, and she was pretty, with curly blond hair and a warm smile. She reminded Sturm of Tika, were Tika about ten years older.

"No, thank you," he said.

"Been in Palanthas long?" she asked.

"A few weeks."

"Thinking of staying, are you?"

"Actually, I'm ready to leave now."

Zerla frowned attractively. "Not on my account, I hope!"

"Not at all. I have business in the south," said Sturm.

"A girl?"

Tervy came to mind, but Sturm's most pressing task was to get back on his father's trail. That meant going to High Clerist Tower. He'd come to Palanthas after his encounter with Merinsaard mainly to rest and get his mind calm and focused again. While there, Sturm heard gossip that some knights were gathering at High Clerist for a conclave. He was certain his father's trail would lead there.

Zerla was talking to him, and Sturm snapped out of his daydream.

"The good-looking ones are usually taken," she was saying. Zerla wiped the table under his cup of sweet cider. "Are you married?"

"What? No, I'm not."

The maid brightened. "Where are you from?"

"Solamnia," he said.

"I thought so! I noticed your helmet and mustache. You're a knight, aren't you?" He admitted that he was. "My grandfather tells me stories of the old days, when the knights watched over the land and saw that justice was done. I wish I'd lived back then. I'd have liked to see the knights on their fine horses, armor all polished, doing good for people." Zerla blushed. "I'm sorry. I'm talking too much."

"I don't mind," Sturm said. "What you said cheers me. I thought most folk had forgotten the Order, or hated it." He finished his cider and put down two Solacian silver pieces. "The change is for you," he said.

"Thank you!" Zerla swept the cup and coins off the table.

Sturm walked out into the afternoon sunshine. In the days he'd been lingering in the city, other reports had come in via the seaport. Tales of strange marauders in other regions were growing. When Sturm got to High Clerist he would have plenty to tell the other knights.

But here in Palanthas, the threat seemed far away. Children played in the streets, wagons and carts moved goods about from the wharves to nearby shops and markets. The citizens were well fed and well dressed. Yes, the danger of war was far removed from the life of the average Palanthan.

He could see from the high street that puffy white sails filled the bay. Were there gnomes down there? he wondered. Did a gleaming white elf ship named *High Crest* ride at anchor beyond the headland? Sturm could not tarry long enough to find out. Too long he'd allowed himself to be diverted by other matters. The time had come to shoulder the responsibility of his knightly name. The burden of duty was as heavy as the armor Sturm now wore. His father's armor, and the Brightblade sword that hung by his side. Sturm rested his right hand on the pommel and let his eyes linger on the polished plate of his armor. He took a deep breath and walked down the street.

So it was south to High Clerist. Nearly a year had passed from the time he'd said good-bye to Tanis, Flint, and all his friends in Solace.

And Tervy.

And south again. Abanasinia and Solace. In due time, his old friends would be gathering at the Inn of the Last Home. They would want to hear about what had happened to him and Kitiara. How could he tell them? How could he explain to Tanis? And what of her brothers? Would they understand any better what Sturm himself did not? So many questions troubled Sturm as he walked the sunny streets of Palanthas.

A cloud passed over the sun, and Sturm looked up. Darker clouds than that were coming. He could shout it from the rooftops, but the Palanthans wouldn't heed him. Life was good, why worry about war? Weren't the mountains high? Was not the bay patrolled by Palanthan galleys, armed and ready? Palanthas was safe, absolutely.

But mountains and warships were no impediment to evil. The seed of that insidious force lay in every heart, in every act of greed and hatred. The land and the sea were merely highways over which ideas flowed as readily as the trade winds, and now the sky was open, too. The gnomes had proved that.

The cloud moved on. Sturm shaded his eyes from the sun's glare and listened for the sound of beating wings.

Calling all fantasy fans –

n the **Penguin/TSR Fantasy Fan Club** for exciting news and fabulous competitions.

For further information write to:

Penguin/TSR Fantasy Fan Club
27 Wrights Lane
London W8 5TZ